# WHEN SHADOWS CREEP

*TALES OF WEIRD LONDON*

Edited by R Poyton

www.innsmouthgold.com

THIS IS AN INNSMOUTH GOLD BOOK

ISBN 978-1-7391756-6-5

Copyright@ 2024 R Poyton.

www.innsmouthgold.com

Art Copyright@2024 Graveheart Designs
www.facebook.com/graveheartdesigns

*Dedicated to all of them who went through it, but especially to a young boy called Michael and his best pal.*

*When shadows creep*
*When I'm asleep*
*To lands of Hope I stray...*

- "I'm Forever Blowing Bubbles"
Jaan Kenbrovin

# Contents

INTRODUCTION                                                    8

THE EYE OF JUPITER              - B Harlan Crawford    10

FROSTFALL                       - Tim Mendees          34

THE SONG FROM THE STATUE        - Simon Bleaken        96

CELL 34                         - A.D. Radford         126

WHEN SHADOWS CREEP              - Robert Poyton         172

WHISPERED CADENCES OF SWEET DELIRIUM  -Lee Clark Zumpe  238

RAG AND BONE                    - David Cartwright      288

SHADOWS AND ECHOES              - Gavin Chappell        322

THE PIERCER OF THE VEILS        - John Houlihan         372

BIOGRAPHIES                                             440

# INTRODUCTION

London has a rich and varied history dating back centuries. Although founded by the Romans in 43AD, there is evidence of people having settled in the area as far back as 4800 BC. Londinium was founded on the point of the river where it was narrow enough to bridge and the strategic location of the city provided easy access to much of Europe. In around 60 AD, it was destroyed by the Iceni led by their queen Boudica. The city was quickly rebuilt, yet later fell into ruin when the Romans abandoned Britain in the 5th century.

London lay mostly empty for a hundred years, until Anglo-Saxons began settling there, naming the city Lundenwic. Since then it has seen perhaps the widest range of settlers, visitors and attackers of any other city in the world. Viking, Norman, Jewish, Irish, Huguenot, Italian, Polish, Maltese, West Indian, Bangladeshi, Nigerian, Indian, London has attracted people from all around the world. It became the heart of the British Empire, attracting 1.25 million migrants between 1841 and 1911.

As such, London has been a constant melting pot of cultures and ideas, a vibrant centre of arts and sciences. As well as our home- growns of the Blakes, Turner, Pepys, Chaucer, Dickens, Shelley, Ray and Dave Davies, Bowie, Bolan, Lydon, etc, London has been home to Mozart, Poe, Marx, Gandhi and countless others. Jimi Hendrix lived for a in the house once owned by Handel (now there's a musical mash-up!) Paul McCartney wrote *Yesterday* while living in Wimpole Street. The city houses several leading museums and scientific establishments, the "mother of all parliaments," and has been a centre of political and social change from Wat Tyler's Peasants Revolt, to the Suffragettes, to Swinging London.

Beyond all of that, London also has a long occult history. Its pre-Roman origin is shrouded in myth. Geoffrey of Monmouth in his *History of the Kings of Britain* (1136) traced London's roots back to King Brutus of Troy settling on the banks of the Thames, building a city called *Troia Nova* (Trinovantium). This city was later fortified by King Lud (buried at Ludgate). Later legends have the head of King Bran buried in London where the White Tower now stands. As long as it remains there, Britain is safe from invasion – a link perhaps to the still-current practice of keeping ravens at the Tower of London (in Welsh *brân* means crow.)

The Elizabethan era saw the birth of empire and a huge growth in interest in the occult. This was the era of Dee, Kelly, and Forman and saw the introduction of the Witchcraft Act in 1563 that was to lead to so much tragedy. Following the Great Fire of 1666, Wren led the great architectural revival, assisted by Nicholas Hawksmoor, whose interesting church alignments continue to intrigue today.

Swedenborg, Falk, Blake and others continued the mystic tradition, bringing us to the Victorian and Edwardian era, complete with tales of Spring-Heeled Jack, Madame Blavatsky, The Golden Dawn and, of course, Crowley. The tradition continued into the 20th century, with Fortune, Beardsely, et al and shows no signs of diminishing today, with a London steeped in supernatural lore, true crime history, and the added myths and legends of incoming incumbents.

My own introduction to London came in the early 1960s, when I arrived in Forest Gate Hospital in the Borough of West Ham – just within earshot of the famous bells at St Mary-le-bow if the wind is blowing the right way! My family roots are deep-set in London, dating back to at least the 17th century. I grew up with so many stories of the old East End, particularly the war years, in which so much hardship was endured.

These days I live out in the sticks, but a part of me is always in London, and I go back there frequently. So when pondering on a theme for a new IG anthology, a certain three word phrase from a well-known London song popped into my head – and this volume was born.

I am honoured to once again bring you the works of my talented colleagues, and to welcome some newcomers to the Innsmouth Writing Circle, too. Each of them has presented a London tale - each from different times, each in different settings, but all within striking distance of the Thames, all with that little tinge of London fog.

So, settle back in your chair, rest your plates, have a little drop of your favourite tiddly, and enjoy this collection of weird jackanories about the finest city in the world...

*- Rob Poyton*
Innsmouth Gold

*A a hulking anthropomorphic shape was ushered into the hall by a half dozen centurions...its aspect was so bizarre Aelred struggled to make sense of it.*

# THE EYE OF JUPITER

### B. HARLAN-CRAWFORD

"I say, Jenkins, here's an interesting piece!"

Conrad's outburst jarred Jenkins from a brown study. Having grown disinterested in Conan Doyle's latest offering in *The Strand*, he had allowed his gaze to wander out of the large picture window of the Pickman Club. A gaggle of filthy street urchins had gathered there, accosting passersby for handouts. One particularly roguish boy had taken up a loose cobble and eyed Conrad with devilish intent. Ere the boy could go through with his fiendish plan that no doubt involved hurling the stone through the window and into Jenkins forehead, a constable arrived and dispersed the menacing horde. The crisis averted, the erstwhile bobby resumed his patrol, keeping an eye on the fleeing youngsters. Jenkins greatly valued his time lounging by the window, and Conrad's stentorian attack on his leisure left him irritable.

"What is it now Conrad?" he grumbled. "Some lurid conspiracy played out in the agony column?"

"Nothing like that." said Conrad, noisily rearranging the pages of the morning edition of the Journal. "Listen!" Conrad began reading aloud: "Extraordinary affray at Dowgate Wharf: brazen escape of nude miscreants ensues!

In the twilight hours of the twenty-third, a most remarkable commotion unfurled near the bustling wharf at Dowgate. PC Newell Middlemass, was swiftly summoned by the clamorous outcry of the local denizens residing in proximity to the waterfront. Upon his arrival, he was abruptly accosted by a scandalous spectacle: two individuals, one of the male persuasion and the other a lady, both bereft of attire. The man brandishing an implement of violence-namely, a prodigious knife.

Without a moment's hesitation, PC Middlemass endeavoured to take these flagrant offenders into custody, bravely upholding the law amidst the chaos. Alas, his valiant efforts were met with stout resistance, for the malefactor and his female accomplice overpowered the constable with audacious force. In the ensuing scuffle, our gallant protector sustained grievous wounds, including a deep gash upon his right forearm and a split scalp, testament to the ferocity of the encounter."

"Balderdash!" erupted Jenkins. "The perfidious hyperbole of Fleet Street!"

"Listen, there's more!" Conrad continued. "Regrettably, the tumult did not cease with the plight of the constable, as three innocent bystanders were also ensnared in the perilous fray, suffering injuries in the melee. As the smoke cleared and order sought to reassert itself, it became apparent that the daring duo had effectuated a daring escape, leaving consternation and bewilderment in their wake.

As the eve wanes and darkness enshrouds the city, the nefarious perpetrators remain at large, their brazen escapade casting a pall over the peaceable denizens of our fair metropolis.

Let us pray that the long arm of justice shall swiftly apprehend these miscreants and deliver them into the custody of the law, lest further havoc be wrought upon our streets." Conrad folded the paper, cast it upon the Ottoman, and turned to Jenkins with an air of defiance. What an extraordinary occurrence! What do you make of it, Jenkins?"

"Opium addled lunatics no doubt, or foreigners, or some combination of the two."

"I disagree! That's the third incident in that area in the past month! There was the lamplighter attacked by knife wielding dwarves."

"Gypsies, escaped Orang-utans!"

"The lady assaulted by a brute in fancy dress, like a midsummer night's dream she said."

"Fantasies dreamt up by a drunken prostitute."

"Now this! I'll tell you Jenkins, something is amiss in Dowgate, and I think we should look into it."

"And I think you should stop taking the Journal!"

---

From the alluvium vomited up from the sluggish Tamesis thrust the moldering corpse of Old Londinium. Though often flooded and overgrown, many of its structures remained relatively intact, a testament to the architectural mastery of the Romans who held sway here for some three centuries. They were gone now, the Romans, the tide of their empire having crested and receded, leaving behind tottering ruins like the detritus left at the edges of an evaporating puddle.

Time had caused the walls surrounding the city to weaken and crumble in places, and here locals would come and gather the loose blocks to repurposed in their own, less exalted structures. This created gaps of varying widths in the wall and it was at such an aperture that a rangy, tawny haired young man clambered over the tumbled masonry and into the old city.

`He was modestly clad in a roughly woven linen tunic, with linen trousers thrust into rawhide boots. A long seax was thrust into the leather belt about his waist. His features marked him for a Saxon, one of the waves of Germanic peoples who insinuated themselves in Britain, filling the vacuum left by the retreating Romans.

He looked back toward the skeletal bridge of rotting timber he had just crossed with great care and effort, eyeing it furtively for signs of pursuit. For the past fortnight, he and a score of other Saxons, erstwhile and restless youths all, had ranged across the countryside in search of distraction from their dull lot during this time of relative quietude.

A young woman of one of the Pictish tribes had fallen into their hands, and the lad, being of a thoughtful and gentle bent for a young man of his environs and era, found himself at odds with his companions on the disposition of the girl. This disagreement escalated into a set-to in which he had been obliged to slay one of his fellows. Faced with the prospect of battling the remainder of his companions, some of whom he'd counted as friends since childhood, he took to his heels. The Pict girl had fled also, and roughly half of the Saxon bucks had set out in pursuit of her, with the balance opting to pursue their former comrade.

For two nights he had fled across the countryside, outpacing his pursuers here, evading them there. He had sustained himself on water from shallow puddles and hastily gathered sprouts or vermin. By night he eschewed sleep and crept along in the darkness, adding distance between himself and those who harried him.

Now he saw no blood-mad Saxons upon his trail. It seemed at last he had thwarted them, but now he was alone and friendless in unfamiliar surroundings, as well as hungry and exhausted. He resolved to find some dry ruin near the wall and spend the night there in relative comfort, he would sleep, then forage for food by the river on the morrow.

Under the last dying rays of the day, he searched among the tottering ruins for suitable shelter. As darkness fell, the ruins took on an increasingly phantasmagorical aspect. The empty black windows and doorways of an old granary became the vacant sockets and gaping maw of a gargantuan skull that once housed the brain of a long-fallen titan. The exposed archways and rafters of a roofless bath house became its rib cage, and the weed-choked streets of dark stone became the dried rivulets of its sluggish blood.

Finding an old bakery whose roof was intact and whose floor was still dry, the Saxon went in and threw himself upon a discoloured mosaic of an ancient warrior battling a bull-headed monstrosity. Having lost his cloak in his flight and having no means to make a fire, he curled up into a ball in one corner of the room. He cursed himself for a sentimental weakling, spilling Saxon blood in defence of a Pict of whom he knew aught. Thus was his mind occupied as he dropped off into a dreamless oblivion born of exhaustion.

Some unknowable interim had passed before the lad was roused from insensate oblivion by rough grasping hands that lifted him bodily from the floor. Harsh, guttural gibbering filled his ears, and he was jostled and buffeted. Striking out fiercely with fists and feet, the scion of Saxony took grim satisfaction in the crunch of bones breaking and flesh splitting wetly beneath his blows. But his assailants were many, and he was soon overwhelmed. Trussed up like a pig and hoisted in the air, he found himself being carried along like a slaughtered deer.

Along rank, overgrown avenues he was paraded. Rats and other vermin peered out from the stygian shadows to cast their mindless, idiot gaze upon the stricken lad. These onlookers cared little for the young Saxon's fate, and soon turned from him to resume the business of survival.

At length, the Saxon found himself shrouded in deeper Cimmerian shadow as his captors carried him to a low overgrown mound. Hidden in that tumble of decayed brick and mortar was the mouth of an ancient shaft that originally directed the effluvia of this quarter into the now disused sewer. Down they went in darkness. The air grew progressively warmer and more humid, the Saxon felt drops of fetid water fall upon his face and heard the feet of his captors splashing in puddles of varying depth. At length they stepped into the lurid glow of sputtering torches and noisomely smoking oil lamps. The Saxon was thrown forcefully to a cobbled floor and set upon by countless foes, rough hands buffeted and restrained him as the garments were torn from his body, save his broad leather belt that proved too difficult to remove. During this he got his first clear look at his attackers.

They were squat, sallow-faced men with lank unkempt black manes. Their features were broad and dull, having the look of caricatures of men moulded by the hands of an inexpert potter. Pummelling the Saxon seemed to bring them some amusement, for their pulpy slashes of mouths twitched a bit at the corners, and short swinish grunts of what might have been laughter sounded in their throats. When receiving the few retaliatory blows the Saxon could muster, they showed little emotion or even awareness, gaping dully at him with lustreless black eyes. They wore the armour of that empire that ruled some half century ago, battered and tarnished, and bore swords and spears of the same make.

The Saxon was lifted and thrown onto a crude chair of loose brick and crumbling mortar and fastened to it with rusted iron chains applied to his neck, wrists, and ankles.

The stunted mockeries of centurions shambled out of what the Saxon saw now to be a crude dungeon, save for two who took up positions by the door. The room was of poorly maintained brick and mortar, with crude attempts at repairs having been made with river rocks and mud. Water dripped from myriad points on the ceiling, forming noisome puddles on the filthy tiled floor.

After a few heartbeats, a creature who bore the grotesquely exaggerated and distorted attributes of a woman entered the room. She was generally of the same type as the centurions. Squat, rotund, and pulpy, with long greasy black hair framing a wide porcine face. Her wide flabby-lipped mouth was spread in a lecherous grin showing an endless array of tiny black and yellow teeth. She was clad in the filthy tatters of a silken robe, left open to reveal pendulously swinging udders.

Without preamble she waddled forward and climbed atop the Saxon, groping, and belabouring him with hands and mouth in a blasphemous mockery of a lover's caress. The Saxon howled and struggled at his bonds, but though the masonry was brittle, and the iron rusted, they did not yield.

The repellent harpy pressed against the lad, enveloping his face in her gelid rolls of sweaty flesh. He retched at the sour reek held therein. Though his mind and spirit recoiled in horror, the Saxons' flesh betrayed him, giving the fulsome hag that which she sought. She cooed and tittered and gurgled unintelligible words in his ear while the dwarfish centurions emitted brittle, wheezing chortles. The noisome hag gratified herself upon the Saxon with an effort that rendered her gasping in laboured gurgling breaths until at last, to his shame and horror, he yielded to her his seed.

The hag sluggishly dismounted the Saxon, and waddled from the dungeon, whistling some airy tune. The centurions followed, laughing, locking the door behind them.

The Saxon sat for a moment in the torchlight, he shivered as the sweat and effluvia left upon his flesh by the brutish harpy evaporated. In this moment of silence his mind reflected upon and correlated what had occurred since he entered the ruins, and the full horror, shame and humiliation settled over him. He wailed and shrieked like a damned soul.

When he had exhausted his anguish. He sat with head slumped on his chest, beseeching Thunor to strike him dead.

"Hist!" came a soft, quiet voice. The Saxon turned toward the sound. In a corner of the dungeon was a young woman, dark haired and dark eyed. She was naked and chained by the neck to a heavy iron ring set in the floor. The chain was so short she could not rise higher than her knees, and even then, her head was held low, forcing her to stoop. From beneath the filth that covered her, the Saxon saw her bronze skin was decorated with elaborate designs.

He recognized her for a Pict, the same Pict he had rescued from the rapacious attentions of his own companions a seeming eternity ago. She spoke again, in the tongue of the Saxons, heavily accented yet perfectly ineligible, her voice was soft and quiet.

"Who are you? Where do you come from?"

"I am Aelred, son of Guthlaf." he groaned.

"I am Eithni of the Crow-Folk. You are the lad that took my side against those Saxons yesterday?"

"I am."

"You have my thanks Aelred, and I am in your debt, yet I think you might have done us both a better service had you held your piece. But who could have known?"

Aelred slumped and groaned. He had saved the girl from the rapacious intent of his fellows, only to have her meet a similar, possibly worse fate at the hands of these wretched troglodytes. Further, she bore witness to his own humiliation. The Saxon found himself fighting the urge to weep. With a heroic effort, he mastered himself and addressed his fellow captive.

"What is this place, who are these folk?"

"I have been here only a little longer than you, Aelred, I sought these ruins to hide me from Saxon eyes, only to be seized by these goblins. They chained me here and..." The Picts voice trembled almost imperceptibly, and she paused, perhaps composing herself before continuing. "They have treated me much the same as they have you. They are all stunted, twisted folk, weak and sickly, yet they are many, at least enough to overcome a Pictish girl and Saxon lad."

"Thunor take me! Better we had both died than be tormented

Thus."

The Pict showed her teeth in a humourless grin. "We live, Saxon. So long as we draw breath, we may find the chance to upend our tormentors! Thunor may do as he pleases with you, I call upon the Dark Man to grant me revenge upon these toads!"

Thus, Aelred and Eithni were held captive by the stunted troglodytes under the ruins of Londinium, for how long Aelred could not tell. They were left chained in place, never allowed to move, and forced to wallow in their own filth for days on end. Occasionally they were fed a thin soup of unidentifiable content and "washed" by having a bucket of cold, bitter water dumped over them. These "baths" were usually followed by a visit from what the Saxon had taken to calling "The Aristocrats," who would take delight in tormenting the prisoners with degradations so vile that Aelred could scarcely believe a human mind could conceive of such abysmal perversity.

Often one captive was forced to witness the humiliation of the other. They were utterly helpless against these assaults, save once when, overcome by base lust, an aristocrat allowed his manhood to stray too close to Eithni's teeth. Oddly, the centurions took no action against the Pict, nor did they aid their stricken master. Instead, they stood by chuckling as the fellow bled his life out on the filthy cobbles.

After some indeterminate time had passed, long enough for Aelred to have grown a light beard, a company of centurions entered the dungeon and unshackled them. They were then forcibly marched along a long tunnel. They struggled at first, their muscles numbed and stiffened by long confinement. But they were young and vital, and as they moved life returned their deadened limbs.

Aelred glanced at Eithni, who now stood fully upright, nearly as tall as the Saxon himself. In the crumbling burrow along which they were led, ruddily illuminated by guttering torches and noisomely smoking oil lamps, the Pict took on a demonic otherworldly appearance. Her raven mane, shaggy and unkempt, bristled wildly about her head. The designs etched on her body seemed to come alive under the lurid glow playing upon the thews coiling under her bronze flesh.

"This must be it." muttered Aelred, "They have grown weary of tormenting us and now we are to die."

"Perhaps they mean to sacrifice us to their gods," snorted Eithni. "I will try to get my teeth in one's throat ere then."

The pair were conducted into a great circular hall. Lit by an array of tarnished bronze lamps, this room was even more decrepit than the dungeon in which the captives had languished, water dribbling from the ceiling, in some places in droplets, in others in steady streams. The floor was treacherously wet, totally submerged in water that ranged from ankle deep to the depth of the first joint of a man's finger. Pale fungi grew freely upon many surfaces, giving the room a foul reek. Crawling things of unnatural size and colour scuttled about to and fro.

There were benches arrayed all about the perimeter, some of fine workmanship but badly decaying, others dully thrown together out of crudely cut timber. Upon them sat a throng of the noisome aristocrats. They swilled wine, gorged on unidentifiable delicacies, and abased themselves with one another in every manner conceivable. they were guarded by a ring of the dull-eyed centurions.

At the wall opposite the captives was a raised dais upon

which was a great metal orb held in place by a rusted iron framework. The orb was about man-high and polished to a mirror finish. Aelred felt his gaze drawn to it. He was not sure, but he felt what was reflected on that mirrored surface was not the room in which he stood.

Before the orb was set a couch of gilded ebony, and upon this sprawled a grotesque figure. Clad in a clean white toga he was broad, stocky, and quite hairy save for the crown of his bulbous head upon which rested a headdress of brass fashioned to look like a wreath of laurel. At first glance he appeared to be of a typical physiognomy. He was perhaps less repellently twisted than the other aristocrats, but in many ways his subtle deformities were more alarming than the broader grotesqueries of his peers. The slight bulging of one eye, the broad elephantine toes of the left foot, the awkwardly larger girth of the right forearm. There was a scaly coarseness to the skin that would have been unremarkable had it not been coupled with a patchy irregular hirsutism. Noting the entrance of the captives he rose grinning; he drew himself up to his full height.

"Behold! The Guests of honour! I, Decimus, Magister of Londinium, welcome thee!" He thundered in a stentorian baritone, the formal Latin reserved for public pronouncements in the old days of the empire. "I trust you have enjoyed your time with us?"

Aelred's grandfather had spoken the tongue of the Romans and had insisted upon teaching it to all his grandchildren, thus the Saxon could understand and reply. "Enjoyed? Dog! I will flay your wretched hide!"

Aelred lunged for the magister. But the spear points of the

guards hindered him long enough for the centurions nearby to restrain him.

"You are strong and spirited!" purred Decimus. "This is good, it will serve you well and provide a rousing spectacle!"

"What do you mean?"

Decimus leaned in and addressed Aelred conspiratorially, rubbing his slightly outsized jaw. "A test if you will, to see if your blood is robust enough to inject new life into our stagnant community. You may have noticed a certain peculiarity among my people, and a lack of children among our number. For centuries we have avoided mixing with the barbarian, but that has proved unwise. I had intended to test your mettle before allowing your seed to be introduced into our people, but the ladies of the court could not be dissuaded from visiting you. Alas, it is unlikely your Pictish friend will bear any offspring from her liaisons with our noblemen. The seed of the men of Londinium has grown thin, and as warped and feeble as their mind and bodies. In keeping to our own bloodlines, we have grown... decadent. What few children we conceive are birthed lifeless heaps of deformed flesh, what few survive to adulthood grow into stunted, idiot troglodytes!"

"You seem hale enough." hissed the Pict.

A shadow passed briefly over the magister's visage, his jocular manner darkened for a heartbeat, then he grinned and continued with mock joviality.

"I was fortunate, perhaps I am a throwback, a last desperate attempt by the bloodline of Romulus to assert itself. There will be time to tell tales later if you survive. Prepare them!"

Decimus stepped aside as servants moved his couch to one side. Aelred and Eithni were herded to the base of the great orb.

Two wretched crones scuttled forward bearing pots of a yellow pigment and brushes; with these they painted an esoteric design on the chests of the captives. The Saxon's skin crawled at the maddening path the brush traced upon his skin.

Aelred found his gaze drawn to the orb. Though polished to a mirror sheen, the Saxon saw not his own reflection, but a swirling, ever changing panoply of shadowy visions that would coalesce to near clarity, only to shift to some new but equally muddled scene.

"Amazing is it not?" boomed Decimus. "It is called The Eye of Jupiter, for it is said to be the eye of the god himself. Jupiter has beheld all of the cosmos with this Eye, and all of the cosmos can be viewed in it! For untold ages combats to the death have been held before the Eye of the Cloud Gatherer, whether he be called Jupiter, Zeus, Dyes, Helios, or Baal. In those glorious days only the noblest and mightiest of warriors would do battle before the Eye, so their prowess might find favour in the gods' gaze. But alas, we must offer less exalted fighters. ``

Aelred stood amazed as these vistas played before him, he longed to embrace the orb, to leap into the eye where he would be whisked away to these wondrous and strange worlds. He pressed forward but was held fast by the centurions.

"Look away, Aelred!" Hissed Eithni. "Look away, lest your soul be forfeit!"

The Picts' words broke the spell upon the Saxon, and he tore his gaze away from the orb. Decimus chuckled. "It is mesmerizing, eh, barbarian? I myself have gazed into the Eye for hours, for days. I sometimes feel I could plunge into the Eye as I might plunge into the sea and be carried away by those phantasms of other worlds. The past, the future, and beyond would open to me, I would walk the paths of eternity!"

Decimus shook off the rambling fascination with the Eye and raised his arms to address the onlookers.

"Now our guests will be given the privilege of exhibiting their prowess, their skill, their fighting spirit. Bring forth Tetraites!"

A previously concealed doorway was opened, and a hulking anthropomorphic shape was ushered into the hall by a half dozen centurions. It towered a head or more taller than its handlers, and its aspect was so bizarre Aelred struggled to make sense of it.

It could have been stated that it was a man, overly large and clad in that odd specialized armors of an old Roman gladiator, but that would have ignored the hugely disproportionate right arm that gripped a broad, double-bitted ax, the comparatively withered and stunted left arm holding a buckler, the painfully crooked, bandy legs that terminated in broad feet with overlarge, thick-nailed spatulate toes. Upon the wide, humped shoulders rested the horned crown of a massive bull. Aelred recoiled in horror at this preposterous creature that stepped out of the myths of antiquity.

The centurions moved away from the behemoth, and formed a ring that circuited the chamber and placed them between the aristocrats and the captives, save for two who approached Aelred and Eithni and thrust objects in their hands. Looking down, Aelred saw they had given him the long seax he was carrying when he was captured. Without thought or hesitation he lashed out, slashing the flabby throat of the toad-like centurion who had given him the blade. Beside him he heard a heavy thud and saw the second centurion with his brains spilling out upon the floor, skull split by the copper ax Eithni now gripped in her fist. From the assembled aristocrats, there was no outcry of shock or outrage, rather a cacophony of riotous laughter rose up from them. It seemed that to the decadent nobility of old Londinium, murder and cruelty were considered jest of the highest order.

Now, with a great bellow the bull-headed Tetraites charged. He swung his great ax, aiming a stupendous blow at the young Saxon's neck with all the force in his grotesquely oversized arm. Aelred, robbed of much of his vigour and agility by captivity and mistreatment, barely avoided the wild slash by hurling himself prostrate. He rose, struggling to keep his footing upon the flooded tiles, and thrust his seax at the brutes' legs, but his clumsy attack was robbed of any potency by the gladiator's tarnished iron greaves. Tetraites swung his ax downward seeking to split Aelred in twain, this time the Saxon deftly sidestepped the blow. Even while fighting for his life, Aelred noted the nightmarish gladiator was slow to recover, sluggish and awkward.

Eithni swung her ax and Tetraites only by the slimmest of margins raised his buckler in time to parry the blow. Sensing Tetraites, for all his outré menace, was a fighter of lesser ability, Aelred pressed the attack with a thrust to the gladiator's kidneys, Tetraites lurched away from the blow, coming away with a cut that was shrewd, but not mortal. He emitted a wheezing bellow and brought his ax down toward Aelred's head. The Saxon ducked and rolled out of the way but suffered a painful gash to the thigh.

With a shriek Eithni leapt upon Tetraites' misshapen back as he was stooped over from delivering his blow against Aelred and began to belabour the Gladiators bull head. Great chunks of fur and horn fell away as the Pict's ax rose and fell over and over. The man-bull reached back and seized the Pict by her raven mane, dashing her to the floor where she lay stunned.

The crowd erupted in repellent, infernal glee, raising their twisted, gurgling voices in calls for blood and suffering. Aelred looked upon his foe in shock, the bull head was gone, having been some sort of bestial helm or mask. In its place was a distended, blob-like bulge of flesh holding drooling flabby lips, crude slashes of nostrils and tiny, piggy eyes that rolled about in pain and confusion. In those eyes Aelred saw only the dimmest of intellects.

As the gladiator stood wheezing and moaning faintly, The Saxon felt a pang of empathy for Tetraites, and even more intense hatred for these self-styled aristocrats who forced the pathetic creature to slay and bleed for their perverse amusement. Aelred struck, and as he drove his seax into Tetraites' heart, he did so with pity, not hatred. With a child-like whimper, the champion of Londinium's debauched Roman aristocracy fell, landing with a splash upon the sodden floor, the filthy pool in which he came to rest reddened. The assembled throng squealed and guffawed in sadistic abandon. Aelred thrust his seax into his belt and took up the gladiator's great ax.

"Eithni!" he shouted. "Slay! You know what awaits us so long as we draw breath under the yoke of these fiends! Slay! Let them feel the wrath of the Picts and the Saxons! Slay! Slay! Slay!" Aelred did not wait to see if the Pict heeded him, instead he waded into the line of stunted centurions, splitting skulls and cleaving breastbones. A hundred times his naked flesh was pricked by spear or gladius, but no centurion could land a killing blow. Smashing through their line he charged into the screaming, milling aristocrats and lay about with the ax, slaying with no regard to the age or sex of his victim. A grim smile played upon the Saxon's lips, and a wordless, guttural song of death was in his throat as through a tide of gore and viscera he did wade.

The aristocrats, had they united their efforts, would likely have overwhelmed and slain their now rampaging captives, but they did not. Selfish fiends that they were, they could not overcome the drive to continue their debauched existence. Sensing that doom was upon them, they fled in disarray.

Decimus stood before the Eye of Jupiter, brandishing his bejewelled gladius. He exhorted the centurions to rally to him, but was roundly ignored, those centurions who did not lay dead in gore-spattered heaps on the floor now fled along with the nobility.

A long rope of entrails, spilled from the slashed belly of one of the aristocrats, threatened to entangle Aelred's feet. The Saxon kicked them aside and closed within fighting distance of the magister. Decimus did not shrink or cower from the blood-drenched apparition that stalked purposefully toward him.

"Barbarian trash!" He spat. "You need to be reminded of your place!" He thrust his blade forcefully at the guts of the young Saxon, who twisted clumsily from the blow, coming away with a gash across his ribs. Aelred countered with an overhead blow with the notched, gore-clotted ax of Tetraites. Decimus sought to parry the blow. He was largely successful, but his blade snapped in twain, and he suffered a glancing blow to his skull that sent him reeling back against the Eye with a bleeding, gashed scalp.

With a guttural whine Decimus lunged forward, aiming a wild blow at the Saxon's neck with the broken gladius. Aelred sidestepped his attack and hurled Decimus headlong into the Eye. The magister's twisted bulk stuck it near the base, and the rusted iron framework gave way, toppling the Eye. It smashed to the ground with such force it shattered the tiles beneath it and shook masonry loose from the ceiling, which caused the water to fall faster. The great mirrored orb began rolling across the floor. It hurtled into a throng of fleeing aristocrats, who vanished from sight as it rolled over them. It smashed into the far wall and recoiled off of it in an explosion of brick and water.

"Thunor!" exclaimed Aelred. "It must weigh a thousand minae! How does it move thus?"

Indeed, the Eye did not roll as a simple earthly object, it smashed and crushed all in its path like some juggernaut yet changed its course as easily as a mote of dust carried upon the wind. Now it came thundering towards Eithni, who, engrossed in cutting the throat of a screeching, sow-like aristocrat, was oblivious to the polished metal juggernaut hurtling toward her. Aelred leapt from the dais and threw himself over Eithni in hopes of shielding her from the worst of the impact. The Eye struck and Aelred was instantly enveloped in icy weightlessness.

He fell.

Through a vast cold neverness he fell past silvery blurs that sped by too quickly for him to be aware of them. But here and there were more distant orbs that floated by at a slower pace, each a duplicate of the Eye which had an instant ago engulfed him.

These orbs passed by slowly enough that he could gaze upon

them and listen to the sounds they made. In each could be viewed scenes which no doubt had once been held in the gaze of Jupiter.

*Resplendent insects buzz through the dense air of a lush mist-shrouded jungle, teeming with outré life.*

*Massive reptiles lounge in inky lagoons. Among the trees are hunters who are not men nor are they serpents.*

*Iron-thewed men, their chests emblazoned with the Yellow Sign, butcher one another with bronze swords at the feet of Titans.*

*A filthy, pale she-ape shrieks among icy crags and brandishes a bloodied stone ax at the cordon of gaunt leering wights encircling her. Black bile drips from their thin lips and bubbles upon the snow.*

*Grim faced men in stiff, drab garments guide ships of glittering steel through the air to rain fiery bolts of death upon unseen foes below.*

*Anthropomorphic shapes of polished steel and translucent crystal fly gracefully on golden pinions in a sky of colourful light. They battle arthropodinous fungi with blades of lightning and beams of sunlight.*

*Sallow, wizened priests with bulbous heads and lips sewn shut with silver wire wallow in the blood and viscera of martyred penitents and abase themselves before a godhead of tangled vegetation. Scarified bronze cannibals sally forth on the backs of ax-beaked birds to slay them as they pray.*

*All that ever was is now a formless cold gray miasma. The Last God languishes in eternal ennui.*

Aelred shut his eyes and screamed, his sanity hanging by a thread. He might have succumbed to madness were it not for the warm flesh of the Pictish girl pressed against him. Eithni served to tether him to the firmament he knew, to a reality of flesh, blood, and iron. To the memory of a life that, as harsh as it was, now served to comfort him. He gripped the girl tighter. Opening his eyes, he saw that one of the myriad orbs now grew closer, looming large before him. Upon it he saw a fog shrouded city, great spires loomed out of the mist, and lurid fires blazed upon its ghoulish courts and spidery avenues. Ever closer it came. Closer and closer...

Icy water struck his face, and he instinctively held his breath. They were underwater. He felt Eithni pull away from him, no doubt shocked into awareness just as he was. There was a faint brightness, and he strove toward it, his lungs screaming in agony for want of air.

His head broke the surface, and seconds later the Pictish girl's head emerged beside him. The pair drew agonized breaths. When Aelred had recovered himself and realized he was no longer in danger of imminent drowning, he looked about to take stock.

They were in a broad river. Aelred thought it must be the Tamesis, but surely it moved too swiftly. The water carried a dismal, unwholesome reek, and that which had entered his mouth tasted of foul and unspeakable things. A dense, noisome mist shrouded all, parting at rare intervals to offer glimpses and hints of dark rows of tall narrow tottering houses and low black huts that looked as though they should be a penal colony for dwarves.

"What has happened?" moaned Eithni.

"I know not."

In the near distance downstream Aelred spied a wall of filthy dark bricks thrusting itself against the oily waters. A crooked, crumbling stair writhed along its face down to a short pier where a few rickety boats were tied. Aelred struck out for it and Eithni followed.

Reaching the pier, he aided Eithni onto it, and then dragged himself out of the water. Naked, wet, and shivering, they climbed up the slimy steps. At the top they found themselves on a cobbled path or street, lining this was a long row of the squat dark houses, some of decrepit stone and brick, others cobbled up from unlovely timbers. Folk began emerging from these. Men, women, children all clad in peculiar clothing the like Aelred had never seen, but yet for all its outlandishness it was all threadbare and filthy.

One woman approached the pair, Aelred could not guess her age, her face was unlined, but her dark hair was shot with gray, her teeth irregular and rotting, her eyes haggard and defeated. She spoke in a high-pitched wheezing screech, punctuated by fits of coughing. The language was almost familiar to Aelred, yet he understood none of it.

More of these wretched folk poured out of their huts and thronged about the pair. Aelred reached to his belt and gave thanks to Thunor that the seax he'd thrust in it earlier was still there. He drew it and the woman recoiled. Behind him Eithni, bereft of any weapon, clenched her fists, and poised to fight. Aelred allowed himself a grim smile. The Pict would fight at his side like a she-devil, should it come to that.

From the back of the throng came a stentorian bellow, and the milling flock of wretches parted. A robust figure stepped into view; a man in a dark tunic festooned with brass. He wore dark trousers and a dark coloured helm perched upon his head. He was cleaner and better formed than the others, and his great moustache was well kept. His eyes brighter and more alert than those of the cretinous horde surrounding them.

Brandishing a short wooden club, he approached the pair with an air of authority. He spoke loudly yet calmly to Aelred, who could not understand his words. The young warrior replied in the tongue of the Saxons.

"I am Aelred, son of Guthlaf, and this is Eithni of the Picts. What is this place?"

This did not please the dark helmed one, and he approached with obvious intent, club on high and arm outstretched with a grasping hand. Aelred crouched, seax poised to strike at the helmeted man's vitals.

*Whoever this fellow was, if he desired battle, he would learn the fury of the Saxons...*

*This humanoid abomination had
antlers like those of a stag and their
faces were almost skeletal. Letting
out a bellow of terror, he turned
and ran...*

# FROSTFALL

*TIM MENDEES*

Bundling himself up in his Chesterfield overcoat and adjusting the Ascot tied in an elaborate bow around his neck, Lord Richmond Tremayne did his best to feign an air of calm and disinterest in the sharply cracking twig that sounded off to his left amidst a scattering of Beech trees. It simply didn't do for one of his lofty station in life to be seen yelping and leaping around like a common scullery maid startled by a wayward rodent. In any case, as newly-appointed secretary to The Order of Tamesis, and armed with a stout, silver-tipped cane to boot, he would have no trouble seeing off a would-be attacker. After all, it wouldn't be the first time he'd had to defend himself from a ruffian intent of relieving him of his valuables on a moonlit stroll through St James's Park. The truth was, he relished a good punch-up from time to time. It got the blood pumping.

A thick fog that had earlier rolled in off the Thames, along with a continuous flurry of snowfall, hung low and frigid over the City of Westminster so visibility was decidedly poor. Partially due to the inclement conditions, Lord Tremayne would have been fibbing if he had denied feeling uneasy, but that wasn't the sole reason. After all, battle seldom took place under ideal conditions. In his experience, it was always either too wet, too dry, tipping it down, or blowing a gale. Nature had a habit of making an already tough job infinitely more arduous. No, his nerves were already jangling by the time he had said goodnight to Magnolia at her rooms near Westminster Abbey... and it wasn't just because she had yet again hinted at marriage.

Hearing another *crack*, followed by the furtive rustling of shrubbery brought him to a stop. Gripping his cane in a defensive position and slapping the decorative metal handle against his left palm, he peered into the gloom. "Alright, you bounder, I know you're there. Why don't you make this easier for both of us and show yourself?" Hearing no further movement, his moustache slanted into a mocking sneer. "What's the matter, scared to take a bit of a thrashing? Be off with you, then, you blasted meater!"

Stirring the gentle snowfall and sending the leafless branches of the trees into a manic dance, a stiff breeze plunged west from the banks of the Thames, cutting at his face and making his eyes water. It was uncommonly cold, even for December. It was being said that it was the coldest on record since 1813, it was certainly the first time the Thames had frozen over since that date, something that was currently baffling those redoubtable fellows at the Royal Meteorological Society. It was one of those chaps, an old chum from Oxford, that had put the wind up him earlier, so to speak. What he had told Tremayne was a curious tale indeed, but he had put most of it down to the man's skittish nature, and his reliance on laudanum to get him through the rigours of daily life. If anything, it had been his date that had been unsettled by the encounter rather than him. Still, it certainly warranted mention the next time he met with members of The Order. Putting those thoughts aside for the moment, he once again scanned the area for any sign of lurking ne'er-do-wells.

It appeared that the coast was clear. "Thought better of it, what?" Tremayne grinned and straightened his back. "A bally good thing too, I'm no stranger to the noble arts." Planting the tip of his cane on the frozen ground, Tremayne paused to take a look over at the pond. It had iced over giving it a spectral aspect as the crystals twinkled under the effect of the diffused moonlight. If he had been a romantic sort, he'd have called it beautiful. As it was, all he could think about was the chilly-looking ducks that huddled around its perimeter. "Poor buggers. Well, at least you've got feathers. My skin feels like it's being flayed from my dratted cheekbones."

Pivoting his well-buffed boots, Lord Tremayne turned with the practised air of a former Army officer and resumed his journey back to his lodgings in Piccadilly. It wasn't a long journey, as flown by a crow or other sundry corvidae, but the bleakness of the weather made it significantly more tortuous than normal. He had briefly considered hailing a Hackney, but that would have deprived him of the spectacle of Buckingham Palace by moonlight. A stirring sight under any condition. His hand twitched into the formation of a salute just at the thought, and, as he followed the path towards The Mall, he forgot all of his worries for a brief, yet blissful, moment. It was fleeting, however, as a commotion in the bushes to his rear brought him back to reality with a bang.

Turning sharply on his heels, Tremayne stifled a gasp as a blood-curdling scream preceded a heavy thump and an unsettling scrape. Fearing the worst, he let his cane fall to the ground and drew his old service revolver from his inside pocket.

The smell of fresh oil on the cylinder gave him hope that, despite it not being fired in anger in several years, his rigorous maintenance routine would see that it functioned as intended. He made to call out but quickly thought better of it. The bushes were shaking furiously and the scraping had been replaced by a disgusting slurp. Edging towards the cluster of evergreen shrubs, he held his breath and cocked the hammer. As it clicked into place, all other noises and movements ceased.

Cautiously, he used his free hand to drag some of the foliage aside. Peering into the gloom, he was surprised to find it devoid of any occupants. "What in the name of sanity, there was definitely someone there." Stepping forward, Tremayne stooped and examined the ground. There were scuff-marks and other signs of a struggle. Returning to an upright position, he planted his fists on his hips and pondered his next move. As he contemplated a further search of the bushes something warm and wet landed in the centre of his forehead. His body froze as it slowly started to trickle down his aquiline nose. He didn't need to see it to know that the substance was red, the coppery smell on the breeze confirmed that. Quickly taking out a monogrammed handkerchief he wiped his face and looked up to its source...

"Good God in Heaven!" A man was bent backwards over the limb of a beech tree, his arms and legs dangling and his neck twisted into a grotesque angle. There was no point checking for a pulse, the vacant eyes and lolling tongue confirmed that the poor chap was most certainly deceased. Crossing himself, Tremayne backed out of the bushes, letting his soiled hankie fall from his trembling fingers. There was nothing else to be done here. "I'd better go and find a Peeler."

Snow swirled and danced around his ashen face as Lord Tremayne retraced his steps towards where he had left his cane. The wind had risen from a whisper to a primal howl that cut through his garments adding more force to the shudders that the discovery had sent through his body. It wasn't late, so he would have no trouble locating a constable, yet all he could think about was fleeing to his rooms and having a hot bath. Clenching his fists to steel his nerves, he prepared to set out towards Buckingham Palace and do what needed to be done. After all, it was his duty as a protector of London. Rejoining the path and retrieving his cane, he turned west and began to adopt a marching pace.

Tremayne hadn't gone far when another strange occurrence stopped him in his tracks. It was yet another unnerving sound, only this time, it was harder to codify than a man's scream. His mind catalogued it as somewhere between a crack and a groan followed by the flap and quack of startled ducks. Turning slowly towards the frozen pond, he squinted out towards the centre. A fissure had opened in the ice and was spreading in a straight line towards the west bank. When it had drawn level with his position, it stopped. His brow furrowed as, for a brief moment, everything was quiet and still. Then, with the force of an explosion, the ice ruptured in a gout that reached the height of the bordering treeline.

Mouthing expletives, Tremayne turned and ran as something under the ice shot in his direction. Water, both frozen and liquid, splashed and spurted from the force of the movement. Whatever it was, it was fast and had already nearly reached the reeds. In the second before his mind snapped, he likened the effect to a shark's fin breaking water. This memory brought comforting thoughts of sun-kissed beaches and lobster buffets as he was gripped roughly around the waist and hauled into the air. Gibbering and weeping, he let his cane fall from one hand and his revolver from the other as the contents of his pockets rained down with the snow. All rational thought deserted him as he saw the park shrink below him and his screams rang out over the streets of London...

A collective gasp sucked the oxygen from the backroom of The Red Lion, Westminster, as the door burst open to admit a visibly flustered young woman. She was clad in a figure-hugging sequin dress in the flapper style, a peacock feather headband, and t-strap shoes, her tight golden curls darting around the edges of her pale features like a miasma of over-excited bees. Raising the painted fingertips of her right hand to her blood-red lips, she fought for composure as all eyes fell upon her. Squaring her shoulders, Magnolia Wakefield assumed the entitled air befitting of a girl with good breeding and addressed the leering horde. "Pardon the intrusion, gentlemen, I'm looking for Uncle Dick."

Once again, it became hard to breathe in that low-ceilinged space. Mutters of, "I say," and "Well I never," punctured the stunned silence. One of the older gentlemen standing around the billiard table had to lower his rump onto a threadbare stool to stop his knees from giving way. One of his fellows mopped his balding pate with a handkerchief and whispered to the startled chap next to him about how much he liked a young lady to be forward. This revelation elicited a tut and a shake of the head from his outraged companion. Polite society had never heard of the like.

Magnolia was nonplussed, her cheeks flushing as her barely contained hysteria threatened to uncork itself and bubble over like an agitated champagne bottle. As she tottered slightly and considered holding onto the door frame for support, a rakish young chap by the name of Freddie Farthingale leapt from the settle along the back wall, a wolfish grin plastered across his face, his pencil moustache fluttering with excitement.

"My, my, you are a fine filly, and no mistake," Farthingale was at Magnolia's side in a fluttering heartbeat. "Allow Freddie to buy you a drink," he lowered his voice and leaned in to whisper in her ear, his boozy breath stinging her left eye, "then we can go up the apples to my rooms and, ahem... look for *Uncle Dick*."

Magnolia bristled and slapped the young oaf across his cheek. "Oh, do go away, there's a good fellow. It wasn't a blasted euphemism, I'm looking for my Uncle Richard, Richard Hampton, the valet to Eugene Angove, has anyone seen him? I was told his employer was here drinking himself silly."

Before anyone could respond, a well-groomed gentleman in an immaculate black suit raised a gloved fist to his mouth and coughed politely. "If you would pardon me, gentlemen, it appears that the young lady is looking for me."

As the focus of attention shifted to the valet in the corner, Magnolia beamed and commenced weaving through the tables. The man looked embarrassed, appearing to fight the urge to hide behind the aspidistra on the corner table as the two somewhat portly gentlemen encased in tweed occupying the domino table looked up at him questioningly. Stifling a heavy sigh, he turned to the man nearest to him and purred, "Apologies, Mr Angove, allow me to introduce my niece, Miss

Magnolia Wakefield," Hampton turned his head ever-so-slightly so that he could side-eye Mr Farthingale, "she's the paramour of Lord Richmond Tremayne."

Eugene Angove's shoulders began to shake, imperceptibly at first but quickly progressing into heaving spasms of mirth. Eventually, his low throaty chuckle became a loud guffaw as two words burst from his lips, "Uncle Dick! ... Oh, Hampton, my dear fellow, I may have to refer to you as such from this day hence."

Hampton rolled his eyes, it was going to be one of *those* nights. Eugene was on his fifth pint of porter and the tone of conversation tended to lower as the alcohol content in his blood-stream rose. It was only a matter of time before the room was treated to his repertoire of bawdy drinking songs. Not wishing to engage and risk any further mockery, he turned his attention to the new arrival. "Miss Wakefield, I fear you shouldn't be in the tap room, this is something of a *traditional* establishment. Perhaps, we should move through to the snug?"

"Nonsense, don't be such a blasted prude, Hampton," Eugene cut in, gesturing for his dominoes opponent to vacate his seat with a flick of his hand, "can't you see that the poor woman is in some distress? In any case, this place could do with brightening up a little, it's like sitting in God's waiting room." Turning to Magnolia, he indicated the now vacant seat. "Take a seat, miss, and Uncle Dick here will go and fetch you a brandy, you look in dire need of fortification."

"Thank you, Mr Angove," Magnolia replied, visibly relieved to sit down. She had felt somewhat on display since her arrival and it felt good to be out of the spotlight, as it were.

"Please, call me Eugene. What are you waiting for, Hampton,

three brandies, if you please. From the look on her face, I think we are all going to be in need of one."

"Very good, sir," Hampton purred as he turned and made his way to the bar, making sure to give Freddie a look that could have curdled milk as he did.

Eugene and Magnolia sat in silence, weighing each other up, while they waited for Hampton's return. His impressions of her were highly complementary and of a well-brought-up young woman, as indicated by her posture and general air of refinement. Her impression of him, on the other hand, was less than flattering. Mr Angove had spent the best part of the day off-loading crates of artefacts from an expedition in Peru to the British Museum. As a result, his clothes were grubby and rumpled and his fingernails clogged with dirt. Couple this with the fact that he was visibly three-sheets-to-the-wind, and he presented a less-than-wholesome figure. In short, he looked like a drunken docker who had pilfered someone's tweeds to try and sneak into a club. She lowered her eyes in fear of giving away her thoughts through an unwanted roll or squint. Eugene grinned boozily, misreading the signals entirely.

"Ah, good work, Hampton," Eugene beamed as his valet placed the tray of drinks on the table. "Now, find yourself a seat, there's a good fellow, we will give ourselves neck ache having to talk to you while you loom over us like a dratted vulture."

Hampton did as instructed and fetched a stool from one of the nearby tables.

"Splendid. Now, why don't you enlighten Uncle Dick, and myself, as to what has got you in such a flap, Miss Wakefield?"

Magnolia took a sip of brandy before beginning, it seemed to help. "I'm probably worrying over nothing, but I'm concerned about Richmond, Lord Tremayne, I mean. We had an early dinner by the Abbey and parted around seven. I called his lodgings just over an hour ago and his butler informed me that he had yet to return."

Eugene pulled out his fob watch and checked the time, it was close to last orders."

"I know it's not what you would deem late, but he was supposed to be heading straight home. I'm worried that something has happened to him in the park. You hear such frightful stories about cut-throats and lunatics running amok, I fear my imagination has run away with me."

Hampton sniffed. "I'm sure he is fine, a stout fellow like him, and you shouldn't believe the hysterical reports in the newspapers..."

"You say that, Hampton, but they have found three bodies there this last week. Drowned, they reckon." Eugene quickly stopped himself as he noticed the panic in Magnolia's eyes. "Apologies, miss. They were probably just drunks who fell into the pond after one-too-many libations. I'm sure it has no bearing on current events."

"Still," Hampton rejoined, hoping to placate his niece, "maybe informing the constabulary might be wise, under the circumstances."

"I already did that," Magnolia huffed, crossing her arms across her chest. "I sought out a Bobby on leaving my abode... The blasted man implied that Richmond had a mistress or that he had gone on to a bawdy house!"

"Is it a possibility?"

Hampton gasped.

Magnolia bristled. "How dare..."

Eugene held up his hands. "I'm sorry, miss, I had to ask. There is no point in us mounting a search if there is a simpler, if less palatable, solution. I mean, he could have popped into another drinking establishment for a nightcap, could he not?"

"I strongly doubt it. The reason we parted so early is that he had an important matter to attend to. He's not the type to shirk responsibility by diving into drink." This last comment came out more pointed than she had intended. Luckily, Mr Angove was either too drunk or too wrapped up in the mystery to notice. In any case, she again lowered her eyes to avoid meeting his gaze.

"I don't suppose you know what those matters pertained to?" Hampton asked.

"I'm afraid not. I assume it has something to do with The Order of Tamesis... he seemed troubled by something that had happened earlier that day."

"The Order of Tamesis?" Hampton cocked an eyebrow, "I'm not familiar with them."

"I am," Eugene replied darkly, "a bunch of crackpots vaguely connected to the Golden Dawn, I believe. I've met one of their number in the past, a chap named Stephenson, a right bounder, by all accounts. We had similar business interests with the museum some time ago. The rotter tried to diddle me out of several shillings with a counterfeit papyrus!"

Hampton rolled his eyes, he knew only too well that his employer's *business* with the museum included the sale of black market artefacts from his less-than-legal expeditions. Since leaving the Army under a dense, and rather noxious, cloud, Mr Angove had returned to his original calling, that of self-styled explorer and archaeologist. The main difference was, that where he had before been attached and regulated by a university, he now acted alone... and sold the discoveries to the highest bidder. If this Stephenson chap was in the same line of work, then he was not to be trusted as far as you could throw a particularly bulbous elephant.

"Well, I'm sure that Richmond isn't mixed up in any funny business."

"I hope you are right, Miss Wakefield. From what I've heard, they get up to some right peculiar things in their lodge above The Mitre... Rituals and practises so kinky that even the bloody Freemasons would baulk at them. There's this one I heard about that involved a plucked turkey and a pot of engine grease..."

Magnolia held her hand to her mouth to stifle a gasp.

"Sir, please!"

"I'm sorry. It's probably all a load of cobblers anyway. I'm just going off what I've heard from loose-lipped publicans and opium-addled barrow boys. Pray, continue. You said he was troubled by something that had happened earlier in the day?"

Magnolia finished her brandy in one gulp, then nodded. "As I mentioned, we had gone for dinner at that new restaurant by Westminster Abbey. Everything was sublime until a man arrived in a state of agitation. I thought he was just some oaf that had wandered in off the street, but it turned out that he knew Richmond, and had discovered his location by pestering Wetherby, his butler. The two went aside to a quiet corner, so I didn't hear what was said, though the conversation was animated, to say the least. The man was waving his arms around like a blasted windmill. I thought for a moment that the maître d'hôtel would be forced to eject him. In the end, he left, but not before stuffing several sheets of paper into Richmond's hand.

"When he returned to the table, my companion was visibly concerned, his mind occupied by what the strange man had told him. When I asked what it was all about, he curtly replied that it was 'Order business' and that he would take care of it upon leaving. After that, we ate our meal as though nothing untoward had happened, though I could tell that his attention was elsewhere. Still, I put it down to some club politics or other such petty nonsense. It was only when he failed to return home that I began to wonder if it was something altogether more serious."

"This man," Eugene asked, "did you catch who he was?"

"Only that his name was Theakston."

"Blast, that's not a lot to go on."

Hampton turned to his employer. "Do I take it that you are going to aid our search?"

"Never let it be said that Eugene Angove turned away a lady in distress... Also, I believe we have missed the last call and I'm dry," Eugene placed his drained glass on the table. "In any case, we can't let Miss Wakefield walk the streets alone at this hour. Where are you lodging?"

"Not far from the Abbey."

"Splendid, then I propose we take a stroll through the park on our way to getting you back."

Magnolia gushed. "Thank you, Mr Angove, you can't begin to understand what a relief this is."

As Eugene rose unsteadily from his seat, waving off her thanks with a practised air of nonchalance. Think nothing of it, miss. Come along, Hampton, there's not a moment to lose. I know of a late-night drinking establishment down that way that has a fine line in absinthe... it's been ages since I smothered the parrot!

Once again, Hampton was forced into an eye-roll. "Very good, sir...

"Bugger me, Hampton, it's cold enough to freeze the barnacles off a whale's backside out here."

"Indeed, sir," Hampton agreed wholeheartedly with his employer, though, what he really wanted to say was that at least Eugene still had his overcoat. He had bundled the freezing Magnolia Wakefield up in his. How she hadn't frozen to death locating them clad only in flimsy nightwear was anyone's guess. Adrenaline was indeed a powerful anaesthetic.

"You say this is the way he always walks?"

"Yes, Mr Angove. Richmond likes to keep to a routine, says it keeps his mind sharp," Magnolia muttered through chattering teeth. "He always enters the park down by Westminster Abbey, rounds the pond, and exits here. He says that he likes to come this way so he can see the palace. He says it makes him proud to be English."

"All it makes me is glad that I don't have to clean the blasted place. Imagine how much dusting a Brobdingnagian monstrosity like that would require."

Hampton ignored Eugene's quip, knowing that whatever patriotic spark he may have once possessed had been fully extinguished in the trenches, and picked up the investigative ball. "Right, then we will follow his footsteps in reverse, and see if we can spot any sign of him. Though, I have to say, the park looks deserted."

If it hadn't been for the late hour and the worrying circumstances for their visit, St James' Park would have looked like the inspiration for an idyllic Christmas card. The constant snow had settled into crisp untouched drifts and the branches of the trees were similarly coated in pristine white. The wind had almost completely dropped by this point, leaving everything still and silent. All it needed was a couple of apple-cheeked urchins in cloth caps building a snowman. In their current mood, however, the almost oppressive calm only added to their unease.

Keeping to the path was difficult due to the frozen blanket occluding the boulders, and the going was treacherous. Eugene had already nearly lost his footing on two separate occasions, though how much of that was down to the snow and how much due to the alcohol was anyone's guess. As the trio made their way down towards the pond, the tip of Hampton's boot connected with something heavy.

"One moment, sir, I think I've found something," he stooped to uncover the object, brushing snow off its length with his gloved hand. "It's a walking cane, an expensive one, by the looks of it."

"Let me see," Magnolia pushed between the two men and gasped. "It's his, it's Richmond's."

"Are you sure?"

"Yes, quite sure. Look at the top there, those are his initials, RLT," she peered at the decorative metal knob on the top of the cane, it was dented. "Oh, God, Richmond. What the Devil could have happened to have caused a dent like that?"

Eugene took the cane and scrutinised the dent. When he was done, he motioned for the others to move aside then tossed it high above them. The cane turned over in the air and came down with a thump on the same spot as the dent. Satisfied, he shrugged his shoulders. "Maybe he used it as a javelin? Though, to have caused a dent like that, it must have dropped from one hell of a height."

"We'd best check the ground as best we can," Hampton asserted, "he may have dropped something else."

Magnolia agreed and started to gingerly nudge snow aside with her shoe. Eugene couldn't help but chuckle, her patent t-straps were designed for doing the Charleston, not Arctic ranging. Taking pity, he recovered the cane and handed it over. "Here, use this, miss. The last thing we want is you getting frost-bitten toes." Grateful, she took the stick and began raking the snow. Eugene smiled and proceeded in the opposite direction. Moments later, Hampton, who was heading towards the trees and bushes, stopped and let out a surprised yelp.

"What is it, Hampton?"

"A revolver, sir," stooping to pick it up, the valet gave the barrel a sniff before checking the chamber. "A Webley. Army issue. It's not been fired but the hammer has been cocked."

"Miss Wakefield, have a look at it."

Magnolia nodded and did so before shrugging.

"Is it Lord Tremayne's?"

"I wouldn't know, Uncle. I know he carried a firearm but he never showed it to me. It's not the sort of thing one produces at the dinner table."

"That's true enough. He's a military man, though?"

"Oh, yes. He's very proud of his time in service."

"Well, this weapon certainly seems to have been cared for. It looks pristine, aside from this dent on the barrel." Hampton gently replaced the hammer, not an easy task due to the freezing effect of the snow, and placed the gun into his inside pocket. "It looks fresh, the dent, I mean."

By this time, Eugene's beer-filled bladder had begun to strain so he stalked off to the bushes to relieve himself. Once nature's call had been answered, he resumed his search. Upon reaching the edge of the shrub-line, he spotted something fluttering out of the corner of his eye. "Hello, what's this?"

"Have you found something, sir?"

"Hmm," Eugene fished a piece of cloth from the snow and held it aloft. "A handkerchief."

Magnolia, knowing that her beau had a set of very distinctive nasal rags, hurried over and snatched it from Mr Angove's fingers. "Yes, this is his. Look, there are his initials again." As she continued her scrutiny, she discovered a brownish smear. "Oh, good heavens, is that..."

Eugene took back the cloth. "Blood? It certainly could be..."

Leaving the others with their potentially grisly find, Hampton decided to poke his head into the trees and instantly regretted his decision. "Good Lord!"

"What is it?" Magnolia asked, her voice growing loud and shrill.

"Stay back, miss."

Eugene joined Hampton and let out a stream of invective. Above them, bent over a branch backwards, was a dead man. An icicle had formed from the saliva at the corner of his mouth and his eyes had iced over. "I think we've found Lord Tremayne. Poor bugger... How in God's name did he get up there?"

"Have you found something?" Magnolia pressed upon hearing Eugene's low muttered words to Hampton. She hadn't caught what he said, but it sounded important. "If you have found something, I simply have to know.

"Stay back, you don't want to see this."

"Rubbish, Mr Angove," Magnolia huffed as she pushed her way between the two men, "I have the constitution of an ox. I'm not one of your shrinking violets." Her affronted squeak was silenced by the sight which greeted her. Gasping for air, she turned and buried her head in her hands.

"I'm sorry you had to see that," Hampton said softly as he produced a hankie from his pocket and waved it in her direction, "I've heard he was a good man. You have my deepest condolences."

Magnolia sniffed back the shock and turned to face her uncle with a puzzled expression. "What are you talking about, I didn't know this poor soul."

"But, surely, this is Lord Tremayne?"

"That's not Richmond, you silly goose! Look at his clothes, this is obviously some local ruffian."

Suitably cowed, Hampton stuffed his handkerchief back into his pocket and ushered her out of the bushes. "Apologies. Now, if you would give us some room, I think we should see if we can work out what happened here. Perhaps you should check the area for more of Lord Tremayne's possessions?"

"Very well, uncle. I'll sing out should I discover anything of note."

Eugene smirked crookedly as Hampton turned to face him. "A spirited one, your niece."

"You don't know the half of it, sir. Anyway," Hampton gestured towards the dangling cadaver, "shall we?"

"I think we should leave it to the Peelers. I'm not sure if this has any bearing on our own mystery."

"Hmm, I suppose it could be a coincidence. I confess, I'm curious as to how he got up there. I'll just check the tree for rope marks."

"Oh, very well, Hampton, let's have a little look." Stamping his feet to ward off the chill that was seeping up from the frozen ground, Eugene approached the corpse and stood on tip-toes to get a better look. "There are no ligature marks on his neck or wrists."

"No, none on his ankles, either," Hampton moved over to the tree and ran his hands over the bark.

"Anything?"

"Not a scuff. If I didn't know better, sir, I'd say this poor chap had been dropped from a great height."

"Like the cane..."

"... and the gun. What in God's name is going on here?"

"I have no idea, Hampton, old chap. Do you remember the circumstances of our first meeting?"

"How could I forget?"

"Quite. Well, I'm getting the same feeling now as I did back in that accursed château."

Hampton shivered.

"Go and find a Bobby. I'll look after Miss Wakefield, the sooner we hand this matter over to the proper authorities, the better."

Hampton nodded. "Agreed, I'll try The Mall, there's usually a couple of them milling about by the palace."

"Good idea, but be quick about it, I'm freezing my vitals off out here... and I think it's getting colder."

Again, Hampton shivered before doffing his bowler hat and marching out of the bushes.

Eugene took one last look at the corpse before turning away and exiting in the opposite direction. The harsh metallic taste of adrenaline was rising in the back of his throat. Simply thinking about some of the strange things he and his valet had encountered since their chance meeting during the war brought him perilously close to panic. Since that time, they had encountered several more uncanny situations. It seems that, in some strange way, he and his valet were forever cursed to encounter what an acquaintance by the name of Carnacki would dub, *the abnatural.* It was one of the reasons that his already insatiable drinking habit had increased to almost critical levels in the intervening years... that and the dreams.

Pulling his coat around him as his mind raced, he scanned the snow-covered park for a sign of Magnolia. She was standing over by the pond holding something in front of her face. Taking out his trusty flask, he took a hearty slug of brandy before walking swiftly to her position. "Have you found something?" Eugene offered Magnolia the drinking vessel, she shook her head to decline.

"I think these are the papers that strange man gave to Richmond," she answered, a slight tremor in her voice, "though, it's hard to tell. The ink has run due to the snow." Passing the wad of saturated paper, and the ribbon they had been held together with, to Mr Angove, she turned and headed towards the frozen water.

Taking the papers and attempting to separate them without them turning to mush, he cursed under his breath. They were utterly ruined. Rolling them up as best he could, he slipped the ribbon around them and stuffed them into his coat. The wetness almost instantly started to seep through his inner jacket and waistcoat, making him curse once more. Turning away from Magnolia, he searched for a sign of Hampton. "Come on, blast it, I'm going to get hyperthermia at this rate."

"Mr Angove!"

Eugene turned in the direction of the shrill voice. "What is it, Miss Wakefield?"

"I'm not sure... I think there is something under the ice."

"Try using His Lordship's cane to smash it," Eugene called out as he hurried towards her.

Holding the cane with both hands and raising it over her head, she brought it down on the ice in a wide ark. Yelping at the impact, she let go of the walnut shaft, letting it spin off into some frozen reeds that were poking above the solid surface. The ice didn't even crack. "Damn it all to Hell! It's no good, it's too thick."

Both taken aback and impressed by her outburst, Eugene joined her at the water's edge. "If it's so thick it resisted that strike, I seriously doubt whatever is under there has anything to do with Lord Tremayne."

"I suppose you're right. It's just..."

Eugene raised an eyebrow. "Go on."

"Well, if you look back towards where we found the cane, the gun and the papers were in an almost direct line to this position."

"Not only spirited, but sharp too. I'm impressed," Angove thought for a second. "Perhaps if we clear the snow off the top, we will be able to see below. Pass me the cane," he instructed as he fished his hankie from his inside pocket. Once she had retrieved it, he took the stick and tied the cloth around the hilt. Stepping forward, he commenced using it like a mop. Almost instantly, he began to see something. It looked like fabric of some sort. Sweeping the cane in a wider angle, he got a sinking feeling in the pit of his stomach.

"Are those... clothes?"

"I think you should look away, miss," Eugene mumbled as he followed the cut of what seemed to be a jacket upwards.

Magnolia refused, and as the stark white of a face frozen in terror was revealed, she let out a wail of despair before swooning and collapsing to the ground in an undignified heap.

Eugene let out a heavy sigh. "Lord Tremayne, I presume," moving over to Magnolia, he crouched and patted her hand, "Magnolia, are you alright?" It was a stupid question, of course she wasn't. She had fainted into blissful oblivion upon seeing her dead lover encased in ice that couldn't have possibly formed in the hours since he was last seen. On reflection, he concluded that it may have been one of the stupidest questions that had ever spilled from his currently chapped lips. "By cripes, Angove, you can be a buffoon at times."

Done chiding himself, Eugene stood upright and pondered his situation. He was alone in St James' Park with two cadavers and an unconscious female. It was freezing cold and his shirt was damp. Worse still, all the pubs were closed and he was low on brandy. As the thought of making it to the after-hours drinking pit seemed increasingly unlikely, he pursed his lips and looked up to the Heavens.

"Well, that's just bloody marvellous..."

Wheezing as the cold air burned his lungs, Eugene Angove struggled onwards. The snow was up to just below his knees and stiff winds buffeted his face. Stopping to rub his stinging eyes, he looked around at the towering lodgepole pines and sugar maple trees that encircled him. "Where the bloody hell am I?" He appeared to be in a forest, that much was clear, but it was unlike any forest he was accustomed to. Many of the trees and shrubs were not native to the British Isles. If he'd been pressed for a guess, he'd have said Canada. A howling gale stirred the trees to his left into a frenzy of movement. Branches strained in his direction like the fingers of skeletal hands straining to claw at his chapped skin. Feeling a mixture of panic and confusion, he began walking again. He was unsure why, but he was certain that he had to keep moving. Why couldn't he remember?

"You must have had a skin-full last night, old chap."

The snapping of a twig to his rear prompted a startled yelp and a sharp turn that almost saw him land on his backside in the snow. "Hello... is someone there?" When no reply was forthcoming, he scanned the snow behind him with puzzlement. There were no tracks. His legs were gouging two trails in the snow as he walked, yet it looked as though it hadn't been touched. His confusion deepened when he realised, to some surprise, that he was wearing little more than a bathrobe and a lace cravat. Realisation started to dawn, and as it did, something arrived on a neighbouring branch that confirmed it.

*'Meow,'* it was a black cat with burning orange eyes.

"Oh, bloody hell, not another nightmare..." Ever since he had been a boy, Eugene Angove had been plagued by strange dreams. The occultist Thomas Carnacki put this down to him taking a snooze over a *weakness* in the fabric between our world and the land of dreams. These slumberous excursions had taken a somewhat darker turn when, during renovations on his family property, he had removed, and burned, the very thing keeping the darker forces within at bay. The horror unleashed had plagued his family, prompting his father to call in specialist help. In the end, it had been contained but the dreams had continued. Since that time, Eugene had dreamt of a cat, the very one now sitting on a log eyeing him with a mixture of pity and reproach. To make matters worse, the things shown to him in his dreams often came to pass in some way, shape, or form. Though often abstract, his nocturnal wanderings contained portents and omens that never boded well. Carnacki had told him that the cat was his guardian... yet he couldn't help wishing that the blasted creature would leave him be.

"Wake up, damn it," Pinching his arm did no good. He seemed to be stuck there for the time being. It was the curse of a lucid dreamer. He knew he was in a *somnum exterreri,* yet was unable to awaken. "Very well, what are you trying to show me, puss?"

More cracking twigs and rustling foliage startled the cat, sending it leaping off the branch in the direction he had been heading. Turning again, Eugene squinted through the dancing snowflakes. Several figures loomed just out of his range of vision. Tall and spindly-limbed, their hunched posture reminded him of the *ghūl* creatures he and Hampton had encountered on a recent trip to Egypt, yet they were somehow different. As one stepped closer, slipping from the masking shadow, that difference became explicit. This humanoid abomination had antlers like those of a stag and their faces were almost skeletal. Letting out a bellow of terror, he turned and ran after the cat.

Sprinting in two feet of snow is not a simple task, he was forced to adopt a rabbit-like half-run-half-hop that was tricky to keep up. As his lungs began to burn and the knot in his stomach tightened, he risked a glance behind him. The creature, and its fellows, were following at a steady pace. "Leave me be, you bastards," he panted as he searched for his little furry friend. As his eyes darted left and right, he noticed, to his horror, that the trees on both sides were lined with more of the horrors. They stood motionless, watching on, and muttering a rhythmic chant consisting of words not meant for human mouths. He was being herded, but towards what?

Another fifty yards of panicked flight saw him crash through some bushes and into a clearing. His left foot connected with a log, sending him crashing forward onto his hands and knees. Raising his head, he was startled to find himself outside the flaps of a brightly-coloured carnival tent. The snow began to melt away, running through his fingers and into the soil. Snapping his head around, he saw that he was now in a vast cavern of some kind. The walls were lit with flaming oil lamps in roughly-hewn sconces and covered in carvings of the same creatures that had hounded him through the trees. Littering the floor were piles of worker's clothing, equipment, and other personal effects mingled with an abundance of gnawed bones.

Careful not to trip over a shattered skull, Eugene picked himself up and looked for an exit. There wasn't one, the walls were completely solid. As he began to panic, the chant of the beasts in the woods started to fill the enclosed space. The acoustics, combined with the rhythm and timbre, made his vision swim and stomach lurch. Finding no other way to progress his nightmare, he approached the tent and reached out for the flap. Above the aperture was a sign consisting of two words. Unfortunately, they, like the chant, were in an unknown language.

"Are you in there puss?" Eugene called out as he swept the heavy canvas aside and entered. "What the Devil?" The inside of the tent was an almost identical replica of the cave down to the lamps and carvings. There was even another tent in the centre, though it was much smaller and its red and blue stripes were inverted. "Bugger me, it's like I'm stuck in some kind of bizarre Russian nesting doll." Finding no other option, he entered the second tent.

"Where the hell are you, Puss?" He asked as he stepped into a smaller still version of the cave. This time, the tent was much smaller and now completely monochrome. "There had better be a point to all this, puss."

As he spoke, there was a soft *'meow'* from inside the squat black and white tent.

Eugene sighed, stooped to fit through the gap, and entered what turned out to be the final door. "Holy Mary," he exclaimed as he found himself peering down into a yawning void. With panic squeezing his heart like a ripe lemon into a large gin and tonic, he flattened his back against the tent and tried not to fall. "Help! Puss, anyone, help!" As he shouted and babbled uncontrollably, an object began to rise from the fathomless depths. Squinting, he saw that it was an enormous block of ice with a cat perched on top of it. It rose with uncanny swiftness and the top was soon level with the bewildered adventurer.

As soon as it ceased movement, the chanting also stopped dead. The silence that now filled that impossible place was in a way more unsettling than the gibbering of those nameless horrors in the trees. It took Eugene a good minute to pull himself together. In all that time, the cat hadn't moved. It had just sat on top of the monolithic lump of frozen water licking its backside and paws, seemingly unphased by the strange world around it. Making that curious *'psp-psp-psp'* sound that humans do to attempt to get the attention of felines, he reached out and tried to scoop it up. Instantly the cat arched its back and hissed.

"Don't be like that, you moody little sod!" Somewhat taken aback by the cat's response, it took him far too long to realise that the cat wasn't hissing at him... it was hissing at something at the dark shape within the ice. Stepping as close as possible without tumbling into infinity, he peered inside... Instantly, two malevolent eyes the size of cart wheels and the colour of cinders snapped open. The cat hissed, the ice shook, and Eugene screamed...

... Then he woke up in an icy sweat.

As daylight streamed through the bathroom window of his rooms at Claridge's in Mayfair, Eugene Angove shuffled over to the mirror and examined his bloodshot eyes and the dark rings that encircled them. "Well, at least you look as bad as you feel, old chap. You can't have had more than three hours sleep." Tightening his white towelling robe around himself, he shrugged at his reflection, at least he was warm. There had been a point as he sat shivering in the interview room at Vine Street Police Station that he doubted that he'd ever thaw out. For some odd reason, it was colder in that unwelcoming building than out in the snowstorm that continued to pour from the sky. Splashing some water on his face in a failed attempt to rouse himself, he sighed and decided to go in search of sustenance.

"Good morning, sir," Hampton called out cheerily as Eugene entered the main living area of the apartment, "I trust you managed to get some rest?"

Eugene grunted and ruffled his sandy hair into a slightly less unruly tangle. "Not much. What time is it?"

"Just after eleven, sir."

"Ah, I was wrong. I had four-and-a-half hours sleep, yet I still feel like I've been flattened by an omnibus. I don't know how you do it, Hampton. You must have had less sleep than I, but you're as bright as a button."

Resisting the urge to point out that all the booze might have something to do with his employer's condition, the valet cocked his head slightly. "Did sir not sleep well?"

Eugene sighed. "I confess, I didn't."

"Bad dreams?"

"Indeed."

"Not..."

"I'm afraid so. There was a cat... *the* cat."

Hampton flinched as though someone, or *something*, had just walked, or slithered, over his grave. "Do you think it was one of your, ahem... omens?"

"I'm afraid so. I know you don't believe what Carnacki told me about the *Dreamlands,* but you can't deny that every time I've dreamt of a blasted moggy, something damned odd has happened. It's always the same one too, black with orange eyes. Carnacki called him my guardian. I thought it was a load of bunkum too, at first, but you can't deny the coincidence."

"I never asked, did you ever see Carnacki after that *incident*?"

Eugene shook his head. "To be completely truthful... I've been afraid to get in touch. He lives not far from here, on the Embankment."

Hampton remained silent, but his eyes said what was needed.

"I know, I know. Blimey, Hampton, sometimes you remind me of my blasted mother... God rest the old battleaxe." Eugene sat at the small dining table next to the window and unfolded the morning paper. "Anyway, have you had word on your niece?"

"I have, sir. My sister, Miss Wakefield's mother, sent a couple of servants to collect her and her belongings. She is, as we speak, on the road back to Buckinghamshire to convalesce."

"Has she spoken since coming around?"

"Not a word, sir."

"Poor girl. Can't say I'm surprised. It was a sight that could have shocked the hardiest of souls into silence. The look on his face will haunt me for a good while, or at least until I drink an entire bottle of brandy."

Hampton rolled his eyes.

Eugene continued. "Can you believe that useless Bobby? An accident, indeed. How in Hades could a man get under a foot of ice by blasted accident?"

"I have no idea, sir."

"It was rhetorical, Hampton. They can't, that's how. The fact that he suggested that the other chap fell out of a neighbouring tree makes me seriously doubt the astuteness of our local constabulary."

"I confess, sir, I can't think of another rational solution."

"Rational be buggered! Would you call half of the things we have seen *rational*?"

"Touché, sir," Hampton decided that changing the subject was probably the wisest course of action. Though a good employer, on the whole, Mr Angove could be a royal pain in the backside when his dander was up. "Can I fetch you something to break your fast, sir."

"I thought you'd never ask. An omelette and three rounds of toast, please."

"Very good, sir," Hampton turned on his heels and headed for the kitchen.

"Oh, and a pot of coffee... strong," as the door closed behind Hampton, Eugene did his best to forget about the previous evening's escapades by burying his head in the newspaper. It didn't work. Most of the front pages were taken up with stories about the weather and how it was causing mayhem in the capital. Several people had died, either through misadventure or sheer stupidity. There were reports of bodies being cut from the frozen river which was mildly disconcerting, considering Lord Tremayne's fate, but he put it down to the usual tendency of local toughs to hurl one another off Tower Bridge over a handful of coins. Other than that, it was the same sordid tales of local dignitaries in bawdy houses as per-usual.

In what seemed to be no time at all, Hampton returned with breakfast and a steaming pot of coffee. Once it was all laid out in front of him and the drink poured, he held the paper up to his valet and pointed at the headline. "It's official, that new trader's group managed to get the mayor to agree to a frost fair... you owe me a shilling."

"Blast," Hampton winced as he fished his purse from his immaculately pressed suit, "well done, sir. I was convinced it would never happen after the last one."

"Oh?" Eugene spluttered as he shovelled egg into his maw.

"The last frost fair, in 1813, was something of a disaster. I recall reading about it at the library when I was waiting for you to come to an arrangement about those horrible books you, ahem, acquired from that estate in Wales. Apparently, they had an elephant on the ice at one point. My theory is that it weakened the integrity of the surface. Whether that was the reason or not, the outcome was the same."

"You mean someone took an icy dip?"

"Several someones,' from what I gather."

"I can see why you didn't think it would happen. I can only assume that the *International Traders, Hoteliers, and Quartermasters Association* greased the old buzzard's palm."

"I fear you may be right in that assumption, sir. Money does indeed grease the wheels. Was there anything in it about Lord Tremayne?"

"Not a sausage. I can only assume that it didn't reach the desk in time for the morning edition. I'd wager it will be featured this evening."

Hampton smiled and held up his hands. "Oh, no. You've had quite enough out of me for one day, sir."

Eugene chuckled and recommenced attacking his food with all the gusto of a starving man.

"Oh, one more thing, sir, then I will leave you to eat in peace. I managed to separate out those pages of notes from your pocket and have dried them out."

"I confess, I'd forgotten all about them. Is any of it still legible?"

"Alas, I'm afraid not. Though, I did manage to make out the letterhead. It seems that Magnolia's *odd chap* is a member of The Royal Meteorological Society."

Pausing to think momentarily, Eugene then shrugged before returning to the important business of loading up a triangle of buttered toast with a fork-full of omelette.

Slightly put out that his revelation wasn't met with a glimmer of interest, Hampton rolled his eyes and left his employer to it. Walking towards the door, he began to put on his gloves and overcoat.

"You off somewhere, old chap?"

"Erm, yes, sir," Hampton shuffled furtively, "I have a couple of errands to run. I won't be long."

"You are as transparent as freshly blown glass, do you know that?"

"Sir?"

"You're following up on this Tremayne business, aren't you?"

"Well..."

"No need to beat around the bush, I heard you promise your niece that you wouldn't let it lie. I deduce that you are thinking of returning to the station to see if the day shift can be more useful than the oaf we saw last time, am I right?"

Hampton nodded sheepishly. "Do you object to me looking into it, sir?"

"What would be the blasted point? You'd do it anyway," Eugene sighed and dropped a crust onto his plate. "Very well, allow me to finish my coffee and I will come with you."

The valet nearly fumbled his bowler hat. "You're coming with me?"

"I am."

"Then, you think we should investigate the matter?"

"No, I think we should leave it to the proper authorities. They may be borderline useless, at times, but they get paid to do it."

"Then why?"

Eugene drained his cup, stood, and headed for the bedroom. "Because, old chap, it's dashedly difficult to find a decent valet in this day and age... I'm not letting you blunder into peril without some form of backup."

Hampton pinched the bridge of his nose and shook his head. "I did ask."

"Ha! You did indeed. When will you ever learn?" Eugene grinned before opening the door. "Hold your horses while I get dressed and fill my flask. I think a good Scotch may be needed for what may lie ahead..."

"Very good, sir."

"Of all the dratted nerve!"

As the door to the police station slammed behind them, Eugene Angove and Hampton stepped out into the snow. It hadn't gone well. Contrary to all hopeful expectations, the daytime desk Sergeant had been even less helpful than the constable they had dealt with previously. After asserting that Tremayne had simply slipped into the water and drowned, he brushed off all questions as though he was either hiding something, or bored with the conversation. Eugene had picked up on this detail and had forced the issue, pointing out the rather glaring problem with the ice. To this, the bulbous Bobby with the jowls like a particularly depressed bloodhound had told him in no uncertain terms to, sling his hook.' Suitably outraged, Mr Angove lost his rag and was promptly ejected from the station by two large constables.

"*Death by misadventure*, my left testicle!" Eugene bellowed, prompting a passing elderly lady bundled up like a table at a church jumble-sale to gasp in outrage. He waved her off before turning the corner and unleashing a barrage of invective that turned the snow around him blue.

"Please try to calm down, sir."

"Calm? Calm be buggered! There's something odd going on here and that damning indictment of our education system in there is either too stupid to see it... or he's hiding something."

"Well, either way, it seems like we have reached a wall."

"Balderdash," Eugene snorted as they hurried along Regent Street in the direction of the river, "I will not be thwarted by some jumped up raw lobster!"

"What do you intend to do, sir?"

Eugene winced, he hadn't gotten that far. "First, I intend to go to the river. I'm hoping the air will clear my head."

Continuing in silence, the two men soon found themselves standing on the embankment of the River Thames east of Westminster Bridge. Below them was a mass of frenzied activity as myriad traders and showmen rushed to erect their tents and stalls for the upcoming frost fair. It was fascinating from their vantage point, dozens upon dozens of humans toiling away like a colony of ants. Hampton couldn't help feeling a pang of unease, after reading about the last one, he couldn't see this one ending well. As his mind raced, he didn't notice that Eugene had turned and started walking east. It was only when he turned to make a comment that realisation dawned.

As Hampton scurried after his employer, it didn't take long for him to spot what had grabbed Eugene's attention. Just over a hundred yards from their previous position, several men in blue uniforms stood around four objects covered in tarpaulin. "Oh, good grief, are those..?"

Eugene nodded. "Look at the river. There are four holes in the ice."

"Didn't you say that there had been others?"

"Indeed I did. The newspaper reported a further six in the past two days. All from this general area," Eugene turned and looked at the preparations for the upcoming event. Flashes of the previous night's dream shot across his vision. He saw the cat, the tent, the ice... those burning eyes. "I can't help feeling that all this, the corpses, the frost fair, Lord Tremayne, are somehow connected to the dream I had. The symbolism is too much to ignore."

Hampton hummed thoughtfully. Eugene had related his nocturnal terror on the way to the police station. It was certainly food for thought. Pulling his bowler down low to keep the flurry of snow off his face, he returned his mind to the task at hand. "So, what's our next move, sir?"

As Eugene pondered the question, two men in uniform appeared with a handcart to carry away the frozen cadavers. This gave him the inspiration he sought. "I've got it. I want you to head over to the library and see if you can dig up anything useful about 1813. Take notes of anything that might have some bearing on the matter, names, incidents, you know the sort of thing I mean. Once you are done, meet me at The Red Lion around two, I think it's about time we tracked down this meteorologist chap."

"Isn't the HQ of the society in Reading?"

"Indeed, but if one of them is in town, I'd wager he's here to speak to the government, or other-such bigwigs. In which case, asking around some of the gentlemen's clubs in the area seems like a safe bet."

"Very good, sir. What are you going to do in the interim?"

Eugene grinned, tapped his nose with his index finger, and wandered off along the river in an easterly direction. Hampton stood, perplexed, it was somehow unsettling to see his employer acting so shifty. Knowing him as well as he did, he knew that what he had planned was most-likely not strictly legal. "Oh well, I guess I'd better go and purchase a notebook and a pencil."

Descending the steps leading below the north tower of Tower Bridge in the current weather conditions was treacherous in the extreme and a chill wind whipping off the frozen Thames cut through Eugene's Inverness cape. His destination was a grim one, the mortuary known locally as *Dead Man's Hole*. It was usually used to house the bodies of the poor souls that perished in the dangerous waters but was also used for corpses found in the surrounding districts. A hunch told Mr Angove that the late Lord Tremayne, and the body on the branch, would have been taken here for examination. Reaching the non-descript alcove that the majority of Londoners were blissfully unaware of, he balled his fist and hammered the heavy iron gate.

While he waited for a response, he turned and scanned the wintery scene. The snow was still coming down in thick flurries, piling upon the ice and completely hiding all traces of the normally fast waters. "Oh, well, at least I don't have to worry about *drifters* today," he chuckled at his own macabre joke before checking himself and adopting a sombre expression. Due to its proximity to the Thames, it was not uncommon for the mortuary to flood and the bodies inside to *escape*. It was a ghoulish sight, seeing several bodies in a state of rigor mortis bobbing around the bridge. Eugene had witnessed it once, after a hearty lunch, an experience he was in no hurry to repeat.

After an interminable wait, there was a jangling of keys followed by the heavy *clunk* of a bolt being shot. Moments later the gate creaked open allowing the odour of decay and carbolic soap to escape into the atmosphere. "Don't tell me there's more," a hoarse voice croaked from within.

"I'm afraid there is, but that's not what I'm here for," Eugene grinned. "Matthews, you old scoundrel, how the Devil are you?"

Blinking from under a pile of scarves and hoods, Matthews, the mortuary attendant, gazed upon his guest with some surprise. "Upon my soul, Angove, what brings you to my circle of Hell, business or pleasure?" He made a drinking motion with his right hand to clarify what he meant by pleasure. "I'm afraid I don't have much in the way of libation but I do have a rather scrumptious bottle of brandy on the go."

Eugene produced a dented hip flask engraved with a Welsh dragon, "you know me, Matthews, I always come prepared."

"Ha, you haven't changed, you old soak," Matthews held the gate open, "come in, you'll catch yer death out there... not that it's much warmer in here, I'm afraid. I've spent the past two days huddled around a blasted oil burner."

Eugene stepped inside. The tiled floor had been covered in a layer of salt to stop the omnipresent standing water freezing. Matthews had done his best to keep the pinkish slush to the sides, but it was still slippery in the extreme. As they followed the corridor down towards his little office-cum-hovel adjacent to the mortuary room, the two old friends shared pleasantries and moaned about the weather. Once the ice was broken, so to speak, Eugene broached the true reason for his visit.

"I don't suppose you've had a *client* by the name of Tremayne, by any chance?"

Matthews winced. "Come on, Eugene, you know I can't give away information like that... for free," he grinned, revealing a maw filled with crooked yellow teeth.

Producing a coin purse from his inner pocket, Eugene chuckled. "I see that I'm not the only one who hasn't changed, you old vulture." Opening the leather pouch, he took out a shilling and placed it on the desk in front of his friend. "I know how this works, and I came prepared."

Rubbing his frost-bitten hands together, Matthews beamed with delight. "You're a Godsend. I can get myself a couple of nights somewhere warm with this."

"There's more where that came from... if you prove to be in a loquacious mood."

"I can feel me lips loosening with every passing second."

"Splendid! Now, did they bring Tremayne here?"

"Yes, him and the other three from the park..."

"Three?" Eugene's eyes widened in alarm.

Matthews nodded. "Two more from the pond and one from up a tree!"

"Bloody Hell... This is getting ridiculous," Eugene rubbed his forehead with the flat of his palm before taking a nip of Scotch from his flask and passing it over. "Fine, we will get to those in due course. On the subject of Tremayne, has anyone done a post mortem."

"Aye, Llewellyn, the police surgeon and a portly peeler. They were here first thing. Opened him from neck to navel and had a good poke about."

"Did they say anything? How he died, I mean?"

Matthews adopted a vague expression. "I think they did, but my memory isn't what it once was."

Eugene sighed and plonked another coin on the desk, a penny this time.

"You know, the mists are clearing... They were somewhat perplexed about the cause of death."

"How come?"

"Well, you'd expect someone who had presumably drowned to have water in their lungs. He, and the other two, were dry as old bones in there."

"You mean, they died *before* they ended up in the water?"

"It appears so. Heart failure, apparently. Llewellyn postulated that all three died of fright."

"Jesus wept..."

"... and that wasn't the oddest thing," Matthews tapped the coins with his index finger.

"Go on," Angove produced yet another coin.

"They didn't seem to be that interested in Tremayne and the other floaters, to be honest. It was the chap from the tree they were most concerned with. The policeman, in particular, seemed to be very interested in him."

"A common ruffian, why?"

"He was no common ruffian. He was a police inspector!"

"The plot thickens... This *portly Peeler*, he wasn't a Sergeant by the name of Blackmore, was he?"

"Got it in one, dear boy."

"That explains why he was in such a hurry to get rid of me. The bodies from the pond, any idea who they were?"

"Market traders, same as the ones that keep coming in from

the river. Nobody special."

"Hmm, very interesting. Thank you, Matthews, you've been most helpful. Now, if you would excuse..."

"Wait," Matthews yelped, fearing the loss of his cash cow, "there was something else... something *odd*. But, I'm afraid, it will cost you."

Tossing another penny in his friend's direction, Eugene tutted and shook his head, "this had better be good, Matthews, or they will be fishing your carcass out of the river next."

"Oh, it's good, alright. Follow me," rising from his seat, Matthews led Eugene into the mortuary proper. The gas lamps hissed and flickered casting the room in a moody half-light where the shadows danced and loomed. The ageing attendant moved to the first of several bodies covered in blankets fashioned from heavy sackcloth. "This is one of the bodies from the river less than a mile from here," with an almost showman-like flourish, he lifted the covering to expose the feet.

"What in God's name?" Eugene moved in to examine the soles and toes. They looked like they had been seared by extreme heat and had an orange tint to them. "Could that have been caused by some post mortem effect due to the ice."

"No. In all my years in the trade, I have seen hundreds of bodies, and never seen anything like this before. It would have been odd to have just found one body like this, but..." Matthews swept his hand around the room, gesturing to each corpse in turn.

"What? Each one?"

"Indeed. Every single one of them came in with orange plates, even the one from the tree."

"Do the police know?"

"Oh, they know alright. They told me to keep mum, or I'd be in trouble, but coin will always win out over petty bully-boy tactics."

"I'm grateful. I was just wondering, could I have a look at the personal effects of the deceased. I'm assuming you still have them?"

"Oh, I have them alright. They're in a trunk in the office. I'm afraid it'll cost you..."

"I figured as much. Here," Eugene produced a pound note and waved it under Matthews' nose, "will this do?"

Snatching the note and stuffing it into his pocket, the attendant grinned. "That will do very nicely, old friend. Here, take this key, the chest is in the corner next to my cot. I'd better get back to work. If you say that they are bringing some more corpsicles in from the river, I'd better make room."

"Thank you. I'll let myself out when I'm done. "Taking the key, he entered Matthews' domain and quickly located the chest. Unlocking it, he began to riffle through the surprisingly neat piles of clothing. It didn't take him long to uncover something of interest. In the pocket of one of the unfortunate traders, he found a folded card. It had been saturated but had dried sufficiently for him to make out some of the printed lettering. It was an invitation to some kind of meeting of local traders and MP's. He wasn't sure it was of use, but he pocketed it anyway.

Digging deeper, he came upon Lord Tremayne's attire. It stuck out amongst the other tattered garments like a badger in a hen coop. "Let's see if you managed to keep hold of anything or if you scattered the lot over the park." Upon first inspection, there was nothing. He was about to cast the coat aside when he discovered an ovoid lump in one of the inside pockets. Fishing it out, he held it up to the light. It was a perfectly smooth stone with a branch-like design carved on its length. "Hmm, something to do with The Order, I presume." Stuffing it into his own pocket, he moved on.

"Now, where's this inspector's coat?" It took some rummaging, but he finally located his prize. He recognised the ripped and tattered jacket from discovering the man up the tree. Giving it a closer look, he was able to confirm that the tears and scuffs had been manufactured deliberately. This was evidently some kind of cunning disguise. "Now, did the Peelers take everything, or are they as sloppy as I suspect?" Running his hands over the fabric, he eventually found something the boys in blue had overlooked. There was a secret pocket in the lining. Squeezing his fingers in, he pulled out a rolled up piece of paper.

"Now, this does look interesting." It was a letter scrawled in barely legible script on a piece of notepaper bearing the letterhead of the Royal Meteorological Society. "I can't make head nor tail of this. I'd better give it to Hampton, he writes like a drunken arachnid, perhaps he will be able to decipher it." One thing he was able to make out was the name of the author... Jeremy Theakston. "Well, Magnolia, I believe I have found the identity of your mysterious chap from the restaurant." As he began to fold the coat and return it to the chest, he felt a suspicious bulge in the lining. Tearing his way in, he pulled out a familiar-looking stone.

"Well... that was unexpected..."

"You suspect that the inspector was a member of the Order of Tamesis?" Hampton was sitting next to his employer in the back of a Hackney as it trundled along at a snail's pace to avoid skidding into some poor blighter on the pavement.

"That's precisely what I suspect. I'd wager that Theakston approached the policeman first before tracking down Tremayne. Could you make out his handwriting?"

"Some, though it makes very little sense. He seems to have something of a disordered mind."

"Don't beat around the bush, Hampton, you mean he's barking mad?"

"That or he is writing a story of a fantastic nature for one of the popular magazines."

"Any more fantastic than the things you and I have seen?"

"Touché, sir. In any case, it's hard to make out what he means. Most of it is about 1813 and something called a *Wind Walker* or *Wendigo.*"

"Well, we will see if we can get any sense out of him in a few minutes. Good work on tracking down his lodgings, by the way. How did you do it?"

"While you were wolfing down your pie and mash in The Red Lion, I popped over to the Junior Ganymede Club and located an acquaintance by the name of Reginald who, in turn, knows Theakston's valet. From there, I was able to check the black book and find his current lodgings. It seems that Mr Theakston is in town for an extended period."

"Well, good work, old chap," Eugene peered through the steamed up windows. They were finally approaching their destination, an imposing terrace in Mayfair. "Right, I think it best that you let me do the talking... I have a certain rapport with his kind."

"His kind, sir?"

"Cambridge chap, isn't he? Have you forgotten that I too attended that grand institution."

"My mistake, sir," as Hampton looked away to avoid being seen smirking, the Hackney came to a halt. Eugene had indeed attended Cambridge but his time there had been less than distinguished. Indeed, he spent most of his time drinking and unsuccessfully attempting to romance any female with a pulse. In many ways, he was the archetypal student. "Ah, I believe we have arrived."

"Splendid, make sure to give the driver a good tip. I'm going to get out and stretch my legs." Stepping out into the early dusk, Eugene was struck by the realisation that the snow was heavier than ever. To make things even more uncomfortable, the wind was getting up. If this continued, there would be a blizzard before the frost fair opened that evening at six. On reflection, due to his mounting suspicions, it wouldn't be a bad thing if it got cancelled. Once Hampton had settled the fare, he joined his employer outside of Theakston's temporary abode, a well-to-do bed and breakfast run by a notorious local woman with a penchant for *discipline*.

"You wouldn't catch me staying with Madame Whiplash," Eugene chuckled as he fished in his pockets, "I hear that this place is frequented by several people in the cabinet. Why someone would lodge in a specialist bawdy house is anyone's guess. Perhaps Mr Theakston is fond of squeezing more than just weather balloons."

Hampton decided not to comment. The three pints and two brandies Mr Angove had imbibed over lunch had succeeded in dragging his mind into the gutter.

"Here," Eugene passed Hampton one of the stones he had

*liberated* from Dead Man's Hole.

"What is it, sir?"

"I confess, I'm not sure. I think it is something to do with The Order. If Theakston is somehow affiliated with them, showing it to him may help loosen his tongue."

Hampton nodded and took the three steps up to the front door. Gripping the knocker, he gave it a gentle rap. Moments later, they could hear the raised voice and clattering heels of a woman getting closer to the door. She sounded like she was reading someone the riot act. Hampton nearly leapt out of his skin when the door was wrenched open and he was confronted by the angry visage of a buxom middle-aged blonde in a black silk nightie, red shoes, and black stockings.

"What?" She barked, forgoing any polite niceties they may have expected.

"Um," Eugene dithered, "we are here to see one of your lodgers, a Mr Theakston."

"Oh, for crying out loud! If I knew my nephew was going to be this much trouble..." The lady of the house turned sharply and raised her voice at a harassed-looking man in a black suit. "Reynolds, they are here for your master. Get rid of them, and tell him that if there's any more funny business he's out on his ear, family or not!"

"Ah," Eugene whispered, "nepotism not naughtiness, I see."

Hampton had to stifle a chuckle as Theakston's browbeaten valet approached the door.

"Can I help you, gentlemen?"

"I believe you can, we need to speak to your master on an urgent matter."

"I'm sorry, Mr?"

"Angove, Eugene Angove. This is my valet, Hampton."

"Well, I'm sorry, Mr Angove, Mr Theakston is *indisposed*."

As he went to shut the door, Eugene stuck his boot in the jamb. "I'm afraid I must insist," flashing the stone he had kept for himself, he barged the door aside.

Reynolds looked at the stone, and the one Hampton then produced, and let his shoulders sag. "Apologies, I had no idea you were with The Order. I'm sure he can spare you a few moments. Though, I must warn you, he's in something of a sorry state."

As they mounted the stairs, against the protestations of the landlady, Eugene asked Reynolds what ailed his employer. The valet responded by stating that he had suffered an *'an attack of nerves.'* Unsatisfied, Eugene pressed the matter but was met with stony silence. In the next heartbeat, they were at the door to Theakston's apartment and being ushered over the threshold.

"He's in the bedroom," Reynolds pointed at a door towards the southern end of the room. "I'll be out here if you need me."

"Are you not going to accompany us?" Hampton asked, perplexed at his laxity.

"I'm afraid not, sirs. I have a lump on the back of my head from our last conversation. For a small man, he is certainly proficient in the art of plate throwing."

"He threw a plate at you?"

"And a jug, and a glass. Like I said... he's had an attack of nerves."

Eugene and Hampton shared a look before approaching the door and knocking. "Mr Theakston," Eugene called out, "we are with The Order of Tamesis. We need to ask you a few questions... about the snow."

The door cracked open and a bloodshot eye appeared in the gap. "Show me your *credentials*."

Eugene and Hampton flashed their stones.

"Good, good, you can't be too careful," Theakston opened the door onto a scene of disorder and vandalism. It was suddenly clear why the landlady was in such a foul mood. It looked like an irate bull had been trying to redecorate. Along with the aforementioned projectiles, there were reams of paper strewn around the room. "You'll have to excuse the mess. I can't find it anywhere."

Eugene stepped inside and spoke in soft, level tones. "Find what, old chap?"

"Evidence, of course! It has to be here somewhere in these calculations."

"Evidence of what?"

"Foul play of course!" Theakston's eyes danced with manic frenzy as he began rummaging in the pile of paper on the bed. "I have to prove to those idiots in charge that the frostfair is dangerous, that *something* is coming. It must be stopped. The tragedy of 1813 will look like a picnic on a warm summer's eve in comparison. They must be stopped!"

"Slow down, dear boy. Who must be stopped?"

Theakston stood upright and fixed Eugene with an intense stare. "Why, The *International Traders, Hoteliers, and Quartermasters Association*, of course!"

"That bunch of market unionists, why?"

Theakston eyed Eugene with suspicion. "I find it odd that you aren't better informed. After all, it was you lot that approached me in the first place."

Thinking fast, Hampton cut in. "I'm afraid we have been out of the country. Taking care of *something* for the British Museum."

"Ah, I see. Very well, allow me to explain. While back in Reading, I was summoned to London by an old friend. Jeremy owns a rare book shop in the back streets of Soho and had been employed by a man named Stefan von Blon to track down a grimoire. It paid well and, as a junior member of The Order, he had access to certain things that other people didn't. To cut a long story short, he *acquired* the book and sold it. Before handing it over to his customer, he flipped through the pages a little. What he saw chilled his soul... literally. This book, *Ventus Secretus,* or *The Secret Wind,* detailed certain chants and rituals associated with the Great Old One, Ithaqua!"

Eugene staggered like he had been struck between the eyes.

"Sir," Hampton asked, a look of concern on his face, "are you alright, Sir.?"

"That name, *Ithaqua*, I've heard it before... in my dream. It was what those creatures were chanting!"

"Dream? What are you talking about?" Theakston began to scratch at his forearms, drawing blood in several places. "Can I continue, or are you just going to babble on?"

"Sorry, pray, continue," Eugene patted the air with both hands in an attempt to calm the troubled weatherman.

"Yes, well, Jeremy said that much of it was concerned with summoning this *Ithaqua* and his minions, the Wendigo. He didn't give it much thought, and put it down to the usual mumbo-jumbo that he encountered in his capacity as a bookseller. If he'd had a shilling for every time he'd been called upon to secure a magic book or grimoire that turned out to be utter tripe, he'd have been able to purchase Big Ben. The problem was, two days after the transaction, the predicted mild weather system changed to that Arctic blast outside."

"And, you think this von Blon chappy did it using the book?"

"I know it sounds far-fetched, Mr Angove, but it seems to be the only option. Jeremy called me to London to investigate and perhaps allay his fears. To the contrary, I'm afraid I only deepened them. The weather we are experiencing currently, is scientifically impossible. It shouldn't be, but here we are.

"My friend took it upon himself to attempt to right his wrong by tracking down Mr von Blon. In the end, it wasn't hard. He was the founder and chairman of The International Traders, Hoteliers, and Quartermasters Association. What's more, he filed a proposal to the council for a frost fair, a day *before* the weather changed. I looked into him and it turns out that his family were somehow involved in what happened in 1813..."

"I knew I recognised the name," Hampton cut in, pulling his newly purchased, and hastily filled, notebook from his pocket, "there was a Mr von Blon that owned a kind of freak show or cabinet of curiosities." He started flicking through the pages. "Aha, here we are, sir. A Mr von Blon was listed in the official reports as the proprietor of the *Tentacular Spectacular.* Apparently, the hole in the ice opened up right next to his tent!"

Eugene's mind flashed back once again to his dream. This time, he pictured the tent in his mind's eye and tried to make out the sign. It was the right length to say *Tentacular Spectacular.* "I don't like this one bit, Hampton. I think Mr Theakston here is right. I'd put a hefty bet on this *International Traders, Hoteliers, and Quartermasters Association* being the cause of all this. Though, why, is a complete mystery."

"You see it, I knew you would," Theakston beamed. "If that

wasn't enough to point the finger of blame at von Blon, just look at the name of his organisation..."

Hampton and Eugene looked at each other, nonplussed.

"It's an acronym!"

"Eh?" Eugene spluttered.

"An acronym Take the letters at the start of each word... I... T... H... A... Qu... A."

"Ithaqua!"

As Theakston shook his head emphatically, there was a colossal bang from downstairs followed by a scream.

"What in blue blazes was that?" Eugene instinctively drew the Webley revolver that he had stuffed in his pocket that morning, just in case.

"They've come for me!" Theakston dived behind the bed and tried to hide. "They are going to kill me like they did to Jeremy, Tremayne, and anyone else who stood in their way!"

"Stay out of sight," Eugene ordered. Rushing out of the room with Hampton on his heels, he was just in time to see Reynolds open the door to investigate, as he did, three shots were fired from the stairs, slamming into the valet's torso and spinning him like a top. One of the shots must have struck an artery as a thick gout of blood hosed the yellow wallpaper.

"Stay back, Hampton," Eugene instructed as he darted behind a chaise longue and took aim. A large man in a flat cap and a boiler suit was nearly through the door. Angove squeezed the trigger and shot him in the chest. He dropped instantly. Scurrying out of cover, he took the dead man's gun and tossed it to Hampton. "Just like the trenches, eh?"

"I bloody hope not, sir," Hampton grimaced as he checked the chamber. There were three shots left.

"Stay behind me and keep low, we don't know how many of them there are," advancing to the door, the former Captain Angove fell snugly back into the rhythm of combat. Poking his weapon through the balustrades on the landing overlooking the foyer, he spotted only the landlady. She was lying flat on her back with a bloody wound on her head. She looked like she had been pistol whipped. "Quick, Hampton, check her pulse, I'll take the other rooms."

As Hampton raced down the stairs and to the unconscious woman's side, Eugene checked the drawing room followed by the dining room and kitchen. The house was free of any other interloper. Once he was sure that the house was clear, he closed the front door as the wind howled, rattling the worm-eaten sash windows. Once it was secured, he joined Hampton who was in the process of placing a cushion from a nearby sofa under her head.

"Is she alright?"

"I think so, sir. Her breathing is steady and her pulse strong. She'll probably have a concussion, though. We should call a doctor."

"Agreed, we'll do it when we call the Peelers to deal with the bodies. Poor Reynolds... he seemed like a nice enough chap. He would have never won valet of the year, but..."

As Eugene spoke, there was a crash from upstairs followed by a shriek of terror.

"Theakston!" Bounding up the stairs, Eugene burst into the apartment and came to an abrupt stop nearly making Hampton collide with him. "What? How is this possible?" The room was frozen. Every inch of the carpet was covered in a blanket of pristine snow and every fitting and item of furniture was coated in a layer of ice, giving it a bluish tint. Both windows had been blown out, sending shards of glass in a wide radius.

"Theakston?" Hampton asked as he sidled towards the bedroom. Once at the door, he paused and poked his head inside. The room was empty and similarly frozen. The main difference to the living area was the window. Where the windows in the other room had simply had their panes obliterated, the window in the bedroom was missing... along with half of the wall.

"Sir, I think you should come and look at this."

"Any sign of Theakston?"

"I'm afraid not, sir."

Eugene stepped into the bedroom. "Well, bugger me..."

"Quite."

"What could have caused this?"

"I have no idea, sir. Ithaqua or one of his wendigos, perhaps?"

"Perhaps... Both you and I have seen what these *Old Ones* can do."

Hampton shuddered as he recalled the yellow horror in France, and the howling monstrosity in Egypt. "What do we do now?"

As Eugene pondered, there was a scream from outside the yawning hole in the building. Racing over, he poked his head out into the gloom. From somewhere high above, he could hear panicked cries and the uncontrolled babble of a broken mind.

"Good grief," Hampton exhaled, "can you make out anything he said, sir?"

"Something about his feet being on fire..."

"Poor chap. At least, we now know how that inspector

found himself up a tree."

Eugene turned away from the hole as Theakston's voice trailed off into the oncoming night. "If what he said is true, about anyone standing in von Blon's way being killed, I can only assume we have now made our way onto that list, Hampton."

"I fear you are right, sir. What I don't understand is the market traders, why target them?"

After pondering the question for a moment, Eugene answered. "Maybe they didn't want to get onboard with the frost fair idea. You know what it's like, Hampton, most committees couldn't agree on what to have for blasted breakfast, never mind making a decision on something potentially dangerous... yet lucrative."

"So, what's our next move?"

Eugene took a handful of bullets from his coat and passed some to Hampton before reloading his revolver. "I for one don't relish the idea of flying over London like a ruddy seagull," he closed the chamber and spun the barrell. "I think it's time someone had a word with this Stefan von Blon cove, don't you?"

Despite the harsh conditions, the frozen surface of the River Thames was a bustle of excitement and commerce. It had taken Eugene and Hampton longer than expected, due to Mr Angove taking a tumble outside of a pawnbroker's, to cross London and arrive at Westminster Bridge. By now, the first frost fair since the tragedy of 1813 was in full swing. Traders and food stalls competed with each other for customers while carnival barkers tried to lure those with a few extra coins to enter their attractions. It was a heady mixture of all that London had to offer. Under normal circumstances, Eugene would have been in the thick of it, downing bottles of ale and shoving jellied eels into his kisser. On that night, however, he wore a pensive expression.

"We have to be grateful for small mercies, sir," Hampton sighed as he looked down on the scene below, "at least they haven't brought an elephant this time."

"That's true enough," Eugene patted his jacket to feel the reassuring bulge caused by his firearm, "come along, Hampton. I think I recognise that tent near the centre."

"From your dream?"

Eugene nodded then turned and headed for the steps leading down to the embankment. Mudlarks and urchins, presumably paid handsomely by the trader group, toiled away with shovels and rock salt in an attempt to keep a clear path down to where a wooden gangplank had been erected to allow people onto the river. Wooden pallets had been placed in rows, providing makeshift roads over the ice that led punters to myriad opportunities to part with their wealth. From their earlier vantage point, it had been impossible to take in the sheer scale of the event and the incredible range of goods and refreshments on offer. Stalls selling Persian rugs rubbed shoulders with greengrocers and local artists attempting to sell their daubs to discerning homeowners.

"I think, if we take this path down past that beer stall, we should be somewhere near the centre," Eugene's mouth was watering. The smells of food originating from the four corners of the globe mingled with the enticing aroma of freshly poured ale. It took supreme force of will to make it past the makeshift bar without ordering a jar. Still, if they were successful in their enterprise, there would be plenty of time for that later. If they failed... Well, that didn't bear thinking about.

"Over here, sir... Is that the tent?"

Eugene turned the corner and stopped in his tracks. "Yes... that's the one." It was identical in every way to the first tent that had appeared in his dream. This time, he could read the sign. "Tentacular Spectacular, proprietor S. Von Blon..."

As they stood and looked at the red and blue striped carnival tent, the flap opened and a short, rotund, and bespectacled man in a tail-coat and top hat stepped out waving a staff tipped with an odd snowflake design. "Roll up, roll up, to the Tentacular Spectacular! Step inside to meet the wonders of the deep. Marvel at the Massachusetts fishboy, gasp at the tentacled horrors from the darkest trenches. All this and more for a single ha 'penny!"

Eugene pushed his way through the gathering throng. "Mr von Blon?"

Von Blon removed his hat and performed a deep and ostentatious bow. "At your service."

Pulling out his revolver in one hand and the stone of Tamesis in the other, he adopted a stern expression. "I think we need to talk."

In a flash, von Blon's demeanour changed. Snarling like a wild beast, he drew his own gun and loosed off three wild shots that, fortunately, only succeeded in thudding into the ice at Eugene's feet. Before Angove could return fire, von Blon held his staff aloft and started chanting. "*Hup yogagll Ithaqua nog. Nog wendigo nog!*" The end of his staff began to glow and the wind, or something riding it, howled furiously. A split-second later, there were screams from all over the frost fair and the already heavy snow became an impenetrable blizzard .

Eugene tried to aim but the terrified crowd running in all directions distracted his eye and knocked him off-balance. Von Blon cackled and flounced back into the tent. "Quickly, Hampton, into the tent!"

Shoving several men and women aside, Hampton drew his revolver and raced into the tent. "What the..." He found himself in a large vestibule containing a ticket booth and a Pacific blue ringed octopus in a hexagonal tank. This wasn't what had surprised him, however it was the multitude of paths leading off into darkness. The scale was impossible. From the outside, the tent looked barely able to contain a jazz quartet and a moderate audience. Inside, it looked bigger than the Houses of Parliament.

Eugene followed his valet and was similarly struck by the size of the interior. "Impossible. This is bloody impossible!"

From one of the passages to the left, a mocking voice called out, "Nothing is impossible, you blind fools. When you are one with the Old Ones, all is possible."

"Come out, von Blon, let's do this the easy way."

"Not on your Nelly, you blithering fopdoodle!" von Blon shot in the general direction of Eugene and Hampton. Again the bullet went wide. "Ha, catch me if you can!"

"Bastard," Eugene spat, "at least, the damned fool couldn't hit a barn at six paces. Come on, Hampton, let's finish this." Von Blon's shot had helped to pinpoint which passage he had used. Keeping to the sides of the passage, the two men hurried into the darkness. After a minute or two, they came to another round chamber housing a mirror maze. "Come out, von Blon, there's nowhere to hide."

"On the contrary, there are plenty of places to hide." On

cue, the lights around the maze were extinguished.

Cursing under his breath, Eugene took out his cigarette lighter and sparked the flint. "What's this all about?" He asked as he entered the maze.

"Respect, of course! My family was once respected in this city. Did you know that my Grandfather organised the last frost fair?"

"I didn't, " Eugene turned to Hampton and mouthed, "*Keep him talking.*"

"He did! If my damned fool father hadn't gotten rid of the book and the staff, we could rule the Empire by now."

Hampton picked up the conversational ball as Eugene navigated the hall of mirrors. "Why did he get rid of them?"

"Because he was a spineless fool, that's why. When he heard about the deaths at the last one, he stole them. He tossed the staff into the river and handed over the book to your blasted Order. We lost everything. Do you know how hard it is to be raised in poverty? My father's bleeding heart ruined my life!"

"It sounds to me, sir, that your motivation is money rather than respect."

Von Blon chortled. "The two go hand in hand."

Eugene had heard enough. "You're as mad as a March hare, you know that?"

"Enough! My Wendigo will deal with you... *Nog wendigo nog!*"

A growl echoed around the cramped corridors of the maze. Eugene had to stop his hands shaking as the hairs on his arms became erect. "My God... it's the *things* from my dream. Hampton, run!" Shielding the flame of his lighter with his hand, he took off towards the centre of the labyrinth. Seconds later, the sound of claws on wooden struts made him spin. "Look out!"

Hampton cried in alarm and dived to his left as an abomination flew in his direction, springing of powerful segmented legs. The wendigo collided with a mirror, shattering it with its antlers. Eugene aimed and took a shot. The bullet ricocheted off its thick bony forehead, ending a small chip into the air. Momentarily stunned, the creature shook it off and prepared to spring. This time Hampton fired, striking the creature in one of its hateful eyes. It howled in pain and crawled back into the darkness.

"Quickly, it will be back," Eugene grabbed his valet by the shoulder and dragged him onward. Soon, they found the centre and recoiled from the sight before them. In a large tank, was the preserved body of a teenage boy. It was half man-half fish.

"Do you like him... he was my grandfather's pride and joy."

Von Blon stepped out from behind the tank flanked by two more wendigos. "As you can see, you may as well drop your weapons."

"And, why would I do such a stupid thing?" Eugene asked.

"Because," von Blon snapped his fingers, "if you don't, I'll have my friends tear your valet limb from limb."

As the creatures started to stalk towards Hampton, Eugene held up his hands. "Fine, you win. Hampton, drop your gun."

Hampton complied, as he did, he felt a warmth in his pocket. Quickly, he stuffed his hand in inside and drew out the object responsible. The branch-like carving on the stone of Tamesis was glowing. Instantly, the wendigo closest to him recoiled and shielded its eyes. "Sir, the stone!"

Eugene took out his own stone and waved it at the other creature. After trying to withstand its lambency for a couple of seconds, they both wailed and leapt off to the shadows.

"Damn you," von Blon bellowed, brandishing his glowing staff.

Both Hampton and Eugene turned to face their tormentor, stoned brandished in their right fists.

"Fools, those won't work on me... and they won't work on my lord! *Iä Ithaqua!*" As he began to chant, his staff began to glow again and the ice began to shake.

As his blood boiled, Eugene had a flash of inspiration. "The inscription on the stone might not work on you," he raised his hand and bowled the stone at von Blon's head. "... But, I'm pretty sure this will."

Von Blon cried in pain as his nose was flattened by the flying stone. Blood poured down in two thick gouts, soaking the white wing-collar shirt beneath his coat, turning it red. As he raised his hands to cradle his busted snout, the staff tumbled to the floor.

"Quick, grab the staff," Eugene directed as he raised his gun and emptied it into their foe. Von Blon crumpled to the floor, expiring with a bitter curse on his lips.

Hampton leapt over and picked up the staff. It was still glowing. "Now what, sir?"

"Break the blasted thing!"

Gripping the staff at both ends, Hampton brought it down over his knee twice to no avail. On the third attempt, it splintered. Instantly, the rumbling stopped but the tent began to shake.

"Oh, Hell," Eugene grumbled as he retrieved the stone, "the bloody tent is shrinking. The staff must have given it its size. Run!"

Hampton didn't need to be told twice. Taking off apace with Eugene by his side, they fumbled their way by flickering flame to the vestibule. Diving out of the flap, they exited back into the fair not a moment too soon. With a horrific *crack,* the ice below the tent split, and the Tentacular Spectacular fell into the murky waters below.

"Blimey, Hampton, that was close."

Looking up at the now clear and snowless sky, Hampton grinned. "Indeed, sir."

"Where do you suppose Mr von Blon's grandfather found all this stuff?"

"From the reports I found in the library, it turns out he was in a similar line of work to yours. Notably, out in the wilds of Canada. I can only assume that he discovered all of his artefacts on an expedition of some sort."

"That makes sense... Right, Let's go to the pub before we deal with the constabulary. I could murder a pint. Plus, I anticipate that I shall soon receive a summons from The Order of Tamesis. I imagine they will want their rocks back... and I refuse to deal with that bunch of crackpots with a clear head."

Hampton shook his head with exasperation. "... Very good, sir..."

*Cyril stood over that horrible relic, pouring blood across it from a bowl as if it were some kind of vampiric cippus.*

# THE SONG FROM THE STATUE

SIMON BLEAKEN

*- London 1925 -*

It was an overcast August morning when I answered the call from Cyril Finnister that led me out into the bustling heart of London's dockland.

As I navigated the busy wharves and maze-like alleyways between the towering warehouses, there was little time to dwell on the reason for his insistence that I come at once. Instead, I was preoccupied with dodging armies of flat-capped dockhands who were ferrying grain and tobacco on sack trucks like a line of worker ants from a newly docked ship, while cranes lifted creaking wooden pallets laden with cargo into the air. Several British seamen and lascars were also hurrying about on deck, their cries echoing out as if competing with the city's background noise.

It was a relief when I got away from all the chaos and reached the side door of the warehouse that Cyril owned in a quieter section of the dock. I had a key and I let myself inside to find him waiting for me, leaning against a long shelf of large crates, hair slicked back and a smile of anticipation on his toad-like face.

"Ah, George, glad you're here," he beamed. "Wait until you see my latest acquisition!"

His official trade lay in the import of cloth, and that was what filled the main body of his warehouse, where cats prowled to keep the rats at bay. But I hadn't been called here for any of that. It was the small, secret back room that held the item that I had been summoned to appraise; his latest purloined treasure from the ancient world. He liked to call himself an antiquarian, but in truth he was little more than a parasite, picking history clean like some tweed-clad vulture with halitosis. His knowledge of archaeology was appallingly dim. He cared little for learning the history of a culture or the provenance of the pieces that came into his sweaty clutches. He only cared if an artefact was rare and valuable.

And that was where I, George Halwood, came in.

I had been a student of some note, a rising star in certain Egyptological circles. My father, a military man, had hoped I would follow in his shoes. But, I was gripped by a love of ancient history that refused to let me go, and had followed that calling against his approval. I excelled in my studies thanks to my passion for the subject matter, and after earning my doctorate I gained a job as a cataloguer within the bowels of the British Museum's archives. But my passion lay in field archaeology. I was soon in line for an assistant researcher post and had strong connections within several prominent Egyptological organisations, all of which seemed to promise that I would realise my dreams of leading expeditions one day.

After all, I was young and gifted, and in the right city to advance my reputation. Curiously, for a land so far removed culturally, chronologically and geographically, London and ancient Egypt had formed a strong and unshakeable connection. It was home to the British Museum, The Horniman Museum, and the Petrie collection at University College. Above the doors of Sotheby's auction house, a genuine bust of the goddess Sekhmet gazed out over New Bond Street. Meanwhile, Cleopatra's Needle, actually a New Kingdom obelisk from Heliopolis, stretched tall and regal beside the Thames. And, just a short walk away, the Egypt Exploration Society founded by Amelia Edwards was busy lobbying funds for new expeditions to that distant land.

I'll admit, I harboured fanciful dreams of being the man to finally discover the location of Imhotep's resting place in Saqqara, or of unearthing an undiscovered tomb in the Valley of the Kings, fuelled by the recent triumph of Howard Carter and Lord Carnarvon that had been the talk of the whole world, and had given rise to a new interest in all things ancient Egyptian among the general populace.

But, the harsh reality was that my current position was a low-paying one, and the rental costs of my tiny London flat loomed like a sword of Damocles above my head. I might have had a promising future ahead, but promises don't pay the rent or put food on the table. Falling quickly on hard times, and finding my current income insufficient to meet the demand, I smuggled several small artefacts from the museum's vaults to make ends meet. I selected the items carefully enough – things that would fetch a fine price, but which were unlikely to be missed any time soon: a few ushabtis, a heart scarab amulet, a Predynastic pot, and a shard of limestone with a cartouche of Rameses II upon it. I felt terrible about it, of course. It violated everything I believed in at the time, but I was desperate.

That was how I first met Cyril Finnister, and how this nefarious arrangement became an established pact. The man was hardly a friend, and yet, in the two years since I had been in his employ, helping to evaluate his ill-gotten goods in return for the money I so desperately needed to survive, he had become more than just a benefactor. Of course, I had protested that my actions would only ever be a one-off, that my integrity as an archaeologist was too important to violate. But, the trouble was I got away with it, and made good money in the process.

"My dear boy," he had laughed at my obvious guilt, clamping an arm around my shoulder as he surveyed his treasures, his voice as always taking on a cultured affectation, as if ashamed of his working-class origins. "You're far too naive. Everything that has come out of Egypt has been stolen. Museums are just storehouses of plunder. Why should we be any different?"

After that, my moral compass stopped working.

I shook myself out of thoughts of the past and followed him down the rows of towering shelves towards the concealed double doors at the far end.

"It's in here!" he declared eagerly as he threw the doors open and turned on the light, as if I hadn't been down in that small hidden storage room a hundred times already. He lifted a covering cloth with a proud flourish, carefully watching my reaction as I got my first look at the artefact.

It was clearly a statue, but it was so heavily eroded it gave only a vague outline of a shape. I wasn't even certain what kind of stone it was carved from. The colour was that of sandstone, but the texture and density of the rock were harder, more like granite, and it sparkled with trapped minerals. I assumed, at first glance, that it might be a block statue, or perhaps a seated scribe. But again, it was difficult to be sure. The brow of the piece appeared to bear a residual nodule, that I suspected might have been the remains of a uraeus, a stylised and protective cobra found only on depictions of certain gods or royalty.

"So, what have I got here?" he smiled.

"Honestly, I'm not certain yet," I replied, crouching and working my way slowly around it. There were rows of inscriptions running up the back in five distinct columns. They were so worn as to be almost illegible, but I thought with care and time it might be possible to make some sense out of them.

"There's something else," Cyril announced eagerly. "Listen to this." He pulled down an old tarpaulin, revealing a small window set high up and let the weak sunlight into the room and onto the relic.

"Listen to what?"

"Give it a moment."

The dusty light coruscated faintly around the hunched outline of the statue. And then, the stone began to emit a strange musical note, soft but clear, like a finger running around the rim of a glass.

"Hear that?" he grinned again. "It sings! I think the light causes it. Oh I know, it's a dull day out today, but it's still enough to make it work. You should hear it when the sun's *really* shining."

"That is curious," I noted as I stood. "Though, it's not the first singing statue connected to Egypt."

He raised an eyebrow.

"One of the so-called 'Colossi of Memnon' was reported as singing in antiquity," I explained. "It was likely just air moving through a fissure in the rock, or perhaps even sunlight warming the dew inside it. Anyway, it all carried on until a Roman emperor, Septimius Severus, had it repaired and it fell silent again. It drew quite a crowd in its day though, according to the records."

"Ah, but look," his smile widened, "this one has no fissures, or at least none that can be observed with the naked eye. You understand why I *had* to have it."

In the increased light, I crouched and took a closer look.

"This could very well be Early Dynastic, perhaps even Predynastic. There's something here that might be a serekh."

I saw a frown crease his brow.

"That's an early precursor of the cartouche that would later encircle the name of the king."

"So, it's connected to royalty?"

"I said it *might* be. I don't know. I'll need to spend more time with it. I'll also make a copy of the carvings and see what I can find at the museum."

"You won't show anyone else?"

"I'll be discrete as always. Do you know where this came from?"

"It was found buried at a site near Abydos."

"Well, that's something at least."

"I'll leave you to get to work then," he smiled, making his way back out into the warehouse.

I spent the next few hours taking notes, sketches and measurements of the relic and the curious writing that covered the back of it. I worked by artificial light to keep that strange sound to a minimum, but still, by the time I finished and gathered my notes my head was pounding.

I drove straight to the museum, intending to spend the first of many evenings burning the midnight oil among the books, records and resources of that venerable establishment. I had an amicable arrangement with the night guards, and was fortunate that my connections made such late visits possible. It reduced the chances of running into any colleagues and associates who might take an undue interest in what I was researching. It didn't entirely remove the risk though, and for that reason Cyril refused to allow me to take any photographs of his objects. He wasn't especially keen on my need to take notes and sketches either, but I needed something to work from.

I haunted the stacks, papers and books like some bleary-eyed wraith, trying to find any leads or clues to that curious writing covering our mysterious statue, and hoping to find other examples of statuary that resembled it. I studied the site reports from various digs at Abydos, paying careful attention to the artefacts that had been dated to the Predynastic or Early Dynastic periods. I drew a blank on all of them. I even widened my search, speculating that perhaps the statue had been buried at a later date, possibly a symbolic offering, but there was so much to look through it was clear this was not going to be a mystery that would be solved quickly.

Thankfully, archaeologists are patient by nature, and I had faith that my careful digging into the records would unearth something in the fullness of time. I just hoped Cyril would be equally as patient.

It was painful work though. The inscriptions were

unusual, not like anything I was familiar with. And, what I first thought to have been a kind of serekh proved instead, under more detailed examination, to be a curious geometric carving that didn't resemble anything on record. The only thing I was feeling relatively certain about was that the lump on the brow was likely a uraeus.

The weathering of the statue was troubling me too. While I still couldn't determine what kind of stone it was, it appeared comparable to granite or dolomite. Certainly not something that would erode easily, especially not in Egypt.

I spent the first part of that week going back and forth between the statue during the day and the museum in the evenings, grabbing sleep and making token appearances at my day job somewhere in between. I was soon exhausted, but Cyril wanted answers and I wanted money, so I vowed to keep at it. I could only work with the statue under artificial light though, and then only in short bursts. Even under those conditions it would eventually start to sing. I hadn't been able to identify any fissure or crack that could be responsible for the sound though. The whole thing looked curiously intact.

I always stopped work at midday. I still needed to eat, and to clear my mind I took walks beside the Thames, usually pausing in my favourite spot beneath the obelisk as I watched the waters flow past, the sounds and vibrancy of London a welcome relief after the tomb-like stillness of that hidden storage area.

It seemed to me that London was, and always had been, a city steeped in secrets. From the countless dingy alleyways and back streets where thieves and beggars lay in wait, to the vast chimneys belching out choking smoke and the avenues of warehouses and workhouses, it was a place that had changed little since Victorian times, only now with the added filth and noise from passing motor cars and the latest developments in industrialisation. Frequently fog-bound, sprawling and unfriendly, it was a place where scholars and magicians, politicians and scoundrels, power and poverty, were all bound together in an expansive stone jungle as ruthless and dangerous as any wilderness.It was the tarnished jewel in the crown of the British Empire, and we were adding our own secrets to it.

Then, on the morning of the Thursday of that week, I arrived as usual to find Coles, the old night watchman that Cyril employed, pacing anxiously outside the warehouse. It was obvious that he had been waiting for me because he hurried across at once.

"Glad you're back, sir," he muttered gruffly. "I've been ever so worried."

"Worried? What's happened?"

"It's Mr Finnister, sir. He didn't go 'ome last night, just sat in that back room with that stone, *whispering* to it. It was the strangest thing. I could hear 'im, all night. But when I went in to check if he was all right, he'd shoo me away."

"That is odd."

"It's not like 'im at all, sir. I was... well, hoping you might have a word. Make sure nothing's wrong, I mean."

"I'll speak to him," I reassured Coles. "Why don't you go on home? Get some sleep."

I waited until Coles was out of sight before hurrying inside. Cyril was protective of his secrets, and I didn't know how much he had shared with his night watchman.

I found Cyril slumped on the floor next to the workbench with the relic atop it. It was already singing, that horrible monotonous tone cutting through the air. Cyril himself looked pale and shaken, half-conscious, with a string of drool hanging from his mouth and a trickle of blood from one nostril. As I knelt beside him, I feared he might have suffered a stroke, but he stirred when I said his name, and I helped him sit up.

"Are you all right?"

"Yes – yes!" he blinked and seemed to shake himself like a man coming out of a trance. "George, did you *hear* it? Tell me you did. It was wonderful!"

I stood and switched off the light, casting the room into darkness and silencing the song of the statue. "It's giving me a headache."

"No... no – not *that*!" he grumbled, his elation turning to irritation at my reaction. "You don't understand. It sang to me, last night."

"It was doing it just then."

"That's not what I mean. I mean it *sang*, not just the single tone, but a whole *chorus*!" His eyes burned with a manic fever as he clutched my shoulder. "It was majestic. A song of a wanderer, falling through the void between worlds, born in fire as it fell to the sands."

"You had a dream by the sound of it."

"It was no dream. It was telling me how it came to be here."

"Are you saying you think it's meteoric?"

"No. It didn't come from the stars... not out there," he shook his head. "But from..."

There was a faint scuffle out in the warehouse, a soft tread of shoe close by, and I realised someone was standing in the doorway to our secret little room. I turned, just as a voice sneered:

"Well now, what the 'ell's all this?"

Startled, I sprang to my feet, only to stagger backwards as the figure struck out with his arm, catching me full in the face. I fell back against a crate, the wooden rim biting into my spine.

"Stay where I can see you," the stranger warned.

I could see he was a heavyset, round-faced man with a stern, joyless face. He was well-dressed though, his clothes impeccably tailored. Behind him lurked another man, thin and scrawny, in shabbier clothes with dark sunken eyes beneath a frayed flat cap. In his bony hands he clutched a crowbar.

"Who the hell are you?" I demanded.

"I'm the one asking questions," the round-face man barked. He looked down at Cyril who peered up sheepishly. "Where's the money you owe, Finnister?"

"I was just coming to see you, Fred!" Cyril answered, though the look of alarm on his face said otherwise. "I got it right here."

"Really?" Fred folded his arms, looking from me to Cyril and then back again. "Then go get it, nice and slow. Or my friend 'ere gets busy."

"Whatever you say," Cyril nodded, standing hastily and fumbling in the dark at the back of the room. He glanced at me. "Get the light, would you? I can't see a thing in here."

"Naw, allow me," Fred said, reaching over for the switch.

The statue started to sing almost as soon as the light came on, and Fred stared down at it in surprise. "What the 'ell is-?"

That was when Cyril turned, and I saw what he had in his hand, an old *Cyclist's Friend* Colt .32 revolver. It must have been well over twenty years old and looked like it had been sitting unused for a long time.

"Now, don't go doing anything stupid," Fred narrowed his eyes, but I saw beads of sweat forming on his brow and the way he was nervously edging towards the door.

"What's wrong?" Cyril smiled, though I could see his hand was trembling. "Didn't think I had it in me?"

"Still don't," Fred scowled. "You're no killer."

Cyril narrowed his eyes. "These walls are thick. Nobody would hear anything."

"We both know that you..."

That was as far as Fred got before the gun fired. In the small space, the sound was deafening and set my ears ringing.

Fred toppled sideways, slumping across the relic. He was making a strange gurgling gasp and I saw blood spatter across the stone and soak the front of his shirt. He seemed to be trying to stand, but his legs weren't able to support him. He pawed weakly at the statue with one hand, his other clutching up near his throat.

The scrawny chap in the doorway turned and started to run. Without thinking I gave chase, quickly catching up with him in one of the long avenues of crates. I tackled him from behind and we went down in a heap, the crowbar slipping from his hands. In desperation he slammed his elbow back, trying to wind me, but I was already reaching for the crowbar and he struck only air.

"Stop him! He's seen everything!" Cyril barked from behind me. My fingers closed around the crowbar and I brought it down hard across the back of the fellow's head. There was a sickening crack and he went limp instantly. I struck him twice more, just to make sure, and then crawled away, feeling sick and shaken.

It had all happened so fast, I hadn't had time to think about any of it. I had reacted purely on instinct and the awareness that to let him get away would destroy everything. Now, with reason and logic catching up, I could only stare at that limp form and my hands speckled with blood that had ended his life.

"You did the right thing," Cyril said, and I realised he was standing over me. "Saved us a lot of bother."

"Who was...?" I swallowed, gesturing at the body.

"No idea. Some low life, I'd imagine. That other fellow, Fred, was an old... business partner, of a sort. He's not somebody the world will miss, trust me."

"What... what do we do now?"

"You go get cleaned up. Take the rest of the day off and keep your mouth shut. I need you to get your focus back. But, be here tomorrow, you still have work to do. As for these, I'll take care of the bodies."

I stared at him, seeing a side of the man I'd never witnessed before. I thought I'd got a pretty good measure of him over our time together: avaricious, but ultimately harmless. Now, I felt like a clueless child who'd been playing with matches, never realising the truth of just what the fire could do, or how deeply it could burn.

As instructed, I went home. My hands were trembling so badly that I was amazed I was able to open the door to my cramped apartment, and the first thing I did upon getting inside was to be violently sick in the toilet. I spent the rest of that day in a daze, the images of that horrible incident playing out in my mind (and later, I discovered, within my dreams as well).

In defiance of Cyril's instructions, I stayed away for the next two days. I was a wreck, I just wallowed in bed, unable to sleep but unable to face the world either.

Finally, I dragged myself from beneath those sheets and crawled into the bath. I stank and my mouth felt furry. I hoped the hot water would scour away the bad memories as it did the sweat, but such things are not so easily shifted.

Then, unable to deny my demons any longer, I went back to the warehouse.

As I scurried through the chaos and noise of the docklands I felt no better than one of the rats that skulked and darted between the crates. I had always known crime and corruption bred in the shadows of the city. I had recognised too that my own existence had come perilously close to that shadowy underworld. But somehow, until that incident with the gun and crowbar, I had managed to convince myself that I had never stepped fully into that world, that I still held onto some vestige of decency. Now, I knew just how far I had fallen.

The place was silent as I approached and unlocked the door. There was no sign of Coles or of any of the cats that usually prowled the crates. And of course, there was no sign of either of the bodies from the other day.

I made my way through the avenues of shelves towards the little back room, aware that I could already hear the song of the statue from halfway down the warehouse.

"Cyril?" I called, but there was no reply. I reached the doorway and froze.

Cyril stood over that horrible relic, pouring blood across it from a bowl as if it were some kind of vampiric *cippus*. But, instead of the act granting its healing boon upon Cyril, it was the stone that was transformed. I could see it becoming more defined as the blood ran across it, as if the erosion were reversing under that gory deluge. If not for the sound coming out of it and the stone it was made from, I would have believed it a different artefact. It was also changing shape as I watched – transforming into a pyramidion, with those strange inscriptions covering every side. That song was getting stronger too.

"Cyril?" I called again, uneasily.

He blinked and looked up at me. It took a moment for his confusion to clear. "That you, George?"

"What's going on?"

"Restoration," he said matter-of-factly.

"Whose blood is that?"

"Does it matter?" he laughed.

"I think it does," I swallowed nervously. "Where's Coles?"

"Never mind all that, *listen*... listen to the song!"

I edged closer, getting a better look at the artefact. "What happened to it? It's completely different."

"It's healing itself."

"What are you talking about? Stone can't do that."

"This one does. It's the primal source of creation. Why shouldn't it reshape itself."

"What did you *say*?"

"It's a gift from the gods, and it's giving me its blessing too. Come closer, see for yourself!"

I took another step and was leaning in to examine it when Cyril grabbed my hand and pressed it against the bloody stone. I let out an involuntary gasp as the world seemed to turn sharply beneath me and an icy cold flooded my limbs.

I saw a pale sky over an expanse of sandy desert that stretched down to the fertile green of cultivated land bordering the flowing waters of the Nile, where crocodiles basked in the sun and people fished on reed rafts. It was a moment in time from thousands of years ago, perfectly preserved. I could feel the warmth of the sun, hear the lapping of the water and the voices of the people. The air was clear and fresh, without the taint of industry or pollution that hung so thickly over my own world.

Then there was a cry of alarm that ran through the fishermen. They pointed upwards, staring in fearful amazement at something that was plummeting downwards, glowing hot, from out of what looked like a tear in the sky.

I recognised it as the relic, in its pyramidion form.

It rippled as it hit the atmosphere, an angel of death descending through the clouds like a gleaming scythe. It slammed into the mud at the edge of the river, sending lethal sound waves bursting out across the land, dropping people where they stood. Those indoors or far enough away had a lucky escape, but those closer to the impact crater were felled instantly, crumpling like marionettes whose strings had been cut, blood oozing from their noses, ears and eyes.

River water now surged into the crater, cooling the object with a hiss. And as the fluid surrounding it boiled away, the tip of the pyramidion rose out of the steam. There was a strange nodule just below the peak, like a glowing uraeus on the brow of a Pharaoh, and this now exploded in a blaze of white light, carrying a sound out across the land, a summons that drew the survivors towards it. I watched the people come, drawn from the fields and nearby settlements, many of them bleeding profusely from their ears and noses, overwhelmed by the potency of the song. And, surrounding the pyramidion, they dropped to their knees in obeisance and pressed their bloody hands upon it. Several of them even seized the bodies of the fallen dead as if in some crazed frenzy, dragging them across to the relic before ripping them open with blades made from chert, letting the still-warm blood spill across the artefact. The crowd bayed and howled wildly at this grisly bloodletting. Then, when the fallen dead had all been offered, the men with the stone blades demanded that the crowd relinquish some from among the living to appease the relic, and the gory spectacle started again...

That was when the connection broke and the vision ended.

I'm not sure if I had snatched my hand away or if the object was too weak to maintain the connection, but I hit the ground and curled up into a ball. My body was covered in a clammy film of sweat, my limbs shaking uncontrollably. There was a single line of blood running from my left nostril and I wiped it away in alarm.

"You understand now?" Cyril asked. I felt his arms around me as he helped me to my feet. "We have to honour it. We must nurse it back to its full power. We are in the presence of the divine!"

I stumbled away from him. "You're crazy! We don't know what this is..."

"How can you be so blind?" he looked disappointed in me. "I thought you would welcome this. All your life you've dreamed of uncovering something wonderful, and we have! We can bring it back into the world together!"

I turned and lurched from the warehouse, feeling sick and

shaken.

When I got home and burst through my front door I was still trembling. The coppery taint of blood from that vision, from those poor dying villagers and fishermen, seemed to cling to my skin and clothes. I tore everything off and crawled into the bath, increasing the temperature until it scalded my skin. But even with the hot steam rising around me, I still felt cold, as if I had been touched by the spectre of death.

When I was dry and dressed in clean clothes, I went out. The apartment felt maddeningly claustrophobic, and I needed space to clear my thoughts.

The city seemed subdued that morning, the roads a little quieter, as if something of that constant and unceasing pulse of life had been drained away. The few people scurrying through the streets also seemed cowed and sullen, a mood matched by the grey haze of fog that lay upon the city, bringing a damp chill with it.

I sought refuge in the galleries of the British Museum's ancient Egyptian collection. It was normally a place that brought me comfort, a sanctuary for a long-dead civilisation that spoke to my heart. But today, I found only accusation in the faces of the gods, and in the stare of those gilded coffins and carved stone visages. I was a traitor to that which I had sworn to study and protect, and the lingering spirits of that lost kingdom knew it. And now, I had betrayed London as well, having facilitated this cancer that was growing secretly in its heart.

I staggered out into the fog once more, feeling nauseated and ashamed of my actions. I had nobody to turn to for help, not without revealing my duplicitous nature and destroying any hopes for my future. To feel so alone in a city of so many was a curious sort of isolation. Having nowhere else to go, I made for the river, my only remaining place of sanctuary.

The grey murk of the Thames lapped softly as I stared at it. I wondered what mysteries it too was hiding within it. So much of London existed below the surface that at times the city felt like a nest of secrets, layer upon layer, obscured by the fog that so frequently cloaked the streets. I saw myself mirrored in that too. Outwardly respectable, and yet concealing a core that had started to rot with a corruption I no longer knew if I could stop. I realised Cyril would have acquired that damnable statue with or without my involvement, and yet my actions were undeniably a part of everything unfolding here.

Had the ancient Egyptians wrestled with this same dilemma all those years ago? Had some of them understood the danger of the relic and tried to protect future generations from it? To me, it was a stark reminder of the futility of all endeavours. Time would eventually strip away all knowledge and memory, reducing everything to dust. I used to believe that as an archaeologist, I played a small part in the process of returning a semblance of life to dead ruins once more, but it was an imperfect process. Our work could grant us an insight into the culture they lived in, the values they held and the gods they worshipped – but we could only ever paint a partial picture. Time would forever deny us a total understanding of all that had been.

And, of course, our own civilisation wasn't immune to the process either. One day, we would be the nameless bones and ruined cities unearthed by some distant explorer, our achievements and discoveries lost. If we were lucky they might struggle to understand us too – drawing a fumbling approximation of our dead language and culture out of the dust to flourish briefly once more in the data archives of some future library or place of learning, at least until the fall of that civilisation and the start of the whole cycle once again.

It was the grim reality of the endless march of time, swallowing all things as it went. Nothing was forever, and eventually, all things would be forgotten, as impermanent as a shadow cast by the sun.

But I wasn't about to admit defeat, as futile as it all might have been. If I could hold back the threat to our city for even just a short time, I had to try. Whatever was in that warehouse was powerful and dangerous and needed to be destroyed, no matter how old and valuable it might be.

That evening, armed with only a vague plan of attack and courage born from desperation, I returned to the warehouse.

I could hear the song from the statue even as I neared the building, even through those thick walls. It was louder than ever, and now was no longer a single note, but a shifting chorus of sounds that seemed to stimulate potent feelings of awe and wonder, of adoration and worship, and also filled my mind with images of shifting colour, like half-formed visions.

I plugged my ears as best I could with shreds of rags before letting myself in, sneaking through the avenues of crates like a burglar. I was hunting for explosives. Cyril had once told me that, as a younger man, he had been involved in the clearing of slums and derelict buildings during the 1880 construction of the Albert Dock. Not one for worrying about the legalities of any situation even then, he had found ways to cut corners through the use of illicit homemade explosives, little more than black powder, but strong enough when used in quantity. He'd mentioned in passing that he still had some left, hidden in the depths of the warehouse. I didn't know how much, or even if it would still work after so long. But I hoped it just might be enough to destroy that infernal relic.

It took half an hour before I finally discovered what I was after, hidden within several old crates at the farthest end of the building. I prayed it hadn't got damp over the years as I moved them up one by one and stashed them near the side door.

I'd set them shortly, but I wanted to try and get Cyril out first, if I could.

I crept towards the back room and was only a few steps away when I noticed a foot sticking out from beside one of the crates in the shelving. I peered into the space between the wooden containers, and gave a startled gasp at the sight of the body of Coles, and at least two dock workers that had been unceremoniously stashed there. Their heads had been bludgeoned, their throats and wrists slashed, and I finally realised where the blood had come from that Cyril had been pouring across the relic. The man had been busy.

"George?" a voice called, hoarsely. "Is that you?"

I turned as Cyril shambled out into the warehouse, barely holding back a second gasp. He looked like a desiccated corpse, a living mummy devoid of wrappings. His sunken eyes blinked weakly, and he stank, a stench of death and corruption as his cells necrotised and his body broke down. He was also bleeding from the ears, eyes and nose.

"Cyril? What happened?"

He stumbled and fell against one of the crates. His eyes squinted as he tried to focus on me. "Can't see you... where are you?"

I hurried over, pulling the plugs from my ears so I could better hear him. That infernal song filled the warehouse, louder than ever before, and I struggled against its call. The colours shifting in my mind seemed to be getting clearer and stronger, more like the vision I had witnessed when I touched the relic with my hand. I pushed through it as best I could. "I'm here!"

"The light... it was too much for me. It drained me... took more than I ever imagined..."

"What light?"

"It's waking, returning to full strength....."

"Cyril, what is it?"

"It's the primal mound... the benben... the first above the waters. They knew, at Heliopolis, where it landed... they knew it well. They fed it with regular offerings of blood, and venerated it."

I frowned. "History has no record of that."

"The stone remembers what we have forgotten. Listen..." he gripped my arm. "Listen to me. I don't think I have much time left..."

"I'm listening," I assured him.

"It fell at Heliopolis, burning like the sun. It rose from the water, transforming it to steam, and summoned the people to it. They came. They built their world and their belief system upon it, but soon realised it was too dangerous to keep in the light. They buried it, cloaked it in myth and symbol. Later Pharaohs took it to Abydos, and made an offering of it to the cult of Osiris, beseeching him to take it safely into the afterlife. They believed only in the west, in the land of the dead, would it be safe. There its powers could no longer harm the living. Only... we dug it up. We brought it into the light again. We brought it here to London."

"How do you know all this?"

"It told me... whispered its history, sometimes in words, and sometimes in visions. You've seen that for yourself, haven't you? A relic that slipped between worlds, passing between the walls that keep realities separated..."

"Can it be destroyed?" I urged him.

"I can't keep it out of my mind..." he gasped, a shudder running through his ravaged frame. "I can't fight it. At first, I was in awe of it. I desired its boon, its blessing. But it drank deeper than I even imagined. It took more than I was willing to give. Its hunger is still growing. Whatever spell it cast has broken for me. I see it for what it is now. What it made me do. I see the truth of all of it. It will consume the city if we let it. Already its voice is calling to the faithful..."

"You need to get outside, get away from here!" I urged, but he waved me away.

"It's too late for me. But not for you."

"I'm going to destroy it," I told him. "You can't stay here."

"I'm already dead. Do what you must."

"You're sure?"

"Hurry! While it's still weak, and before they come!"

I ran over to the side door and looked outside. The light of that relic was so bright it lit the warehouse from within, blasting out of the cracks and spaces around the doors and through the narrow windows and loading bays. It shone like a beacon even through the dense pea-souper fog now smothering the streets and turning the once-familiar landmarks into vague and eerie shapes.

And it carried that song with it.

Even as I watched, figures were emerging from that thick yellow smog like people under a mesmerist's spell. The relic had seduced and beguiled them the same way it had put Cyril under its thrall. It had drawn dockhands and workers from nearby, as well as beggars from the alleys and the poor and sick from the workhouses. They came, summoned by the light and the song, and in return it drew from their essence and whispered in their minds with visions. There must have been eighty people now converging on the warehouse.

Had such a scene once played out thousands of years earlier in Heliopolis, that ancient city of the sun? Had the people there also been drawn to the dazzling light and sound of this noxious relic, and had that over time become conflated with the worship of the god Atum?

I didn't wait to find out. I darted back inside and bolted the door before rolling each of the crates of black powder explosives over to the back room one by one. I prayed this would work, at the rate the relic's power was increasing I suspected I'd not get a second attempt.

The light from that tiny room was blinding as I approached. I had once more plugged my ears against that sound, but even so it still rang within my head, taking all of my willpower to resist its seductive allure. I felt the tickling trickle of blood running from my nose, and knew the plugs in my ears were failing me.

Inside the room, the uraeus atop the relic blazed like a

white-hot flame, a lethal beacon that would absorb the essence of anyone it snared.

"Hurry..." Cyril called, the sound barely audible over the song and the rags in my ears. "They're pounding on the doors..."

I kept my gaze on the floor. I didn't dare raise them to meet that object as I set each of the explosive barrels around the relic, careful not to touch it with my hands. It was agonising work. I had to fight against the insidious pull of that object, and the images clouding my mind, obscuring my thoughts. It was hard to focus on the task at hand as I dragged each barrel across to that room of hellish light and sound.

Finally, my face slick with blood, I led a small powder trail out into the warehouse.

There was a muffled crash from behind me, a window breaking.

I heard Cyril shouting something, but it was lost to the intensity of the note that now pulsed through me in defiance of the rags in my ears. My hands shook as I fished a small box of matches from my jacket pocket, my body already trembling with the energy surging through it. Those shifting colours in my mind were already starting to coalesce into an actual vision. I was finding it hard to concentrate on the real world and the task I was trying to complete.

There was another faint crash, almost swallowed by the song.

People were breaking into the building, under the thrall of the relic that now blazed like a star.

I blinked away bloody tears and struck the match, setting the end of the powder trail alight with a fizzing spark.

Then I ran.

I had almost reached the side door when it burst inwards, admitting a shambling mass of glassy-eyed tramps, vagrants and dockhands. They too were bleeding from the nose and ears. They surged inside, shoving past me in their desperate haste to reach the room where the relic waited – and I in turn battled against them, like a swimmer against an incoming tide, in my frantic attempts to escape the building before the flame reached the rest of the black powder.

I was fortunate that they seemed to have no interest or awareness of me. The relic was the only thing they seemed to be conscious of.

Finally, I made it to the door, fighting to squeeze through the bottleneck of people desperate to get inside. I punched and kicked, shoving and clawing to get past them. And finally, I did. The night air was cool on my face as I squeezed through and started to run past the figures still emerging from the fog.

I wasn't sure how long I had, or if the powder would be dry enough to ignite.

I just had to get as far away as possible before...

The explosion that came lifted me on a wave of burning pressure and threw me forward six feet. I landed heavily, face-down and winded, as behind me a fireball ripped through the warehouse, blasting the windows outwards and blowing chunks out of the walls and roof with a thunderous roar.

My ears rang and my body screamed in pain where I had skinned myself against the ground's hard surface. I tried to stand, but could only stagger at first, a thin whine cutting through my skull. I could smell something burning, and see the flames that licked up high at the broken windows. It must have been the bodies of the dead inside, and what remained of the crates.

A second explosion went off, smaller than the first.

The sides of the building groaned, a sound of fracturing brick and protesting metal, and then the whole thing seemed to collapse in a dense cloud of gritty dust and tumbling rubble.

For a moment I could only stare, stunned and numb. Everything felt dreamlike and unreal. Then, as the flames rose higher and the screams of the trapped and dying began, I hurried away down the docks as fast as my battered body allowed, before the police or fire crews arrived.

I went straight home, to lick my wounds and lie low.

By some miracle, I avoided being connected to the place in the days that followed. A lot of dirt was dredged up about Cyril and his past dealings in the newspapers, but my name wasn't among them. Somehow, I had scraped through it all with my reputation intact and my involvement unknown.

My promising future at least seemed secure.

I made my excuses and stayed away from work until my wounds had started to recover. It took several days before that awful ringing in my ears finally dissipated, but I knew I had been extremely fortunate not to have done any permanent damage.

It was well over a week before I dared go anywhere near the docks again. When I finally did, one hazy afternoon, I kept to the shadows as much as possible, avoiding people until I turned off to where Cyril's building had been. The rubble still lay where it had fallen, aside from a few places where police and firemen had scoured the ruins trying to retrieve the dead. A few fragments of wall and broken metal still stood defiantly, but the rest had collapsed, and more importantly, the small back room where the relic had been was buried deeply.

I prayed it would be a long time before they ever cleared the site for rebuilding.

I also prayed that the relic had been blown to dust.

"I'm sorry it came to this, Cyril," I whispered, watching shadows dance across the broken stones as the clouds moved overhead. It seemed so peaceful there now, so still, it was hard to imagine the horrors that had once taken place there.

It wasn't until I turned, planning to head home and get some more sleep, that I caught a single faint note on the morning breeze, and froze in terror.

It was a thin, almost indiscernible note, but it came from deep beneath that pile of rubble at my feet.

It was the song of that infernal statue.

I dropped to my knees amid the grime, frantically clawing at the blocks and debris, finally seizing a length of twisted metal and hacking at the rubble and trying to smash or break the blocks of fallen stone that blocked my access to that buried horror. I never even felt the metal as it cut into my palms. My only thought was that I had to unearth the foul relic, to smash it apart with my own hands. It couldn't be allowed to be discovered ever again.

I never heard the raw howl of anguish and rage that tore from my throat, but others did.

It took me a little while to notice that my wild outburst had been witnessed and that a small crowd was gathering nearby, watching the madman attacking the debris. I must have looked a sight, filthy, raving, and brandishing that length of metal like a club.

But once I saw them, once I realised there was a danger I might be recognised, my resolve left me. I dropped my weapon and staggered away, palms bleeding. I pushed through the unresisting crowd as I limped off in hopeless defeat, cold fingers of terror clawing deep into my heart.

I had failed.

After everything I had done, after all the lives that thing had claimed, it was still down there, beneath all that rubble.

Just waiting to be unearthed once more...

*My ears picked up a faint noise. A clicking, scuttling, cockroach-like noise, as if a hundred tiny feet at the far end of the corridor were treading as lightly as possible lest they wake the patients up.*

# CELL 34

*A. D. Radford*

Prologue

5.16am on Saturday 28th July 1929

The Royal Nazarene Hospital, London

A heart lay in the middle of the office. Dawn cautiously peeked through thin purple curtains, casting a gentle light that revealed intricate geometric patterns etched into the skin. Around it was a seemingly chaotic arrangement of lines, runes, hieroglyphs, dots, and dashes, the chalk long since tattooed into the smoothed grain of boot-polished floorboards. Like many of the raids of late, the suspects had been tipped off and had fled in advance.

It was not until mid-morning, when the gloom could no longer conceal its secrets that the police constable on duty screamed down the corridor for the inspectors to come "most urgently." The lines had begun swirling around his head like a colossal murmuration of starlings, pausing occasionally to depict unfamiliar stellar constellations of foreboding mythical beasts. Although the meaning of the symbols on the floor would be deciphered within six months, neither of the case's inspectors, Andrew Blythe or Ruth Oakwood, would ever be told.

A cluster of stout barrels in the corner of the room caught Blythe's attention. He pried the lid off one, only to jerk his head back in primal revulsion as an overpowering smell of rotting meat flooded his nostrils. A thin black slurry coated the inside, just about covering a carving that matched the pattern on the heart. Blythe failed to notice this as he was too busy fumbling in his breast pocket for a handkerchief and dashing to a nearby window to retch out of.

Oakwood slid on her gloves and glided to the mahogany desk, a grand piece with emerald green upholstery and beautifully carved legs. Her eyes darted around, zoning in on details and comparing them with the linked premises she had recently investigated. Glancing at Blythe's pitiful form slumped over the windowsill, she mentally noted to once again request his secondment to end as soon as possible. Or, at least, for the superintendent to find her a different partner. She had no need for somebody as queasy as Blythe, especially as the most recent cases all suggested ritualistic sacrifice, hardly something for the faint-hearted or faint-stomached. Besides, she thought, it didn't take a genius to figure out why they were always one step behind and had yet to catch anybody. She needed someone she could trust, not the chief inspector's golfing partner.

Unfortunately for Oakwood, although her sergeant confided in her that he also thought Blythe was "limp-spirited," he also maintained that the only cure for this was "character building," and that she would have to "soldier on." Oakwood would add these to her ever-lengthening list of meaningless clichés from meaningless people.

She noticed a pile of dumped envelopes cascading from the bureau to the floor. The scale of the crimes became evident as she flicked through bundle after bundle of letters, each addressed to different people. Most of the names were new, but she recognized a couple from recent missing person reports.

Oakwood sucked in her teeth to suppress some 'colourful' language as she felt something sharp cut through her glove and across the pad of her index finger. A scalpel had been left underneath the paper. It was gold-plated with a decorative handle. Macabre thoughts whispering from the crevices within her consciousness were quickly hushed when she found the name she was looking for on one of the stacks of letters. It was the name of the man they had rushed to find two hours ago: Mr Frank Green.

Chapter 1
Letter from Mr Frank Green to Dr Henry Smith
Tuesday 22nd May 1928

Dear Henry,
I stood outside the vets holding the newly empty cat basket as innumerable identical sharp-suited businessmen with newspapers crumpled under their arms rushed past me. They mingled seamlessly with packs of overcrowded omnibuses and the evening's first dog walkers. A couple of minutes later, I found myself in a nearby alleyway with my forehead pressed against a wall and sobbing like a child.

I used to seek the comfort of warm friends and room-temperature ales in The Albert Arms. We'd sit for hours at our corner booth by the fireplace on the first Friday of every month to discuss society, poetry, philosophy, literature, and, of course, cricket. I'd always arrive early to secure a couple of extra seats and while away the time until the others came with a pint and a newspaper; the evening stretched ahead of me like at the start of those endless childhood school summer holidays. We called it 'The Alcove'.

When the Great War broke out, we all signed up and vowed to meet again on the first Friday after peace was declared. The last one to turn up would buy the first round of drinks. Looking back, I can see the tragic naivety of this, but when we were caught up in that heatwave of patriotism, anything felt possible.

When that day arrived four years later, I hobbled to the pub, pulled the tables together, grabbed a discarded newspaper, and sat with a pint as usual. My eyes involuntary checked the door every time it opened, just like a dog waiting for its owner outside a shop. The moment of realization hit as I shuffled home late that night. I'd asked other pubs whether they recognized anybody from a photograph I kept of us and even checked with restaurants whether they had taken any bookings in their names. That was why I finally decided to let Charlie into the flat.

He was an affectionate black and white short-hair I had often seen slinking between the bins on my street. He more than filled the emptiness left by the absence of my friends, gave days a sense of purpose, and was always waiting for me whenever I returned home. I found him in the middle of the road this morning. His killer, presumably some motorist showing off, hadn't even the decency to leave a note. It is an awful thing, Henry, to go to a vet and ask them to bury your cat because you have no garden.

Besides Charlie's warm presence, it's no secret that my life over the last decade enjoyed little variety, urgency, or structure, and the days blur together. I write, read, eat, drink, sleep, and smoke, although none to a desirable degree. With unpaid tabs barring me from most pubs, my afternoons are often spent reading and watching the world go by from my window.

The only regular punctuations are when I feed a stray tabby three times a day. He's an affectionate creature, so I'm unsure whether he was recently abandoned or is simply after a couple of extra meals. Henry, this will sound terribly self-pitying, but caring for an animal transforms anybody for the better. It isn't just the structure it provides for the day but also knowing I make a difference, however slight, to somebody else. We should all feel like we matter to somebody.

For as long as I can remember, the weather has been ghastly, which provides a ready-made excuse for almost anything. It's why I can't sleep until dawn or rise until noon. It's why I don't go outside. It's why I have receded from the world and neglected the last of my friendships (except yours, of course). While I'm aware this is purely a comforting fantasy, as it provides something outside my control to blame, it is nonetheless a convincing fantasy to tell oneself.

The weather also reminds me of the night we met, I can't believe it was over a decade ago. The rain fell like ball bearings, and there was nothing we could do to keep the cold out from that draughty medical tent. I remember repeating the same fact in my head over and over again as if it were a mantra: the Victorians only needed thirty seconds to amputate a leg. It would be over before I realized, I thought; all I had to do was bite down on the rag in my mouth. That, alongside the near-half pint of whisky I had drank, would soak up all the pain. I couldn't bear imagining the back-and-forth-and-back-and-forth of the saw cutting through my shinbone, sending vibrations throughout the rest of my body. Then, I would feel the weight of my leg drop away, and the real horror would begin.

Into this bleakness wafted velveteen pipe smoke and a chipper New England accent. I wish I could replay your heated discussion with the chief surgeon, but those words have been lost to time and alcohol. You sat me up, took the bandage from my mouth, and reassured me that I would keep my leg. Hopefully, you won't find it too embarrassing to hear that every night since then, I have said two prayers: one for the strength to carry on and the other for Him to watch over you.

Our friendship has kept me afloat amid life's gradual decay and loss of meaning. More than a handful of times, I have dangled my toes over the edge of a bridge or railway platform, counting down to zero. That memory alone has held me back.

If you had asked me a decade ago what the worst aspect of being long-term unemployed was, I would have said emasculation or feeling a burden to others. In reality, it's the insidious and persistent whisper in your head. A voice that reminds you how useless or inadequate you are, how everybody you know is more successful than you, and that the gap between you and them grows daily. While you can try to run away (or addle your thoughts) at the bottom of a bottle. The trouble is that you'll sober up at some point, and when the noise dies, that unrelenting whisper is always waiting.

Due to my liberation from this misery, there are over a dozen failed attempts of this letter in the bin as I write this.

Words have failed me thus far, so thank you, Henry. Truly. I find myself once again indebted to you and, of course, to your uncle for the offer to take me on at the Royal Nazarene. It was even more of a shock because I had no idea you had family in London. Has he moved here recently?

Although I start next week, I have already written a list of the (roughly) fifty people to whom I owe money and when I will be able to pay them back. Truth be told, this list could serve as a local directory for pubs, tobacconists, and greengrocers. Just the thought of regaining a little dignity with every settled debt has cheered my spirit on even the most dismal days.

I also hope to gradually chip away at the debt I owe my landlady, the kindly but increasingly elusive Mrs Miller. For almost ten years, she has deferred my rent payments and taken care of my post, including the cost of sending letters to you. I've never received a straight answer as to why she is so generous with me, but I have learned that she lost all three sons to the war. I've also heard that she is old enough to be my mother. So, I hope that by accepting her kindness, I'm not taking advantage of her grief. Not once has she asked when I would get a job, and not once has she uttered a word of complaint. I've not actually met her, truth be told, but I have always gone through one of her nephews, and still, she trusts me. Being trusted is the most wonderful feeling, is it not?

I hope it comes as no surprise to hear that my response to your final question is simple: I'm as disgusted as you at how society treats those in need of mental care. Though by no means all, certain members of the public have revealed themselves to have brittle compassion (which indicates that they actually had no compassion to begin with, doesn't it?). Is it not the case that some who shed tears every Remembrance Day, dressed up in their Sunday finery, also mock victims of shell shock or even deny its existence? Is it not true that some would never dream of mocking physical 'abnormalities' but will freely tell 'jokes' about the mentally unwell or use brutish language to dehumanise them?

Why would anybody do this except for a profound lack of empathy? A poor intellectual understanding on their behalf is no excuse to err on the side of cruelty when they could just as easily err on the side of decency. Libraries contain boundless information on long-term afflictions of war, and wilfully choosing to remain ignorant while continuing to behave savagely is lazy and uncivilized. This should not be a radical message in our day and age.

Therefore, I was naturally delighted to be offered the job opportunity. It will change my life, and I hope to do what I can in my capacity to help others who, but for sheer luck, could be me.

Now, to turn to the other matter you raised: the clipping from the National Geographic you enclosed with your previous letter. I, too, was captivated by the statuette in the Australian Museum. Its description, 'Carved and polished obsidian idol. Unknown origin. Exquisite condition, circa 9th Century,' was initially difficult to believe. How is it possible that something so perverse from the norms of any known civilization was undiscovered until now, and how is it in such perfect condition given its age? Undoubtedly, this icon has been revered, protected, and lovingly maintained from generation to generation.

Having said that, its ruby eyes burned through a tangle of tentacles and glared back at me from the page, conveying an unmistakable sense of tyrannical dominance. One can easily imagine howling fanatics laying prostrate before it in open-air ceremonies during full moons. Who knows what barbarous worship rituals its believers partook in and of the misery carried out in this idol's name?

Seeing it reminded me of a recent report from The Times, which I have enclosed. A group of hikers, whom various search missions had failed to locate, emerged from a Moravian forest about a month ago. They had lost all their bearings for a couple of days, whereupon they stumbled into a village long forgotten by the world. A Stygian monolith at the heart of the village square depicted a globular-eyed, pot-bellied figure which, although clearly different from your article's idol, appears to be of a similar cultural or religious background, possibly even from the same pantheon.

At its base was an offering bowl where the police found human remains charred and partly eaten, possibly by wildlife, but also possibly by the inhabitants, who were unashamed of their customs and worship. Photographs and all other information remain censored by the Czechoslovak authorities, leaving fertile space to speculate about who, or what, they were worshiping and how both of these gods (the one in the village and the idol from the National Geographic) managed to cascade through the ages concealed by their believers.

I look forward to hearing from you soon.

Thank you again.

Yours,

Frank

Chapter 2
Monday 2nd July 1928
Letter from Mr Frank Green to Dr Henry Smith

Dear Henry,

I wake every morning at five, smoke my first cigarette, wash, shave, drink a coffee, eat breakfast (two slices of toast with jam), make lunch (grated cheese and pickle sandwiches cut into triangles), gulp down a second cup of coffee and, put food out for the cat (I'll return to him later). It's always in that order, and I'm always out the door within half an hour. I cannot put into words how motivated one becomes when one is to be expected somewhere.

Waking so early is beastly only if you choose to ignore its rewards. I witness London waking up lazily at first, and then suddenly it's teeming with life. I hear the chorus of chaffinches, song thrushes, and blackbirds as a greengrocer whistle *When The Saints Go Marching In* at the same time every morning while he lays out his produce carefully. I see the milkman placing bottles on doorsteps with a swagger and yet also with great care. I smell bread baking in unpolluted, trafficless streets. How many grey years I've had, deaf to the street's charming symphony of morning rituals.

I arrive at the hospital's front gates by six forty, chat briefly with the ever-beaming guard, Gurung, and change into my overalls. My mop hits the floor by six fifty-five.

I work twelve hours a day, Monday to Friday, with an hour for lunch and two fifteen-minute tea breaks, which I usually spend in the shade of a mature oak in the grounds (when the weather allows). From there, The Nazarene seems more like a sprawling colonial mansion than a hospital. A copper-domed, Doric-columned entrance is flanked by two wings, one male and one female, whose three floors loom over the gardens and stretch out towards the perimeter wall in the distance. Although the work can be rather mundane at times, it is agreeable. The patients and staff are all friendly and calm, unlike in the horror stories I've heard about this place.

Occasionally, I've been lucky enough to take lunch with Dr Antonio Perez. He arrived in London about twenty years ago to study and has never quite managed to leave. The Nazarene, he has told me at length, was revolutionary when it opened its doors a hundred years ago. Separate criminal and non-criminal wings, large windows to flood the rooms with light, and even a kitchen garden for patients to grow some of their own food set it apart from any psychiatric hospital at the time. It paved the way for actually treating patients for mental illnesses rather than warehousing them in the shadows.

However, much to our mutual disgust, permission was only granted for construction should the aforementioned perimeter wall, which stands at ten feet tall, be built. "No other hospitals," Dr Perez says, "have such walls except those in prisons." It's a line he repeats once a week and punctuates the end by pointing with his pipe with such force it's as if he were holding the air around him responsible for this mistreatment.

I have to say, I agree with him. It only reinforces the prejudice that the mentally unwell are dangerous. I'm sure you would agree(?)

Grand promises delivered with such priestly earnestness at the inauguration turned out to be platitudes. Reports of mistreatment have been rife for decades, with some inspectors remarking it is nothing more than a gilded cage. Beatings used to be commonplace, as was the humiliation of the patients. Its once-proud appearance has long since fallen into a state of decay. Peeling paint and cracked tiles at every turn. In fact, I don't think I've seen a single floor or wall tile which isn't damaged. Not one. The heating works in overdrive in the summer, it's too cold in the winter, and some parts of the hospital are even without electricity. Dr Perez has told me that it would cost a fortune to renovate, redecorate, and refurbish everything up to standard. This, combined with the high land value (it is central Lambeth, after all), means that relocation is likely. Selfishly, I wonder if I can work after the move. I can't say I'd be too sorry to see the back of London and start a new chapter.

The pay is five pounds a week, which I collect in an envelope after Friday's shift. It's a handsome wage for a cleaner, but to be honest, even half would feel wonderful after having relied on charity for so long. My first port of call is always to settle the entire debt of at least one person on my list, ensuring just enough is left over to buy food for me and Claude for the week. That's the name I've given the street cat I mentioned in my previous letter. I don't know whether I took him in for my benefit or for his, but I know we are both better off with each other. He's settled in well and has developed a taste for digestive biscuits and corned beef mixed together.

I've rediscovered the feeling of lounging in my armchair with a good book, food bubbling on the stove, and a cat purring on my lap. There is no satisfaction like the unspoken knowledge that one is independent and relied upon. I've enclosed a present as a token of my gratitude. I would never

have rediscovered this feeling without your selfless help.
Best wishes,
Frank

Chapter 3
Monday 10th September 1928
Letter from Mr Frank Green to Dr Henry Smith

Dear Henry,

I'm glad that you enjoyed the gift! One day, I hope to properly repay your kindness should you ever visit your uncle in London. Do you have any such plans?

It's hard to answer your question directly. There are colleagues who I like, but none I would consider to be close to. I talk to the patients far more than I was expecting. Usually, it's while I'm cleaning nearby, and they ask me questions. I'm glad, to be honest, as without it, I could go for a few days without talking to anybody, such is the under-staffing of this ward.

While taking a cigarette break, I sometimes speak with the gentleman in Cell 34, Smethwick. We're about the same age although, it has to be said, the hospital has aged him even worse than my poverty. He refuses to bathe or to hand his clothes over to be cleaned. This has led to a pungency from body odour and layered grime, which I've only ever seen during my brief spell of rough sleeping.

For the first couple of weeks, I tried to make small talk with him about the birdsong that drifts into the ward, and all he could muster were grunts. This, I assumed, was due to his condition. However, after a chance discovery that he, too, is a long-suffering West Ham fan, his behaviour shifted dramatically. He allowed me to clean his room, which felt like a great privilege given his deep distrust of other members of staff. This provided plenty of time to discuss several topics. In a single morning, Smethwick's speech had transformed from monosyllabic mumbling to flowing, elegant conversation.

He has demonstrated himself to be a well-read and eloquent speaker on a range of subjects, from history and classics to philosophy and literature. However, one time, when I asked him why he turns down any meals prepared at the hospital in the gentlest way I could, the coherence of his speech broke down almost completely. Vibrant jade eyes gleamed from behind a greasy fringe as words tumbled from his mouth. He told me his name isn't actually Smethwick, that he used to work here until the staff turned on him, that he is being poisoned through his food, and that there are things in the walls listening to everything he says.

While tragic and debilitating, they are, I have been told on several occasions, fairly standard thoughts for somebody in his state of mind. Still, I was unsettled enough to check his overview notes when I left his cell. They confirmed he's been at the hospital for several years, always in the same cell, and suffers from paranoid delusions.

Since then, my mind has put to bed almost every lingering doubt about his claims and 'theories.' For example, there's no sign that the patients have been poisoned. While I don't doubt his sincerity, I can't see what makes Smethwick so important that the hospital would want to listen to everything he says.

However, he made one claim that has occupied my mind for days because there's no easy way to disprove it. He believes none of the patients in the ward are actually unwell. He clarified that this is not to say that mental health problems don't exist, far from it, but that something sinister is happening at the Nazarene. Given Smethwick's diagnosis, this feels silly, but I can see where he's coming from. Despite a range of different diagnoses on their summary charts, the patients all exhibit similar symptoms. In particular, their auditory and visual hallucinations are almost identical. They all report hearing the same nonsense language spoken in their dreams (a jumble of guttural sounds based on Smethwick's impression) and seeing a figure stalk the corridors at night. Even their dreams are similar, of a city on the ocean floor cloaked in shadow. This is consistent with what scraps I've been told by patients during my rounds, as many freely tell me about their experiences.

Smethwick described how each patient's auditory and visual 'experience' represents a single jigsaw piece in what he calls the 'Great Puzzle.' This is to say, two patients' experiences might appear like disjointed scraps at first. But, by connecting them in the right way, Smethwick says he can step back and see the picture formed when the puzzle is complete. The completed image, he claims, proves that all the patients are experiencing real sights and sounds and are not hallucinating at all. Instead, Smethwick claims, they are imprisoned here under the dominion of the same source: a malevolent power of unparalleled strength. It must be hideous for one's mind to be gripped by such ruinous thoughts.

While I was finishing my shift yesterday, my mind adrift, Smethwick found me and pressed a coin into my hand. He insisted over and over, until I agreed several times, that I must promise to always keep it on my person. It was a twopenny piece onto which he had engraved a curious symbol of a five-pointed star. The shape is as unfamiliar as it is unsettling, reminiscent of some sketches by Crowley that I've chanced across. I have included a rubbing of the coin in the envelope, lest you can shed any light on the shape's meaning.

As I walked out, I noticed that he had begun to carve a larger version on the inside of his cell door. The doors here wouldn't look out of place from a prison. They're thick, heavy, and made of steel. They all have a hatch, presumably to monitor those on suicide watch and to pass food through. All except Smethwick's, whose door is missing one. That's a little strange, isn't it?

I look forward to reading your reply,

Frank

Chapter 4

Thursday 8th November 1928

Letter from Mr Frank Green to Dr Henry Smith

Dear Henry,

A spate of ritualistic murders has dominated the news since I last wrote to you. The hearts and livers of the victims have been removed, and there have been runes and glyphs found surrounding the bodies, as well as carved or tattooed into the victims' skin. The Times reported that one body had more than three hundred symbols carved into its torso and legs alone. Has this news made it to the US?

I have received your package; thank you! While I appreciate the gesture, I must admit that I was surprised by the selection of books. I'm all for broadening my horizons, but in the interests of honesty, I must confess that I haven't placed some of them on my bookshelf, as others may judge me harshly.

Nonetheless, they are in my ever-growing pile of books I plan on reading, alongside others I picked up at Watkins Books this weekend. I took the engraved coin there to see if any of the staff could tell me what the symbol Smethwick carved onto it means. It's a charming little store tucked down an alleyway near Leicester Square. The smell of years of incense burning hangs in the air. Its shop floor is overseen by mystical statues, who stand guard between the seemingly endless shelves of grimoires, bestiaries, and other forgotten lore.

When I arrived, I showed the coin to an earnest manager, who carefully examined it and simply said it was a protective symbol against evil. She demanded to know, with great forcefulness and concern, who had made it. I told her a sanitized version, afraid she wouldn't listen beyond the words "patient" and "Royal Nazarene," after which she vanished into a back room. She emerged after several minutes with an armful of ornate, yet nonetheless decaying due to the passage of time, leather-bound books. The manager insisted that I take them for free, on the sole condition that I write to a professor at Brichester University, whose details she scribbled on a note, and to tell him of everything Smethwick has said and done that is unusual. I agreed, of course, but I couldn't find the note when I intended to write such a letter earlier today. I searched the entire flat for it to no avail. I guess I lost it on the way home from the shop.

Smethwick has deteriorated considerably in the last couple of weeks. He hasn't slept without the aid of sedatives, which have to be administered forcefully. He's carved the symbol into every surface and item in his room. They're on the floor, the wall tiles, his bed frame, his chair, and there must be at least a hundred on the door alone. Even the inside of his toilet (including below the 'waterline') hasn't been spared. Standing inside the cell, it feels as though the symbols are swarming around you.

I previously thought Smethwick smuggled knives from the dining hall to do this, but I have been violently disabused of this notion. One day, as I passed by his cell, he was on his hands and knees, smashing his mouth against the floor in a practically mechanical motion. I raised the alarm, and while assistance arrived, he was flailing with such unexpected energy that it required three men to restrain him while another injected a sedative.

Then followed the worst experience of my job: to clean it up. I came across half a dozen teeth worn down to stubs and mopped the mixture of blood and 'fresh' teeth. It's a horrendous thing, hearing teeth 'plop' into a bucket, in which the blood and soap lather to form pink bubbles, which one proceeds to push around the floor tiles with a mop, watching it soak into and discolour the grout. I don't think I will ever forget that scene or stop my mind lingering on dark questions such as: how did he decide which tooth was next? Was there any hesitation? When did he first get the idea? The more I've stewed on these questions (with no meaningful conclusion), the more I'm convinced that I would be better off not knowing the answers to any.

While some patients have always been asleep during my shifts, I've recently started to pay attention to what they're calling out from their dreams. Mostly, it appears to be in some form of gobbledygook language. I'm aware that this will come across as xenophobic, but I assure you I'm merely trying to convey how incoherent it is and also how it's distinct from any language I've ever heard. Occasionally, a word or two of English or Latin will get through, though.

However, an even more unsettling thing is that patients have started occasionally chanting. One day last week, every patient, whether or not they were asleep, began chanting the words' the gate' repeatedly, building from a whisper to screaming at the top of their lungs. I later found out that this was the same for male patients exercising in the gardens and those in isolated confinement; they all did it.

I've wracked my mind for a rational explanation, but the seed Smethwick planted in my mind a couple of months ago has begun germinating. Has anything like that happened at your hospital or in your career? Any light you can shed on this phenomenon would ease my mind.

I close with a confession. I strayed from my designated area. You see, I was mopping a corridor, and my mind, occupied as it is with recent events, wandered also. There was no sign demarcating where the general ward ends, and the research and criminal wards begin, not that this is any excuse. It wasn't until I bumped into a rather large fellow, who introduced himself as Dr Voigt that I was told I wasn't authorized to be in that part of the hospital. He didn't quite give me a dressing-down but grinned and told me "as a friend" that it really would be best to never repeat this.

However, a few days have passed, and nobody has

approached me about this, so I guess Dr Voigt didn't report me. I am very grateful for his discretion, but I feel guilty for this mistake nonetheless, so I wanted to get it off my chest.

Write soon,

Frank

Chapter 5

Monday 16th January 1929

Letter from Mr Frank Green to Dr Henry Smith

Dear Henry,

It's lovely to hear how you and your family enjoyed Christmas; it sounds idyllic! I was hoping you wouldn't ask about my celebrations, as they were too quiet for my liking. I simply can't justify spending money while I still have debts to settle. Aside from attending Church, I spent a couple of hours serving lunch at the Royal Legion. It would be nice to claim this was for altruistic reasons, but it was mainly in the hope of seeing familiar faces. While there, I managed to wrap some turkey in some newspaper and smuggle it out for the cat.

Your present is fascinating, thank you! In fact, I've almost finished reading it already! Isn't it funny how we bought each other the same book? Even six months ago, if you'd asked whether I would enjoy reading about the occult, I would have dismissed the idea, but it's grown on me. Not as something I hold true, you understand, but there is something darkly fascinating about it.

.After I confessed to you in my last letter, guards are now stationed round the clock by the entrance to the research ward. This means I spend roughly an hour of each shift in the line of sight of an unmoving, silent figure standing in the gloom at the far end of the corridor. It's uncomfortable, to say the least, and time crawls by, but I'm just grateful to have kept my job.

The other significant change is I learned from Dr Voigt (Dr Perez is away visiting family) that Smethwick is the heir to a fortune and that his family came to collect him last night to pay for private care at the comfort of his estate. While it isn't unusual to find rooms no longer occupied due to overnight discharges, I was disappointed to not be able to say goodbye. I hope he gets the help he deserves and that I'll bump into him someday.

His sudden departure surprised me for two reasons. Firstly, if his family is so wealthy, why have they only come to move him now? Secondly, his recent behaviours suggest a deterioration rather than somebody on the mend and ready to be discharged. These concerns were heightened when, later that same day, a young doctor I hadn't seen before informed me cheerfully that Smethwick had been moved to the research ward for some "cutting-edge treatment" and would doubtless be back soon.

Hearing this chilled me, not just because at least one of those doctors can't be telling the truth, but also because there is something deeply unnerving about the research wing. Every day, four cleaning staff arrive in their van during my lunch shift and leave within the hour. All four are covered from head to toe like plague doctors, including boots, gloves, and those horrid bird-like masks. Perhaps most unsettling is that they softly hum a slow minor-key tune together while they load barrels into the van. I'm never within sixty yards, but the smell is unlike any I have experienced: a sharp, fetid stench as if something is rotting or fermenting. Do you have a team like this at your hospital in the States?

Please pass on my best wishes to your family,

Frank

## Chapter 6

Friday 28th March 1928

Letter from Mr Frank Green to Dr Henry Smith

Dear Henry,

Last week, I ate lunch with Dr Perez for the first time in several weeks (he has just returned from visiting his family), and I mentioned the differing accounts of Smethwick's whereabouts. Since then, he has sought to find out what has really happened to the poor fellow, which has taken a toll on his health. His eyes are bloodshot and vacant, his skin is pallid, and he clearly hasn't been sleeping well. However, perhaps the most notable change is he has given up his pipe and has started chain-smoking cigarettes; his shaking hands leave a trail of tobacco flakes on the floor.

His nerves reached a climax when, yesterday, he firmly grabbed my shoulder in the corridor and told me, in a hurried whisper, that he had also received different stories about what has happened to Smethwick. Dr Perez went on to say that all of the patients in the ward are showing the same symptoms. They have the same visions in their nightmares, the same visual and auditory hallucinations, even down to the same tone of voice that speaks to them in the same unintelligible tongue. He had even noticed that the new patients, despite a wide range of diagnoses, always rapidly deteriorate to our current patients' conditions and report the same symptoms.

He concluded that not only does some psychological disorder seem to have taken hold, but it is also inexorably spreading like a virus and needs to be quarantined lest it infect those beyond the hospital's walls.

Hearing this, I froze. Could it be the case that Smethwick had been right after all? Was I wrong to so quickly distrust his perspective?

However, I didn't dare share Smethwick's hypothesis. Besides, Dr Perez was more shocked that his colleagues had hidden this development from him. He confided in me that roughly eight months ago, all his colleagues had stopped discussing their cases with him in any meaningful detail and consistently disavowed any peculiarities. Hence, he had to read the patient notes to garner this information.

Have you ever encountered such a scene in all your years of service? Is it even possible for conditions like these to spread? Dr Perez hadn't experienced this before and told me he had already begun writing requests for an urgent visit by other experts to examine the patients further. The suggestion of asking you to visit was brushed aside, but maybe you could use the trip to also see your uncle? Please consider it.

Should you come, I'm sure you will have no shortage of invitations to dinner or offers to host you for your stay in houses much more opulent than mine. But my door is always open to you, and the kettle is always on.

I look forward to hearing from you again,

Frank

Chapter 7

Tuesday 14th May 1929

Letter from Mr Frank Green to Dr Henry Smith

Dear Henry,

I'm a little worried, as I haven't seen Dr Perez since writing my previous letter. Due to the hospital's reputation, our doctors regularly attend conferences to deliver talks, and many are university guest lecturers. Dr Perez is no exception to this, but it struck me as odd that he didn't tell me in passing that he'd be away for a prolonged period. I fear that his absence has not been planned.

Only when I cleaned the staff changing rooms were these suspicions aroused. You see, staff have to change into their uniform upon arrival, whether into blue cleaning overalls or the white suit jackets of medical staff. I noticed the same casual clothes hanging from a particular hook in the men's changing room a good deal longer than usual. The coat had a much slimmer waist, the kind that is popular in Perez's native Spain.

Much like with Smethwick, there were only inconsistent answers from the other staff members regarding Dr Perez's whereabouts.

I wish to speak with him urgently, as I heard a deep and prolonged agonized howling coming from the direction of the research wing last week. I've replayed it in my mind countless times, but I can't work out whether the noise was made by man or beast.

I took my concerns about the wailing straight to Dr Voigt, who has been covering for Dr Perez in his absence. At first, he responded as if his mind was in another room, and then his face broke into an overly broad, strained smile. There was absolutely nothing for me to worry about, he said quite firmly, as the patients in the experimental wing are so chronically disoriented that "cutting-edge" experimental treatments must be deployed. "Trust me," he said with vacant, shark-like eyes, "the patients are well taken care of."

I've seen more of Dr Voigt recently, but I'm sorry to say that I haven't warmed to him. Despite their efforts to spark conversations, he ignores the patients. He is too quick to forcefully restrain them for even the most minor infractions, such as interrupting him or not completely finishing their meals. Not only can he do this without assistance, but he also seems to take great pleasure in it. What sort of man would be so unsavoury, except one chronically unloved himself?

I've also noticed that despite his youth, he dribbles constantly and can't seem to close his mouth properly. This, alongside the fact that he never blinks, makes him rather unpleasant to be around.

His start at the Nazarene coincided with mass discharges of patients. It used to be the case that nearly all of the cells were occupied. Now, about two-thirds are empty. One night, as many as ten patients were discharged - ten! Dr Voigt said the public would not react well to seeing psychiatric patients in the street as they are being transferred, so it is always done at night. Although I didn't challenge him at the time, this simply isn't true. In my first couple of weeks here, I saw, on several occasions, patients being taken away from their cells for transfer in broad daylight. I also remember that they carried all their belongings, whereas the empty cells we have now still have the personal effects of their previous tenants.

Furthermore, none of the patients I've seen recently seem to be recovering, and yet I'm expected to believe that some of them are ready to be discharged or moved to hospitals that are not as well-equipped as the Nazarene?

Some of them must have been transferred to the research wing, as I've noticed an increased number of waste collections by those vans with the curiously dressed workmen I mentioned in a previous letter. The patients who have remained are practically mute. Most mumble under their breath, where previously they might have called out to me. Mopping the main corridor feels as though I'm walking through a forest, but all of the birds have forgotten how to sing or are too anxious to do so.

I long for the day they feel healthy enough to talk with each other again. God willing, in a place without barred windows and barbed wire fences.

Yours,

Frank

Chapter 8

Monday 15th July 1929

Letter from Mr Frank Green to Dr Henry Smith

Dear Henry,

Forgive the brevity of this letter, and please do not divulge its contents to anybody.

This evening, I was informed that Dr Perez had not actually left for a series of conference engagements but had accepted a job elsewhere. Therefore, his locker needed cleaning out so his personal effects could be returned to him. A clipboard with notes from his last ward round was among a couple of dog-eared novels, research papers, and a half-empty carton of cigarettes. I was alarmed to see that these were dated just one day after I sent my previous letter.

Naturally, these can't be thrown out, so I searched for someone to hand them to. However, the wing was deserted, other than the now-handful of patients, all of whom were unconscious. So, I thought, perhaps naively, I could return the notes directly to your uncle. After hearing so much about him in your letters, I couldn't pass up this opportunity.

His office is next to the research wing, and the thought of going near filled me with an intense dread. However, this evaporated when I saw the guard not at his post. Pausing with my hand on his door, I stopped and listened. I couldn't hear a thing. No telephones ringing, no murmurings from meetings, no clattering of typewriters or scratching of pens on paper. None of the other offices even had their lights on.

There was no response when I knocked hesitantly on his door; the noise amplified as it echoed off the tiles. I knocked again. Nothing. I paused for another moment in the gloom, the evening's lazy rays filtering through a couple of dusty skylights above me. Then, bowing my head and opening the door gently, I began to apologize "for disturbing you at this hour, as I'm sure you're a very busy man -." The breath was knocked out of my lungs by the scene I beheld.

An enormous frayed Persian rug had been pulled to one side of the room to reveal hundreds of chalk lines crisscrossing the floor. Well-used (but unlit) candles sat where large numbers of these lines converged. In the centre sat an alabaster idol, no larger than a teacup. Aside from the colour, it appeared identical to the grotesque octopoid god in the National Geographic article you shared last year. I didn't dare meet its gaze at first, and I practically felt it grasp at my overalls as I slowly walked over. My mind raced between what I had read in those archaic books from Watkins and the news story of that cult in the Moravian forest.

Picking up the figure, I noted that the craftsmanship was even more impressive up close. The texture of the tentacles, the veins running across its pulpy head, the intricate creases of skin on its knuckles. Were it not so hideous, I could have just as easily been staring at a Bernini or Puget masterpiece. Finding the courage to stare into its glinting emerald eyes, a faint whisper spoke to me from inside my head in a tongue I had never heard before, the same language I had heard the patients scream aloud occasionally. The voice grew louder and louder until it crescendoed as a deep, furious, deafening roar.

I heard a sizzling and smelt burning. In my trance, I had failed to notice the idol heat up in my hands. Shocked, I dropped it with a heavy clang. The sudden screeching of chairs being pulled out and startled voices barking at each other made it clear that I was not alone after all. Flooded with raw, primal terror, I ran, my footsteps echoing off the walls.

Since then, until writing this letter, I've been unable to stop looking over my shoulder. My unforgiving mind constantly expects to see the silent, beshadowed guard watching me or for him to be waiting for me when I open my wardrobe or go into my bathroom. Occasionally, if I concentrate, I can hear the idol's voice as clearly as if it were a faint scream coming from down the street. I must pull myself together for Claude's sake, as my erratic behaviour has put him on edge.

I must confess that yours is actually the third letter I have written upon returning home. I have already prepared two letters: one for the Secretary of State for the Home Office and the other for the Minister of Health, both of which will be hand-delivered tonight. Although they will not be spared any grisly details (I need them to act decisively), forgive me for not sharing everything with you. Some of the information may be used to link your uncle to crimes, and I do not wish to place you in an impossible position.

A note is attached to the envelope, asking Ms Miller whether she could send your letter first class so that you are notified as soon as possible.

Looking forward to writing to you with happier news soon,
Frank

## Chapter 9
Undated letter by Mr Frank Green to Dr Henry Smith. Labelled "first"

Henry,
If you are reading this, the cleaner has made good on his promise.

The night after writing to you last, I was dragged from bed. The only thing I can remember is a couple of my fingernails tore off because I was clinging to the mattress. Then, darkness. I woke up in Smethwick's old room by the dawn chorus through barred windows and the jarring rattle of the tea trolley on the tiles floating through my open cell door. I must admit, even just writing the words' my cell' leads to such a rush of dread and panic that I question the reality of this whole situation.

Smethwick's cell, like all the others, measures six feet wide by nine feet long with a ceiling only slightly higher than a man is tall. While the logic behind this is noble (to make it impossible for a patient to hang themselves), it creates a stifling atmosphere, as though the walls and ceiling are always poised to move an inch narrower and lower should I dare look away. A barred window scarcely illuminates the room, its glass too greasy to allow any clear shafts of light in, even at midday.

However, unlike all the other cells, mine had been recently repainted a brilliant white, and the floor tiles had been replaced so recently that the grouting wasn't even fully dry. I suppose the bloodstains from Smethwick smashing his teeth out were too stubborn. I also suspect the star symbols he etched were too deep for a fresh layer of paint to fully conceal. The paint's metallic stench was nauseating, so much so that I requested if I could open the door. The door handle and the catch were removed as a response, possibly as a cruel joke, possibly for purely pragmatic reasons.

The result is that it always swings open almost entirely. In any other building, I could simply lie next to the door to stop it opening at night, but all the cell doors here open outwards. I guess this is the same in the US as well(?)

While working my rounds, I was told this was to stop patients from barricading themselves in. Accurate as that may be, now I'm inside, it makes me feel utterly vulnerable. The best I can do is to hook my finger into the hole where the handle used to be and swing the door closed. As soon as I let go to step away from the door, it swings silently and slowly outwards again.

I must have only been here for a couple of days. Repeated memories flicker on and off in my mind of my bare feet slip-slapping on the cold tiles down the gallery as I hobble towards the entrance hall as fast as I can. From there, it's a clear run across the grounds and freedom beyond.

Yet, each time it happens, I wake up inside the cell again, with a cup of tea and a hot bowl of porridge in the doorway, without a headache or signs of being restrained (or marks from being injected with a sedative). I know I tried to escape; I could picture everything so vividly. Yet, why wouldn't I wake up in a more secure cell, strapped to my bed, or punished?

Unanswerable questions gang up with sleep deprivation. They ask me if I'm so sure I've tried to escape that maybe I've just been imagining things due to the stress. They ask whether all my memories might be as fictitious as dreams and how can I be absolutely sure that I've not been a patient here for years.

To steady my nerves, I started scratching a tally on the underside of the bowl of porridge after each escape attempt. This worked for a while. I would wake up each time and check the bottom of the bowl. Sure enough, there were my tally lines scratched there. Each time I woke up, I would eat the porridge first, then drink the tea in one gulp before marking another line neatly onto the bottom of the bowl. Then I'd run for the exit. Sometimes, my hand would touch the brass door handle into the entrance hall, where I could just about glimpse the flower beds outside.

Other times, it seemed like I would only set one step outside my cell before I woke up. For a while, it was easy to lose myself to the notion that my existence has always been this and that this loop will continue again and again: an eternal neo-Sisyphean torment.

Then, one time, I woke up in the middle of the afternoon with a police officer peering through the cell's door hatch, which was, much to my surprise, fully closed and fitted with a handle. Although my heart leaped when I saw him, his response was a look of poorly concealed disgust. I could hear Dr Voigt telling the officer that I was "Smethwick, a long-term patient here and a dangerous fantasist" and "obsessed with the overlap of the occult and the fascistic." This was, Voigt explained, evidenced by such books in my flat.

I felt the urge to scream aloud that somebody had sent them to me, but I couldn't. While I could move my body sluggishly, as though weights were attached to my arms and legs, I couldn't speak. I strained to open my mouth, and a faint yet incomprehensible babble fell out. At first, I thought this could be due to being paralysed with fear; I have been unable to forge sentences or even whole words since then, as though I were a right-handed painter who has been forced to paint with his left.

When I heard them walk away from my cell, I moved to the door and held open the hatch to hear better as he continued to regale the officer of my apparent "grand conspiracy that the hospital staff harvest the patients" and that I kept "telling people that he, Smethwick had died, and refers to himself in the third person, can you believe that!?"

He laughed, slapping the policeman jovially on the shoulder. The officer turned his head and looked at me with unspoken, unbroken pity. I turned away partly out of shame, partly lest it become contagious, and partly because I don't know what I would have done if Dr Voigt had glanced a dishonest smile at me.

A cup of tea and a bowl of porridge both sat steaming on my windowsill. Next to these lay some sheets of paper, a couple of new pencils, and a note with "I know who you are. Write down everything, and I will send it to Henry," in kind handwriting.

I have to place my faith entirely in the ministers (to whom I posted those letters) and in you to secure my release and to investigate this hospital.

I pray to the Almighty that this letter reaches you, and I pray for His strength to prevent the disintegration of my sanity. I would appreciate it greatly, my dear friend, should you, upon reading these words, beseech the heavens on my behalf, as I cannot ask them aloud.

Frank

Chapter 10
Undated letter by Mr Frank Green to Dr Henry Smith. Labelled "Second"

Henry,
I know you will not have received my previous letter by the time you read this, nor can I read any replies until I'm back home, but I know not to whom else I can turn or unapologetically outpour my conscience.

A couple of nights have passed since my last letter. The cleaner, who kindly assured me that he posted it, visits me every few hours. It wasn't until yesterday that I realized he is wearing my old overalls. I still haven't regained my ability to speak anything other than a jumble of confused noises, so I have to write my responses to any of his questions. In my naivety, I had hoped for a flash of panic or concern, but it only elicited the unmistakably vacant smile of pity and a cup of weak tea. Deep within my desperate soul, the sight of my overalls comforts me.

The tea is the only thing keeping me awake at the moment. I figured my porridge was most likely being drugged, so I always empty my bowl into the flower bed below my window when nobody else is around. However, as the cleaner always pours a cup of tea for himself from the same urn as the cups he pours for me, I have continued to drink. This has the happy side effect of avoiding the prospect of being force-fed.

However, more than anything, the nights are the worst part of being imprisoned here.

What little sleep I have is full of moving scenes fluttering around me, like a hundred thousand living photographs in a storm. They all depict dank and gloomy scenes of a murky city, with charcoal-grey buildings overgrown with slimy emerald vine-like algae and a viscous sludge. Tower blocks, which seem to have been put forth by the very earth upon which they sit, huddle overcrowded and irregular, like row upon row of crooked teeth, looming ominously over deserted streets and joyless town squares. I can't see anybody in this decaying place, wherever it is, but occasionally, I'll see flickers of movement. Whoever, or whatever, lives there is always just out of shot or out of focus.

If I'm careful, I can interact with these images. I can smell the salt of the ocean and even touch the dank stone of the buildings. One night, the dream was so vivid that my ceiling was ripped away, leaving me staring up from one of those empty town squares at rocky skyscrapers, except this time, they were full of glowing blue dots watching me. The thick black ooze dripped onto the floor from somewhere fathoms above me in the darkness, algae started to grow on the walls, and fish with glowing eyes like piercing headlights swirled around me. I swear, they even seemed to mutter amongst themselves as if they were plotting. I frantically thrashed at these demonic aberrations and tore at my walls. When I woke up, I noticed some scraps of algae under my fingernails. It was then that I realized I was losing my faculties.

But this is not what is most terrifying about nights here. The most horrifying thing is whatever lurks in the corridor after sunset.

Last night, when I woke, my eyes darted to the open door as they always do. I squinted to adjust to the darkness. My ears picked up a faint noise. A clicking, scuttling, cockroach-like noise, as if a hundred tiny feet at the far end of the corridor were treading as lightly as possible lest they wake the patients up. I sat up in bed. The scuttling stopped.

All I could think about was the need to close my door. If it could hear me sit up, it would notice my feet patter on the tiles. So, I lay my blanket as softly as I could on the floor. I heard it take some careful steps as it sniffed the air hurriedly and animistically, desperate to locate which cell the noise had come from.

Holding my breath, I swivelled my body on the bed. A spring in the mattress gave a muffled squeak.

THUD

Two electric blue shafts of light, as if from spotlights, shone on the patch of floor directly outside my cell. Some feet shuffled cautiously from the far end of the corridor.

People think that fear makes you scream. It doesn't. Not always. Not real fear. Real fear robs you of your breath. It freezes you.

Then, a shattering noise, presumably a dropped coffee mug, came from a cell further up the corridor. The shafts of lights vanished, followed by that repulsive, hurried scrabbling noises. Then, a muffled, piteous, agonized moaning. This was my chance.

I leaped onto the floor and ran, arms stretched out to pull the door inwards. A deafening crack echoed off the wall tiles, and the shafts of light shone outside my cell door again, but this time they were crimson. Whatever the creature was, it let out a furious pig-like squeal. Then came the horrifying frenzied scuttling as those hundreds of legs raced towards me from the shadows.

I didn't dare look. I plunged my fingers into the cavity where the door handle should be, curled them into a hook, and yanked at the door. I had half-closed it when the door was slammed shut with such force that I was thrown across the floor.

The force had been so great that the metal frame had buckled, and chunks of plaster had already fallen to the floor. The sheer power with which the door was slammed shut fixed it into place. I instinctively mumbled a prayer under my breath, but just a tangle of noises tumbled out despite the cadence of regular speech.

This is not the first time this has happened. Sometimes, the doors are torn open; other times, I can just about hear the unmistakable noise of a key being softly turned in a nearby lock. Each time, we are informed the next day with absolute sincerity that any empty cells have been unoccupied for months. What adds to my confusion is that some of the cells really have been vacant for a while... haven't they?

I saw it once. During the first night, before I knew better, I casually walked over to my (open) door in the middle of the night to swing it shut. There it was, standing in the shadows at the far end of the corridor. Tall. Broad. Hairy. The beast's raspy breathing paused when it noticed me. Then, it opened its eyes, revealing bright cyan, cat-like eyes, that scanned me up and down. It stood up, a thin, crescent grin forming on its face, if I could call it a face. I froze with panic, but the thing was not interested. Instead, it was inspecting the cell it was standing next to. Holding my breath, I reached into the darkness for the cold metal door and swung it closed, cursing as the hinges squeaked.

I exhaled, my heart still racing. I heard a noise outside my door, so I opened the hatch, and the thing took up my entire field of vision. Its turquoise eyes blinded me, my legs gave way, and I fell, the hatch closing as I did so with a metallic clang. I forced my eyes closed as if by tensing my eyelids, I could somehow speed up the coming of dawn and end this nightmare. The hatch above me slid open cautiously and carefully to make as little sound as possible. The thing must have peered its head into my cell. I could feel it looking down at me, and I could feel its breath on my ears and neck, its muzzle touching them lightly as it did so.

Is this what drove Smethwick to take such drastic steps? Every time I pace in the cell during the day, I'm reminded of when he dashed his teeth out on the floor and the sound of the blood dripping into the metal bucket as I squeezed the mop, and the teeth fragments swimming about. But, whenever I try to disremember this, all I see is the mysterious, murky city on the ocean floor instead.

Is that why he carved those symbols into the tiles and onto the coin he gifted me? Did he dream how I dream? Was he even Smethwick? What if he was just like me and had been captured and placed here under a false name?

Only you know I'm here. You and the secretaries of state whom I warned of this place, should they ever read my letters. Everybody here except for the cleaner and Dr Voigt ignore me. Both smile at me, although one does clearly out of pity. The other's smile is because his signature alone can release me. Not that he will sign anything of the sort. He likes me being here. He wants to hear the fumbled attempt at speaking and enjoys the spectacle of my desperation.

I know I don't have long left, so I promised the cleaner that should he deliver this letter, I won't bother him again or put him in this uncomfortable position of going behind the back of the hospital authorities. That means this is the final letter you will receive from me while I am here. All I'm hanging onto is the thought that the policeman sent to the hospital before felt something was wrong enough to warrant a search. It is a withering hope, but it is hope, nonetheless. In the meantime, I beg of you, send help as soon as you read this. I look forward to writing to you again once I'm out.

Your good friend,

Frank

Chapter 11

Wednesday 28th August 1929

Investigation Summary by Inspector Ruth Oakwood for Chief Inspector Edward Parker

Sir,

I have attached all the letters sent by Mr Frank Green that we seized from the Royal Nazarene on 28th July as well as letters received last week from Dr Henry Smith and Dr Antonio Perez. Summary of forensic analysis conducted since the 28th of July: It has yet to be confirmed whose heart was discovered during the raid on the 28th of July. However, I suspect that it is Mr Green's, given the circumstances of his disappearance.

The scalpel blade had traces of liver and heart tissue. There are some indications that the heart was still beating when it was removed from the victim's body. The coroner believes this butchery took place only hours before we arrived.

Summary of my investigations:

We have one male suspect in custody. Mr Green wrote his address on the back of every envelope in case of delivery problems. Whilst efforts had been made to cross these out by the actual recipient, he got sloppy over time. Thus, I could piece together Mr Green's address through the occasional flicker of a letter here and there which had not been sufficiently scratched out. This allowed me to track down Mr Green's address to a boarding house in Spitalfields. I took five officers with me and arrested the suspect last week. It appears that somebody had tipped him off, as he was frantically burning evidence when we arrived. He has refused to answer even the most rudimentary of questions posed to him during interviews.

Hundreds of letters were seized during this raid. This amounts to a similar quantity to July's raid at the hospital, further highlighting the scale of this deception. They are still being trawled through to provide as much insight as possible. It appears that the suspect had been impersonating others, as we found a number of unfinished letters all bearing the same handwriting. Officers also found entire folders of unused postage stamps from other countries, presumably to fool victims into thinking they were actually corresponding with a foreign pen-pal. It is worth noting that none of the letters sent by the victims themselves had any post office stamps on. This means that they never actually entered the postal system.

In total, 43 victims have been identified. Of those, only 12 could be located. They are all due to provide statements and hand in all of their letters within the next few days. If, as I suspect, the handwriting matches those found at the boarding house, we should be able to charge the suspect. Several letters from Dr Perez addressed to Mr Green were also found in possession of the suspect. All express a grave concern for Mr Green's wellbeing and urge him to leave the Royal Nazarene as soon as possible, with the offer of employment at his new hospital.

No other letters sent to Mr Green, or any letters sent by him before the 22nd of May 1928, have been found. I suspect that these have been destroyed.

Of course, Mr Green's flat itself was also searched. We found his diary, which was secured with a combination lock. The number for this was found on the collar of his old cat, which is now being cared for by the new tenant, Mr Montague Breakespear. Alarmingly, he had very recently started working as a cleaner at the hospital, and it was he who gave Frank the paper and pens to write his final letters. Police protection has been provided, and we are in the process of finding him a safe place to live.

The public appeal for information yielded hundreds of responses. Despite our best efforts, Inspector Blythe and I have barely made a dent in reading and categorizing them. For Mr Green alone, we have had warm correspondence from Dr Antonio Perez, Dr Henry Smith, numerous landlords, shopkeepers, ex-servicemen, and the hospital's security guard, Mr Kulbir Gurung. I have read several alarming references to Inspector Blythe, including in Dr Perez's letter, which warrant his immediate removal from the investigation.

Despite repeated requests to remain on this case, my (surprise) promotion to a Chief Inspector position in the Highlands requires an immediate start, so I will be relocating tomorrow and will be unable to offer any further assistance.

I wish you every success in bringing the perpetrators to justice.

Sincerely,

Inspector Ruth Oakwood

Metropolitan Police

Chapter 12

Tuesday August 27th, 1929.

Letter from Dr Henry Smith to Inspector Ruth Oakwood

Dear Inspector Oakwood,

Your telegram shocked me so much that I could scarcely believe its authenticity. Whilst it is indeed true that I met Frank whilst he was recovering from a severe leg wound sustained in the war, I never heard from him again after he was discharged.

Although I can't say we got to know each other well, I remember his warmth and would very much have liked to have met him again.

In response to your other questions, I have no family living in England, nor do I have any connections to the Royal Nazarene. For this reason, I would appreciate if you could inform me should you come across similar instances of my name being used fraudulently. As cold as it sounds, given the sheer scale of the depravity involved, this could cause irreparable damage to my reputation.

I'm afraid that there is very little I can do to aid your investigation. However, should you think of anything, I beg you to inform me immediately.

Dr Henry Smith

Saint Joseph's Hospital

Salem, Massachusetts

Chapter 13

Friday 23rd August 1929

Letter from Dr Antonio Perez to Inspector Ruth Oakwood

Dear Inspector Oakwood,

I was distraught to hear of the appeal for information regarding Frank Green earlier today, as I understand it was first made a month ago. It was back in March when I initially spoke to a colleague of yours, Inspector Andrew Blythe, with my grave concerns regarding the Royal Nazarene. Although I was repeatedly reassured that everything possible was being done, it appears as though you have failed to protect Frank.

Shortly after first contacting your colleague, I was transferred to a hospital in the town of Stonehouse, Gloucestershire. Due to the urgency of the transfer, I was unable to even say a formal goodbye to Frank. After moving away, I wrote to him a few times, but I heard nothing from him.

My relocation, this lack of direct contact with Frank, and of not having maintained contact with any of my former hospital colleagues means I am unable to shed any new light on the situation there.

For a few years I have given guest lectures at Brichester University and have collaborated with them on various research projects regarding patient audiovisual hallucinations. Naturally, I have been in regular contact with them regarding some of the patients at the Royal Nazarene. Over the years they have consistently provided insightful, though unsettling, analyses, and I am sure that they will be able to provide such assistance to your investigation.

I took the liberty of speaking with them after the public appeal for information, and they are very keen to collaborate with you and your colleagues directly to assist with the case in any way they can.

If there is anything else that I can possibly do, however small, please contact me immediately.

Your most humble servant,

Dr Antonio Perez,

St Arilda's Hospital

Stonehouse

*Sightings of a large figure, fuelled by
fear, prejudice, gossip and speculation,
had led to the appellation of this
apparent fiend  - the Whitechapel Golem.*

# WHEN SHADOWS CREEP

*ROBERT POYTON*

### September 13th

J ones the caretaker winced again, his knees complaining with every step that took him deeper into the bowels of the museum. Most of the exhibits had been evacuated out at the start of the Phoney War to safer locations. Some still remained, however, particularly the stored items locked away down here in what the staff referred to as the Vault. Jones had only been down here once before, it was not part of his usual rounds. But tonight had been a bad raid, worse even than those of the preceding week, and the Natural History museum had been hit. It seemed that Hitler, having failed to break the RAF, had directed his rage upon the people of London instead. Most of the bombs had fallen to the east, the docks had got it especially hard. But a few had strayed west - there were even reports that Buckingham Palace had been hit. Friday the thirteenth was living up to its reputation.

He had already covered the west wing upstairs, at least those parts he was allowed access to. Some of the museum galleries had been closed off, with MPs stood on guard. "Hush hush operations" was the only official announcement, though Jones had heard whispers of something called SOE. Regardless, the east wing had caught a packet, the fire crews were still damping down the blaze. The rest of building appeared untouched but Mr Pavitt had asked Jones to check everything, so here he was, checking everything. The heavy door at the foot of the stairs seemed undamaged, and opened with a loud click of the large key. The room beyond lay in thick darkness though, even here, there was no escape from the smell of burning.

Jones groped around the wall, finding and flicking the large light switch. No need to worry about blackout, this room was twenty feet below ground with no windows. Only half the lights came on and those flickered, leaving dark shadows among the racks before him. Row upon row of metal shelves filled with crates, boxes, bags, vague shapes in canvas sacks. Each one neatly labelled, each one carefully catalogued. Jones' torch flickered alongside the lights, then went out. He grumbled again and shook it, to no avail. No matter, there was just enough light from above to see by.

Wandering through the stacks, he could find nothing obviously wrong. However, the acrid smell grew stronger the further he went, and soon its source was revealed - the series of smaller rooms at the far end of the main chamber. Three of the doors were hanging from their hinges, the air was tinged with a vague haze of smoke and dust. Jones wafted a hand before him. There was no sign of fire but he advanced cautiously, nonetheless. One door had suffered more damage than the others, a thick door, locked and padlocked. Or at least, it had been. Now it tilted outwards, presumably damaged by the shock wave of the bomb that had hit the ground directly above.

Jones peered through the gap. Impenetrable darkness met his eyes. He swore and sharply rattled his torch again, this time being rewarded with a flicker, then a growing glow. The yellow beam revealed a trestle table at the opposite end, now partly covered in rubble. The wall above it had bulged in, damp earth spilling through the distorted brick. Most of it had fallen onto the table, displacing a small crate, tumbling it onto the floor. Jones squeezed his way past the blasted door and over to the table. He glanced up as he went, shining the torch above him. The ceiling seemed undamaged but he felt disinclined to linger. Who knew how buildings as old as the museum might stand up against the power of modern bombs? Yet some impulse drew him on. He brushed aside some dirt from the tabletop, revealing a manila folder beneath. Some words were stenciled on the cover, but they were difficult to make out in the gloom.

The caretaker was about to open the folder when a sound caught his attention. A vague scuffling somewhere behind him. *Rats*, was his first thought, or was this more earth spilling into the room? He turned as the noise sounded again - no, it was coming from the crate. Jones shone his torch across it, noting how the impact of the blast had broken the container open at one corner. The sound was definitely coming from inside. Intrigued, Jones squatted beside it, wincing at the stabbing pain in his leg. Placing a hand on the rough wooden surface he directed the torchlight into the crate, revealing a metal box. Not large, perhaps three inches square, it would just about fit in the palm of a hand. Another scuffle. It was coming from within the metal box.

Knees creaking and his back adding to the chorus of dissent, Jones leaned in, closed his fingers around the box, and pulled it out. It felt odd to the touch. A sensation of intense cold momentarily ran through the old soldier's bones, causing him to shiver. He rose, placing the box on the table. All was quiet.

Jones jumped as more earth rattled through the ruined wall. Then came that noise again, from inside the box. He could see now that there were strange markings engraved into its sides and a clasp at its top. Before he knew it, without any apparent conscious thought, Jones' bony fingers were reaching for the clasp, touching it, twisting it open. The box lid released with a slight hiss and fell with a soft clatter. Jones swallowed hard and shone the torch within.

Nothing met his eyes. Nothing. Not an empty box - for he could not see its interior. No, the box was filled... but with nothing. A void that neither reflected the yellow torchlight, nor was illuminated by it. An absence of light... but not an absence of movement. By some strange process, Jones' eyes detected a movement within that box of nothing... a curious ripple, like the undulation of a wave on oil covered water. An impossible extension of shadow that moved towards him, or was he falling away from it? Too late, Jones tried to take a step back. He didn't even get time to scream.

Albert shrank back into the shadows at the first hint of a sound. Sure enough, steady, heavy footsteps presaged the appearance of a copper, little more than a vague silhouette in the darkened street. A routine patrol, Albert guessed. Now that the bombers had gone the Old Bill would be out and about, checking for looters and other "undesirables." Into which category Albert definitely fell. A burglar, mind, rather than a looter. A professional and a bloody good one at that. As an in-and-out man, he prided himself on leaving no trace of his incursions - save the disappearance of various choice items, of course.

The footsteps faded into the night and silence fell once more. Well, silence apart from the distant cries of the fire-fighters. The docks were still ablaze, the sky glowed red above the river. Burnt flakes, pieces of charred paper and ash dropped from the sky, carried across London on a wave of heat.

Luckily, the Germans and Albert had different targets tonight. He was in the back streets of Poplar, heading for the home of Tommy the Pop. Tommy was away in hospital with a broken arm, courtesy of the Luftwaffe. That meant his gaff was empty for a couple of days, leaving it ripe for the plucking for an enterprising burglar. Sure, there was a code, but in Albert's mind all was fair in love and war. Besides which, Tommy was no saint. He was happy to fence the proceeds of any robbery, with no questions asked. And look at how he fleeced the refugees, paying them peanuts for the few valuables they'd managed to snatch before fleeing the Nazis. People desperate for money to survive, and Tommy was always there with an offer of cash. A low offer, but what choice did the people have? Jack Spot looked after his own as best he could, but he'd been called up. And with Billy Hill away on a two stretch, toe rags like Tommy had free rein.

No, Albert had no qualms about paying Tommy's place a visit. After waiting a few minutes, the wiry young man shinned over the wall at the end of the alley to drop quietly into the yard below. A cat streaked out of nowhere, Albert gasped, his heart pounding. Swearing under his breath, he turned his attention to the paint-peeled door before him. With a final look round, Albert removed a pick from his pocket, knelt and within seconds was in.

Detective Inspector Harry Lane rubbed his tired eyes, yawned and stretched. Another sleepless night. Reports were coming into the station every five minutes, it seemed. As if the bombing wasn't bad enough, crime levels had shot through the roof since the start of the blackout. Burglaries mostly but also robbery, looting and assaults. Then there were the gang disputes, over territory usually or some perceived slight.

Lane turned as Detective Sergeant Bert Bull came into the office. His face was blackened with soot and smoke, his eyes red-rimmed.

"Give us a cup of tea, for Gawd's sake," he croaked.

"Bad one?" Lane asked, pouring the over-stewed brew into an enamel mug.

Bull gulped down the proffered tea, winced, and nodded. "Yes, sir. On the way in. Tapley Street. Three houses gone, whole road blocked."

"And the inhabitants?"

"Most of 'em made the shelter. Three hadn't. Well, we think it's three. Hard to tell." He sighed heavily, eyes glazed. "What sort of swine drops bombs on women and children, sir? What sort of murderous swine?"

Lane had no reply. He grit his teeth and patted the grizzled Sergeant on the shoulder.

"I know, I know. Get yourself home, Bert. I'll finish up here."

September 14<sup>th</sup>

The thing that had been Jones blinked slowly in the morning sunlight and, following some deep impulse, fell in with the queue of people boarding the number nine bus. He took the first vacant seat and sat perfectly motionless, even when the conductress approached.

"Where you off to, love?" the young lady asked.

Jones remained still, eyes fixed ahead in a glassy stare, even when the conductress nudged him. "It's tuppence a ticket if you're going all the way to Aldwych."

The old man still made no move, save to open his mouth slowly with a soft hiss of breath.

"Sir? Sir?" The conductress tried again, until the lady sat in the seat opposite tugged her sleeve.

"Leave him be, dear. Shell shock, I reckon. Poor old sod. No wonder with all this going on."

The conductress nodded and, with a soft smile, moved on to the next passenger, leaving Jones staring into space.

At a certain point he arose, moving stiffly off the bus. The sunlight was even fiercer now, the weather was unseasonably hot for the time of year. Hand shading eyes, Jones walked slowly, following his feet to the door of a small terraced house. Fumbling for a key, he unlocked the front door and, with a last glance around the bright street, went inside.

Albert nudged his way into the smoky interior of the White Horse. He nodded to some, avoided the gaze of others, and ordered a pint at the bar. None of the afternoon drinkers owed him money, and he didn't owe anyone, so he could be assured of a quiet drink. Besides which, the landlady, Betty Snape, ran the pub with an iron hand. A local legend, Betty was feared and respected in equal measure and most knew better than to act up in her pub. That had led to the place becoming a sort of no-man's land, a neutral ground for doing deals and hatching schemes.

"Pint of Oscar, please, Betty." He slid a few coins across the bar, took a sip of the warm beer and walked over to sit opposite Jimmy the Leg.

"Got something for me, son?" the old man wheezed.

"Few bits of moody tom, Jimmy, not much else."

The old man grinned, revealing tobacco-stained teeth. "I hear Tommy the Pop is in 'orspital. Pay him a visit, did yer?"

Albert shrugged. "Now, now, Jimmy. Ask no questions, tell no lies."

"Alright. Let's see it."

The young burglar glanced around before sliding a burlap sack across the beer-stained wood. Jimmy rifled through the contents, squinting at each item in turn.

"You were right, not much. Still, that ring and brooch, I'll take those off yer hands. Pay the usual?"

Albert nodded and began rolling himself a fag, looking up at Jimmy's exclamation.

"What's this?" He pulled out an large, oilskin-wrapped packet from the sack.

"Some papers and stuff. Not really had a proper butchers at them."

"Not a treasure map is it, Albert? Does it tell us where the gold is?" The old fence gave a wheezing laugh, replaced the packet and stowed the items of interest in his jacket pocket. "I'll nip back in a day or so, sort you out. I don't carry much cash in here. Too many thieves around."

Albert nodded as Jimmy rose, patted him on the shoulder and limped his way laughing and coughing to the door.

"You orf out again?" Mrs Creswell folded her arms and scowled in disapproval.

Annie rolled her eyes. "Yes, I am, Mrs C. Not that it's any of your business."

The older woman glanced disapprovingly at her young lodger, noting the scarlet lipstick, the nylons, the just-above-the-knees skirt. "Disgraceful. And what goes on under my roof is entirely my business!"

"Which is why I'm going out, Mrs C. Keep your neighbours from gossiping, eh? Besides, I pay me rent, don't I? What I do to earn it is up to me. Donch'a know there's a war on?"

"Disgraceful!" Mrs Creswell repeated. "But as long as you are on the way out, you might as well make yourself useful. Hang on." She ducked back into her doorway, returning with a tray on which sat a covered plate and a mug of tea. "Take Mr Jones his supper, would you? I've not heard from him all day. Just check he's alright, there's a love."

Annie sighed but nodded. Despite her moaning, Mrs C wasn't a bad sort for a landlady and finding decent digs was hard enough at the moment. She carried the tray along the narrow hallway to Mr Jones' room by the front door. She tapped and called, both went unanswered. She tapped again, then paused. She thought she'd heard a low groan from within. Resting the tray on the hall table, Annie pressed down on the handle and pushed the creaking door open. The room beyond was gloomy, the curtains drawn, the sunlight only visible as a glow along their top edge.

Something felt wrong. A street girl quickly developed a sixth sense and Annie's inner voice was screaming at her now. But this was Mr Jones, the harmless old codger who worked at the museum... *what harm could he do?* Annie moved slowly into the room, wrinkling her nose at the musty odour. The door swung shut with a soft click behind her. Ahead was a chair, a dressing table in the window, a wardrobe, a single bed against the far wall. Where was he?

"Mr Jones?" she called, throat suddenly dry. "It's Annie from upstairs. I've brought you your supper."

The response was a vague stirring in the shadows. Squinting in the gloom, Annie reached back to flick the Bakelite switch behind her. The bulb flared a dull yellow and, in its glare, Annie's eyes were drawn upwards to the far corner of the room. There, crouched impossibly at the junction of walls and ceiling, like some huge, sinewy spider, was Mr Jones. Strands of opalescent goo hung from his pale, naked body. His lips were drawn back in a rictus grin, revealing yellowed teeth. And his eyes... Annie found herself unable to tear her gaze away from those dark pits. Flinging her hands up as if to block out the terrible sight, Annie stumbled back against the closed door. Mr Jones swivelled his head like a predatory insect, following her movement. With a soft ping, the bulb expired and the thing in the shadows pounced.

"And stay out!"

The door slammed behind the hulking figure of Frank Sadler as he was bodily ejected from the White Horse.

"Fucking cow," he swore as he staggered out into the street. All he'd done was pay the barmaid a compliment, chatted her up a bit. Then that interfering old boot Betty had stuck her oar in. Frank wasn't having that, he'd drawn back his hand to give her a proper slap. Then he'd felt something press against his groin. It wasn't a pleasant sensation. Glancing down he'd caught the glint of the cut throat razor Betty was holding against him.

"Which one shall I take, Frank, left or right?" she'd hissed. Naturally, he'd shrunk back, only to be seized by a couple of regulars and bundled out the door.

"Bitch," he cursed again. The big docker was used to getting his own way, usually relying on his reputation of being handy with his fists and not averse to pulling the knife at his belt. For a minute he considered hanging round until closing time, then popping back in to stripe Betty up. She wouldn't be first woman he'd left with an unsightly scar. Then another thought struck him. He'd head up to the Ship in Brick Lane. There was a tidy little tart working there now who'd be pleased to see him. Or see his money at least. And if he roughed her up a bit after? Well, who would care, no-one would take the word of a tuppeny whore against a working man. Chuckling, he set out on his way.

September 15<sup>th</sup>

DI Lane glanced up again at the morning sun. The late hot spell showed no signs of finishing. He tugged on his collar, nodded to the wan faced PC stood at the front door and knocked. A call had come in regarding the discovery of a body in Aldwych, a rather unusual corpse, apparently. The door was opened by a middle-aged woman, equally as pale as the PC.

"Mrs Creswell?" Lane touched the brim of his hat. "DC Lane. Here about the, er... you know."

The woman hustled him and DS Bull inside, peering round perhaps in search of twitching curtains.

"Yes, of course, Inspector. Please do come in. It... he... is in here." She indicated the door of the first room off the hall. "I knocked for Mr Jones first thing. Bringing him his breakfast, you see. Well, when there was no answer I grew concerned. I hadn't seen him the day before, either. And as I said to Annie, well, it's not like Mr Jones to miss his meals. " She indicated the congealed plate of food on the hall table. "He was very fastidious about that. Did you know he – "

"Yes, thank you, Mrs Creswell, we'll handle it from here. I take it no-one has been in since you discovered Mr Jones?"

"Only your young constable." She rolled her eyes. "Left a pile of sick on the carpet, he did. And who's going to clear that up, then?"

Lane sighed. "I'll see to it, don't you worry. Now, how about you go and put the kettle on for us, while me and the Sergeant here have a look round, eh?"

Mollified, the housekeep bustled off. Lane raised an eyebrow at Bull, stepped carefully to the door and pushed it open. The first thing to hit them was the smell. Fresh vomit, yes, but also a deeper, more insidious tang. Not the odour of decomposition, a smell all too familiar to a copper of Lane's years. In fact , all too familiar to many Londoners these days. This was different. Unusual. Acidic, catching at the back of the throat. Chemical, somehow, with a faint undertow of musty staleness.

Jones was crouched face down on the floor a few feet from the door. Bull coughed, moving into the room to pull aside the drawn curtains, filling the room with sunlight. Lane grimaced as he examined the body. The features locked in a wild grimace. The eyes sockets gaping, shadowed pits. The hands almost fleshless claws that dug into the faded lino.

"That's one Samuel Jones, then?" Bull said.

"I gather so. Been dead a while from the look of him."

As he continued his inspection, Bull inspected the room. "Notice something, sir?" He asked.

"Go on."

"Well, it's been proper warm all week, and he's been dead for a while in here. But not one fly."

"You're right." Lane straightened up. "Room should be heaving with bluebottles. And look, what's this?"

He pointed to several strands of a slime-like substance that hung from the ceiling in the far corner. Bull moved closer to look, placing a hand to his nose.

"Don't know, sir, but that pen and ink is worse here."

"No signs of violence. Yet his skin looks odd, almost charred. Who was the last person to see him?"

Bull consulted the PC's notes. "Annie McKenzie it seems. The other lodger."

"Right. Let's have a chat with her then."

"Oh I'm afraid that won't be possible, Inspector," Mrs Creswell called from the hall, the rattle of teacups signalling the arrival of refreshments. "You see, she went out yesterday, And I haven't seen her since. Young people today. Out all hours, up to all sorts. It's a blooming disgrace is what it is."

Lane moved quickly to the doorway, though the housekeeper showed no sign of wanting to enter the room. "I see. Any idea where she may have gone? Friends, family?"

"She ain't got none of neither, as far as I know."

"Right. Well, if we could have a look at her room, I'd be grateful. Then we'll have that cup of tea and leave you in peace, Mrs Creswell."

"Peace? Peace he says! Bombs falling all over the place, a body in me front parlour, and he says peace!"

Twenty minutes later, the pair were back out in the sunshine. Bull had a few words with the PC on the door, then joined Lane, stood smoking by the front gate.

"What do you reckon, sir? This Annie did him in, and ran off with his cash?"

"Could be. You think there was something going on between them, perhaps?"

Bull grinned. "Well, he was in the nuddy. And he was an old geezer, she's a young woman. Maybe it was that what done for him?"

"Alright, alright. Well, let's keep an open mind. I've a few questions for young Annie McKenzie. We'll get an alert out for her. In the meantime let's get back to the shop and write all this – " He was interrupted by the mournful howl of the air raid sirens.

"Bloody hell, " Bull muttered through gritted teeth. "Those bastards are early today. Come on sir, I know where the nearest shelter is."

The mood in the White Horse that evening was subdued, even more subdued than normal. It had been the heaviest series of raids yet that day, from late morning til dusk. Many regulars coming in were coated in brick dust. Some stared vacantly as they sipped their drink. Others would never be seen in the pub again. Yet the low murmur of conversation was stilled with the appearance of an elderly man in the doorway. Bearded, wearing a heavy coat and a fedora despite the heat, he glanced nervously around the room .

"Cabaret's arrived, then," came a voice from the back.

"Shut it, Henry." Betty snapped before sliding off her stool to greet the man. "You alright, love? Are you lost? I don't think this is the place you're looking for."

"This is the White Horse?" the old man replied in a thick European accent. Betty nodded. "Then it is the place. I have been informed that there are people here who deal in certain things. Things that," he shrugged, "might not strictly belong to them?"

"Here, you're not Old Bill, are you?" growled another regular, prompting a menacing murmur around the room.

"Shut up!" Betty called again. "Look at him, you think he looks like a rozzer? Tell you what, my love, you come in the back room with me, we'll have a little chat. Doris, watch the bar, will you?"

With that, the man was led away into the depths of the pub, leaving the room buzzing with speculation.

Albert nodded to Doris as she lifted the bar counter for him to go through.

"Betty's in the back," she gestured as he passed.

"Wotcha, Betty. What's up then?"

The landlady took a puff on her cigarette and gestured to the elderly man sat on the sofa.

"This is Mr Falk. I think you might have something of his."

Albert's innate response was denial, and a step back towards the door.

Betty laughed. "Calm down, Albert. He ain't Old Bill. He's – well, why don't you tell him what you told me, Mr Falk? Sit down, Albert, I'll have Doris fetch you a drink."

Albert did as he was bade, taking the armchair, closely watched by the old man's piercing blue eyes.

Falk raised a hand. "Please don't be alarmed, I'm not here to judge, Mr...?"

"Albert will do," he grunted, feeling increasingly nervous. "What's this about, then?"

The man nodded. "Well, as your friend here said, my name is Falk. Rabbi Falk to be precise. Myself, my daughter and my grandson and granddaughter here have not long arrived in London."

"Fled from the Nazis, they did." Betty added, as Doris came in with a pint of mild.

"Precisely, Mrs Snape. Naturally, we could bring little with us, save some treasured family items. Items which have been lost."

"I don't know nothing about no jewellery," Albert replied quickly.

Falk waved a hand. "No matter, no matter, that is not why I am here. You see, jewellery, rings, lockets and the like, they can be replaced. Certainly, they might be of value but, all things considered, they are just pieces of metal. What is more precious is knowledge. What I am looking for, Mr Albert, are some papers. And I believe you may be in possession of some papers that, well, came into your reach, so to speak."

"Papers?" Albert shifted in the armchair.

"Yes, papers." Betty blew a cloud of cigarette smoke towards the ceiling. "I overheard you talking about them to Jimmy the other night. A big wodge of them, from what I could see."

Albert wasn't surprised. Nothing that happened in the White Horse escaped Betty's attention.

"Well, yes, I got some papers. What are they? Secret documents or something?"

"In a manner of speaking. " Falk leaned forward. "I shall try and explain."

Albert took a grateful sip of the beer and listened as the old man explained.

"They are secret in terms of being hidden. What we might call *occult*. But they are not documents. More... instructions. Instructions on a means of protection, to be exact. You see, Mr Albert, my people have often had the need for protection. The recent troubles, our flight from our homes..." he shrugged. "They are not new to us. Though I fear today they are on a scale unparalleled."

"I was telling Mr Falk how we had it with all that Mosley lot, didn't we?" Betty interjected.

"We did," Albert replied, "But we seen them off sharpish, didn't we? Him and his blackshirts. I'll rob anyone, Mr Falk, Christian, heathen or Jew. But I know a bully when I see one. Besides, who needs another posho coming round here telling us who we can and can't be pals with, eh?"

"I understand." Falk  smiled. " Well you see, the papers in question form part of a collection handed down to rabbis such as myself for generations. They are ancient indeed, said originally to be copied from a text whose name I will not utter here."

"So they're valuable, then?" Albert sat upright in the chair.

"Yes... and no. Their pecuniary worth might be appreciable to a scholar or collector. Outside of that, their only value would be as kindling for a fire.  For my community, though, they are extremely valuable, both as cultural heritage and as a powerful defence against the forces of darkness. Have you heard of a *golem*, Mr Albert?

Albert shook his head.

"Ah. There was a motion picture some years back, very popular in the United States, I believe. Well, in short, a golem is a creature of clay, brought to life by certain means, that will work for and protect its creator. This is all detailed in our *Sefer Yetzirah*, which may itself draw from the same sources as the papers. Old wisdom, we might say. Older and darker."

Albert could think only that this sounded like a load of old pony but politely kept his thoughts to himself. He took another sip of beer as the rabbi continued.

"You see, my people's history and legends stretch back centuries, But there are far older mysteries still. And some say - at least those that dare countenance such a thing - that fragments of the elder lore can be found not only in our legends and religion but in those of other peoples, too. Well, that is for others to debate. In any event, some part of that old knowledge came down to my people, particularly the secret of bestowing life onto inanimate matter in order to create a golem."

Albert puffed out his cheeks. "Righty-ho. And what's this got to do with me and these papers?"

Falk sighed. "The information contained in the papers can be used for good or evil, Mr Albert. I desire only to protect my people, and only in their greatest need. Others, though, would seek to use this arcane knowledge for their own power. To twist the role of the servitor from protector to conqueror. I need not remind you, particularly after a day such as we have had today, of the utter lack of mercy and relentless drive for dominance that our foes possess. Should they discover these papers... well... even the events of today would be the merest foreshadowing of what might come."

"And if I did have these papers? Then what?"

"Then I would appeal to your good nature, Mr Albert, to your common decency. For we have nothing left of value to offer other than our heartfelt gratitude."

Albert flicked a glance at Betty. She was staring at him hard. He knew that look. Betty stubbed out her fag in the ashtray. "It's true, Albert. You know the state of these poor people fleeing from Europe. Nothing but the clothes on their backs, most of them. And if these papers are something the Nazis are after, then, well, I reckon it's your duty to see they don't get hold of 'em."

Albert sighed and finished his pint. "Alright. I'll bring them in." That awful, all too familiar sound brought the conversation to a halt. The wail of the sirens had everyone standing, moving quickly to the door, joining the crowd outside in the stream towards the nearest shelters. "Tomorrow!" Betty mouthed to Albert. He nodded before rushing away.

September 16th

"They found that tart you were looking for, sir. She's brown bread." PC Gossage called to Lane as he came into the office that morning. The DI immediately halted and rounded on the young officer.

"Are you telling me, constable, the young lady we were looking for to assist us with our enquiries has been found and is, in fact, deceased?"

Gossage paled and swallowed hard. "Y-yes, sir. The report just came in." He replied, proffering a sheet of paper. Lane didn't pause.

"Bull!" he called out. "With me!"

The short drive to Brick Lane took some time. Many of the roads were still choked with rubble, a thin pall of smoke and the smell of burning still hung over the city. Two days of solid raids had stretched the services to breaking point, let alone the nerves of the people. The authorities had eventually bowed to public pressure and opened the underground stations as shelters. Still, hundreds had died, many were missing. Despite that, Lane noted with a grim smile the sign hanging from a shattered shop window. *Bombed but not defeated.* He turned his attention back to the road as Bull parked the car outside the Ship.

"We'll leave the car here, sir. Easier to get to the scene on foot. Besides, you might want to have a word with the landlord here. Seems our Annie was last seen in the pub."

Lane followed the sergeant over some rubble, down a side alley, and past a PC stood guard at an open doorway. The place stank of piss and death. Inside, pale sun through grimy windows softly lit the interior of the disused warehouse. The woman lay in the corner.

"Who found her?" Lane asked.

"Some local kids. They come in here to play and lark about. Found her this morning."

Lane took in the crouched posture, the clawing hands, the vacant eye sockets. "Same as Jones, then. She looks burned, too." He glanced around. "But again, no sign of fire. No blood, no obvious wounds." He spent a few more minutes studying the scene, scribbling in pencil in his notebook.

"Right, then. Get her moved. Let's pop in the Ship, have a word with the guvnor."

The guvnor turned out to be a nervous, sweaty man named Greaves. He ushered the two officers into the cool pub interior and offered them a drink. Lane declined and got straight to the point.

"Annie McKenzie, found dead a couple of hundred yards from here. We gather she was last seen in this pub?"

Greaves nodded and poured himself a shot, downing it in one. "Yes. Two nights ago. She came in as usual. "

"She was a regular, then?" Lane asked. Greaves nodded. "And did she work here, Mr Greaves? If you catch my drift?"

Greaves mopped his brow with a beer mat and fidgeted on the bar stool. Lane sighed.

"Listen. I don't give a monkey's what goes on in here. Everyone knows what sort of place this is. But a young girl has been found dead in suspicious circumstances, which means there may be a killer on the loose. If that's the case, we need to nab him quick. I don't need to tell you how this might play out otherwise, eh?"

"Okay, okay. Yes, she was a Piccadilly Commando, quite new to it, mind. I gives them a place to work from, they bung me a few bob in return, that's it. I keeps an eye out for 'em too, you know, in case they get any bother."

"Proper little guardian angel, ainch'a?" Bull growled.

"So the last time you saw her, who was she with?" Lane pressed.

"Big feller. Frank. Don't know his last name. All I know is he's a docker from down Poplar way. You can't miss him. Huge bastard, big scar on his cheek. Nasty bit of work. Don't tell him I said anything!"

"Alright. If he comes back, you give us a shout, right?" Lane took one look around the drab, dingy interior of the Ship, then turned to Bull. "Let's get down to Poplar, see if we can pick up this Frank character.

"They say our lads shot down 175 Germans yesterday," Jimmy the Leg indicated the front page of the *Daily Herald* as Betty poured his pint of mild.

"You believe that?" the landlady responded, placing the beer on the soggy beer mat front of him.

"Given the amount of bastards overhead dropping bombs on us…. nah, not really." He took a sip of beer and smacked his lips. "Still, this place is still standing, so it ain't all bad, eh? Ah, young Albert. Just the feller I came in to see."

Albert nodded as he made his way to the bar, taking the stool next to the old fence. "Alright, Jimmy? Usual please, Bet."

"Got something for you, son." Jimmy reached inside his jacket to remove a brown envelope.

"Oh, that reminds me." Albert repeated the movement, bringing out the bundle of papers to hand to Betty.

"Well, now. What have we got going on here, then?"

The voice came from one of the two men who'd just entered the pub. All conversation immediately ceased. Some stared with undisguised contempt at the newcomers, others made a point of looking somewhere else.

"Mr Lane," nodded Betty as Lane and Bull strode the bar.

"Betty," the DI nodded. "And Jimmy the Leg, having a little chat with young Albert Seagrott. Interesting."

"Nothing much interesting, Mr Lane," Jimmy responded. "Just giving Albert here his winnings. I put a bet on for him at the dogs the other night."

"Did you, now? And I thought West Ham stadium was shut this week," Lane smiled.

"I wouldn't know about that, Mr Lane. " Jimmy returned the smile. "I went to Hackney dogs, didn't I?"

Lane shook his head. "Course you did. And how about you Albert, you behaving yourself these days?"

"Yes, Mr Lane, of course. " Albert tried to stop his fingers drumming on his leg.

The policeman regarded him sideways then turned to Betty. "Anyway. We're look for a man called Frank. Big lump, apparently, a docker, scar on one cheek."

"Sounds like Frank Sadler," she replied, wiping a glass. "Slung him out the other night. What of it?"

"Do you know where we might find him?"

Betty shrugged. Normally she'd deny all knowledge when the coppers came nosing. But Frank was trouble, everyone knew it. If the cops were out to lock him up then, well, no-one would be that bothered, even round here. "I hear he often drinks in the Buccaneer as well."

"Tried there," Bull interjected. "And the Eagle. And the Duke of York. No sign in any of 'em for a couple of days."

"Can't help, then. Why, what's he done?"

"That's what we're trying to find out. Alright, then. If you see or hear anything, you let me know. It's important. I know you look after your girls here, Betty. That's all I'll say." Lane was about to leave when he noticed the package of papers on the bar. "What's all this, then?" He reached out and undid the oilskin wrapping to reveal a loosely bound collection of pages. Lane flicked the cover aside and glanced through the first few sheets. He grimaced at one of the diagrams on a stained and yellowed page. "What the hell is that? And what language is this? These yours, Albert?"

"Actually, sir, those documents are mine." Rabbi Falk had slipped into the pub unnoticed. "Albert here has been looking after them for me. Isn't that right, Albert?"

Albert nodded, pleased to be out of the spotlight of attention.

"And you are?" Lane turned to face the newcomer.

"Falk. Rabbi Falk. As I said, these are some old family documents, thought lost, that Albert found. And now he has returned them to me. Will there be anything else, officer?"

Lane looked between the four faces. Jimmy and his sardonic grin, the fidgeting Albert, the impassive Betty and the elderly rabbi. He shook his head and sighed. "Perhaps. But not for now. Come on Bull, let's get an address for this Sadler, go pay him a visit."

## September 18<sup>th</sup>

Dr Carpenter removed his glasses and pinched the bridge of his nose. "Well, it's all there in the report, Harry. But the long and short of it is... I don't have a clue."

Lane flicked through the pages in the folder and raised an eyebrow. "Do you have a cause of death, Matthew?"

The white-haired coroner leaned across his desk, offering Lane a cigarette from a silver case. Lane waved the offer away. Carpenter sat back, lit, inhaled, and exhaled a cloud of blue-grey smoke. "Technically, in both cases, heart failure. I mean, for both the man and the woman, their hearts gave out. The question is, why? In both cases the heart had *shrivelled*. In a normal cardiac arrest, there'll be signs of damage. A rupture, or similar. Yet for these... well, I have the hearts down in the lab if you'd like to see them."

Again, Lane waved the offer away. "And the apparent burns?"

"Equally strange. Bodies burnt from the outside exhibit

particular qualities. God knows, I've seen enough of those this last few weeks."

"But these two?"

"The heat seems to have been generated from inside. " The Doctor waved his cigarette. "Again, it makes no sense. The nearest thing I can compare it to is if you put too strong an electric charge through a wire and into a 40 watt bulb. The wire melts, and the bulb blows, right?"

"So electrocution, then?"

"Not quite. Again, the burns would be different. And I gather there were no nearby electrics or wires in both circumstances?"

"Correct. Jones was in his room, McKenzie in a disused warehouse. There was nothing of note in either location to indicate anything dangerous. There was that unusual slime, though. We found that in both places."

"Another mystery, I'm afraid." Carpenter indicated a sheet of paper on his desk. "Initial reports came back marked *substance unknown.* I'm sending the remaining samples off for further testing."

"What's your best guess, then?"

"No signs of overt violence and strange slime aside, nothing unusual at either scene. Death from what looks to be some internal cause. To be honest, I'm shooting in the dark here, Harry. You don't think this could be some new German weapon do you? I mean, it's a bit out there but I have nothing else."

Lane shrugged. "I'm as in the dark as you. If there's a chance of that, though, I'll have to kick this upstairs. The military will need to be informed."

The Doctor nodded and stubbed out his cigarette, rising to shake Lane's hand. "Absolutely. Well, if there's anything else you need, let me know. I'll get those chemical reports over to you as soon as they come in."

Tom Kirby stumbled out of the pub and leaned against the nearest lamppost. When the world had stopped spinning quite so much, he took a breath, squared his shoulders and staggered diagonally across the street. He'd been in the Grave Maurice since they'd opened, drinking until his money ran out. Automatically he began heading along St Leonard's Road, set on home. He pulled himself up short with a sob. *Home.* There was no such thing anymore. Gone. All gone. The house, his lovely girls...

He wiped the back of his hand across his eyes and pressed his forehead against the cool brickwork in a nearby alleyway. His stomach roiled, his head pounded and nothing could control the raging grief in his heart. A voice brought him out of his stupor. Confused, he looked up, peering in vain to pierce the shadowed gloom of the twilit alley. There was a scuffle of movement, a vague shape in the dark. Then that voice again. But in his head... *Come*, it said. *Come. I can give you peace... peace...*

One hand steadying himself against the wall, Tom took a faltering step towards the gloom, a gloom rolled out to meet him, enfolding him in soft, shadowy wings. He felt those wings close around him, gently pulling him forward, enfolding him in a curious sensation that was neither warmth nor cold.

A figure emerged now, a man... a large man, pale face floating before him, a thin smile on its lips. And when he looked into those fathomless pools of eyes, Tom did, indeed forget his cares. His earthly woes left him as he welcomed the embrace of the shadow, welcomed the sweet oblivion that it promised...

September 26th

Albert rummaged in his pocket and found only a few coins - just enough to cover the price of a pint. He nodded to Doris and sighed as she poured. The past couple of weeks had been awful. London was burning. Not one part of the East End had gone untouched from the sustained attentions of the Luftwaffe. Every night the bombers had visited, dropping their deadly loads, seemingly oblivious to the barrage of flak sent up by the AA guns. Indeed, whispers were that as many Londoners had been killed by falling shell casings as the bombs. Still, at least the underground stations had been opened now, providing safer shelter for the beleaguered Londoners. That did leave certain places and premises unguarded for a man like Albert. It also made it extremely dangerous to be out and about at night. Not just for the duration of the raid, but the aftermath. Whole streets blazed with raging fires that could change direction in an instant. Buildings collapsed, there were unexploded bombs, burst gas and water pipes... no, the streets were a mess, and, as a consequence, business was down.

Truth be told, he wasn't feeling too good, either. Before bringing the old man's papers to the pub, he'd had a quick glance through them. Idle curiosity, he supposed, or perhaps the lingering thought that the old man wasn't being totally straight with him, and they contained some valuables-related secret. That was not the case. First off, he couldn't understand the writing. Some of it used normal characters, though in a foreign language. Other parts were in characters he'd never seen before. What's more, those characters appeared to squirm or wriggle on the page. But they'd not been the most disturbing things. It was the diagrams that got to him. Those and the drawings.

The diagrams showed geometric patterns that hurt Albert's eyes just to look at them, and made his head spin trying to make sense of them. Impossible angles and weird perspectives. Then he'd turned the page and seen that drawing. Even now, he struggled to make sense of the eyes, the shapeless bulk, the insectoid legs, the contorted, almost-human face. Just thinking about it set him into a cold sweat. And it was that face above all else that haunted his dreams.

No-one in London was sleeping well right now. But this was different. Not the fitful slumber of a person with one ear out for the air-raid siren, nor the disturbed sleep of a person packed with dozens of others in a dank, fug-filled underground station. No, this was a deep slumber punctuated by the strangest of dreams. They began with a sense of falling, not through space but through time. He was aware of vast, shadowy forms in the void around him, of unsettling glows of unearthly, violet light, before a panoramic vista suddenly opened out. Albert was flying above an immense city, whose architecture was as confusing to the eye as the diagrams in the papers. There was no sign of life in the cyclopean metropolis below, yet there was a sense of brooding presence, of something that lurked unseen or crept in the dark shadows of the numerous towers and palisades. For while their peaks and spires were rose-tinged in the light of the weak sun, the streets and thoroughfares of that dread place were mired in gloom, forever hidden in crepuscular obscurity.

Albert shook his head, carrying his pint to his usual table, nodding to some cronies. They were chewing over the other main talking point of the day, the disappearances.

"Another one gorn last night," Billy Boyce was saying.

"Vanished, they say, like a puff of smoke!"

Charlie Flowers shook his head. "Summink strange, I tell you. This could be worse than Saucy Jack. At least he only murdered tarts. Now, it's all sorts disappearing. Respectable folks, too!"

"Like you know any respectable folks, Charlie Flowers," Betty chided as she collected the empties. "There's a war on. Bombs and the like, of course people will go missing. Killed likely, or gone off to the countryside. Who can blame 'em, escaping from this hell-hole."

"Nah, Betty, it's more than that!" Billy gazed up, wide-eyed. "I seen it, I tells yer. Three nights ago, I was walking back home after the all clear. Stopped for a Jimmy Riddle in an alleyway and I seen it. A great, hulking brute of a thing it were. It's eyes shone fiery red in the shadows! It weren't 'uman!"

"And how come it didn't grab you, then?" asked Albert.

"Looked like it already had someone. It bent down, picked up a body and slung it over its shoulder. I couldn't see no more as it faded back in the shadows. Pissed all over me shoes, I did!"

"Garn, Billy," Betty scoffed. "Keep up with that, and they'll put you in Barmy Park."

The old man muttered and stood up. "Bollocks to the lot of yer. I'm off home. You'll see, mark my words."

Albert nudged Betty. "Did that old boy come in for his papers?"

"Yes, love, the day after you brought them in. Oh, he asked me to pass on his thanks, and he stood you a drink."

Albert grinned, perking up at the news. "Lovely. I'll have a double scotch!"

Lane rapped on the door and entered his Area Commander's

office. He saluted, eyeing the two civilians sat in front of the desk. The Commander nodded motioned him to a chair.

"Thanks for coming in, Lane. I know you're busy. But we have a matter arising."

Lane removed his hat and took a seat. The Commander continued.

"These gentlemen are from... where was it again?"

"MI5, sir." The younger of the two men spoke. Typical officer looking type, Lane thought, with his Ronald Coleman 'tache and well-tailored suit.

"I'm Clifton-Brown, and this is Professor Alec Smith of the Natural History Museum." He indicted the edlerly, studious looking gent next to him, sat with hands folded atop a walking stick. "I understand you are investigating the case of one Samuel Jones, recently deceased?"

"Yes," Lane nodded. "Though, to be honest, the investigation isn't moving. We've uncovered very little evidence."

"I see. Do you have a cause of death?"

"Well, that is the strange thing. Technically it was a heart attack, but the body was like nothing I've seen before. It seemed burnt, but from the inside, if that makes any sense."

"I'm afraid it does, Inspector, I'm afraid it does." The Professor spoke now. " I appreciate you are a busy man, so I'll be as succinct as possible. Jones was a caretaker at the museum. You may have heard it took a direct hit in the air raids. I was present at the time, hence the stick." He gave a small smile. "Part of the museum sustained heavy damage. This resulted in certain artefacts becoming... unsecured. We believe that the unfortunate Mr Jones came into contact with one such artefact, and suffered... well, you know more than we do what he suffered."

Lane raised an eyebrow. "What kind of artefact causes such a thing?" he asked.

"That is on what we call a need to know basis," Clifton-Brown interjected.

"I see. Well, I can get you the autopsy reports, such as they are."

"Reports?" Asked Smith

"Yes. You know the same thing happened to a young woman, too?"

Smith gasped. "When was this? Where?"

"Near Brick Lane. Last week."

The Professor took out a handkerchief and mopped his brow. "This might be more serious than we originally thought. I'd like to see the bodies if that is permissible, Commander?"

"Indeed, it is." The Commander leaned back in his chair with a creak. "Lane, you are to give these gentlemen every assistance in their investigations. Clear?"

"Clear, sir." He inwardly sighed. As if he didn't have enough in his plate, now he had to nursemaid a spook and a boffin.

September 27th

The mood of the crowd was ugly. Rabbi Falk could understand it, in part. These people were suffering terribly under the German assault. They felt helpless against the endless hail of bombs, it was natural for them to be angry. But there was more to it than this - the recent disappearances that were the talk of the area. No bodies had been found, but everyone was thinking the same thing....*the Ripper is back*... And now, as then, the finger of suspicion pointed to the outsider. Sightings of a large figure, fuelled by fear, old prejudices, gossip and speculation, had led to the appellation of this apparent fiend - the Whitechapel Golem. As such, the finger once again pointed to the Jews.

Falk's clothing and hair marked him out immediately. People were already shouting as he rushed through the busy street. He narrowly dodged a thrown bottle that smashed on the wall behind him. With a gasp he darted down a nearby alleyway, hoping to escape the attentions of the mob. But some followed, hurling abuse. Approaching a state of panic, he desperately tried the first door he came to, but it resisted his efforts. The cries grew louder and he fled deeper along the alleyway, hoping to find some concealment in its shadows. The shout of "there's the bastard!" from behind dashed his hopes. Breathing heavily, Falk made the end of the alleyway, turning to face his attackers. *That is should come to this... finished in what had promised to be a place of asylum.* He closed his eyes in prayer as heavy feet thundered towards him.

Abruptly he pitched back, pulled physically into the suddenly opened door behind him, which immediately slammed shut. Bolts cracked into place as an accented woman's voice whispered to him, "This way. Quickly! *Vite, vite!*"

Boots and fists thudded on the door as Falk followed his saviour along a dark hallway.

Lane offered his guests cigarettes as Bull brought in the tea and arrowroot biscuits. They were back at the station, both men were reading the autopsy reports, having earlier visited the morgue. Lane glanced at Bull, lit a fag, perched himself on the corner of his desk and waited.

"Well?" Clifton-Brown asked his companion.

Smith, still pale from the corpse viewing, nodded. "Yes. I'm afraid so. It is as I feared. Our artefact has become animate. This is extremely serious."

"You mentioned this artefact before," Lane asked. "What exactly is it? I don't understand?"

Clifton-Brown brushed a speck of lint from his lapel. "I don't expect you to understand, Lane. To be honest, this is something way above the level of a London copper. No offence."

"None taken," Lane replied through gritted teeth.

"What I can tell you is this. The thing is a potential weapon of great value. To us, or to the other fellow. Now, of course, we like to play with a straight bat. It's not the sort of thing any decent chap would countenance using. But your Jerry... well, we know what swine they can be, eh?"

The more Clifton-Brown talked, the less Lane liked him. "Indeed, sir," was his laconic response.

"So here's what we need from you and your *wallahs* here." The MI5 man waved a hand. "Reports of strange occurrences. Any sightings of odd things, anything untoward or out of sorts."

"You mean apart from the bombs, devastation and general mayhem?"

"Well, yes, of course, man, of course. I appreciate these are difficult times, but anything that stands apart."

"There's the disappearances, sir?" Bull offered.

"Disappearances?" the Professor echoed? "Locally?"

Bull nodded. "At least nine or ten over the last week or so. No pattern to them." He glanced at a sheet of paper on the desk. "The latest one was reported just last night. A Canadian airman named Kevin J Donachie."

"The bombings?"

"Not as far as we know. I mean obviously, people are going missing all the time. But we find all of them. Or what's left of them. No, it seems these mispers have simply vanished off the face of the earth."

"And you say the last person seen with the dead woman was this Sadler character?" Clifton-Brown asked.

"Yes, sir." Lane confirmed. "And despite extensive searches in the area, we've not been able to locate him. He remains our prime suspect."

Clifton-Brown clapped his hands together. "Well, if I can use your telephone, I'll get onto Fleming back at HQ, see if we can't rustle up a few more bloodhounds, so to speak. Our chaps will run this fellow down in no time. Capital! Sounds like we could have our blighter, eh, Professor?"

Smith glanced at Lane and rolled his eyes. The policeman had the distinct impression things were about to take a turn for the worse.

Falk sipped the tea and sat back with a sigh. He was in a comfortable armchair in a modest but well-appointed parlour. The middle-aged, well dressed lady opposite sipped her own tea and placed the china cup on a side-table.

"How are you feeling now, Mr Falk?"

"Much better, much better. Thanks to you, Madame Courbet."

His rescuer had led him out through one building and a couple of streets away to her rooms. She had introduced herself as Madame Courbet, like him a refugee, having fled the Nazi occupation of France. She further explained how she had spotted him earlier, watching as the situation had developed, moving quickly into place to save the rabbi from his would-be attackers.

As they chatted, they shared experiences, both talking of their families. She mentioned, with a brief grimace of pain, the husband she was separated from in France. Whether he was alive or dead, she knew not. "He was part of the force covering the English retreat at Dunkirk," she explained. Eventually, noting the clock on the mantelpiece, Falk stood and gave a small bow.

"My word, the time. I really must be going. My family will be expecting me." Madame Courbet accompanied him to the door. "I cannot thank you enough, Madame, you may have very well saved my life! Please do come and visit. We do not have a lot but would be honoured if you joined us for dinner one evening?"

"That would be nice. I know so few people here, I would very much like to meet your family."

"Then I shall be in touch." Falk touched the brim of his hat. "Bonsoir, Madame."

## September 28th

Having taken them to the morgue yesterday, and the scenes of both crimes earlier that morning, Lane was now showing Smith and Clifton-Brown around the local area. They had been joined by two other plain clothes investigators, introduced only as Morris and Cowley, who were conducting door-to-door enquiries in the properties closest to Sadler's lodgings.

At lunchtime the group convened in the Guy Earl Of Warwick pub on Chrisp Street. Despite the situation, the market outside was buzzing with life, the locals keen to *carry on as normal* even in the most trying of circumstances. There was little new information to be had, and no sightings of Sadler, though Morris and Cowley had noticed something.

"There's a lot of talk about these disappearances," Morris stated, eyeing the cloudy pint before him with suspicion. "Several sightings of what has been described as 'a large man', or 'a huge brute' lurking in the shadows."

"Could be our chap?" Professor Smith winced as he shifted his weight on the unconformable chair.

"Could be sir," Lane added. "Though the locals are calling him something else. After DS Bull mentioned the disappearances yesterday, I looked into them. Seems we had a letter come into the station warning us about something called The Whitechapel Golem. Not a name I've heard before. It was signed *Anonymous*, of course. Bit like the old Ripper letters, eh?""

"Golem, you say?" Smith leaned forward. "Interesting."

"Some sort of Jew superstition, what?" Clifton-Brown had already drained his whisky.

Smith ignored the remark and turned to Lane, gesturing with his pipe stem. "A golem is a mythical creature. A man of earth and stone brought to life by a mystical incantation. Its primary role was to defend the community, I believe. Tobias of Newmarket mentions them in his *Chronica majora*. There were legends of their use at the time of the Jewish expulsions in the late 13<sup>th</sup> century. Josephus mentions them in his *Antiquities of the Jews*. And I believe they are also referenced in many occult works, from Trithemius' *Liber Octo Questionum* to more modern works such as Spare's *The Book of Pleasure*."

Clifton-Brown loudly harrumphed. "Well, that's all well and good, Professor, but we are dealing with the real world here. So let's save the fairy stories for the children, shall we? Inspector -" he turned to Lane, "how many men can you get out here for a thorough search? Every street, every alleyway, every hidey-hole."

Lane looked at the man as though he were mad. "At present, sir, maybe four or five. We are little... stretched, you might say." He turned to Smith. "This golem thing, it's Jewish, you say?"

The Professor nodded. Lane's mind turned to the old gent he'd seen in the White Horse a week or so back. The man and his papers, who had seemed so out of place in that thieves' den. But Clifton-Brown was speaking again.

"Dashed poor show, Lane, but I suppose there's a war on. Well, I'll see what I can do, but we're up against it too, you know." He tapped the side of his nose. "Fifth columnists and all that. Don't know who you can trust these days, eh?" He eyed the drab interior of the pub and its inhabitants. "Well. Must be off. Drinks at the club at three. You coming, Professor?"

Smith shook his head. "I'll stay a little longer if that's alright. I'd like to ask some of these locals about the golem."

The MI5 man shrugged and stood, retrieving his hat from the stand in the corner. "Very well. Toodle pip then, gents." As Clifton-Brown and his agents left, Lane ordered himself and Smith another pint from the bar. Sitting, he regarded the Professor with a firm stare.

"Well then, Professor," he leaned in. "Now that idiot has gone, how about you tell me all about this artefact , and what's really going on here?"

September 29th

Michael craned his neck as he lowered the push-bike to the ground and called out again. "Scuff! Scruff!" Most Sundays the lad took to his bike and cycled round the East End, Scruff trotting along by his side, tail wagging. Today he'd come as far as Beckton

Gas Works, a place that fascinated him with its steam trains, huge gasometers and strange sounds and smells. Of course, the main gate was guarded now, but you could still see a lot of stuff through the perimeter fence. Scruff was normally a good dog, but something had spooked him.

Wincing as his leg brushed a stinging nettle, Michael swore and peered through the wire. There was nothing for it, he'd have to go in. There were a few gaps just large enough for a small boy to wriggle through.

Once in, Michael darted for cover behind a big, old hut. The site was huge, stretching all the way down to the river, the shoreline marked by the presence of the barrage balloons floating serenely above. That part of the works was still very busy, manufacturing gas as it did for virtually the whole of London north of the Thames. But other parts, less vital to the war effort, had effectively been closed down. So Michael had little trouble moving about this edge of the works, pausing to call softly for his dog every now and then.

A whimpering alerted the boy to Scruff's whereabouts. The black dog was calling and pawing at the door of what looked like an old tool shed.

"What'ya found, boy?" Michael crouched at the dog's side, clipping the lead back on Scruff's collar. His pet secured, Michael stood and peered in through the grimy window. The interior was gloomy, wreathed in shadow, but he could make out some shapes on the floor around the edges of the room. It looked like people, lying down and sleeping. Workers on a shift? But there was no sign of how they got here, most people went about on bikes these days. And no blankets that he could see. Curious, Michael wiggled the latch on the door. It gave beneath his hand with a loud creak and, tying the still whimpering dog to a post, the boy entered the shed.

The first thing to hit him was the smell - a curious, chemical reek that made his eyes water. That was not uncommon in the gasworks, but this was like nothing he had smelled here before. Placing a hand over his nose and mouth, Michael walked over to the nearest shape. He had been right, it was a person. Were they asleep? It was difficult to tell. In the dark he could make out little of the person's features, what with the odd-looking goo that covered much of them. It reminded him of the tadpole spawn they'd collected for school once. This was the source of the pong, it seemed.

He moved again, counting six recumbent forms in all on the dusty boarded floor, each one motionless. He wasn't even sure he could see them breathing, and felt no urge to draw closer for a more thorough examination. A noise made him start, a thud from outside. Heart in his mouth, Michael wheeled and rushed for the door, yanking it open, snatching up Scruff's lead. "Time to scarper, boy!" he explained to the dog. Yet before he could make his escape, Michael's collar was grabbed in a powerful grip and he was pulled sharply back, jerked off his feet, the sky wheeling above him, Scruff's barking ringing in his ears.

Lane rubbed his temples again in an attempt to ease the throbbing in his head. He wasn't sure what had caused it the most, the several drinks he'd had last night after his chat with Smith, or the, on the face of it, fantastical information the Professor had imparted. The man had been reluctant to speak at first, it had taken a few drinks to get him loosened up. They had quickly left the Guy Earl Of Warwick for a place just round the corner that Lane described as "copper-friendly." Certainly, the Professor had agreed, they served a better class of whisky there.

Flicking open his notebook, Lane squinted at his handwriting. He was glad he'd taken notes, the old copper's habit, as most of what Smith had told him went in one ear and out the other. It had started off normal enough. The arrival at the museum of a shipment from the States, from a university in New England, containing some samples from a recent Antarctic expedition. Apparently, one of the samples had excited considerable interest and speculation, it being totally unknown and unclassifiable to modern science. Hence the shipment to London, for examination and assessment by experts from the various English museums and universities. But then the war had begun, and speculative science had been forced to take a back seat to more pragmatic concerns. And so the sample had been locked away, safely, everyone thought, until recent circumstances proved otherwise.

"So what exactly is it then?" Lane had asked, eliciting a shrug from the Professor.

"Simple answer - we don't know. We had very little time to make a thorough examination before this whole shooting match began. But our best educated guess is that the protoplasmic lump we received is its own form of life. In effect, it is a cell, but a cell of colossal proportions."

"We're made up of cells, right?"

"Indeed. Yet, if I can put it this way, our sample is a single cell made up entirely of itself." He smiled at Lane's obvious confusion. "Don't worry, Inspector, it baffled us, too."

There had been more talk, as the whisky flowed, veering off into all sorts of wild theories and speculations. From the origins of man to the potential existence of beings from other planets and galaxies, to the primordial survival instincts of even the most basic life forms. Lane had made notes but reviewing them in the cold light of day, very little made much sense. His cogitations were interrupted by the desk sergeant tapping on the door.

"Sorry to bother you, sir, but we've just had a call come in that might be of interest. Half a dozen bodies have been discovered at Beckton."

Lane's headache wasn't improved by the smell in the shed. Beckton Gasworks was hardly London's most scenic spot, even less so when standing amid six corpses. Or were they corpses? No-one seemed quite sure and no-one seemed that eager to check. Something about the white, glutinous substance covering each provoked an extreme revulsion in even the most experienced there. Bull was outside with the boy and, while waiting for the medical officer to arrive, Lane went out to chat to him, glad for the relatively fresher air. The boy sat wide eyed, his arm protectively around a black dog of indeterminate breed next to him.

"Michael, is it?" Lane squatted on his haunches and extended the back of his hand for the dog to sniff. "And who's this then?"

"Scruff. My dog," came the answer. "Am I in trouble, mister?"

"No, Michael, you're not. In fact, you might have done us a big favour here. So why don't you tell me exactly what happened?"

The lad recounted his experiences, from losing his dog to being grabbed by the watchman. Lane stood, beckoning a WPC over. "Good lad, well done. Now, I'll get WPC Colledge here to see you back home. I expect your mum will be wondering where you are?"

As soon as he saw the lad's face fall, Lane regretted the question.

"I'm staying with me Aunt Edie," Michael replied quietly.

Lane sighed and dug in his pocket. "I see. Well, tell you what, here's a sixpence. Buy Scruff a treat, eh? Off you go now, son."

As the boy was led away, Clifton-Brown and Professor Smith approached.

"We got your call, " the MI5 man nodded. Lane was pleased to see Smith was in an even more fragile looking state than himself. "What do we have?"

Lane motioned the pair into the shed. Clifton-Brown glanced around, wrinkling his nose. Smith, hangover forgotten, moved straight in to examine the nearest body. He took out a pen from his jacket pocket and scooped up a little of the substance coating it.

"Fascinating." He turned to look up at the others. "I need to get a full analysis on this back at the lab. But my first impression is that this is very similar material to our sample. It certainly carries the same odour." He turned back to further examine the body.

As he did so, Bull called Lane over to the wall.

"I just noticed these markings, sir," he indicated, shining his torch on the wall. The yellow glow revealed a series of words or sigils, apparently scorched into the wood. If either man had the disturbing impression of *undulation* in the carvings, neither mentioned it.

"These look familiar," Lane mused, though he had no idea what language the words represented. "I'm sure I've seen these before..."

"Medical officer's here, sir," Bull noted. Lane was glad for a reason to turn away from the squiggles.

"Ah, thanks for coming, Doctor. Afraid we have six bodies for you to examine. Place is a bit of a tomb, you might say."

"Actually, we don't." Smith interjected, standing, wiping his hands. "These aren't corpses. Each of these people is still alive." He stroked his chin. "And something else. Ever heard of a *Glyptapanteles,* Inspector?"

Lane frowned and shook his head.

"That's the wasps, isn't it, Professor? The ones what lay their eggs in living caterpillars?" Bull responded, earning him a glare from Lane.

"Correct, Sergeant!" Smith gave a wan smile. "You see, Inspector, this isn't a tomb... it's a nursery."

### September 30th

The White Horse was quiet, even for a Monday lunchtime. It had been a bad one last night. There were mounting calls for more evacuations and for better shelters for the people. Bethnal Green tube, so the rumours went, was getting its own cafe and library, the underground station becoming a virtual subterranean town in its own right. Lane strode to the bar, oblivious to the usual hostility.

"Betty," he nodded. "This is Professor Smith of the Natural History Museum."

"Well, technically it's the British Museum," Smith explained, "You see - "

He was halted by Lane's upright palm. "Point is Betty, we're looking for that old Jewish gent who was in here last time I popped in. Falk, I believe his name was?"

"The rabbi?" Betty moved to pour a pint, Lane motioned again to halt.

"That's the one. And we don't have time for a drink. Do you know where we can find him?"

"Why? " Betty scowled. "Is he in trouble? Haven't his lot been through enough?"

"No, it's nothing like that," Lane explained, "I just need to talk to him about his papers, that's all."

Betty stared at him for a moment. "Well, in that case, reckon he won't mind me telling you his address."


Half an hour later, Lane and Smith were sipping tea in a small sitting room not far from the pub. Falk's daughter fussed around until the old man waved her away with a smile.

"So, gentlemen," Falk sat back in his chair. "You wished to see me about something?"

"Yes." Lane put down his cup and saucer. "We're currently involved in investigating some local disappearances. You are aware of them?"

"Only too aware." Falk raised his palms. "Some claim to have spotted what they are calling a golem. But this is impossible. Golems are created to protect, not to harm."

"I see. Well, that aside, we are following up some strange writings we found just recently at a scene. Writings that very much resembled those I saw in your collection of papers recently. Do you have the papers here?"

Falk's gaze hardened. "The papers are safe, Inspector. But they are not for casual browsing."

Professor Smith intervened. "If I may, Rabbi Falk. I believe that your papers may contain information pertaining to a situation that has developed as the result of a certain sample going missing from the Natural History museum. A sample with some unique properties, that may be part of something way, way older than any of us here could truly comprehend."

Falk eyed the Professor with curiosity. "You are a scientist I take it, Mr Smith?"

"Indeed, I am. But I like to think of myself as an open-minded scientist. One prepared to accept that we are far from knowing everything, despite all our recent advances in technology. One prepared to accept that there are things which may defy our current, logical modes of thinking."

"Then you are far wiser than most scientists I have met. Very well, I will show you the papers. But on one condition. That you take me to this scene. It may be that I can be of more assistance in this matter than you think."

Lane thought for a moment. "Alright. It's a deal. But we have to go the morgue now, and I'm not sure I can whistle up any transport for you. You can imagine how things are."

"This is not a problem," Falk smiled. "I have a friend who I'm sure won't mind driving me there. Following which, I can meet you at the morgue later and bring the papers. I keep them somewhere safe, you see. They are far more dangerous than you might imagine."

"Very well." Lane stood. "We shall see you later at the morgue."

Falk's visitors had barely gone when there came another knock at his door.

"Albert," he said, somewhat surprised. "What can I do for you , young man?"

"May I come in, Mr Falk?" the obviously disturbed visitor replied. "I have some questions to ask you."

"I'm afraid I am just on my way out," the rabbi replied. "Tell you what, why don't you come with me. My friend Madame Courbet lives just around the corner, I'm asking her to drive me somewhere. I have a feeling it may relate to the questions you wish to ask me."

The car journey took longer than expected, given the numerous detours made to by-pass rubble blocked streets. During it, Falk again reminded Albert of the ancient provenance of the papers, and the secrets held therein. Last time, Albert had scoffed. This time, he listened, though he still had a sense that the rabbi was not giving him the full picture.

If anything, Falk turned even quieter at the crime scene, particularly when he examined the strange marks on the all. They made Albert feel uneasy too, he felt a vague familiarity with the sinuous figures. Scene examined, Falk asked the WPC for directions to the morgue and Madame Courbet once again took the wheel.

"Well there's never a dull moment, is there?" Dr Carpenter was drying his hands, having finished a preliminary examination of the six individuals lying prone on the slabs. Smith was looking decidedly green around the gills thought Lane, though the Doctor hadn't even reached for a scalpel yet.

"You were quite correct in your assessment, Professor," the medic continued. "There do seem to be signs of life in each person, though extremely faint. Most intriguing. They should really be in a hospital, not here."

"No space," Clifton-Brown explained. "And official secrecy,

you know. No need to panic the public and all that. But if these aren't murder victims, then what on earth is this chap kidnapping them for? Some sort of sexual deviancy, I'll be bound!"

Carpenter shook his head. "There is no sign of sexual assault or activity on any of them, male or female. Having removed the slime, the only other oddities are small burn marks around the ears and nostrils, and that curious marbling of the skin." He gestured to the nearest slab, on which reposed the body of a young woman. Her bare shoulders, above the crisp, white sheet did indeed display an odd green and purplish mottling, as though something other than blood ran in her veins. "Further than that..." Carpenter shrugged and lit a cigarette.

Lane spoke up. "You said something about a *nursery*, Professor, and this wasp thing. What did you mean?"

Smith appeared hesitant. "It's hard to explain. You'll think me mad. But it relates to the information we received from our American colleagues attached to the missing sample. This is something that goes back in the depths of time. Not decades or even century, but millennia."

"What nonsense is this?" Clifton-Brown interjected? "Surely this is the work of some deranged lunatic, that's all. God knows, there's plenty of 'em round these parts. Millennia? What rot!"

"Not rot at all, " came another voice. Falk and Albert had arrived and been ushered in by Carpenter's assistant. The rabbi smiled and wagged a finger at Smith. "You know, don't you Professor? I suspect your sources may be different from my own, but they both point to the same conclusion, am I right?"

"What on earth is a Jew doing in here," Clifton-Brown spluttered.

Lane glared at the MI5 man. "Mr Falk his helping us with our enquiries," he responded. "Well, Smith? Out with it, with all the madness I've seen these last few months, there's not much that can surprise me."

Smith sighed and continued. "As you know, the sample and connected papers came from the Miskatonic University over in the States. Some years back, they chartered a series of Antarctic explorations that made something of a splash in the scientific community. Well, I say splash, a lot of it was quickly hushed up. Went against the grain, you see? Would seem that science can be every bit as dogmatic as religion. The long and short of it is that mankind are not the first intelligent species on Earth, and our predecessors date way, way back. Those expeditions found evidence of ancient civilisations way older than anything previously discovered."

"And what does all this have to do with the price of fish?" Clifton-Brown asked.

"That sample... the missing artefact... was something from that ancient civilisation... and we think it was still alive."

"There is more in here." Falk proffered Smith the oilskin-wrapped bundle of papers. "The language and terminology is far from what you might be used to, Professor, but I can assist with translation."

"It's weird stuff in there, alright." Albert added from behind Falk.

"Albert Seagrott, what on Earth are you doing wrapped up in this?" Lane demanded.

Falk raised a placating palm. "Albert has been looking after the papers for me. Unfortunately, he read some of the text without taking the preliminary precautions. But to echo the Professor, I believe what we are dealing with is a section, a sliver of a very ancient being, one that wishes to reform itself, or to spread its seed, as it were. I believe each of these unfortunates lying here before us has been inseminated in some way with that seed. Notice how all the victims are young, strong people. They will make excellent hosts for the parasitic organism when it hatches, so to speak. My advice would be to incinerate all of these people without delay."

"Incinerate? You swine!" cried Clifton-Brown. "These are decent British people! I'll not.."

His tirade was interrupted by a hideous wheezing sound as the woman on the slab behind him sat suddenly bolt upright. The sheet fell away, exposing more of that hideous mottling, black drool hung in strands from her slack lips and her eyes rolled pure jet in their sockets. With a lurch, she reached out for Clifton-Brown, her discoloured fingernails tearing a rent in the sleeve of his jacket. Clifton-Brown sprang back with a shout, throwing up his arms in a fruitless effort to ward off the assault. The only thing that saved him was the sheet twining around the woman's hips and legs, causing her to stagger off balance. Lane seized his opportunity, drawing his truncheon and bringing it down with a dull thud onto the woman's shoulder. She shrugged off the heavy blow as though it were nothing, and span to face her attacker. Fingers curled into claws, lips pulled back over black-stained teeth she swung for him, slashing for his eyes or throat. But Lane had been a boxer in his youth, and he weaved his head sharply to the side, hitting out at the hands with his truncheon. There was a sickening crack as bone snapped, but the woman was not slowed.

Albert leapt forward, grabbing the woman's shoulder from behind. She lashed out with an elbow, catching the young man in the nose, sending a gobbet of blood down his shirt. Behind him, Falk was waving his hands and chanting, Smith stood frozen to the spot. Clifton-Brown was fumbling desperately for his revolver.

"Stand clear," he shouted, putting two shots into the woman's chest. The report was deafening, the air filled with cordite as the woman was hurled back into the wall, sliding down the smooth, white tiles to slump to the floor. A thick, aqueous goo ran from the holes in her chest.

Clifton-Brown cricked his neck, replacing his revolver. "There. My word. That's an end to-"

The woman sprang impossibly upright from her slumped position, spraying ichor, giving a high pitched shriek that froze the marrow. Clifton-Brown stood like a deer in headlights, face ashen, hands raised in a last ditch attempt to stave off the inevitable.

"Get back! "shouted Dr Carpenter hefting a large, glass jar above his head. With a crash, he brought it down onto the woman's skull, the glass shattering to release the clear, colourless liquid within. Immediately, a putrid smoke began to arise as first the woman's scalp, then her face, then her upper body dissolved in a gory, streaming mess, leaving the men retching and gagging from both the sight and the stench.

Within a minute or so, there was little left of the woman but a discoloured jumble of bones and glutinous matter on the floor. The group reeled from the room, eyes streaming, expressions shocked, senses numbed. Only Falk appeared to maintain a level of composure.

"So. What do you advise now?" He pointedly asked Clifton-Brown.

The MI5 man wiped the snot from his nose and glared up with red rimmed eyes. "I-I-incinerate them!" he spluttered. "Incinerate the fucking lot!"

"Bull, get on the blower, I want as many bodies as you can get for a search party. Now!" Lane hurtled into the office like a rocket. Bull took one look at him and the faces the men following, and obeyed immediately without question. Lane rummaged in a filing cabinet and pulled out a map. Laying it across the desk, he began pointing.

"The gasworks has gates here, here and here. All of them are guarded. But it's a huge site and, as we know, even a small boy can find his way in. I'll bet a dollar to a quid that our man Frank.... or whatever he is now... has the rest of the victims stashed away there. There must be dozens of empty sheds and workshops."

Clifton-Brown interjected. "I'll see if we can get some of our chaps along, too. The more eyes on we have, the better."

"And when you find it?" Falk asked quietly.

"Well, we shoot it!" Clifton-Brown replied indignantly.

"That did not work so well last time, as I recall." the rabbi pointed out. "If it hadn't had been for the good Doctor and his jar of sulphuric acid then, well..." He shrugged. "And that was only a hatchling. A chick. What you have in Frank Sadler is the thing itself. Bullets won't stop it."

"What will, Mr Falk?" Smith asked. "Is there anything in your papers that will help?"

"Some things, maybe. But those sigils and incantations were used to control golems. I do not know what effectiveness they will have against something so ancient and powerful."

Smith tapped the briefcase under his arm. "I have the file

here from the Miskatonic University, and the box the thing was kept in. It has sigils on the outside. Perhaps we should review the information we have in each? The combination of the two sources might yield something useful."

"You said to incinerate the others," Lane said, adding, "Bull, put your eyes back in your head and get those officers here!"

"Fire is ever cleansing," Falk replied. "The sacrificial flame..."

"Can we trap this thing somewhere and burn it?" Albert asked.

Lane turned to Clifton-Brown. "Not with police equipment. Your people got access to flame-throwers? My old man told me about them in the last lot. Terrifying things, he said."

"I'll do my best," Clifton-Brown replied, picking up another phone. "But it's specialist kit. Might take a while."

"Time that we do not have." Falk looked grave. "I suggest we research as the Professor suggests, find the thing as quickly as possible and see if we can't contain it with the words of power. That might, at least, buy us some time. "

"Shit." Lane rubbed his sore eyes. "Well then. It's the only shot we've got right now. You two get cracking, I'll round our people up, then we'll get down to Beckton, sharpish."

The gate guard waved the cars through, they disgorged the group of police officers, and Lane, standing on a box he'd found, addressed them. "Right, listen up, you lot. We're looking for one Frank Sadler. Big lump, scarred face, you'll know him when you see him. This bloke is dangerous, mark my words. And I mean dangerous. No-one is to approach him! If you see him, get word back to me or Clifton-Brown, here. Monitor, follow, observe, that's it. Work in pairs at least, threes would be better. We're also on the lookout for his victims. Might be ten or more, stashed away somewhere quiet. Again, don't approach. If you find them, let me know. That's it." He glanced up at the dusk-tinged sky. "God help us all. Off you go."

Albert stayed close to the rabbi, clutching the papers, ready to hand them over. Smith and Clifton-Brown also stayed close, while Lane spoke to the site foremen and some of the workers. He returned.

"That's all the groups off. We managed to get a decent number, but it will take us all night to cover this area. The foremen has got his men to help, they know which areas are not currently in use."

"My men should be arriving soon," Clifton-Brown said.

"Good. Mr Falk, Professor, I suggest you stick by me. If we find Sadler, I want you there quick as, understood?"

As it happened, they didn't have to wait too long for the first news. Albert earwigged as a Sergeant rushed over to speak to Lane.

"We got something, sir. Right queer it is, too."

"Blimey, Jack," Lane replied, "If it's given you the wobbles, it must be odd. Professor? Mr Falk? With me please."

Sergeant Warner led them through the warren of buildings, over a railway line, and into the north-west corner of the site. He motioned to an open door, outside which a constable stood guard. "It's in here, sir."

Inside the large open space, arranged in a circle around the centre of the room, lay eight bodies. They were similar to those previously found, though far more covered in the strange, pearly residue. In fact, each was fully enclosed in a cocoon of the stuff, with the faces barely visible. That chemical odour was way stronger too, each person there placing a hand over nose and mouth. The Professor indicated the sigils present on the walls.

"My God, they're glowing," exclaimed Clifton-Brown. Indeed they were, each with a steady pulse, a violet glow that leant a strange tinge to the air. Albert cried out. That lambent glow had brought back the full vivid memory of his dreams. He half fancied he heard a voice whispering to him, beckoning him on, bidding him to close his eyes and just fall.... fall....

"Albert!" Rabbi Falk had gripped his arm tightly and shaken him. "Don't look too close! Try and ignore the sigils." The old man turned to Lane. "Let's get back outside. We have little time to lose. I suspect these bodies are close to hatching. And see how near to the perimeter we are. If they get out, there will be little any of us can do."

Once outside, Lane called to Sergeant Warner. "Jack, bring the petrol up, as much as you can." He turned to Falk. "What do you and the Professor advise now?"

"Clear your men from the area, Inspector. If these things hatch, they will be helpless in any case." Falk responded. "The Professor and I will see if we can't do something to counter these sigils, hopefully slow things down a bit, give us time to burn these things."

Lane was about to respond when that chill sound drifted out across the site, across the whole of London. The air raid sirens were calling again.

"No, you bastards!" Lane swore at the sky. "Not now! Not now!"

PC Carter glanced up at the wail of the siren. He nudged his colleague. "Reckon that's torn it, Alf. The boss'll be calling us all back in."

"I'll go check," Alf responded. "You wait here, mate, I'll be back in a jiffy."

Carter nodded and leant against a wall. His hand moved to take a his pack of ciggies out before he remembered he was in the middle of a gasworks. Grinning to himself, he stayed his hand and glanced up again. Already he fancied he could hear the low drone of the bombers, though he knew they couldn't be that close yet. Then another sound caught his attention. A steady tread, heavy, deliberate... approaching from around the corner of the large hut in whose lee he stood.

"Who's there?" he called, drawing the truncheon at his hip. There came no reply, only a sense of movement in the long shadows fallen between the buildings. No, more than that. It seemed as though the shadow itself was moving, as though whatever was coming was wreathed in gloom.

"Stop there!" Carter cried, feeling overcome with a sense of nameless dread. He grabbed and flicked on his torch, shining its beam straight up into the pallid, corpse like face that loomed above him. The figure of Sadler, oddly swollen and expanded, lifted huge hands and, with mouth agape, smashed them down onto the screaming man before it.

Lane was waiting with the others for the petrol when the shout came through.

"We've found him! We've found Sadler! We think he got Carter!"

Lane swore again and made a quick decision. He turned to the PC on the door. "When Warner gets back with the petrol, tell him to clear everyone out, get them to a shelter. You too." He spun round to the others. "Let's see if we can nab Sadler and get back here before anything else happens. Clifton-Brown, any sign of your people yet?"

"They should be here any moment. Tell you what, why don't I wait here for them? At least we can set to dousing those things inside."

Lane nodded and led the group off towards the growing hue and cry. They burst onto a scene that chilled the blood. In the light of several torches Sadler, or what used to be Sadler, stood motionless above the crumpled form of Carter.

"Stay back!" Lane ordered. "Surround him! Don't let him out, but don't go near him!"

Sadler stood like a marble statue, almost monotone in the torchlight. His stillness was unnatural. Lane was put in mind of a praying mantis he'd seen at the zoo once. A terrible, focused stillness that presaged death for whatever stood before it. All accounts of Sadler had marked him as a large man, but that terrible form in the torchlight must have stood close to seven feet tall. The head was swollen, misshapen and, Lane could swear it was pulsating. The eyes were solid black, strands of a black viscous substance dripped from corpse-pale lips. The overgrown hands were held up and forward in a claw-like position, again bringing to mind the mantis.

When Sadler moved it was almost too fast for the eye to follow. The nearest officer was brushed aside, hurled with a sickening crunch into a wall. Sadler looked ready to go through the resulting gap, but Falk and the Professor stepped forward now, both simultaneously chanting in a language that rang on the ears like the tolling of a discordant bell. The rabbi brandished a medallion above his head, a Hebrew sigil perhaps, that emitted a clean, white glow.

Remarkably, the huge figure reared back, turning its

grotesque head this way and that, seeking another avenue of escape. The pair pressed home their advantage, forcing Sadler back, getting as close as they dared to that terrifying form. The rest of the officers kept a respectful distance, yet none broke the line. They were joined by soldiers form the gate, levelling their rifles, one swearing loudly at the sight of the thing.

"Don't fire!" Lane ordered, "It won't do any good! Let the rabbi handle it!"

Now Lane could see what the pair had in mind. Close by were some large furnaces, cool now but presumably able to be fired up. Could they possible trap Sadler in one and switch it on? It seemed like madness, but what other option was there? And for a time, it seemed it might work. The power of the chanting and that strange, pulsing sigil appeared to be having a marked effect on the creature. Foot by foot, yard by yard, the furnace drew closer.

There came a sudden crack, the firing of guns. Lane swore - *no, not the soldiers... AA guns.* The bombers were coming, that gut-wrenching drone growing steadily louder. He shouted out to his officers. "Get out of here, all of you! Go, leave us! Go!"

Reluctantly they obeyed, streaming past him for the relative safety of the shelters at the edge of the site. And not before time. As the pair pressed their advantage, as Sadler's back touched the cold iron of the furnace, there came the hellish whistle of the first bombs.

Clifton-Brown glanced up at the sky and looked again at his watch. Warner had delivered several jerry cans of petrol and then, as ordered, departed. *Where were his men? They should be here by now.* He wandered over to the nearby perimeter fence, struggling to make out anything in the gloom. He thought he'd caught a glimpse of movement out there. Seeing nothing, he returned to the doorway, took out his cigarette case and lit a fag, oblivious to the jerry cans at his feet. A voice pulled him up short.

"Please make no sudden movements, monsieur." A middle-aged woman had appeared from the shadows, remarkable enough in this place. Even more remarkable was the pistol she had levelled at him.

"Who the devil are you?"

The woman smiled. "Who I am is of no importance. What is important is what lies in that hut. It is of great interest to a very important man. And I intend to see he takes delivery of at least one of those things."

Clifton-Brown considered his options. A quick jump forward, grab the gun arm, chop to the throat. No. The woman had judged the distance well, and the way she held the gun denoted experience, or good training.

"You're a German spy!" he snarled.

"French, actually," she smiled. "But yes, I do work for the Germans. For the Reichsführer himself, to be precise. You have heard of the Ahnenerbe, perhaps?"

Clifton-Brown had. A covert group set up by Himmler to retrieve so called occult artefacts of interest to the crazed leaders of the Third Reich. He nodded. "And how do you propose to affect the acquisition of one of these bodies?" he asked, sneering.

"Why, with your help, monsieur," replied Madame Courbet. She waved the gun. "Now, into the hut, and pick one of them up!"

As that first whistle began, Lane abandoned all hope of capturing Sadler, and sprang instead towards Falk and the Professor.

Ignoring the rabbi's protestations, he man-handled both of them away from the scene. He spotted Albert lurking uncertainly near-by. "Help me, man!" he shouted, "Get them out of here!"

Albert complied and the group raced for the perimeter fence, the first crump of explosives sounding behind them... behind them, but ominously drawing nearer. They'd made a couple of hundred yards when there came a deafening scream from above, a tremendous crash and thud, a wall of flame, and Lane fell into merciful oblivion.

Clifton-Brown grunted as he hefted the body through the gap in the fence. From here he could see a car parked a short distance away. The woman had kept her distance the whole time, the pistol had never wavered.

"To the car," she motioned. Clifton-Brown feigned shortness of breath.

"Need a moment," he gasped.

The heavy drone of aircraft overhead drew Courbet's gaze upwards, and Clifton-Brown seized his chance. He leapt for her, desperately clutching for the pistol. But the woman had indeed been well trained. A single crack sent a bullet directly between Clifton-Brown's eyes, and the MI5 man fell heavily into the dirt.

Courbet swore, glancing around, then up again at the sound of the bombs. She dragged the body over to the car and placed it along the back seat. Quickly, she jumped in, started the engine and drove off at speed. Fortunately, the air raid would give her cover... provided, of course, she was not hit. But once out of East London she would be safe, barring any security patrols. Her first stop was an isolated farmhouse in Essex, home to a fellow agent, to put in a radio call. Then out to the coast for a special rendezvous. Her cover here was blown know, she must return to her masters. But to return with such a prize would no doubt elevate her standing in the eyes of the Reichsführer. As London began to burn around her, she smiled.

*Lane tilted his face up, enjoying the warmth of the sun on his skin. For the first time in weeks, the sky above was clear… clear of dust, clear of the bombers, clear of the odours of death and destruction. Strangely, a bluebird fluttered and flapped in the air directly above him, and he watched, delighted, as the sunlight flashed off its bright feathers…*

He came to with a start, opening his eyes to the beaming face of Sergeant Bull.

"What you cowing about", Lane muttered, the dream bird fading quickly away from his mind. "And where am I?"

"Queen Mary's, sir," replied the still grinning Bull. "You copped a right packet. Your missus has been sat here all night watching over you. I just arrived, she's gone off to get some tea. How are you feeling?"

"My leg hurts," Lane replied. "In fact, everything hurts. What happened?"

"You were lucky. The place was hit by a string of incendiaries. You got buried under some rubble. Doc says you've got a broken leg. Whole lot went up in flames."

Lane digested this information. "And I have you to thank for dragging me out?"

"Actually it was me, Mr Lane." Albert's face appeared round the screens.

Bull nodded. "Yep, young Albert here managed to get you out

before the fire reached you."

"I see. Well, in that case, thank you Albert. Hope you weren't hurt?"

Albert held up his bandaged hands. "Well, I won't be playing the joanna for a bit. But you know, I reckon it was worth it. Always pays to have the gratitude of a copper, eh? See you around, Mr Lane." With a cheeky grin, he was gone.

"Everyone else alright?" Lane asked, closing his eyes against the renewed throbbing in his head.

"Yes. All our lot got out okay, and the Professor and Falk. Strange thing, though. We found Clifton-Brown's body just outside the perimeter fence. Been shot. Right between the eyes. Professional, like."

Lane's eyes flickered open again. "Shot? Who by?"

Bull shrugged. "No idea. But his spook pals have been down, swarming all over the place. I caught some talk of an enemy agent, but that's it. They took Smith and Falk off, too. Seems the intelligence bods are taking this weird stuff seriously now. We all got questioned, they made us sign some documents."

"Official secrets, I imagine?"

"Yes, that's it. Oh, and I heard from Dr Carpenter that the same crowd took those bodies away from the morgue. He was just about to torch them he said, as ordered. Anyway, they stopped him and took those poor people away."

"I see. Strange."

"Ain't it? I did a bit of asking around. Pal of mine at Special Branch reckons they were taken to a place called Porton Down. Hush hush and all that."

"What about Sadler?"

"No trace. But then there's no trace of anything. The place is still burning. If anything was there, it would have gone up in the flames. At least, we hope so. Ah, here's Daisy back. I'll leave you two alone. I'll see you back at the shop when your all mended, eh sir?"

Lane gave a thin smile. "That you will, Bert. That you will."

Kapitan Schulte, commander of U13, waved a hand at his bosun as the woman was brought on board.

"Yes, yes, I know, Karl. It is considered bad luck to have a woman on board a boat. Might I suggest that if you or any of the crew has an issue with this, they take it up with the Reichsführer on our return to port?"

The old sailor scowled, but nonetheless gave the woman a helping hand down into the bridge. She immediately turned to Schulte, snapping off a Nazi salute, and asking, "My cargo is most important. It is to be kept secure, Kapitan!"

"Yes, Madame, " he replied, deigning not to return the salute, glancing at the sweating, swearing sailors manhandling the bulky crate into the narrow confines of the U-boat. He knew only that it contained a corpse, having picked it and their passenger up from the English coast following certain communications that came direct form the top. Any U-boat crew felt nervous about surfacing so near to enemy territory, but the pick up had gone smoothly and swiftly. Despite that, and the crew's relief at now heading back to base, Schulte took the decision not to divulge the contents of the crate. Two harbingers of bad luck in one go might be enough even for his men.

"Dive, dive, dive," he gave the order. "Take us down to 30 metres. Chart a course for home."

As the klaxon sounded and the boat tilted, Schulte congratulated himself on a successful operation, the ending, in fact, to a successful tour. It was a little more than thirty minutes later when he heard the first screams echoing through the boat.

"We've picked something up, sir," the radar operator reported to Captain David Heath, on the bridge of HMS Weston. The sloop was on routine patrol along the east coast and had received a report of a local fishermen seeing what looked like signalling lights out at sea. "What do we have, Cooper?" he asked.

"Not sure, sir. Bit of an odd one. I thought I picked up an engine sound but now it's gone. There is something else, though."

"Put it on the speaker, will you."

The bridge crew fell silent as the noise sounded over the tinny tannoy. *Clink-clink... clink-clink... clink-clink.*

"Thoughts, gentlemen?"

"Could be a U-boat gone down, sir," his Number Two responded.

"That would account for the engine stopping. But if they were trying to silence it out, why would someone be banging on the side of the hull? At least, that's what it sounds like." Cooper offered.

Heath nodded. "Very well. If a boat had gone down, how much air would they have?"

"In normal circumstances, keeping silent, maybe twelve hours. If the boat was damaged and chlorine gas escaped, no more than ten minutes. Even less if the hull was breached, sir.

And then we'd likely see an oil slick, too." Cooper replied.

"I see. In that case, we will maintain position for now. Stop all engines. Let's wait a while, shall we?"

And yet even hours later, only that faint clanging could still be heard. The Captain made a decision.

"Alright. Some trick of sound, or something banging on an old wreck, I reckon. Make a note in the log, Jenkins. Nothing for us here. Continue our course. One more sweep, then we'll head for home."

## Postscript

DS Bull's contact was correct, Sadler's surviving victims were indeed taken to Porton Down. Little was discovered or achieved during wartime, but post-war scientific advances yielded more results. Some maintain that the white substance encasing each body formed the basis of a guard-servitor creature developed for use in a top secret establishment known only as the Village, located somewhere on the Welsh Coast.

As for Betty, Harry, Albert and the rest, their ilk are long gone, the streets they walked are changed. But London remains a buzzing and vibrant place, home to millions who continue to weave their own threads into the city's rich tapestry. And in the shadows of the steel and glass towers, you can still find the scars from those days, as well as even older remnants of London's long history.

Beckton Gasworks are also a thing of the past. Even the once bustling docks have disappeared, replaced by luxury flats and marinas. Consequently there is far less traffic on the river, far less freight brought up the Thames. But if you head out of the

Thames Estuary, head out to a certain spot to the east and a little to the south... should you cut your engine and listen very, very carefully, you might just hear a faint and distant sound rising up from the cold, grey, shadow-haunted depths.... *clink-clink... clink-clink... clink-clink...*

*In the distance, the ragged peaks of the Tower Bridge that once spanned the glassy Thames now stabbed impotently at the blighted heavens, set amidst a landscape of destruction and desolation.*

# WHISPERED CADENCES OF SWEET DELIRIUM

*LEE CLARK ZUMPE*

*... there are twilight states between sanity and insanity which are clearly recognised not only by experts but by all sagacious men of the world. There are many who are not sufficiently mad to be shut up, or to be deprived of the management of their properties, or to be exempted from punishment if they have committed a crime, but who, in the common expressive phrase, "are not all there" - whose eccentricities, illusions and caprices are on the verge of madness, whose judgments are hopelessly disordered; whose wills, though not completely atrophied, are manifestly diseased.*
- William Edward Hartpole Lecky, The Map of Life, 1899

i.

Adrian Laird stared at a dizzying array of constellations, defined by strings of stars clustered in distant myriads. London fell away from him like a vague dream, its crooked, narrow streets strangely vacated; its neighbourhoods curiously quiet. The black silhouettes of familiar buildings and monuments hinted at some great cataclysm that reduced the ancient city to rubble and ashes. The stubborn carcasses of its once imposing architecture towered over the ruins of an endless city.

A cracked, greenish moon tottered drunkenly on the edge of oblivion, looming low in a cloudless sky. All was still and petrified, with no sound save a faint lilt of harsh undertones, as if cacophonous ghosts of dead musicians performed a prelude to a coming storm in some distant, dilapidated coliseum.

"You still with us, Adrian?" Malcolm McCrorie, the band's guitarist, nudged Adrian. "One more track and we can go home." For the tenth consecutive night, the members of Ultrastellar Phantasmagoria had gathered in a ramshackle recording studio on Broadhurst Gardens in West Hampstead, North London, to work on songs for their sophomore effort. One of a handful of up-and-coming psychedelic acts on the London scene, the band had developed a small but loyal following since the release of their debut album the previous summer.

"Still here, mate," Adrian said, his voice barely audible. The mirage gradually dissipated, replaced by the panelled walls of the recording studio. Still, he could hear that inharmonious dirge continue to reverberate like rolling thunder. "Ready to go. Just say the word."

At Malcolm's command, Gareth Sinclair started playing the organ intro to the next song on the schedule. After a minute-long solo, drummer Callum Ramsden would join him, followed by Malcolm's guitar, and Iain Greenslade's driving bass. Adrian closed his eyes - his thoughts still entangled in the inextricable web of suspended stars and strewn debris he had witnessed in his unsettling vision - and waited patiently for his cue to sing. Somewhere in that anaemic phantasmagoria, the dying cries of some tortured soul mingled with the shrill requiem.

ii.

No keen observer of high strangeness and cosmic synchronicity could ever account for how it came to be that Marcellus Conrad travelled halfway around the world to find himself sitting on a woollen picnic blanket beneath a black mulberry in St. James's Park on that specific day in June 1968.

The 20-year-old American rock journalist had been exiled by his scheming siblings, most of whom were still squabbling over how to divvy up their late father's publishing empire. Seeking to appease Marcellus - the youngest member of the clan - and keep him from staking a larger claim in the enterprise, Granville - the eldest brother - struck a bargain: Marcellus would serve as editor-in-chief of *Kaleidoscopic Velocity*, Conrad Media Group's half-hearted attempt to compete with the fledgling music magazine *Rolling Stone*. Eager to immerse himself in the emerging hippie counterculture, Marcellus seized the opportunity.

Granville also encouraged his little brother to base his operations in London, effectively eliminating him from any contentious and costly probate battles and ongoing litigation in the United States. Though Marcellus readily consented to the arrangement, he did not succumb to the illusion that this pact had been negotiated on his behalf. As always, he could see through Granville at a glance. He could always outpace his siblings in a battle of wits and logic.

Marcellus wanted to be in London, though he had never set foot in the city before his arrival six months earlier. More importantly, he wanted to be away from New York City, away from his family, and away from an ingrained ethos of materialism and self-indulgence.

Despite it being the largest city in Western Europe, and one of the most significant financial centres in the world, Marcellus found something quite different here: layer upon layer of cultural diversity and learned traditions that stretched back to antiquity and reverberated with undertones of primordial invocations. He relished London's many charms and eccentric absurdities. He marvelled at its stark contrasts, with opulence cohabitating with poverty, modern architecture towering alongside Romanesque churches, and teeming streets pushing the boundaries of urban expansion while obscuring the buried bones of the city's archaic past in subterranean charnel houses, abandoned tube stations, and forgotten war bunkers.

In London, Marcellus could feel the sediment of history crunch beneath the heels of his Chelsea boots with each footfall.

"Well, what about it?" Agnes Humphrey could only tolerate his silence for so long. She appreciated the fact that Marcellus had an introspective disposition, and that he often felt the need to focus on observation and reflection, even though it might seem rude and aloof to those around him. "The poetry reading is tomorrow night, at Better Books on Charing Cross Road. I do have other friends, if you aren't interested."

"Of course, I'm interested," Marcellus said, his gaze shifting back to the young woman who had invited him on this lovely summer outing. He suddenly realized he had not spoken since they finished their picnic lunch. He offered her a genuine smile as he banished whatever thoughts had kept him so absorbed in deep contemplation during their midday rendezvous. "I'm sorry." He brushed aside a tuft of wavy auburn hair that had fallen over her eyes. "I haven't been very good company this afternoon, have I?"

"Not particularly." Agnes laughed softly. "But that's not unusual."

"That's a bit cruel. You know how I am some days."

"Lost in the miasma of your soul? Yes, I know how you slip into unfathomable thought and rumination." Agnes sighed. She had grown accustomed to being the center of attention in practically every setting. It surprised her that she had found an adequate supply of patience to cope with his chronic daydreaming. They met shortly after his arrival, but it was in the last month that they began to spend time together almost daily.

"What is it about you that fascinates me so, Mr. Conrad?" Her fondness for him both irritated and amused her. "Why am I stuck on you?"

"Certainly not my rugged good looks and gentlemanly manner," Marcellus said. "It can't be money, because I'm likely to run out of that sooner or later."

"No, that's not it," Agnes said. "I'm heir to a fortune -"

"Yes, I believe you've mentioned that a few times: a large estate in Berkshire outside Cookham Dean, with countless acres and a winding, tree-lined driveway that leads to the front doors of the manor." As he described her family's residence, he made wild dramatic gestures. "Great halls and ballrooms and banquets and a hierarchy of punctual and responsible servants."

"Now who's being cruel?" She feigned injury with a pout on her lip. "You ought not be so discourteous, considering your estrangement from your family. I might well be your saviour someday."

"I don't think I could play the role of a gigolo, my dear."

"I don't think I asked you to, my dear," Agnes quickly replied. "I might be willing to employ you. A butler, perhaps? Or a kitchen boy?"

"Well," Marcellus said, rolling his eyes. "That's very considerate of you."

"I thought so." She paused, studying the young American who was five years her junior. "You are somewhat handsome, in a sombre, saturnine way," she admitted. "Not unpleasant to look upon, I would say. Though it wasn't until we spoke that you sparked my interest."

"I mesmerized you with my intellectual hogwash, no doubt." Marcellus scanned the landscape. The sun had fallen behind a nearby scarlet oak. In the distance, clutches of stern-faced businessmen wearing bowler hats and carrying umbrellas negotiated meandering pathways along the lake as waterfowl congregated on the fringes of Duck Island. "I suppose when I do choose to speak, I do so rather eloquently."

"You aren't that persuasive," Agnes said. "No, it must be your unreasonable obstinance that first attracted me to you - that streak of rebelliousness and contradiction I see in you when you're deconstructing the façade of existence."

"Really?" Marcellus was simultaneously appreciative and unsettled. "Do I do that?"

"I think so," Agnes said, and there was a hint of sadness in her voice. "I think that's where you go when you drift away from me. You perceive what goes unseen by the rest of us. You detect whispers when others hear only silence."

Her statement, no matter how innocent and innocuous she had intended it to be, struck him with the force of a battering ram. In that moment, he felt the mechanism that propels the universe momentarily slip out of alignment. His fragile construct of reality trembled, and his perception of their immediate surroundings grew hazy and distorted. St. James's

Park, Buckingham Palace, Horse Guards and Birdcage Walk all ceased to exist in the interval between two successive beats of his heart - an interlude that, to Marcellus, could have lasted as little as an instant or as long as an eternity.

Before the notion of a scream could form in his throat, the moment passed.

"I'm not sure what to say." Marcellus pushed himself off the blanket and stretched his legs, trying to shake off the aftereffects of the episode. The colour had drained from his face. He turned his gaze toward the sky, spectacularly hued with an ethereal blue and devoid of any hint of cloud or rain.

Marcellus wanted to praise her for her insight. He wanted to throw his arms around her and weep uncontrollably and tell her how grateful he was that someone finally understood him, though he could not begin to fathom how she had so successfully dissected his innermost thoughts. He wanted to bury himself inside of the cocoon of her essence to segregate himself from the unrelenting horror he had experienced since childhood - a private trauma so grievous that no amount of psychoanalysis could defuse the ticking time bomb that would eventually obliterate his fundamental nature.

"I'm sorry," Agnes said. "I shouldn't have said anything."

"It's not your fault," Marcellus said. He looked down at her and offered her a hand. His genial expression had returned and there was a spark of sardonic humour in his eye. "That sounds a little bit like you're saying I might be a - what's your term? - a nutter?"

"No," Agnes said. "Just - sensitive. Tuned into a station we can't find on the dial. Sometimes, you remind me of my brother's friend, Adrian." She grasped his hand, but instead of standing up, she pulled him back down on top of her. She kissed him insistently, conscious of her growing desire to anchor him against some celestial tide that threatened to sweep him away from her. "Let's stay here a while longer."

"I don't have anywhere else to be," Marcellus said.

After a few more moments of shared intimacy, cosmic synchronicity intervened. At first, the old woman's jarring shriek sounded no different than the cries of cormorants that congregate on Duck Island seeking shelter from the clamour of the world. Her screams quickly became more piercing, increasing exponentially in both timbre and terror. The clamour drew all eyes in one direction, and neither Marcellus nor Agnes could resist the urge to seek its source.

The old woman, dressed in gray with a black shawl tied over her head, stood alongside a centuries-old willow tree, its wide boughs stretching out over the pond and hanging low over the water. Those pendulous branches swayed gracefully in the summer breeze, forming a nearly impenetrable canopy, and limiting the amount of sunlight that could penetrate the natural enclosure. Through breaks in the foliage, splashes of crimson emerged.

Onlookers approached the scene cautiously, as if already aware that what they would see would forever defile their sense of safety in the world and diminish their hold on sanity. By now, the old woman had dropped to her knees. She buried her face in her hands and sobbed. Close to the willow, the thick air stank with the pungent reek of death and rot. Carrion flies, going about their macabre work with an unbiased fastidiousness, created a buzzing cacophony around the corpse.

Those who drew too close to the gruesome tableau quickly

recoiled. Some backed away slowly, unable to stop themselves from scrutinizing every horrid detail of the scene. Some turned and ran, hoping that by putting distance between them and what they had glimpsed would somehow make it less real. Some put aside their compulsion to retreat and comforted the old woman.

Marcellus joined the inherently inquisitive few whose morbid curiosity could not be constrained. He discerned something more devastating than the lurid hues amidst that inexplicably dark space beneath the willow tree. He saw bits of meat and bone and flesh that had once been a living being, now completely deconstructed and discarded. What remained had been dismembered and disfigured, marred beyond any semblance to humanity. It was a grisly mockery of mortality. It jeered at the delusion of consequence and worth.

He fought the urge to stay and stare into the abyss.

As Marcellus retraced his steps, he saw that Agnes had finally succumb to curiosity, too - but the distraught look on his face, and the sepulchral dread swirling in his eyes instantly froze her where she stood. She knew in that moment she did not want to venture into that breach.

As they hastily gathered their belongings, Agnes suddenly felt grateful for his introspective disposition. She was thankful he did not want to share the burden of what he had witnessed. She knew it was his way of keeping her safe - of showing her that he cared about something ... about her.

iii.

Despite the ghastliness of the crime, the next day's edition of

*The Sun* buried the story in its back pages. The two-deck headline proclaiming "Remains found in St. James's Park" downplayed the reality of the incident, as if seeking to deter readers from pressing peelers for updates on the investigation. London's Metropolitan Police had questioned everyone in the park upon their arrival as they tried to establish a timeline for the homicide.

No one could explain why the corpse - or what was left of it - went unnoticed for more than six hours, or how the body parts had been deposited beneath the willow tree without anyone witnessing the act. No one could recall seeing any suspicious characters wandering along the park's meandering pathways or idling on the banks of the lake.

The only enlightening piece of information mentioned in the article was the victim's identity: Authorities had quickly surmised that the remains belonged to Irvine Laird, head of Laird Research Laboratories, a multinational pharmaceutical company with facilities in Hertfordshire, Kent, London and Verona. He had been reported missing more than a month prior, though family members were convinced he had simply taken an unannounced sabbatical.

"I met him a few times," Agnes said after finishing the story in *The Sun*. "He always seemed very focused, very intense. Of course, his son couldn't stand to be in the same room with him." The morning sun spilled through the slats in the window blinds, illuminating Marcellus' flat on Westbourne Terrace. GhostCat - a willowy black cat that had adopted Marcellus shortly after he moved into the apartment - stretched his paws and sprawled in a patch of sunlight.

For her overnight visits, Agnes always had a fresh change

of clothes tucked away in a dresser drawer or in the Victorian mahogany armoire that came with the furnished apartment. Sitting at small kitchen table, Agnes took miniscule sips of what Marcellus insisted was "genuine American tea," while he downed a cup of coffee without cream or sugar.

"There is no Venn diagram in which your social circles intersect mine." Marcellus imagined some exclusive social gala where she had met this affluent fellow: some ostentatious affair replete with elegance and opulence, and celebrants eagerly expressing their disdain for commonplace pursuits. "I'm sure you found him absolutely princely and posh."

"As if you haven't benefited from your family's fortunes." She vented a muffled laugh as she tousled his curly black hair playfully. "Your life has been just as pampered as mine."

"I suppose," he said. "But I'd just as soon move to Hooterville with Eddie Albert and Eva Gabor given the opportunity." Marcellus could see by the look of confusion on her face that she did not know the reference - as was always the case when he alluded to American television programs. He did not feel the need to enlighten her. "I guess I'm just not comfortable around the landed gentry."

"You do fine around me," Agnes said. "Although, you are a little rough around the edges - not embarrassingly so, though."

"Give me more time. I'll embarrass you eventually." He offered her a charred bit of bread and a jar of marmalade. "This is breakfast, unless you want to go grab a bite somewhere."

"Not hungry," she said. Her appetite had not returned since the incident in the park the previous day. All night, her mind spat up vivid images and impressions. She struggled to fill in gaps in her memory. She could neither fully visualise it nor erase it. She could not stifle the echo of a distant scream, nor banish the spectacle of such a brutal act. "Did you get any sleep?"

"I slept," he said. "Not well, but I slept."

What he had seen beneath the willow haunted his dreams - dreams that, like most nights, ran along a precarious ledge overlooking a swirling vortex of obliquity. Marcellus always felt its pull on him, tempting him to fall into the abode of chaos. Drifting up from those depths, he often heard a murmured cadence, mellifluous but unsettling. He thought he heard its measure yesterday as he gazed upon Irvine Laird's mutilated body.

"You talk in your sleep, you know," Agnes said. "Nothing comprehensible. No secrets of the universe, as far as I can tell. Just incoherent gibbering." She stood, walked to the sink, and dumped her tea before running the tap. "Are you ready for your interview this morning?"

"As much as I can be, I guess." He finished his coffee and tossed the toast in the waste bin. He had scheduled the meeting through a record company executive recommended by his friend Bruno Sawyer, a freelance journalist. Details were sketchy, and he felt as though the whole affair could go pear-shaped if he failed to follow the band's strict protocols. "I'm still not clear on just who I'm going to be interviewing. They initially promised both Mick and Brian. But Brian may be in court, and Mick is still working on *Beggars Banquet* at Olympic Sound Studios. That leaves either Keith Richards or Bill Wyman as the likeliest to show up."

Although Marcellus could have lived comfortably in London for years without producing a single issue of *Kaleidoscopic Velocity*, he eagerly sought success by respectable means. He had nothing to prove to his siblings: Their narcissistic attempts to legitimise their ascendency within the Conrad Media Group's wide-ranging portfolio made them unmindful of his marginal endeavours. His passion for showcasing avant-garde art and emerging counterculture musicians furnished enough impetus and inspiration to push him to knuckle down, persist and persevere as a fledgling magazine editor.

Since arriving in London, Marcellus had worked tirelessly to produce and promote his publication. He launched the new periodical in January, billing it as a "highly curated repository for new music news, outsider art, and counterculture trends." Until he secured a dependable distributor, he personally delivered *Kaleidoscopic Velocity* to newsagents throughout the metropolitan area. He established a bimonthly publishing schedule, with the first three issues featuring interviews and profiles of both established bands as well as up-and-coming British musical acts, including members of Mabel Greer's Toyshop, Black Botlzhi, Andromeda, Skip Bifferty, Scions of Sholattha, Traffic, Piccadilly Line, The Nice, and Velvett Fogg.

In addition to that afternoon's interview with unspecified members of The Rolling Stones, the next issue would also include a short travelogue written by Nepenthe of Oblivion's guitarist Truman Moss about the band's recent holiday in Marrakesh; and an article on Pink Floyd's first album following the departure of Syd Barrett.

"No matter who shows up for the interview, this is a coup, isn't it?" Agnes looked through his eyes, trying to tease out a few strands of his thoughts. The gesture pleased him, and he smiled and pressed his chin against her forehead. "It's a big deal," she said, tugging his arm as she led him down the short hallway to the bedroom. She stopped in front of the wardrobe and inspected its contents. "What are you going to wear, my sweet?"

"Where did you meet him?"

"Sorry?"

"Irvine Laird," Marcellus said, sitting down on the foot of the unmade bed. "If you didn't meet him at some fancy fairy tale ball or something, where did you meet him?"

"Oh - you're still thinking about that?" Agnes had already settled on her first clothing selection: a double-breasted suit of crushed velvet. To this, she would add a brocade waistcoat featuring a traditional Chinese motif and three black glass buttons; and a ruffled shirt. "I met him several times because my brother used to go to school with his son Adrian. Adrian is the lyricist and lead vocalist for Ultrastellar Phantasmagoria."

Although Marcellus Conrad had heard of Ultrastellar Phantasmagoria, he had never encountered them performing in any of London's clubs. Their debut album was limited to a few hundred pressings, making it virtually impossible to secure through standard channels. The underground band had nurtured a reputation as an outlier even amongst the most radical counterculture artists, appealing to way-out Bohemians and other outré inhabitants of the psychedelic scene.

"I'm surprised you haven't mentioned it before," Marcellus said, with a hint of disappointment. "An interview with those fellows would be a nice addition to an upcoming issue."

"I suppose you're right." Agnes hesitated for a moment, in doubt as to how much her confession might wound him. "I think I've been avoiding it, actually. I told you yesterday that you sometimes remind me of Adrian; but he's different. When he settles into deep reflection, he sometimes becomes catatonic. My brother says he can stay frozen and unresponsive for days."

"You think that might happen to me?"

"I can't bear the thought of seeing you like that," she said. "Swallowed by the shadows. I'm afraid Adrian will end up in Fulbourn Hospital in Cambridgeshire one of these days. I don't want to have to visit both of you there."

"I don't think it's likely," Marcellus said. "Not while you're around, tugging on the rope." He checked the time on his pocket watch and realized he should start getting dressed for the interview. "If you happen to own a copy of their album -"

"I don't," she admitted. "But my brother has an autographed copy of *Shrieking through the Starlit Darkness*."

"Will he loan it to me temporarily so I can give it a listen?" "I seriously doubt it." She giggled, registering the frustration in his expression. A mischievous look took hold in her bright, green eyes. "Oh, don't fret, my sweet. I have no intention of asking Gerald's permission."

"Where did you find these again, mate?" Gerald Humphrey stared at a curious cache of specimens strewn across a teakwood dining table in Adrian Laird's Ladbroke Grove mansion-block flat. The assortment included several bundles of incense rods, dried and pressed hemp leaves collected in paper bags, colourful petals of exotic blossoms, alien-looking mushrooms and other fungi, and a multi-coloured assortment of gelatin pill capsules. "Seem a bit dodgy, don't you think? You'd have to be off your nut to take one of those."

"They were in an aluminium Halliburton case that was sent by special courier," Adrian said. He yawned and stretched, still drained from the night's long recording session in West Hampstead. The band was behind schedule, despite the long hours they had put into the new album. Though none of them would say it out loud, Adrian knew they placed the blame on him. "It arrived early this morning. The fellow who delivered it seemed rather agitated that I came to the door, as if he was expecting someone else."

"Did you ask who sent it? Where it came from?"

"He had nothing much to say about it, really." Adrian had arranged the collection with a fastidiousness that betrayed his fascination with the contents of the case. He had - when the opportunity presented itself - sampled products fashioned by his father's pharmaceutical company, Laird Research Laboratories. He had never had an opportunity like this, though.

"This was meant for my father, wasn't it? But he's not here to claim it, is he?"

"Bloody hell, Adrian!" Gerald knew Adrian and his father had a contentious relationship. Their estrangement from each other had taken root when Adrian refused to pursue an advanced education in biochemistry and physiology, rejecting his father's wishes that he would eventually take over the company. "You're a hard man, aren't you? Your dad's found hacked to pieces in St. James's bloody Park yesterday, and today you're chuffed to bits that he's not around to stop you from taking this lot."

"I am at that," Adrian said, showing more acquiescence than elation. "He was a maggot - a right arse. Maybe when he was younger, he was different. Maybe he wanted to make a difference, cure diseases, give people better lives. But he got greedy, didn't he? Wanted more and bigger things. He did their dirty work for them, didn't he?"

"What are you talking about?"

"The government," Adrian said. "Or whoever was funding his research. Whoever wanted him to develop drugs that could be used to control the masses." Adrian sat at the table, eyeing all the specimens. With the index finger of his left hand, he corralled several of the multi-coloured gelatin pills, methodically aligning them into three neat columns. "I want no part of the deals he negotiated." He summoned a smile to his thin lips. "But this - this is compensation."

"Compensation for what?"

"For not understanding," Adrian said. "For not even trying to see the world from my perspective."

Irvine Laird had never been particularly attentive or considerate. He spent more time travelling the world than raising his only child. He took no notice of his wife's infrequent infidelities - all fleeting affairs that seemed more embarrassing than satisfying to her. When visiting foreign countries to investigate medicinal plants, he corresponded directly with his primary assistants at Laird Research Laboratories, who would relay any pertinent information about his travels to his immediate family. He never conveyed any inkling of wistfulness about his long absences. He never expressed any token of affection.

Adrian's father took great pride in his many discoveries. Part botanist, part chemist, and part anthropologist, he had travelled to some of the most remote and inaccessible destinations in the farthest corners of the world, met and lived with indigenous peoples who had little contact with civilization, and explored regions that climate and geography had made practically impenetrable.

His last known destination - before his disappearance a month earlier - had taken him to Southeast Asia in search of a specific species of fungi that parasitizes cave-dwelling salamanders. The day he returned, he recounted select elements of the experience, telling Adrian that the as-yet unnamed Psilocybe he acquired may possess properties that would be useful in the treatment of various psychiatric conditions.

Adrian knew enough about pharmacology to realize that such a substance had other applications, either as a mind-expanding narcotic or as a tool for mind control or psychological torture.

Thinking back to their conversation, Adrian suddenly realized how extraordinary it had been. The fact that they spoke at all was unusual - but Irvine's unexpected willingness to share details of his expedition went against a lifetime of secrecy and reticence. His father, he recalled, seemed more than inclined to talk about it: Something compelled him to utter his curtailed confession.

"I spoke to him," Adrian said, calling up the memory of that exchange. "Right before he went missing." Adrian found himself reevaluating that brief encounter at the family's estate. He wondered now if his father had known he was in danger. He wondered if what he had presumed was fatigue was in fact dread. "He said he had just returned from an ancient place 'where the silent ones walk.' I didn't know what he meant. I thought he was spinning some barmy yarn."

"Did you tell the coppers?"

"Didn't think of it 'til just now, mate." Adrian picked up a jar containing the mushrooms. "What did the old man get himself into, I wonder."

A few days after that conversation, Irvine had vanished. He left without speaking to his wife or his younger brothers, each of whom served in management roles at Laird Research Laboratories. He failed to notify his assistant of his plans. Though his sudden departure caused some concern, both Adrian and his mother assumed he had just hurried off to some new destination to follow another lead.

With the discovery of Irvine's mutilated corpse, Adrian could not help but speculate about his grisly demise. Those lucrative deals he brokered with clandestine government agencies and other proxies representing organizations with dark designs might have brought him to this tragic end.

"Look, I have to get going." Gerald terminated an uncomfortable silence. "You won't experiment with any of these, I hope."

"No, not today," Adrian said. "The band's got a gig tonight in Kensington, then it's back in the studio until dawn. Can't take the chance. Maybe another time, though. Best find a good place to stash these until then."

"Not here," Gerald said. "They may want to search the place."

"Your place then?"

"I'd rather not, frankly." At age 20, he still lived at home with his parents on a large estate in Berkshire outside Cookham Dean. "Bloody housekeeper will find it without a doubt. She has her nose in everything."

"No worries, mate," Adrian said. "I'll think of a suitable spot." And as Gerald departed, Adrian began the search, recognizing the need to assign it the utmost priority. After all, he conceded - at least to himself - that something in that aluminium Halliburton case may have been what got his father cut into little pieces.

iv.

Agnes Humphrey glared disapprovingly at Marcellus Conrad when he strolled into Better Books on Charing Cross Road an hour after the poetry reading began. On stage, Walker Prite - a lesser-known Liverpool author associated with the Mersey Beat poets - continued a recitation of one of his newest works, titled *Swift Mud*. Other poets taking part in the evening's reading included Mark Papeon and Alwyn Banns Rogers, as well as 80-year-old British occultist and metaphysical poet Carrie Herdtz Wells, who read selections from her epic piece *My Macabre Spell*.

Inside, bookshelves lined much of the wall space, their ranks interrupted only to accommodate narrow doorways into adjacent chambers or gaps that offered occasional glimpses at the dull glow of street lamps. Shadows pooled in certain corners of the shop that even the brightest daylight would not likely penetrate. The place attracted bohemians and hippies, intellectuals and the cultured elite, and all manner of individuals at the forefront of creative expression. Allen Ginsberg had once done a series of readings in this very brick-and-mortar establishment.

Marcellus waited for an appropriate moment to weave his way through the crowd and take a seat next to Agnes. Her sour expression warned him that whatever explanation he had to offer for arriving late would be inadequate.

"It's been a rotten day for me, too," he whispered, leaning close to her so as not to disturb others attending the reading. "I am very sorry. You have every right to tell me to piss off."

"I may well do that." Agnes folded her arms sullenly. She kept her eyes on the poet at the podium, listening to his presentation with solemn attention, admiring his genius, his insight, and his brazen confidence. "Say nothing. Listen."

Marcellus obeyed her instructions, yielding to her wishes. The poet read his work with spirit and sincerity, soothing inflection, and slow, deliberate intensity. As he proceeded, his face grew flushed and his eyes glimmered with genuine tears. There was a marvellous eloquence in his delivery that elicited a deeply emotional response among some listeners. Even Agnes - who rarely revealed any hint of sentiment or melancholy in public - teetered on the verge of weeping.

Once the applause had subsided, guests began to wander around Better Books. Some formed a circle around the evening's presenting poets, eager to interact with them, to shower them with praise and to ask them to autograph copies of their chapbooks. Some aspiring authors approached them seeking practical advice - or hoping that being in the presence of such gifted creatives might inspire them, as if they could siphon off some of that raw ingenuity.

"Are you going to have him sign that for you?" Marcellus noticed that Agnes carried a copy of Papeon's *Holy Diseases* collection. "I'll wait in line with you if you'd like."

"No, thank you," she said. "I think I'd rather go by myself. Why don't you go browse the shelves for a little while. I may come looking for you eventually. Don't be surprised if I don't." With that, she turned and walked toward the poet's table.

Not only did he understand her anger with him, Marcellus knew he deserved it. He consistently let her down - missing dates, forgetting promises he made, not paying attention to her when she needed him to be focused. Although Agnes had no need for chivalry - even as a girl, she had never been fond of stories about damsels in distress pining for knights in shining armour - nor liberation, she did need someone with whom she could connect with on an intimate level. She needed someone she could trust to see inside her soul, and to know that no barriers stood between them. She had her own inventory of secrets and fears and unspoken aspirations, and she wanted to find one person in the world to help her manage that exhausting emotional portfolio.

Truly, Marcellus wanted to be that person.

But how could he be? How could he explain that, since childhood, he had experienced intermittent fractures in reality? That he could perceive all the discontinuity in the universe? That he could sometimes feel himself being pulled into unseen gaps that spill into some awful abyss, as if something unknowable sought his very extinction? He would start by telling her the truth about why he arrived late this evening, assuming she was willing to listen.

Agnes found him outside Better Books, perched on a bench on the street corner and scanning the pages of Oldfield Godolphin's *The History and Antiquities of Dorsetshire*, a tattered old tome he had purchased because he felt a moral obligation to support the business. Somewhere overhead, the pallid stars of the Milky Way sketched vague ghosts of forgotten, monstrous gods. She lingered halfway between the door of the business and that bench for some time, watching as other patrons exited and quietly made their way down the sidewalk. Some would go home to their families, bury their noses in newly acquired books or tune into programming on the idiot box. Some would head to nearby pubs and happily down a few pints with nameless friends.

A few might simply disappear into the shadows, Agnes speculated - swept out of existence by unseen predators. She thought it possible, no matter how far-fetched it seemed. She knew people sometimes just vanished, and unless they were someone wealthy and important like Irvine Laird, no one really seemed terribly concerned about it.

The thought of being forgotten prompted her to suppress her disappointment in Marcellus, at least for the moment.

"Well," she said, sitting down next to him. "Let's have it then."

"Stones didn't show." He waited for their representatives to materialize to either reschedule or offer some explanation, but after three hours he felt confident that they would not extend him even that small courtesy. "Phoned a few times, left messages with my contact's secretary. She wasn't particularly helpful, or friendly for that matter."

"Sorry," Agnes said, and she meant it. "You still have plenty of material for the next issue."

"I guess." Marcellus frowned. "Just a bit put off by the whole thing. They approached me about the interview, after all."

"Maybe they just got their days mixed up."

"Maybe," he said. "But that's not why I was late. It was - "
Marcellus closed his eyes, worried that the words he wanted to express might be enough to trigger another episode. They had been happening more frequently over the last few weeks,

increasing in intensity. He felt on edge all the time, waiting for it to come for him - waiting for it to overpower his meagre defences and consume him. That afternoon, as he made his way back to his flat on Westbourne Terrace, he had heard its whispered intonation once again. He heard three distinct notes, shrill yet hauntingly mournful, uttered by an unseen piper.

"It's OK." Agnes comforted him with the touch of her hand and words of comfort. "Whatever it is, just tell me. I promise you that I will listen until I understand."

"I got lost."

"Is that all?" She laughed a little, surprised that he had been so wary of admitting it. Her American boyfriend still had not memorized London's higgledy-piggledy historic street-layout. "That wasn't the revelation I was expecting, my sweet."

"You don't understand," he said. "I got lost - pushed out of space and time, for at least an hour. I was nowhere. I was adrift on some passage to oblivion, through middle darkness borne toward some vast immeasurable abyss." He was conscious for the duration of his temporary exile, aware of the fact that he had been dislodged from existence. "I had no idea if I would escape - or see you again."

"That's - " Agnes stopped herself from saying what logic dictated. She sensed both his sincerity and his fear. "It must have been some kind of seizure." Agnes wrapped her arms around him. She tried to reassure him by holding him tightly.

"I've got you," she said, as if by voicing those words she made a vow to protect him - to be his paladin. As she pressed herself closer to him, she could feel the aftershocks of what had happened to him. He felt slightly askew and strangely detached. "I've got you."

"There's more," Marcellus said. "Something else you need to know. Someone needs to know."

"What is it?"

"When I woke up, I wasn't sure where I was at first. It was dark, and I could feel something binding me, wrapping itself around me." Marcellus shuddered as he recalled the sensation. "The more I struggled to free myself, the more it tore at my hands." He showed her his upturned palms in the dull light of the street lamp, and she gasped. His flesh had been savagely ripped and rent. "I finally fought my way out of it - and I realized where I was."

"Where?" Agnes closed her eyes as she asked. She already knew the answer.

"You have to understand: I didn't go anywhere near St. James's Park today," Marcellus said. "But when I woke up, I was underneath the willow tree - the same tree where Laird's body was found yesterday."

v.

When Adrian Laird chose to attend the Cambridgeshire College of Arts and Technology to study painting, his father had all but disowned him. His mother secretly paid for his tuition, his flat, and other expenses through a trust fund. During his first year at the school, he fell in with Malcolm McCrorie and Iain Greenslade. The three students frequented London's hottest spots for trending music, plunging into the psychedelic atmosphere of places like the UFO Club, the Goings On Club, St. Toad's Shrine, the Marquee Club, and Club Cassilda.

Seeing Pink Floyd perform on Tottenham Court Road had

been a transcendent experience. It blurred the boundaries of his consciousness and opened portals to alternate worlds. Adrian had experienced brief glimpses of these other dimensions since childhood, but he lacked the focus and discipline to pass through the barriers that separated them. He could only peer longingly through the keyhole at the grandeur and the terror of realms beyond the perception of the masses. Music provided him with a point of reference. Buried in Pink Floyd's psychedelic sounds he could distinguish that otherworldly strain, atonal and jarring yet seductively hypnotic. Like a siren's song, it pressed Adrian to chip away at the partition, promising to grant him access to unimaginable vistas. It sought both reverence and surrender.

That evening, sometime after most wayward wanderers had cleared the streets of Kensington, Ultrastellar Phantasmagoria took the stage at St. Toad's Shrine, playing selections from their debut album. Adrian Laird, the band's lead vocalist and primary songwriter, considered their music an offering to appease the myriad gods dwelling in the chaos of infinite space.

No one knew exactly when St. Toad's opened its doors. No one could confirm the name of the proprietor or remember the face of the fellow who left cash payments for the musical acts with the manager. Even the staff seemed to exist in a chronic state of bewilderment, blundering around the dancefloor like boozy somnambulists, offering any combination of liquor, weed, and hallucinogens to guests who wished to sample them. Holdovers from the days of the mods sometimes infiltrated the club, asking for pills such as purple hearts, yellow dex and black bombers. Most attendees arrived at the club in a state of acid-fuelled euphoria, ready to yield to dulcet, improvised mantras that broadened the boundaries of live music performances.

A dingy basement club, the place could only be found by those who had already visited and had paid close attention to the labyrinthine twists and turns of the corridors that meandered through an otherwise abandoned building on St. Ervan's Road in Kensington. Some claimed the building itself once housed a degenerate cult led by a violent miscreant connected to a series of brutal crimes throughout London in the 1880s. Some also claimed that anyone foolish enough to attempt an exploration of the building's upper floors would never return from their ill-fated expedition.

Far below ground level, St. Toad's Shrine cloaked itself in a violet midnight haze, eager to embrace shunned gods and sympathetic pilgrims.

Agnes Humphrey had attended more than a few shows at St. Toad's. She had rested her head upon eiderdown pillows in the club's backrooms, partying with members of underground bands that would form and disperse over a matter of months. She had been bathed in colourful liquid projections produced by light show pioneers, swimming through vibrant, multihued constellations of dazzling pigments. She had experimented with some mind-altering substances, though none had delivered a particularly vivid or memorable experience.

"Come on," Agnes said, leading Marcellus Conrad through the incomprehensible maze of corridors. "After the day you've had, I think you will really enjoy this. It's a surprise."

Although Marcellus would have preferred to go back to his flat on Westbourne Terrace for the evening, he felt as though he owed Agnes some recompense for arriving late to the poetry reading. She assured him that he would forget about his ordeal earlier that afternoon, continuing to insist that it had been some form of seizure brought on by stress and anxiety. The loss of an interview with members of the Rolling Stones had undoubtedly pushed him over the edge, she said. Marcellus knew better - but he had revealed enough about his situation for now.

As they trudged through the begrimed hallways, it became increasingly evident that the building had been abandoned for some time. The far corners of vacant rooms along the route disappeared in muddy shadows. Mildew and mold thrived in the dank climate, taking root in porous surfaces and forging vast empires across the walls and ceilings. The place reeked of putrefaction and rottenness.

They finally arrived at a doorway to a winding, dimly lit staircase that descended far below the streets of London - much too far, Marcellus thought, to be a common basement. The deeper they travelled, the darker the passage became until only a faint hint of illumination - from an unseen source - remained. By now, they could hear the throbbing pulse of distant music, a psychedelic sound that promised to evoke indescribable visions painted in garish colours. With each footfall, Marcellus felt the pull of the music. With each reverberation, he detected a familiar undertone, ethereal and enthralling.

After traversing a seemingly infinite number of steps, they arrived at St. Toad's Shrine - an underground temple crowded with devotees worshiping the lurid, anarchic ceremony of Ultrastellar Phantasmagoria's avant-garde performance in lysergic frenzy. Agnes turned toward Marcellus, confident he would be grateful she had escorted him to the band's temporary sanctuary where he could experience their innovative, improvisational performance and become acquainted with Adrian. She knew she could convince the lead singer to sit down with him for an exclusive interview. But when Agnes looked at Marcellus, she did not see gratitude. She saw only acute unease, and anticipation of imminent danger.

Instead of walls enclosing the subterranean space, Marcellus found only the sprawling abyss of the cosmos surrounding them. He saw dying stars tenanted by dead worlds - charred and fractured spheres that stood as grim monuments to long-dead civilizations. Marcellus saw unimaginable things squatting along the cosmic periphery, eager to quash any remnant of light and life from the moribund universe.

"Marcellus?" Agnes grasped his shoulders and leaned close so he would not a miss a single word. "Marcellus - I've still got you. I won't let you go."

She held on to him as unseen forces struggled to displace him, even as the band continued to perform and the fulgent lights continued to pulse with such chaotic fury that reality seemed to flicker in and out of existence. Each vibrant shade rippled across the dancefloor, submerging Ultrastellar Phantasmagoria and their enthusiastic disciples in hues of aubergine, cerulean blue, viridian green, xanthic yellow and heliotropic purple. His eyes rolled wildly from side to side and his body warped and stiffened as if twisted by sudden paralysis.

For an instant - no more than the interval between two successive beats of her heart - she felt as if St. Toad's Shrine ceased to exist. She felt as if the underground chamber had grown astonishingly cavernous, its perimeters eradicated and its contents dissolved and transferred to some inorganic realm. The music of Ultrastellar Phantasmagoria ricocheted through that black and terrifyingly empty species of nothingness, mingling with its endemic sounds - a mournful, ill-sounding nocturne composed of shrill pipes and haunting whispers. In that awful abyss, she felt the gaze of something searing its way into her consciousness.

The moment passed, and Agnes found herself alone in a sea of turned-on, tuned-in teens and young adults, their rhythmically undulating bodies lost in entrancement beneath the rapture of frantic obliviousness. Marcellus Conrad had evaporated - snatched from her as though he had never even been.

vi.

*Today, we collected samples of some fungi along the western edge of a remote plateau in Burma where a series of mountain ranges rise to heights nearing 20,000 feet. To reach this place, we set out from Myitkyina on one of two headstreams of the Ayeyarwady River, leaving all trace of civilization far behind, striking out across a landscape that is as unambiguously belligerent as it is otherworldly. The guides abandoned us five days into the journey, muttering some nonsense about forbidden grounds and ancient curses. That we found this place without them is a miracle - or a calamity. Time will bear the rich fruit of our endeavour, or the scourge of some nameless god's wrath.*
From the journal of Irvine Laird

In the weeks before Irvine Laird disappeared, his behaviour

grew increasingly erratic. As he made the journey home from Southeast Asia, he exhibited paranoia and vivid delusions, telling his colleagues that he felt as though something was targeting him. In a journal entry, he wrote that "some agent or entity is systematically removing the building blocks of reality, gradually revealing the abomination of contrivances that constitute the impression of consciousness." He questioned the loyalty of his closest friends and isolated himself upon his arrival in London.

As London's Metropolitan Police continued to investigate his murder, they amassed a significant amount of testimony suggesting that the CEO of Laird Research Laboratories may have been experiencing some form of dissociative identity disorder that caused memory gaps and persistent personality states. His executive assistant claimed she had discovered him on the floor of his office one afternoon completely naked, bleeding from multiple minor lacerations, and clawing at the carpet. After calling for medical aide, she also disposed of a plate containing half-eaten mushrooms.

Irvine's estranged wife, now residing in Bournemouth as Earnestine Snow, saw him only once after his arrival at Heathrow, meeting him for lunch one afternoon at Au Pere de Nico on Lincoln Street in Chelsea. In an interview conducted the day after the discovery of the victim's body, she told investigators that her husband seemed "different, out of sorts, anxious and preoccupied," and that he indicated that he "may be leaving England, possibly for an extended period of time."

A single line of text scribbled on a notepad found on a desk in Irvine's home are believed to be the last words he communicated, though to whom he hoped to convey the

message remains unknown. The message read:
*The days of the darkening are upon him, and his untethered mind is adrift upon a pool of throbbing nothingness.*

Adrian Larid examined the scrap of paper carefully, studying the writing while trying to ascertain some meaning or significance behind the cryptic inscription. Two officials with the Metropolitan Police stood in the doorway of Adrian's Ladbroke Grove mansion-block flat, sullen and reserved, their disposition only tempered by the fact that they felt obliged to show some respect due to his recent loss. They had provided a brief update on their investigation, which included the admission that they had no tangible evidence to assess and no viable suspects to interrogate.

They also returned certain items they no longer considered pertinent to case, including Irvine Laird's personal journal.

"Well, what about it?" One of the two officers grew impatient with Adrian's delayed response. "Does this mean anything to you, sir?"

"I wish I could say that it does." Adrian suppressed the instinct to reveal how his father might use such terms to describe his son's seeming lack of direction and struggle to find purposefulness in the world. What his father saw as aimlessness, Adrian embraced as creative freedom. "If he was talking about himself, I can see why some of his closest colleagues were concerned for him. It doesn't sound like something my old man would say, does it?"

An unexpected wave of regret washed over Adrian as the full extent of loss made itself felt. Despite his lingering disdain for his father, he found room for something akin to grief.

"Well, if anything comes to mind, please ring us," the officer said. "We'll let you know if there's any progress in the case." Adrian nodded in reluctant recognition of their diligence before closing the door to his flat. Though he had not slept since last night's gig at St. Toad's Shrine, his father's journal beckoned him. He wondered what revelations awaited him - and what insights might those entries bring to his understanding of a man who had rejected his family in favour of his career.

After spending hours searching the crowd of unfamiliar faces deep underground in St. Toad's Shrine, Agnes Humphrey had made her way back up the winding, dimly lit staircase; through the incomprehensible maze of corridors that snaked through the abandoned building on St. Ervan's Road; and out into the faint light of the coming dawn. Instead of a vivid and prophetic burst of radiance, she saw only a dull and mysterious pallor gathering in the east. She felt only brooding stillness and wretched solitude overspreading London, as if creation itself had been forcibly disarticulated.

She knew, though - she had been dislodged. She had been put out of place. She shambled down familiar streets that exhibited an inexplicable aspect of malformation and incongruity. The London scenery mocked her: Nothing quite matched her memory or expectation. Everything seemed identifiable yet un recognizable. When lucidity and perception have receded into ruin, the world becomes a hideous anomaly - and for Agnes, the inconsistencies were ubiquitous.

She tried to take no notice of the jarring milieu in which she found herself, focusing instead on finding her way back to

Marcellus Conrad's flat on Westbourne Terrace. She wanted to believe she would find him there, sleeping on the satin sheets she bought for him, wearing his jim-jams and snoring like a foghorn. She wanted to find him there and crawl into bed with him, close her eyes and rest her head on his shoulder, and welcome sleep with its promise of pleasant, uncomplicated dreams.

When Agnes arrived at his place, she found no sign he had returned. She was thankful, nonetheless, that his possessions remained intact - that evidence of his existence had not been wholly expunged, as she had half expected. She chided herself for thinking such demented thoughts, and - for at least a moment - wondered if everything she had experienced over the last few hours could be evidence that she had become unhinged. She had, after all, done a short stretch at Fulbourn Hospital in Cambridgeshire a few years earlier, having suffered a nervous breakdown that required months of ongoing therapy. Memories of the place still haunted her, its halls filled with lost and broken souls in desperate need of compassion and counselling, some raging and rampant, some just formless shapes.

No - she would not jump to that conclusion. First, she had to find out what happened to Marcellus. She knew only one person who might listen to her implausible tale without labelling it utter madness. She knew only one person who might be capable of finding Marcellus and bringing him back to her.

By the time Agnes Humphrey appeared on the doorstep of Adrian Laird's Ladbroke Grove mansion-block flat, he had completed his second reading of his father's journal entries recounting his trials and tribulations in Burma. Adrian had found a detailed account of those alien-looking mushrooms and other fungi - where his father had obtained them, who had shared knowledge of their existence and of their miraculous psychoactive and regenerative properties, and what tactics rival agencies had adopted in their struggle to control access to the asset.

Convinced that Irvine Larid's murder had been the work of a homicidal maniac, the Metropolitan Police found nothing in the journal to support their assumptions. Either they could not conceive of a shadow conspiracy working behind the scenes to acquire and develop mind-control drugs - or someone higher up the chain of command had directed them to abandon that line of inquiry.

These thoughts rolled through Adrian's unsettled mind as he heard some unexpected guest knocking on his door. The interruption fretted him, though he doubted anyone connected to those nefarious agencies would bother knocking before barrelling through the door.

Seeing his friend Gerald's sister standing in the hallway came as a pleasant - though strangely timed - surprise.

"Adrian: I need your help," Agnes said, her eyes red-rimmed with angst and anguish. "I know you'll understand. I don't have anyone else to turn to."

vii.

Marcellus Conrad, editor-in-chief of *Kaleidoscopic Velocity*, sat on a high, square stone slab amongst dead shrubs and charred timber. He felt the base may have once been part of a prominent monument, admired and respected by the dwellers of this city. In the distance, the ragged peaks of the Tower Bridge that once spanned the glassy Thames now stabbed impotently at the blighted heavens, set amidst a landscape of destruction and desolation.

Before he had been thrown into exile by whatever unknown and incomprehensible forces governed this graveyard of the universe, he had witnessed ancient worshippers summoning forgotten gods across thousands of millennia in an unsanctified underground sanctuary - a holy place that had been given the name St. Toad's Shrine only in recent decades. He had observed centuries of secret adulation and veneration among those few who heard the whispered cadences of sweet delirium bleeding through the barrier. He saw them meeting in hidden alleyways, secluded courtyards, and long-neglected squares. He saw them dance beneath an absinthe-hued moon, entranced in their phosphorescent metamorphosis as the shell of reality fractured and imploded.

He felt both horror and bliss - both admiration and revulsion - as he scanned the grim chaos, the blasted panorama, and the myriad voices of sorrow and loneliness. He saw his countless counterparts inhabiting detached shadows, unapproachable and oblivious to all the other souls living in monstrous exile. They drifted like wretched ghosts across the shattered relics of their lost worlds, with lips of purple flesh and eyes like dead blossoms. Many of them, unable to find meaning in their short lives, had sought this destination. Many of them had expedited their banishment, spellbound by that hypnotic melody, as honeyed and soothing as it was unnerving.

Marcellus understood how they had arrived at that tragic decision - but he had not chosen this fate. He still felt a fragile link connecting him to the world. He had purpose, and he had resolve.

He knew only one path that could carry him back to Agnes - and he knew it would not allow him to pass through without a vicious fight.

"I can't imagine how anyone could believe a word of all this." Agnes Humphrey sat in a high-backed, intricately carved oaken chair in the parlour of Adrian Laird's Ladbroke Grove mansion-block flat. Pleasantly furnished, the room was surprisingly bright and cozy, adorned with antique ornaments and historical pieces. On the walls hung old paintings alongside unique examples of modern art: Bridget Riley, Victor Vasarely, Nell Blaine, Grace Hartigan and Jesús Rafael Soto. "Hearing the story out loud makes me question its validity. What if I imagined all of it? What if I'm the one losing my grip on reality?"

"Not to worry," Adrian said, showing both empathy and concern. "You are not crazy, Agnes. I believe you."

"How can you, though?" Agnes took another sip of the brandy Adrian had offered her as she recounted the events of the last few days. "People don't just vanish into thin air, do they?"

"Most people don't." Adrian gave a sad smile that signified understanding as well as a modicum of pity. "But most people aren't attuned to the real world." Like Marcellus, Adrian had glimpsed the harrowing essence of being and the glut of impenetrable darkness that mercifully lies beyond the comprehension of most individuals. "Most people aren't inclined to tug at the curtain any more than they are willing to throw aside the masks they wear."

275

"You sound like Marcellus," Agnes said, and tears spilled from her blue eyes. "You would like him, Adrian. He's smart, charming, witty - full of life and fire. He's ambitious, but not pushy. Most of the time, he's kindhearted and considerate, fuelled by optimism and self-confidence." She paused, momentarily distracted by the passing of an incongruous shadow down a nearby corridor. "But sometimes, he squanders his momentum. Sometimes, something makes him lose the thread. He gets so preoccupied with it that he's barely there."

"We hear the same summoning," Adrian admitted. For him, it was always close at hand, threatening to bewitch and beguile him. That soft, understated rhythm so inharmoniously expressed. It seeped through porous fissures and drifted along cosmic strings, searching impatiently for a direction and a shape - striving to find ears to hear the cacophonous medley of unnatural sounds, and minds to darken and enslave. "We listen to the same song, the same spectral musicians. For me, it's a source of inspiration. For some, it unlocks despair and madness."

As the lead singer and songwriter for Ultrastellar Phantasmagoria, Adrian had tapped into that dark energy as he composed the music and lyrics for their debut album, *Shrieking through the Starlit Darkness*. As work progressed on the new album, he had returned to that perilous source seeking his melancholy muse. Creative commerce with such entities, though, sometimes proved so overwhelming that he lapsed into inattention and prolonged unresponsiveness. It overstretched his fortitude and threatened to dismantle his sanity.

The conductors of that infernal conclave had no names any living being would recognize. Shapeless, primal entities dwelling in the far reaches of eternity, they orchestrated their uncannily mellifluous harmonies - gratingly harsh yet captivating - and channeled them throughout time and space.

"Last night, at St. Toad's Shrine, I heard it," Agnes said. "We came to see Ultrastellar Phantasmagoria play, but there was something else. It's like the walls of reality melted, and for a moment I saw the bare framework of the universe. I heard the awful dirge of chaos." She shuddered at the thought of it, recalling her first and only glimpse beyond the veil. "An instant later, I was back in the club. Marcellus was gone."

"There are certain places where the barrier has grown weak." Because of its long history as a place of pagan worship, a conduit connected St. Toad's Shrine to the swirling vortex. "Marcellus must have been swept up in the current."

"How can I get him back?"

"I'm not sure that you can," Adrian said. The fact that Marcellus had somehow managed to unfetter himself from their dark designs once offered a shred of hope. "You said that the last time this happened, he woke up underneath the willow tree in St. James's Park?"

"That's what Marcellus told me," Agnes said. "His hands were still bleeding, like he had to fight his way out of it."

"The same spot where my father's remains were found a day earlier," Adrian said. "That seems like more than a coincidence, doesn't it?"

Adrian's mind raced as he recalled his last, curious conversation with his father. Irvine had taken the time to track down his estranged son that day, anxious to reveal certain aspects of his recent expedition. In retrospect, Adrian saw it as an overdue apology and an admission that he had failed to truly connect with his son. Maybe that trip had nothing to do with

Laird Research Laboratories, or the other agencies funding his research. Maybe his old man had been searching for a way to better understand him - to break through the barrier and share his experience in the grim abode of eternal chaos.

Maybe he had found a means to that devastating end in those alien-looking mushrooms plucked from caves along the western edge of a remote plateau in Burma.

Adrian never realized his father even knew. He never thought he cared.

"I thought maybe Marcellus had been drawn back there because of the trauma it must have caused him seeing it," Agnes said. "I thought maybe he went back hoping to find something that would help him make sense of it."

"No," Adrian said. "He went back to escape. And I think my father may have guided him there."

I n a nearby corridor that ran the length of Adrian Laird's Ladbroke Grove mansion-block flat, the incongruous shadow Agnes had seen earlier uttered a soft appreciative murmur, pleased to find a spark of faith in his child.

viii.

*The visions were not blurred or uncertain. They were sharply focused, the lines and colours being so sharp that they seemed more real to me than anything I had ever seen with my own eyes. I felt that I was now seeing plain, whereas ordinary vision gives us an imperfect view; I was seeing the archetypes, the Platonic ideas, that underlie the imperfect images of everyday life.*
R. Gordon Wasson, *Seeking the Magic Mushroom*, published in 1957 in *Life*.

Months before Irvine Laird's mutilated remains mysteriously appeared beneath a willow tree on the well-maintained banks of a scenic pond in St. James's Park, the celebrated CEO of Laird Research Laboratories found himself seated on the hard ground of a remote plateau in Southeast Asia, wedged together in a close circle with an assemblage of colleagues and indigenous people. These natives bore little resemblance to their closest Burmese neighbours who dwelled in small villages many miles from this isolated tribe. Upon their arrival, Irvine's team had made repeated inquiries as to the origins of this far-flung clan, but neither government officials nor the expedition's salaried guides could provide a plausible history.

Before those guides abandoned the trekkers, one had warned Irvine that the people of the plateau came from "a realm of mist and solitude," and that many of their customs alarmed travellers who passed through the region.

Only Irvine could speak their ancient tongue - and his knowledge of it proved inadequate for all but the most basic dialogue. Somehow he managed to convey his interest in experiencing the traditional communion rite involving what they considered divine mushrooms, assuring his hosts - as best he could - that he and his teammates would treat the ceremony with utmost respect and solemnity.

One of the elders, acting as a high priest for the ritual, washed the mushrooms in a wide, shallow gully that snaked its way across the plateau. Uttering incomprehensible prayers as he passed each of them through serpentine curls of incense smoke, he next distributed the mushrooms to all those present, allotting four to each man and woman. Irvine guessed that younger members of the nomadic tribe would not be allowed to participate, though no one in his party had seen any children in their encampment during their stay.

As Irvine described in his journal, he and his colleagues ate the mushrooms, chewing them deliberately, wincing as the pungent taste made stomachs turn and senses reel. There was no resisting the immediate effects - Irvine felt his perception of the world as a constrained continuum splinter. He felt the far horizons retreat, growing ever paler as their ability to limit the visible world diminished. Visions emanated from every niche in an intensifying expanse, and reality tapered into inconsequential residue clinging to an insignificant outcropping overlooking a yawning void, featureless and vast.

Within that eternal abyss, dusky as chaos, Irvine encountered that murmured cadence, mellifluous but unsettling. Where crownless gods in darkness sit, his enraptured soul hungered for the bleak serenity of an ethereal existence - but he knew, instinctively, that even here he could not escape the tedium of mindfulness.

The visions gradually faded, and Irvine and his colleagues resigned themselves to the flawed and feeble paradigm that provided the underpinning of their understanding of reality. Despite Irvine's repeated requests, other members of his team refused to discuss their own experiences. He could not determine that they shared identical or dissimilar visions. He could not confirm that their perception of the world had been altered. He could not make any conclusions about the efficacy of hallucinogen nor its applications.

The indigenous people had vanished, leaving no indication where their roving lifestyle would take them next. They seemed eager to lose themselves in isolated corners of the landscape, journeying as far as necessary to avoid both interactions with the modern world and the penetrating gaze of those unnamable things sitting astride the cosmic periphery.

Irvine Laird felt their eyes upon him, too.

Only a short walk from Adrian Laird's flat was Manlike Bones, an exclusive club hidden in a narrow alleyway behind a nondescript door off Hobbs Lane and Kensington Park Road. The place catered to a certain segment of London's affluent: The young, well-heeled, slightly decadent, and decidedly nonconformist mavericks met here in secreted chambers serviced by scrupulously vetted, discreet personnel.

The name, according to local legend, came from a macabre discovery made by workers when working on an extension to the London Underground. A mass grave, dating back centuries, contained more than a dozen malformed bodies. Some experts insisted that the "manlike bones" belonged to an otherwise unknown primate species.

Adrian led Agnes Humphrey to the private chamber he had acquired the previous day. There, he retrieved the aluminium Halliburton case which had recently come into his possession, and which contained incense rods, dried and pressed hemp leaves collected in paper bags, colourful petals of exotic blossoms, alien-looking mushrooms and other fungi, and a multi-coloured assortment of gelatin pill capsules.

"Four mushrooms," Adrian said. "That should be enough to push one of us across the boundary and into their realm."

"I will go," Agnes said. "He'll follow me. If he doesn't, I'll stay with him."

"Are you sure that's what you want to do?"

"It's the only way." Agnes did not make her decision lightly. She understood the risks involved, and she knew once she immersed herself in that nightmare she would always carry its suffering and misery. She also knew that life presented a continual procession of dread and disappointment, alleviated by fleeting moments of joy and belonging. For her, those moments represented more than brief respite. Strung together across a lifetime, they provided both purpose and vindication. "I promised him I wouldn't let him go. I'll find him, and I'll stay with him in whatever world he chooses. If fate allows it, I will be with him when the galaxies start unravelling."

"Go," Adrian said. "Find him. Bring him back. I'll be waiting at the willow tree."

The fact that Agnes Humphrey did not fear the spectre of mortality had nothing to do with her youth and good health. If she allowed herself the luxury of personifying death, she knew the grim reaper might delay his visitation for decades - or he might find time to call on her that very afternoon. She understood both the impermanence of existence and the insignificance of the individual in the unimaginably vast scope of an apathetic universe. Neither concept troubled her. Neither engendered uncontrollable fear.

For Agnes, isolation evoked a sense of dread and failure. She yearned for one meaningful connection in her life. Without it, she felt only emptiness and worthlessness. She admitted to herself that her affection for Marcellus Conrad enhanced every other facet of her life. For that, she would go to great lengths to retrieve him.

It took little time for the mushrooms to transport her across the bridge to that grim echo of the world.

She found Marcellus drifting down one of the meandering pathways along the lake in St. James's Park - except, this iteration of the park was a blighted, ugly facsimile filled with rotting vegetation, scattered rubble, and the carcasses of long-dead fauna. The pathways had disintegrated. The lake had dried up leaving its once green shores cluttered with ashes.

This iteration of London, likewise, was a sprawling wasteland, traversed by vacant streets and cluttered with the charred remnants of Victorian edifices devoid of life. Wandering through the sepulchral ruins, countless lost souls cycled through forgotten tragedies. Wretchedness and misfortune undercoated this bleak panorama, and Agnes felt its doleful magnetism pulling her down and inviting her to self-annihilation.

By the time she reached him, Marcellus had curled into a foetal position on the tattered fragments of her woollen picnic blanket. Above him, the leafless branches of a black mulberry stood like a stubborn skeleton cursing its deaf god.

Agnes grasped his hand, but instead of standing up, he pulled her down on top of him. He kissed her repentantly, convinced that he had doomed her to an eternity of sorrow. He had hoped she would anchor him against a celestial tide that had always threatened to sweep him into oblivion; instead, he had dragged her into the void with him.

"We can't stay here," Agnes whispered, and her declaration drew the attention of shapeless, primal entities dwelling in the chaos of infinite space. The hypnotic melody of harsh undertones grew so thunderous that they could barely communicate. "We have to go - now."

Those who reigned over the cosmic necropolis saw no reason to intervene: The toxic environment would impede any attempt at escape. They watched as two young lovers struggled against a sudden maelstrom that scoured the landscape. They jeered as one abomination after another cleaved itself from shadow to stand in their way. They howled when the topography restructured itself, obscuring their route.

Through it all, Agnes kept her promise: She would not let Marcellus go, even when she realized they might never find their way home. Just as she felt faith slipping away from her, she saw Adrian standing beneath the willow tree. She grabbed Marcellus and together they sprinted across the last stretch of wasteland, speeding toward the same breach Irvine Larid had tried to navigate.

Agnes hoped they would not meet the same fate.

ix.

*A living Gallery of aged Trees;*
*Bold sons of earth that thrust their armes so high*
*As if once more they would invade the sky.*
*In such green Palaces the first Kings reign'd,*
*Slept in their shades, and Angels entertain'd:*
*With such old Counsellors they did advise*
*And by frequenting sacred Groves grew wise;*
*Free from th' impediments of light and noise*
*Man thus retir'd his nobler thoughts imploys.*
Edmund Waller, On St. James's Park as Lately Improved by his Majesty

For an incalculable interval, heavy darkness surrounded and subjugated them. They drifted through a shadowy abyss, its numbing blackness enfolding them in its coils. In this wilderness of nonexistence, the nothingness offered no confirmation they had survived their flight and no proof that anything palpable and perceptible might eventually manifest itself in their presence. Marcellus Conrad could escape the thought that some pragmatic component of part of his brain had intentionally blinded him from vistas too great for the eye of man.

For that duration, he and Agnes Humphrey had no means of communication and no discernment of external stimuli. Somehow, though, they knew they were still together.

Then, through the boughs, a spark of radiance materialized. A path shrouded for eons led them through to their destination.

"Is this tomorrow, or the threshold of forever?" Marcellus watched the first light of the sun shining through the willow branches. He turned to Agnes, kissing her forehead. "You found me."

"Again, yes." She spied Adrian Laird running across St. James's Park. "If it hadn't been for you, we might still be on the other side."

"What do mean?" Adrian glanced at his watch. "I've only just arrived. It took me 10 minutes to get here."

"If that wasn't you," Agnes said.

"Father." Adrian offered his hand to Marcellus. "Splendid to meet you, sir. Rather peculiar way to approach me for an interview, though. I'd be happy to oblige, any time."

November brought omens of an early winter to London. Gray

skies and cold rain kept most people from St. James's Park that afternoon, but Agnes and Marcellus walked side by side, sharing an umbrella.

"No more seizures, then?" Agnes rested her head upon his shoulder as they strolled. "It's as if the doorway closed."

"It's still ajar, I think." Marcellus continued to publish new issues of *Kaleidoscopic Velocity*, including the latest edition with a cover story detailing the recording of Ultrastellar Phantasmagoria's new album. His friend Bruno Sawyer penned an article on Mind Esteem, a new Canterbury scene band whose debut album, *Robot Entropy*, had caused a stir on the charts.

"But I don't feel at risk of being dislodged anymore. This reality - whether it's real or not - feels stable."

"For me as well," Agnes said. "But - there is something." She hesitated, not certain how to explain the phenomena.

"Sometimes, I feel like we're surrounded by invisible people - ghosts, I guess. I never much believed in ghosts."

"They're all around us, all the time." Marcellus stopped and scanned their surroundings. "Not ghosts: Shadows of the people that ended up in that eternal nightmare."

He saw them, too - lost souls doomed to walk an empty shadow world, existing on the periphery as phantoms and night terrors. They are a shallow, incomplete reflection of who they were in life, worn down until all that's left is sadness and remorse.

"That's awful," Agnes said. "What can we do for them?"

"Acknowledge them." Marcellus glanced toward the willow tree. Seeing an aberrant shade beneath its branches, he tipped his hat. "Let them know they aren't forgotten."

LONDON - Ultrastellar Phantasmagoria released their second album on All Hallows' Eve. Titled *Whispered Cadences of Sweet Delirium,* the new album from London's wildest psychedelic outfit features eight brand-new tracks, including the first single *Violet Midnight.* According to Lindström Records, a second pressing has already been confirmed as the album races up the charts. Theo Hopper, the band's manager, is currently working on the itinerary for a string of shows throughout the UK, followed by a North American tour in the spring.

Adrian Laird, the band's vocalist and songwriter, dedicated the work to the memory of his father, Irvine Laird.

Following is the track list for the new album:

*Whispered Cadences of Sweet Delirium*

Side One
1. Prelude to a Coming Storm / Primordial Invocations
2. Where the Silent Ones Walk
3. The Pallid Stars
4. Violet Midnight

Side Two
1. Days of the Darkening
2. Lips of Purple Flesh
3. Where Crownless Gods in Darkness Sit
4. Too Great for the Eye of Man

- Marcellus Conrad, *Kaleidoscopic Velocity*, Issue 6, November 1968

*Jeanne's head whipped around as that same silhouette emerged from the fog. The cloak opened and a long, silver blade emerged, glistening in the muted light.*

# RAG AND BONE

DAVID CARTWRIGHT

Spitalfields London, April 14th - 1892

Dearest Mama,

I hope this letter finds you well and Father's health improved.

I have arrived in London and taken rooms in Brune Street, near Spitalfields market, quite a blessing as it puts me so close to Lombard Street and my new employment with Alexander and Haynes. I know it also has proximity to Whitechapel, but it has been nearly ten years since those most regrettable incidents and I am sure I will be quite safe, the Ripper is long gone by now. I have great hope that the year of our Lord nineteen hundred will usher in an age of enlightenment for us all, a time of progress and intellectualism that will raise us above the fear and superstitions of the past.

I have allowed myself additional time and funds with which to furnish my rooms and allow for a visit to a tailor, the streets of London will find me no know-nothing from the country, I shall have a new suit to suit my new employ and, should you find time to visit me, you will not find me living in the squalor of bachelordom.

I send kind regards to Uncle Henry for making introductions with Mister Folkstone and securing my position here. I had feared the unrest in Europe might hinder my chances at gainful employment but, with much thanks to Henry, not only am I employed, but at an accountancy firm of no small reputation.

I shall write again once I have settled and have more to tell of the rigours of city life.

Yours in Faith,

Your son, Charles Fortesque

"Rag and bone! Any old iron!"

Jeanne Yatumbe frowned before the rumble of a truck and rattle of glass heralded the departure of the bin men. Strange they should call that antiquated phrase, but a faint gale of laughter followed them down the street. She shrugged, some joke or something.

She held the letter carefully. She couldn't be one-hundred percent certain of its provenance but her limited experience of vintage documents was assuring her that this was genuine. But how did it get here? Delivered to her door with a bright new Post Office 'Redirected' sticker bearing her address slapped irreverently on the original envelope.

Most people would've disregarded the letter entirely, but then most people weren't research journalists.

She read it again, then turned the brittle paper over in her hands. Maybe it was a prank, the result of her ad seeking source material in the financials. Her current piece was a commission item on the history of the financial sector in London. Not the most exciting material sure but, as a freelancer Jeanne went where the work was and, should the work come to her it at least saved her mileage. Although she had tried working in offices, writing for a wage, it was the worst kind of purgatory for someone like her. She shrugged, she had interviews to line up, research to do and emails to send. She made a note to look for 'Alexander and Haynes' or their descendent company (if they still existed) and slipped the letter into her desk drawer.

Three days later and the article had stalled.

The information was there, laid out in perfect format but dry, lifeless. A knock on the door called Jeanne away from her computer screen. The letter flap rattled, a bundle dropping through onto the mat. Jeanne shuffled to the door, snatching up the post. Junk, junk, crap, catalogue, bill... what?

Another antique envelope, written with scrolling script and slapped with another bright 'Redirected' label, and a small package, wrapped in brown paper and tied with frayed twine. Discarding the modern mail Jeanne took the two anomalies back to her desk and carefully opened the letter first.

*Spitalfields London, May 20th 1892*

*Dear Mother,*

*I hope this letter finds you well.*

*The news of father's failing health has reached me via Uncle Henry. I am saddened that you did not feel that you could tell me yourself, in truth I am surprised not to have heard from you since my arrival in London.*

*I regret that I cannot come home. Mister Folkstone has been steadily increasing my responsibilities. It would seem that I have a bright future ahead of me at Alexander and Haynes and, perhaps, it will allow me to provide better care for father, should his keepsake from the Crimea continue to plague him.*

*I shall attempt to write more frequently however, Mister Folkstone has said I am to take on an important client and the whispers from around the other employees indicate that this is no small matter of import. I have resolved to keep detailed notes in my journal (without, of course, violating client privilege) as an assurance of accuracy.*

*My sincerest hopes for father's recovery.*

*In Faith*

*Your son, Charles Fortesque*

*No wonder mama didn't write you back, pet,* Jeanne thought, your letter got redirected to a hack journalist a hundred years in the future. But, if the letters got sent to her, then the package might be...

She ripped open the paper, heedless of the age. A small leather-bound book, a little larger than her palm, sat in the sundered wrapping, a golden monogram on the cover.

C.F.

*Curiouser and curiouser*, thought Jeanne.

The journal, for that was all it could be, had a slim, cloth mark slipped between the pages so, on impulse, Jeanne opened to the marked page. *It is most curious. Isn't it just sweetie,* Jeanne thought. The same well formed, flowing handwriting as the letter, just smaller to fit the journal's pages.

*Mister Folkstone brought me before Mister Alexander himself, who has charged me, upon strictest confidence, with maintaining these accounts, but no-one has, at any point, mentioned who they belong to. Equally there is no notation on the documents themselves of names, addresses, even the purposes of the payments. I am to work in figures alone and I am cautioned endlessly to ensure the figures match. Should they not, I am to inform Mister Alexander directly.*

*I can only assume that it is some matter of Government, perhaps the Crown itself? What else would warrant this level of secrecy and I, Charles Fortesque, am charged with its delicate upkeep. I would that I had the slightest inkling, that I would then know just how proud I should be of my secret endeavours.*

Jeanne frowned, the journalist in her smirking, cynically. Her first impulse was that poor Charlie was being set up. Oh perhaps it was something secret. 1892? In a little over twenty years the First World War would begin, surely there were rumblings of something in the financial markets. Perhaps these letters would help her write her article after all.

She flipped ahead a few pages. *This cannot be.* Charles' handwriting betrayed the slight shake in his hand.

*As I reconciled amounts this very morning I had the newspaper upon my desk, the headline story that of a daring robbery staged some days prior, the police making requests for anyone with knowledge to come forth. The auction house that was the target lost many fine antiques and the contents of their safe, a sum of some six and a half thousand pounds.*

Jeanne pulled her phone, searched 'historical currency conversion' and tapped in the figure. She whistled in surprise; that was about a million in today's money. Satisfied she turned back to the page.

*How alarmed I was then, to see a cash deposit into the very accounts I was reconciling for the same amount! At first I tried*

293

*to disregard my misgivings, to convince myself it was mere coincidence but the feeling would not leave me. Upon closure of business I ventured to the offices of the newspaper. I have noted the dates and figures of a number of high value thefts and will see if those dates align with deposits in my accounts. If they do not, then might I put my mind at ease.*

Jeanne didn't for a moment believe that Charlie's mind was going to be put at ease but, before she could continue, an alarm on her phone chimed, reminding her of an interview she'd scheduled with a historian specialising in the commercial sector and finance.

As she shifted the journal to look at her phone a small square of card fell from the back pages. Reaching to retrieve the fallen card she was surprised to see an old photograph, a young man in pinstripe with a boater hat, stiff upright collar and bamboo cane. His features were set in a furiously serious expression which made his pencil moustache all the more comical to Jeanne. On the back, someone had written *C.F. May 1892.*

So, he'd bought the swank new suit and got a picture taken before he made his unfortunate discovery.

Jeanne went to her cloud files, pulling up the very brief references she'd found to Alexander and Haynes, and her resolve to get more information about them from her source reinvigorated.

"Of course, Alexander and Haynes was founded long before the turn of the century," Dominick Allen, historian, a kindly figure who lived the stereotype of a cardigan and tweed academic, announced, reaching behind him to pull a well-thumbed volume from his shelf. "Two catholic clerks, James Alexander and Rufus Haynes went into partnership shortly after the reinstatement of Charles the Second."

"Huh, are they still around?" Jeanne asked, looking up from her phone screen where she tapped her notes.

"Not the original gentlemen, no. That was over three-hundred and sixty years ago." He chided her with a gentle smirk.

She returned the smile, "I mean, the business."

Allen nodded, "Oh yes, the company continued as Alexander and Haynes, passed through family, until the nineteen eighties when it was renamed A and H Holdings of London. Not that many outside the inner circle of financiers will even be aware of it."

Jeanne quirked an eyebrow, "Why not?"

The historian looked up, surprised. "Well, A and H have held a very exclusive clientele for a very long time. I have no idea who is on their books but I know that they've no more than two-dozen clients. Besides that they've never traded publicly and, if they have any external shareholders I've never found any clear reference to them."

Frowning, Jeanne chewed the end of her stylus. "Is that legal? Possible even? They've survived every modern financial crisis without taking on outside investment and apparently don't answer requests based on the Freedom of Information Act?"

Dominick shared the smile of a kindly grandparent, "You'd have to know about them to submit a request, my dear."

Jeanne answered his smile with a determined one of her own. "Well, I know, and I'm asking."

Allen cocked his head to one side, "This seems to be very

important to you, why?"

Jeanne thought about the photo, the journal and the letters.

"I think they did something, something bad, and if you don't know about it, then they never paid for it. It might be too late for the law, but it's never too late for the truth."

The older man's eyes hardened at the corners.

"An admirable sentiment, but be sure of your accusations before you make them, and be prepared for the repercussions."

Jeanne met his earnest gaze and nodded.

"Oh and, when you find your answers, do let me know. For the records," he winked.

Outside Allen's home-cum-office Jeanne took a deep breath. He was right of course, she needed to be sure a crime had been committed so, what to do? She still had the most recent letter and journal with her. Taking the letter carefully from her shoulder bag she examined the envelope. The original delivery address was somewhere near Bristol. Pulling out her phone, she fired off an email to an old college friend, someone she'd worked with on her first work placement, to look into Charles Fortesque. That done, she checked a bus timetable to take her to the London Library. If there had been a scandal, perhaps a murder even, it would have made the papers of the time. She had dates, and the journal to guide her so it shouldn't take that long, right?

"The library closes in twenty minutes." The voice snatched Jeanne from her research. She glanced around, then looked at her phone screen. 17:10 "Fuck!" she swore aloud, then added, "Sorry," quietly as she remembered where she was.

Not a note, not a by-line or an obituary for Charles Fortesque. Well, not entirely true. There were plenty of 'Charles Fortesques', it was a very common name, but none of them where her Charles Fortesque.

She snatched up the journal, flitting the pages more roughly than she might otherwise until...

*I am a fool.* She read. *I have confirmed my suspicions, at least to the satisfaction of my own mind.*

Charlie's script was still tremulous like before, a man ill-at-ease.

*But in my earnest attempts to seek some justice I have been vain, ignorant of the world and its machinations.*

Jeanne imagined a pause as his hand trembled over the waiting page.

*I took the accounts from the office, smuggled them in secret, along with my findings, and took them to Scotland Yard! There I hoped someone might listen, that Alexander and Haynes has been, at the least, laundering stolen monies. I could not simply go to the constabulary; the amounts I have identified constitute the ransom of Creosote! No, I thought, Scotland Yard it must be. What a fool I was.*

*I had yet to make my accusation, had only hinted, made vagaries of 'inconsistencies' to the desk sergeant and yet when mention of Alexander and Haynes left my lips I was escorted to a room and met by a senior inspector, a Rothschild no less! I began my story but he interrupted me, fixed my gaze and said, "Come, come sir, you wouldn't wish to cause a fuss, would you?"*

Jeanne took a sharp breath through her teeth. What was this? She continued reading.

*The look in his eye, I realise now, he knew. But at that moment*

*I did not comprehend, I became insistent. Before I could act in my own defence he struck me, dragged me out of my chair, pressed me to the wall and told me to be away, and to go back to my work. He said I didn't want to 'upset The Man'.*

"What man?" Jeanne asked aloud, unable to contain her desire to know.

*I had no clue, had lost my composure, I asked in desperation "What man?"*

*In his reply, he feared the words but he spoke them anyway.*

*'The Rag and Bone Man'.*

*Those words uttered he stood me on my feet, brushed me down and couldn't eject me from the building fast enough, though he took pains to ensure no mark of our altercation showed.*

*I fear, I fear that there is more than mere malfeasance at work here, and I fear that I am in a dire predicament.*

*I don't know what to do.*

Jeanne shut the book carefully.

Squaring up her notes and returning her things to her bag, she left the library.

The sun was falling, late autumn in London, and the chill crept through her. She'd moved to the city some years ago and had been wary walking the streets at first, prudently so. The big cities hold their dangers, perhaps not Jack the Ripper, but she'd seen the 'Happy Slap' craze run through, acid attacks and increased racial violence against Muslims and the east-Asian community during Covid. The city wasn't always as shiny as the big chrome and glass buildings would have you believe. It still held much of the darkness, the appetites of its past and it was a fool indeed who denied it. It could still swallow you whole in ways no-one would even know you were gone.

She closed her eyes and pinched the bridge of her nose.

*I've been reading too much Edwardian prose,* she thought, I'd never have used a term like 'a fool indeed' if it hadn't been for Charlie. Still, she pulled her jacket tight, and couldn't shake the sensation of eyes upon her as she made the journey home.

"The offices were recently rebuilt to accommodate advances in information infrastructure. An entirely revamped Wi-Fi system, fibre optic hard lines, solid-state storage, backups and state of the art global stock market tracking. We have only a small staff but we like to see that they have the best working environment and tools at their disposal."

The shining corporate shill giving Jeanne the tour looked like he'd been ordered from a catalogue. After the library, she'd put the journal in her drawer, not looking at it for several days. But...For a start she'd already emailed A and H Holdings for an interview. She hadn't expected to get anywhere at the time but, when their reply email arrived it stated they'd be happy to accommodate her, to 'highlight the part A and H had played in making London's Financial sector the *internationally recognised component of the global economy it was today*. The email itself made good copy, corporations being arrogant always made the readership chuckle.

Also, the itch had started again. Whenever Jeanne found herself on the thrill of a story she could never leave it without the itch starting up, the need to see it through to the end. She brushed off her misgivings of that evening outside the library as ghost-story creeps and resolved to find out just what had happened to Charlie and this Rag and Bone Man, whoever he was.

Another reply from her friend in Bristol had also galvanised her.

*Charles Fortesque, son of Elizabeth and Durham Fortesque (cousin to a minor branch of one of the more important Fortesque families), born eighteen seventy-three, moved to London eighteen ninety-two, no further communication with family. Father died of complications from injuries suffered during the Crimean War, eighteen ninety-six, Elizabeth was 'sequestered' (a direct quote from the papers there) to Bristol sanatorium, died eighteen ninety-nine calling for her son. The family line ended with Charles, missing, presumed dead, possibly caught up in World War One.*

So, poor Charlie moved to London at nineteen on the promise of a good job, got caught up in something that included corrupt cops within Scotland Yard, and disappeared. *Like hell he got himself killed in the trenches, he was probably already dead in a ditch somewhere long before*, Jeanne thought venomously.

"News is only the first rough draft of history."

The quote came back to her from her college days.

Well, no-one had even written this draft and, if not for Charlie, and whoever had sent her his letters and journal, no-one would have.

So now, here she was, in the belly of the beast, listening to a man who looked like he'd stepped out of a glossy Polaroid, talking about 'proud history', 'family values' and 'core business ethics' like he was selling her on a stock portfolio.

"That's all very impressive," she smiled innocently, "but surely the company has come into contact with wrongdoing at some point in time? Think of the legacy of the East India

Company, Jordan Belfort, the so-called 'Wolf of Wall Street', the Lehman Brothers' scandal? We're in a time where holding your hands up and saying 'Yeah, we fucked up' is great copy, you might even get a movie deal out of it."

The agent looked uncertain for a moment, then the smile came back even brighter.

"I'm sure I don't know what you mean."

Jeanne's own smile never wavered. "I've come into some information that, in the late eighteen-hundreds, Alexander and Haynes served as a laundering house for large figures of stolen money, that they ran the books for someone only referenced as the Rag and Bone Man? Some kind of underworld kingpin..."

Her voice trailed off. The agent stood too straight, too tall and so stiff he trembled. His smile was suddenly too wide but the fear in his eyes was very real.

"I'm sure," he rasped before clearing his throat and starting over, "I'm sure that any events of past wrongdoing would have been handled with the same due diligence as we would apply today."

His skin was waxen, his voice devoid of its previous corporate brand warmth. "Any discrepancy would be thoroughly internally investigated and all findings presented to the appropriate legal or industry body," he finished lamely. "Now, if you'll excuse me, this interview is over."

Even before he turned to sweep her away, Jeanne felt the presence at her back, a tall and broad-shouldered security guard who looked like she'd been born devoid of a sense of humour, and definitely wasn't in the market for one today.

"Look, I get it." Rickie tried to reassure Jeanne as she took a drink.

The Joiners Arms in Camberwell wasn't exactly Jeanne's local, but it was as good a place as any.

"But you've got to realise," Rickie went on, "he was probably just afraid of dropping himself in it. Just think, years ago you didn't talk about Pablo Escobar, or the Krays, now they get Pedro Pascal and Tom Hardy in movies about them. And what kind of name is the 'Rag and Bone Man'? Talk about melodrama. This is probably a similar thing to the Krays thing, y'know? The company's secret shame. He was only afraid to lose his job, his shares and his pension. Talk to my dad, the train company tried to short him out of his pension, but he wouldn't let them, stubborn old bastard. What was I saying?"

Rickie was a screenplay writer and a generally sympathetic ear, if ever free with the drinks. He smiled in a vaguely bemused way.

"Go easy on the gin there, Rix," Jeanne cautioned. "In fact, let's get you home."

Rickie waved Jeanne away. "I'm fine, Hayley's coming around later so if you want to go, go. I'll be right here."

Frowning slightly, Jeanne gathered her things and made her way home.

Opening the journal, she moved ahead a few pages. She tried to identify with Charles' self-indulgent laments, but really it just came across as whiny. A good deal of 'Who is the Rag and Bone Man?' and 'How shall I extricate myself from this mess?' until a further entry, the writing looking less like the tremor of a man in fear, but the loose hand of a man deep in drink.

*I have a plan*, he stated.

*I cannot go to Mr Alexander, he is most obviously complicit. But Mr Haynes? I have not oft seen him at the office. Perhaps he sequesters himself, or is kept apart because he does not know, or does not approve. I will hope for the former and try to reach him. I know not his address, and would not go direct to his home in any case, for fear of being followed but, in the portrait of him that hangs in the company offices I noticed a ring, like that of a gentleman's club, emblazoned in the image of antlers surrounding a dog's head. It took but little effort to identify the Herns Hounds Club on Singer Street, not far from Spitalfields itself.*

*I shall enter under guise of a porter, locate Mr Haynes and inform him of the criminal enterprise that his company has become embroiled in.*

Jeanne found herself holding her breath as she turned the page. Here the handwriting held an urgency, spiked with near panic.

*Disaster.*

*Having gained entry to the club Mr Haynes was nowhere to be found. I searched, and waited for such a time as I was almost discovered.*

*Worse still, upon my return to my lodgings the hour was late, the gas lamps providing naught but fitful light. I entered my rooms when my bell chimed and, like a fool, I went to answer.*

*Upon the step lay a body, a woman, her clothing rent, face and throat slashed, her belly cut wide, all within open, on display to the world.*

*God forgive me I slammed and bolted my door, running up the stairs to my rooms. I flung the window wide to yell for a constable when I saw him, beneath the gaslight of the street lamp opposite. Stovepipe hat, long cloak and cane, simply staring up at me through my window, bloody blade in hand.*

*The Ripper.*

*The Rag and Bone Man knows, he knows I persist in my investigation, and he has set Jack the Ripper upon me!*

Another pause in the writing. When it picked up over the page the words were simply shaky rather than spiked with fear.

*The police did come, but the body was gone, without trace. The officer suggested I had been the worse for drink, that I had suffered a nightmare, brought on by ill-humours, as if such antiquated ideas still held truth.*

*I did not dream it.*

*I am not wrong.*

*I am hunted.*

*He knows.*

Jeanne's phone chirped, the ringtone snatching her violently from the page.

"Shit," she gasped breathlessly as she answered. "Hello?"

"Jeanne?" the caller ID and voice identified her friend Hayley, she could hear sounds of the Joiners in the background.

"Hi Hayley, what's up?" she asked, calming herself.

"Do you know where Rickie is?" Hayley asked, "He said he was meeting you here, and that he'd be here waiting for me but he's not and I can't get hold of him."

Jeanne frowned, "Huh, that's odd. He was there when I left. Wait there, I'll be right along." Hanging up she grabbed for her coat as the doorbell chimed. "What now?" she breathed, hurrying to the door.

As the door opened, the crisp night air carried the sharp note of copper, shit and piss. In the muted yellow tones of the street lamps, Jeanne's eyes fell upon a shape, like a person but her brain would not accept it as such. The legs were splayed, ankles bound up by the jeans and briefs that had been dragged down. The jacket was thrown wide, t-shirt raised to show pale skin, except where dark wounds marred it.

Her breathing coming in quick, increasingly panicked gasps, Jeanne's eyes took in the details. Slashed across the eyes and cheeks, the throat opened almost down to the bone. Stomach split raggedly from sternum to crotch, a brief flutter of the glistening organs in the upper chest. A spasm of the limbs brought her hand to her mouth. Her gaze dropped lower, the sex organs had been carved from the body, blood pooling on the pavement. Her breath caught, eyes snapping up from the ruined abdomen to see, just visible on the shirt, a red and white name badge, always worn with a certain sense of irony.

*Hello, My Name Is Rickie.*

Taking a deep breath to scream, Jeanne caught a hint of a figure and the scream died in her throat. Across the street, under the lamplight, a silhouette. Tall, and dressed in a floor length cape and stovepipe hat. Cane in one hand and a long butcher's knife in the other, dark fluid dripping from its length.

With a hiss of breath she slammed the door. Running upstairs, she shut every door behind her and swiped her phone screen to dial 999.

"What service do you require?" the operator asked calmly.

"Police, police!" Jeanne demanded.

"What's the nature of your emergency?" a second voice asked.

"He killed him! He killed my friend and he's going to kill me!" Jeanne babbled frantically.

"Please try to remain calm," the voice instructed, "are you safe?"

Swallowing her panic Jeanne went to the window, twitching the curtain aside. No sign of 'Jack'. "I, I think so. But there's a gutted body on my doorstep!" she insisted tearfully.

"Stay on the line, we're sending officers now. What's your address?"

No more than a couple of minutes later, Jeanne opened the door to two uniformed and unimpressed officers stood there, alongside a decided lack of Rickie. Jeanne shoved past the confused officers, gawping at the pavement. No trace, not a drop of blood.

"Are you Jeanne Yatumbe?" the older officer inquired.

Jeanne turned, eyes wide, mouth open. "I don't understand. He was here, Rickie was right here!"

"This would be the victim?" the second officer drew out a notebook.

Jeanne nodded.

"And you say you saw the assailant?" the first officer asked.

Again, Jeanne nodded wordlessly.

"Can you describe him?"

Jeanne's mouth made soundless shapes for a moment before... "It was Jack the Ripper."

The officers shared a glance before the junior folded his notebook closed, slipping it back in his pocket.

"You're aware that wasting police time is a serious matter?" the older officer asked casually.

Jeanne nodded slowly.

"Are you on any medication?" the younger officer enquired.

Shaking her head, Jeanne lifted her arms to hug herself, shame and embarrassment taking the place of terror.

The two officers exchanged another glance, the older man twitching his head toward the car.

"Why don't you call in the false alarm, I'll do the follow-up. I don't think this needs to go any further," he said quietly.

As the young officer left, Jeanne rallied some.

"I know what I saw," she insisted firmly.

The officer tilted his head, the brim of his hat shading his eyes and his smile broadening to show very white teeth.

"Come, come miss, you wouldn't wish to cause a fuss, would you?"

The front door closed behind the police. Jeanne's apartment door closed behind her. She pressed her back to the smooth fire door, her breath coming in short, sharp gasps. She sank to the floor, arms wrapped around her knees, gasping for breath.

Her phone buzzed unheeded in her hand, her mind spinning through a lunatics' asylum of fear, disbelief and paranoia.

*Was that? Did that? Did he?*

She tried to hold back the ragged sobs that tugged at her chest, clenching her teeth against the rising tide, but the vision of Rickie splayed for all the world to see broke her resolve and she sobbed, heartrending sounds of animal pain.

She didn't stop until her heart felt about to burst, her chest felt like it had been gripped in giant hands and wrung out like a rag.

She took a couple of steadying breaths before looking at her phone.

Missed Call: Hayley

Missed Call: Hayley

Message: Where are you?

Message: I can't find Rickie!

Message: You said you'd be here!

Bile rose in her throat as she thumbed the phone, turning it screen down on the carpet only to turn it up again.

*I can't come right now.* She typed.

Delete.

*Rickie's dead.*

Delete.

*You have to stay...*

The doorbell rang. Jeanne held her breath. The bell rang again, her phone pinging.

Message: *I'm outside.*

"Shit!"

Scrambling to her feet she raced back down the stairs, hitting the front door with a thump! Her hand was on the latch before a sudden stab of acute paranoia stopped her. Gently she slipped the security chain in place before opening the door a crack.

Sullen faced, cheeks streaked with mascara tears, Hayley stood on the doorstep. Jeanne craned to see past her to the pavement on either side.

"Where were you?" Hayley demanded bluntly.

Still trying to scan the street Jeanne didn't reply.

"Let me in!" Hayley made to push the door open but the chain arrested it.

"Don't!" Jeanne snapped, more in shock than anger, "You can't come in, you shouldn't even be here!"

Her friend simply gawped at her, like she'd lost her mind which, perhaps she had.

"I still haven't found Rickie," Hayley blurted, "I'm getting really worried, Jeanne. Why didn't you come help me?"

Jeanne bit her lip, tears pricking her eyes.

"I couldn't, I can't. Seriously, you don't want to be here. I'm sorry!" and she slammed the door, scurrying back up the stairs to her apartment.

Out in the street she heard Hayley shouting, "What's going on? Are you in trouble? Jeannie!"

But she threw herself down on the floor in front of her sofa. Snatching up a cushion she screamed and sobbed her fear, frustration and pain into its wadding.

Panting, dripping from her nose and mouth she set the sodden cushion aside. Hayley was gone, long gone. She'd been sat there a while. Panting she glanced around her room, looking for options. She could run. But he might be out there, watching the flat. Hide? No. Same problem, they knew where she lived.

Part of her pleaded that someone was fucking with her, that it was all an extended gag like that Michael Douglas movie, or the Mystery Gift co. It was a setup, a scam, but...

She'd seen the quiver in that violated flesh.

Oh god, had Rickie still been alive? However briefly? Lifeblood flooding out into the night, cold, terrified and alone? And she'd... oh god!

In a fit of desperation to think of something else she snatched up the journal. Maybe, some clue, some get out clause lay within...

Pages and pages of scrawled, desperate words.

*He knows! He's coming for me! I'm dead, I'm dead, I'm dead!*

*I hear the calling of the carters, 'Rag and bone! Rag and bone!'*
*I cannot escape it!*

*Rag and Bone, Hair and Hide. Thought and Breath, Nowhere*
*to Hide!*

*Any old iron, String and twine. A penny for your fate, A knife's*
*work for mine!*

Until, a later page with neater writing.

*Mr Alexander visited me today.*

*I regret I had allowed myself to become overawed by matters*
*I did not understand. Mister Alexander explained that I could not*
*go running willy-nilly about chasing shadows and spectres, that*
*I must return to work and perform my assigned duties.*

She frowned, what was this?

*He regrets, however, that I will not be returning to the*
*company premises, that I must perform my duties for the client,*
*in-house, so to speak, and so I will be escorted to offices held by*
*the same at 122 Leadenhall.*

There, one detail. She drew her sleeve across her sopping
face. Run? Hide? What was she thinking? Did correspondents
in warzones run and hide? Watergate, the Wagner exposé,
journalists covering people trafficking in Brazil or corruption
in Mexico?

*You are a journalist*, she told herself, *this is your story and*
*your friend is dead.*

It didn't matter who the 'Rag and Bone Man' was, what kind
of Dread Pirate bullshit he was running or what kind of
Halloween hack-job theatrics he used. If he had his claws in the

London Financial scene, and the police? There was no telling how far his influence might extend.

But that was the joy of being freelance. She'd find someone he didn't own to run the story, or she'd flood the internet with it, make it so he couldn't move for scrutiny. Setting her jaw she picked up her phone and typed in the address.

An hour later, still hunched in the same space on the floor, she had a confusing picture in front of her. The address Charlie had been taken to was, at the time, the offices of a ferry company. That didn't dissuade her, organised crime had ways of worming its way behind the veil of legitimate business and, to be brutally honest, 'legitimate' and 'moral' were not the same thing in this case.

What confused her was a clause in the building's design proposal from 1846, allowing office space for a long-term tenant in the King's Arms Hotel, the building that'd been bought and razed to make room for the Ferry company's offices. The tenant had apparently occupied the site since at least 1720.

While all of this was completely irrelevant to Jeanne's situation, it had led her to uncover something even stranger. The same provision that had been made before the rebuild in the 1840's had been renewed, both when the ferry group redeveloped in the 1960's and when the offices were sold, demolished and rebuilt into the famous 'Cheesegrater' that occupied the site today.

They were still there. The fucks who'd taken Charlie were. Still. There.

Jumping to her feet she called a cab. It might be just gone two in the morning but Jeanne didn't care. Her mind was flying. A secret criminal organisation, operating in London for hundreds of years, was about to be dragged out into the light.

She hesitated, but snatched up the journal and letters, stuffing them in her bag just in case before throwing a short jacket over her shoulders and hurting down stairs. At the honk of a horn she dashed from door to curb, throwing herself inside.

"St Mary's Axe, please," she ordered.

The streetlight whipped past, the streets near deserted, shadows and shapes under a pall of cloud and the onset of morning mist. Ahead, she swore she saw a figure in a stovepipe and cloak. She was about to shout a warning to the driver but the figure morphed into a street lamp and roadside junction box.

Rubbing her thumb and forefinger into her eyes she tried to blink away the fatigue, exhaustion and distress that had wrapped itself around her like a heavy shawl. There would be time to sleep once the story broke.

Twice more she flinched from the window as 'the Ripper' loomed out of the dark as the car sped by. Twice more the dark figure resolved itself into oddments of light and shadow in the night.

The driver pulled up. "Getting an early start?" he asked jovially.

"No," Jeanne replied coldly, "this is something I have to finish."

Shrugging he took the tap of her phone for the fare and drove off, his car engulfed by rising mist and darkness.

Standing on the curb, breath mingling with the mist, Jeanne looked up and down St Mary's Axe. She'd intended to walk the perimeter, try and form some idea of how to gain entry to the metal and glass monolith at number 122. Shoving her hands in her pockets she started for the Undershaft, thinking to avoid Leadenhall Street and its occasional traffic.

A video screen in a building to her left glowed like a ghost-light in the thickening mist. A wrought-iron gate in the churchyard to her right creaked ominously. The sounds of hustle and civilization, lessened by the night, but never gone, seemed swallowed by the thickening fog.

Up ahead was the glittering tower known as the Gherkin and, in its pale glow, a figure, swathed in a long cloak and topped with a stovepipe hat.

"It's not real, it's not real," Jeanne told herself, striding forward.

A click on the pavement behind her, a cane hitting flagstone. Jeanne's head whipped around as that same silhouette emerged from the fog. The cloak opened and a long, silver blade emerged, glistening in the muted light.

"Oh fuck," she breathed.

She launched into a run, veering toward the church and Great St Helens Street, but the cowled, behatted figure was upon her, leaping past her with great loping strides. Vague memories of the legend of Spring-Heeled Jack sailed through her panicked mind as she back-pedalled, stumbling over closely arranged bollards to spill and tumble into the descending mouth of the Undershaft car park, landing with a jarring thump on the road below.

With a whistling noise like a falling bomb, her pursuer vaulted over her, leather-soled shoes slapping the tarmac as he landed, cutting off her escape. For the briefest second, the silhouette distorted into something huge, monstrous and reaching, causing Jeanne to flinch away. Pushing painfully to her feet, she ran for the yellow security gate, hitting it with all her weight, trying to force a gap big enough for her. The cold metal bit at her hands, her jacket ripping as she forced her way through, spilling onto the concrete on her already scuffed and bloodied palms.

The lighting in the car park flickered. What should have been pristine electrical lighting sputtered fitfully, casting shadows and leaping shapes in the dark and, beyond the yellow gates, the 'click, clack, click' of the cane sounded on the stone.

A glance told her that the security office was deserted so she turned tail, hurrying deeper into the dark, underground garage. The sputtering lights showed her several doors, access and emergency, her cries turned despairing as each one turned out to be tightly locked, ringing louder in the concrete silence.

Behind her, the sound of metal scraping on stone.

Breathing in sharp gasps she turned a circle, trapped at the farthest corner of the subterranean structure until...

A light, clean and strong.

She followed to a lift door, tapping the button urgently.

The doors slid open to reveal the lift car, walnut, brass and black and white tile, strangely art-deco, but Jeanne didn't care. She stepped inside, turning to the button panel.

One button, unmarked.

She was struck for a moment with indecision. This wasn't right, but what choice did she have? Out in the dark a low, rumbling chuckle decided for her. With an anguished cry she slapped the button and the doors slid silently closed.

In the polished metal of the lift she locked eyes with herself, trying to make some sense of her scattered thoughts and take stock of her dishevelled appearance.

Her chin was bloodied from the fall, likewise her hands and knees. Her coat was ripped at the shoulders but she still had her bag, slung across her body in the manner she'd long ago adopted to deter thieves.

If only that were the worst of her worries now.

The lift eased to a stop, the doors whispering open.

The room beyond didn't seem like any part of a modern London office structure. The decor was dated, brass and wood, the carpet bronze and black checkerboard, like something from the high-end offices of the 1970's. This small reception area, with art-deco table, plastic plants and vinyl armchairs, was all that fronted a frosted glass wall with a single door. Some slight, muffled sounds came from beyond.

She'd stepped from the lift almost in a trance, and jumped as the doors closed and she heard it begin its descent.

Jeanne knew she only had the time it took to make the return journey and that knife-wielding monster would be upon her again. Could she ambush him here? Maybe take him?

No, the memory of the distorted shape returned and, she was certain, there had been no engine noise, no passing headlights to throw out his shadow like that.

She edged forward, taking hold of the door handle and, with a slight push, opened it wide.

Dim yellow lights, a dark, open plan office. The ceiling was either swathed in darkness, or much higher than the floors of the building allowed for. Either way the space seemed unreal. There was a sound of keystrokes and a waft of old cigarette smoke. She stepped through into the sepia-stained gloom. A desk to her right had one of those old-time green glass lamps and the figure, dimly illuminated, seemed like she'd stepped straight out of a war-time drama. Her hair high curled, dress ruched at the sleeves and blue-chequed, half-glasses on a chain around her neck, she seemed not to be aware of Jeanne's presence.

Taking a hesitant step, Jeanne leaned down, laying a hand on the lamp to tilt its shade up, bringing light to the shadow-shrouded face.

Deep black holes swallowed the light in place of bright, sparkling eyes.

Jeanne recoiled, bumping the desk across the way.

A figure in Tudor dress, full neck ruff, bald head and pinched beard turned empty eyes up to her, quill pen stilled from its scritching passage across parchment. Hand to her mouth, Jeanne recoiled, bumping from desk to desk as empty chasms in place of eyes dragged at her from figures in all manner of out-dated dress.

Finally she collided with a desk, staring down at the top of a straw boater. Anxious premonition gripped her as the brim started to rise and a face from an old photograph stared up at her.

Charlie.

That pencil moustache didn't seem nearly as funny, with the gaping dark pits in place of his eyes above it.

In that silent moment, the shade who had been Charles Fortesque reached out a pale hand, palm upward.

Not knowing what compelled her, Jeanne reached slowly into her bag, withdrawing the journal and letters, passing them over.

Not looking away from her face, Charles took the journal, laid it in a piece of brown paper on his desk, and started, with deliberate care, to wrap its leather-bound cover in brown paper, binding the package in twine.

The sound of the door snapped Jeanne from her mesmerised state. A glance over her shoulder revealed the familiar, dreaded silhouette of her pursuer.

A glint from Charlie's desk, she snatched up a gleaming letter opener and fled, taking a side corridor, the walls of which seemed to be ancient, crumbling plaster and lathe, backlit by a deep, hellish glow. The dusty air scratched at her lungs with every breath as she ran.

A dark door, fast approaching, seemed her only salvation and she threw herself against it, all too aware of ringing footsteps behind her, wrenching it open and flinging herself behind its thick, old wood.

She fumbled for the lock. Finding none, she turned to reach for a chair to jam under the handle. There was a soft sound in the shadows and she froze.

The room before her was cast in shafts of dim light, the edge of a heavy old desk was just visible and a pair of withered, desiccated hands rested upon it just beyond in the shadows.

The sound was a soft, rasping inhalation preceding a single, dry, word.

"Welcome."

Jeanne foundered, all thought of barricading the door forgotten. The room smelled of dry rot and old death.

"You're, you're him," she breathed. "The Rag and Bone man."

The hands turned outward in a gracious gesture, the shape of a head dipping in assent further into the shadow.

"I thought, you couldn't be..." she stammered.

A rasped half-laugh. "The original and only," said a voice like dry paper. "Ms Yatumbe."

"How do you know my...?" she stammered, sudden realisation striking through her panic.

"You sent me the journal," she realised. "You paid for the article."

A creak like old leather preceded withered, dried lips pulling back from yellowed, cracked teeth in a wide smile. Too wide.

Jeanne backed away, "What are you?"

The hands turned down to grasp on the desk's polished wood. "A collector, a snapper-up of unconsidered trifles, a businessman," was the only reply.

"What do you want from me?" Jeanne's investigator's instincts fought against the rising impression that she really didn't want to know.

A slight shrug. "Like anyone who works in the city, every so often it falls upon us to... upgrade the mechanisms or our infrastructure. Take on new skill sets."

Jeanne's mind raced, "All this, this horror? You're recruiting me? You killed my friend!"

Another smile, this one disturbingly predatory. "The city has its appetites and we find ourselves with an opening."

The voice was wrong, dry and husky, yet flowing and with an odd tempo.

Jeanne reached behind her back for the doorknob, the letter opener still in hand. "What's the term?" she tried to stall.

Another shrug. "From now, until then."

"And if I refuse?" her breath deepened, dragging in the dry air in readiness to fight.

The hands, planted on the desk, pushed down, fingers elongating, knuckles cracking at unnatural angles, skin splitting like corn husk. The shape in the shadow beyond started to deform like a stop-motion animation, the voice changing, deepening as it spoke.

"That would be... unfortunate." The last word was drawn out like bare flesh over broken glass.

With a cry, Jeanne wrenched open the door. Turning to face the hatted and caped figure she knew would be waiting, she drove the letter opener out with a shout of defiance.

She felt it strike home, sink into flesh, but the Ripper didn't so much as flinch.

A spurt of fluid across her hand stung like scalding water and she recoiled.

Slowly, the Ripper drew Jeanne's makeshift weapon from his body, holding it between thumb and forefinger before dropping it casually to the floor.

A brief sensation of movement, a thud of impact.

Jeanne looked down to see the Ripper's hand release the hilt of the long knife, now embedded in her stomach.

She looked up, not fully understanding, as the figure divested itself of hat and cloak, hanging them beside the door, setting the cane in an elephant's foot umbrella stand.

"Jack, Jack the Ripper?" she gasped in the face of the all too mundane seeming man dressed in a modestly cut, modern suit.

"It's just Jack." The man's voice held an edge like a blade.

She grunted, stepping back into a stumbling half turn, the sensation of sharp-edged steel sawing at her with every agonising movement. The looming monster in the dark seemed amused.

"You are dying Ms Yatumbe or, you will die. But you have a choice, here and now. Work for me. Facilitate my dealings with the mortal world in this... new age, and you live, after a fashion."

"What," she swallowed, her throat dry, limbs shaking, "What are you?"

"Those appetites I mentioned? Well..." Lengthening arms spread wide, head dipped in a modest bow, distorted features and torn leather lips pulled back in a monstrous, condescending, smile.

"What, what's my alternative?" Jeanne asked weakly, holding her stomach, feeling her blood pool in her hands.

A rush of sudden, savage motion, then came stabbing pain and the flash of deformed, exaggerated features in her face.

"You die and I swallow down your flesh, bones and soul, you pathetic, irrelevant vermin!"

Shaken like a rag doll, Jeanne was cast bodily to the floor, rolling, jarring the knife deeper into her gut.

"I'll give you a moment to think about it," the voice continued, once more calm, if uneven, as the Rag and Bone Man turned his hunched back to her.

"I don't know why you make me wear this stuff," Jack was complaining.

"It's a statement," the Man replied like there wasn't a woman bleeding to death on his floor.

"It's derivative," Jack shot back. "Worse, it's cliché."

The monstrous figure reduced, drawing back into the shadows, becoming once more the husk of a man sitting behind a desk.

"You should know, it's your look. You shouldn't have made such an enduring legend to go with it."

Fingers drummed on the desk.

"Come now Ms Yatumbe, what's your answer?"

Cold gripped her chest, wrestling with fear and uncertainty. Visions of the office, the figures sat in hollow-eyed servitude, flashed in her memory. An eternal purgatory of servitude to these monsters.

"No," she gasped, finally.

The decrepit, desiccated figure sighed, then swarmed over the desk like a spider, coming to rest inches from her face before, it seemed, a thought struck it.

"Jack?" It's mummified, patchwork face turned up to the killer. "Have Charlie send the journal out again, I'm sure he's packaged it by now."

Jeanne let out a strangled sob, pushing at the thing atop her, her fingers sinking into powdery, brittle rags, finding only leathery flesh, and cold, dry bone before the face flashed down, ragged teeth clamping around her throat.

Jack closed the door to the screaming and sounds of violated flesh.

"Oh well," he sighed, "time to vet another candidate."

*The shimmering seemed to spread... the walls were now ancient brick. The ceiling was lower. Candles flickered in the corners. A flight of steps led up to a door on the far wall.*

# SHADOWS AND ECHOES

*GAVIN CHAPPELL*

## 1   The Labyrinth

"Stop here," Jason Steele said hoarsely.

Rain lashed down. The black cab they had been following had pulled into a parking space outside the towering art deco building. It was dark and depressing, the city streets were awash. As Jason's taxi driver parked a short way down from it, a burly figure, wearing a long coat with the lapels pulled up to hide his face, exited the other cab.

"Okay, can you just wait here, mate?" Jason asked the driver, a Sikh with a massive beard. "I could be a while."

"It'll cost you, squire," the taxi driver told him.

"All on the expense account," Jason assured him absently, watching as the man he'd been tailing waited for the traffic to ebb before hurrying across the narrow street.

In the rain streaked pool of lamplight at the entrance to Freemasons' Hall, his burly quarry encountered another man, this one tall and sepulchral in appearance, holding an umbrella. But rather than lead the first man into the building, he beckoned him to follow and took him to a side door.

"I'll be back." Jason opened the passenger door and jumped out, landing in a puddle with a splash.

Socks and shoes soaking wet, he slammed the door behind him, grinned in embarrassment to the Sikh, and darted round the cab.

From somewhere drifted the tantalising aroma of cooking meat. Elsewhere chips were frying. Traffic hissed past him in either direction, headlights slicing up the night. Light streamed from the open door.

Jason tensed when it shone briefly on the face of the burly man, who now held the umbrella while the other man unlocked the side door. For the first time since he'd got into his taxi outside his hotel, Jason was a hundred percent certain of his identity. *Mike Blake*, he thought. *Tracy's new boyfriend*.

Now, first the tall man, then Mike—having closed the umbrella—entered the building. A clang reverberated across the street as they shut the door behind them.

Jason crossed the road, dodging cars. Drivers blared horns, shouted curses. Jason raised his middle finger at a man who wound down the window to yell at him before his feet touched the wet pavement. He darted round a passing couple, then halted at the door. It was locked.

Could he use his skeleton keys? He looked up and down the street. More people were hurrying past. They'd see him, wonder why he was taking so long to unlock the door. They might even call the police. He had to find another way in.

Some way down the street he found the mouth of an alley. It seemed to run the length of the Freemasons' Hall, but only the light from the street lamps lit it. Pools of shadow flooded it, like the puddles that swamped the pavement.

Squelching in his wet socks, sweat running down his back despite the cold of the night, Jason made his way up the alley, running a gauntlet of the new wheelie bins. But he was disappointed to find no doors. Then his feet scuffed on something metallic. He glanced downwards.

A hatch or manhole stood to one side of the alley, in the lee of the Hall's back wall.

"I'm worried about Mike," Tracy had told him a week earlier.

Jason had been sitting on her sofa in the living room. In the house they had once shared. The very sofa, in fact, he had slept on for several months after losing his job with Essex Police. He'd moved out a while later, first living in a dingy bedsit, then renting a flat over a chip shop after his private detective business—Steele Investigations—started to take off.

After a couple of lucrative cases he'd thought he could support himself. Now those halcyon days were over, he thought; the work had dried up, and he was back on housing benefit.

"Mike?" Jason had asked. "What's up with him? From everything you've said, he's doing pretty well for himself. Chance of promotion, you said."

Mike Blake was a sergeant in Suffolk CID. Unlike Jason, who had been sacked from the force after an unfortunate incident involving a medium, a car chase, and a supposed black magician. Unlike Jason—whose private detective business brought in less than he would have earned as an itinerant gardener—he was going places. Mike had a career.

He was also dating Tracy.

What was worse was, he was a cool guy and Jason got on with him really well. A shared love of comedy shows like *Reeves and Mortimer* and *Bottom* had a lot to do with it. If he'd been a right cunt, things might have been preferable.

"Oh yeah, his career's really taking off, babe." Tracy turned off the TV, which had been burbling away in the background about the latest cabinet reshuffle. She worked in traffic in Colchester nick. Her dad had been a copper. She always dated coppers. "But that's the problem. I think he's been approached about joining the Masons."

Jason chuckled. His laugh cut off when Tracy flung him a hurt look. "Well," he said. "Aren't they all? I mean, the real high flyers?" He frowned. "No one suggested I should join, when I was a copper."

"No surprise there!" Tracy replied tartly. "My dad was in the Masons. I've not got anything against them. I don't believe in any of the rumours. About corruption and murder and devil worship. Do me a favour, I think that's all a pack of lies. They're just men who do a lot of work for charity."

"You make them sound like Smashey and Nicey." Jason was watching her closely. She was searching for the right words. "Why are you so worried about Mike? Everything's coming up roses."

"He's been having these weird dreams." Tracy looked anxious. "I don't set much store in dreams, you know it. I mean, if it really sticks in my mind, I might look it up in my dream dictionary." She'd bought it in a remaindered bookshop in town, he remembered. "But that's all."

"What kind of dreams? Apart from weird ones, I mean."

"That's just it, I don't know. He won't tell me. In the morning he says he just can't remember."

"How do you know he's having weird dreams, then?" Jason was getting a headache. Conversations with Tracy often followed this pattern. They usually ended with a row. He tried to control himself.

"Because of what he's been saying in his sleep," she said. "Strange words. What sounds like… I dunno, chanting. And he's frightened. So frightened. One night he woke me up by kicking me! I didn't know what was going on, but then I see his legs are moving. Almost like he's running. Running to get away from something."

"What was he saying?"

She frowned. "I remember one word. *Valusia*, it was. And another. *Corineus*. And a third. Except I don't even know if it was a word, not really. *Yig*."

"Yig?"

"Yig." She shrugged.

"Maybe he should see a doctor," Jason suggested. "Maybe he needs sleeping pills. Valium, even."

She shook her head. "I think he's got himself mixed up in something. Something bad. Like, you know… occult. Some masonic lodges are occult, you know. I read it in a book once. Not that Dad's lodge was! But maybe Mike's got mixed up in one of the really sinister ones. And the other night I heard him say something about… killing someone."

Jason sat up. "Killing someone?"

She nodded. "Like he's been told he has to *assassinate* someone. You know, like, to prove himself. He's so career driven! I think he might even do it."

"Mike? Murder someone? I can't imagine it."

"Stop laughing, Jason," Tracy insisted. "Look, you've not had any jobs recently, have you?"

She was hitting below the belt tonight. "I'm doing my best!"

Jason protested. "It's just not been my busy time recently. Not even for lost pets."

"Well, here's a job for you," she told him brusquely. "An *assignment*. I want you to follow Mike, see where he goes and who he meets. I want you to find out what's going on. You've had these kinds of cases before, haven't you? Occult crime? You and that professor friend of yours. I just know you could do this."

"What, spy?" Jason was outraged. "Spy on your boyfriend? You're asking me, your ex, to spy on Mike? Haven't you tried asking him about it?"

"I did," she replied distantly. "Once. He got real nasty. I've never seen him like that." She shook her head. "It was scary. Look, Jason, I don't ask much of you, but I did give you a roof over your head when you were homeless…"

Jason looked away. He couldn't meet her eyes. Not when she did that thing. When she looked at him like that.

"You're right," he said with a sigh. "I've not had any work for a while. But we'll have to do this properly. You've got to pay my expenses, you understand? Well, okay then. And Professor Flint will be bound to take it on. He's got a real bee in his bonnet about the Freemasons…"

Jason was drenched. The rain lashed down on the dark alley, puddling around the edges of the mysterious manhole cover. It wasn't a sewer entrance, he could see that much. Rectangular, made of rusty metal. Padlocked. It was more like some kind of cellar entrance. Maybe this was where they dropped barrels into the cellars. A place like the Freemasons' Hall must have huge wine cellars…

He wiped the rain from his face. A nostalgic reek of beer, sex, and cigarettes drifted from somewhere, reminding him of times when he was younger, when he was a police cadet, before he ever met Tracy. It was about time he got inside. Somewhere warm and dry.

He produced his ring of skeleton keys and tried several on the padlock before finally it sprang open.

Before making any kind of move, he looked up and down the alley. From somewhere nearby floated a catch of music. *Jump Around* by House of Pain. It cut off partway through the chorus as someone shut a pub door behind them.

Jason gazed into the pit. Brick lined walls led downwards. A metal ladder had been bolted to one wall. It looked treacherous, rusty and corroded. As he began to descend, it creaked metallically.

The bottom of the shaft opened out into darkness. Turning on his pen torch he saw a cellar lined by wine barrels. On the far side a half open doorway stood in the brick wall. Wondering what he might see next, he peered cautiously round the door frame.

A large, brick lined chamber led away into the gloom, pervaded by an air of immeasurable antiquity. At the far end was a flight of steps. A susurrus of distant voices filtered down into the cellar, resolving into some strange kind of chant, arcane words that Jason failed to recognise. He thought it might be the chant that Tracy had heard from Mike's sleeping lips.

He made his way towards the steps at the far end as quietly as he could. The door at the top opened to a crack. Jason, heart pounding, quietly pushed it further open. The screech of the hinges was muffled by the distant, full throated chanting.

Stepping out into a dark, marble lined corridor, Jason received an impression of opulent surroundings, like some kind of palace or temple. It seemed to him as if a time travelling Tutankhamen had snatched up William Van Alen to decorate his tomb.

As quietly as he could, he crept up the corridor. The polished marble floor was adorned with abstract, arabesque, cabalistic designs. The walls resembled something from a technicolour Cecil B DeMille movie, he thought. The whole place had that sense of sterile grandeur he had noticed in public buildings everywhere.

The chanting voices were louder here but they were still some way off. He followed the drifting sound along the imposing corridor until it came out into a vestibule. As furtive as he was his footsteps seemed to ring out as loud as Big Ben.

In the vestibule he came to a halt before a large door. A bas relief on its surface depicted what looked like the construction of Solomon's temple. From behind the door came the sound of chanting, louder now. He guessed he had almost reached its source.

He thrust at the door and it opened easily, despite its size. As candlelight streamed out he peeked inside. His face paled at what he saw.

The room was vast, lined with seats like an auditorium, big enough to hold a large concert. The walls and ceiling were ornamented with frescoes depicting scenes from Biblical and Classical mythology. Down in the centre, where the stage might have been were this a concert, stood several throne like chairs. But this was not what seized Jason's attention.

The floor had been chalked with the swirling pattern of a

Cretan labyrinth, at the centre of which stood a kind of simple altar. On a cushion upon the altar glinted an elaborate dagger; its blade winked in the light of candles that burned in large, many branched candlesticks that stood in the corners, casting eerie shadows across the chamber. A scent of incense hung in the air, almost causing Jason to sneeze.

Hooded figures were circling the altar, following the twists and turns of the labyrinth, chanting words Jason could not identify. They looked sinister, anonymous. He could not see their faces. But even as he peered round the door, the chant broke off.

The hooded figures stood unmoving. Silence fell and all Jason could hear was the beating of his heart. Had they seen him? Was that why they had broken off?

Down from the biggest throne stepped a tall figure in black robes, face hidden by a cowl. He stood by the altar, raised his arms so the sleeves of the robe drooped downwards. "We welcome a stranger to our midst." The man's voice rang through the large auditorium. *A stranger.* Did they know he was here?

"Step forward," the man added. "Step forward and let us see your face that we may know who we have invited into our lodge."

Jason gulped. *Invited?* He gripped tight hold of the doorknob, ready to push the door open and brazen it out. Desperately he tried to cook up some story to explain his presence.

The door began to swing open on well-oiled hinges, but he grabbed it the moment he saw a burly figure step out from the ranks of cowled shapes. As the figure approached the centre of the labyrinth it pulled down its own hood to reveal Mike Blake's perspiring face.

Jason almost laughed out loud. The man had been addressing Mike! That must have been what they meant, a stranger in their midst. Mike had yet to join this Masonic lodge, he realised. They didn't have a clue that he, Jason, was here.

He watched curiously as Mike stepped up to the altar. "Are you Detective Sergeant Michael Blake?" asked the tall man.

"Yes," replied Mike and his voice cracked. "Yes," he repeated in more assertive tones. "I'm Blake."

"You stand before us as a probationary member." The tall man's voice was sonorous, resonant, booming. "Long ago the Trojans came to Albion. Infesting the island were folk stamped in non-human mould—in the form of serpents. It was Corineus who led the fight against them, and when he was victor he established the Trojan Rite in New Troy. It has been handed down from generation to generation, the duty to hunt down the serpent folk, whatever faces they wear, and to destroy them."

He lifted up the dagger and proffered it. "They lurk in the shadows. They take on the faces of men. Will you swear in the Holy Name of Valusia to join our fight and strike down those votaries of Yig who would oppress us?"

Jason watched in horror. It was true, he thought. It was all true. The Freemasons did indeed carry out murders. It was the only explanation for this mumbo-jumbo. They were going to pressure Mike Blake into committing murder, and then there would be no going back for him.

"I will," Mike replied solemnly, and Jason suppressed a groan.

It was a gang. That was all it was. And a good copper like

Mike had fallen for it.

Mike Blake reached out and took the dagger from the robed man, holding it high so it glinted in the candlelight. "I swear in the Holy Name of Valusia that I will join your fight and strike down those votaries of Yig who would oppress us."

So intent was Jason on his thoughts he let go of the door. It swung open with a booming crash that echoed through the huge room. He stood surprised, silhouetted in the doorway. Cowled heads swung round, eyes glinting hatefully beneath hoods, and he found himself suddenly the centre of attention.

"A spy! A spy!" The whispers chased themselves round the room.

Jason gulped. Mike, following the gaze of his fellow Masons, caught his eye for an instant. He looked as shocked as Jason felt.

Jason bolted.

The marble vestibule thundered to the pounding of his feet. Robed figures streamed out of the room, hot on his heels. Desperately Jason searched for the corridor he had come through, and the way out, but he was lost in a maze.

Looking back, he saw the robed figures were almost on him.

He ran down a polished marble corridor shrouded in darkness. Light from windows high above showed the ghostly shapes of ornate walls. It led into an anteroom where electric light blazed. A middle aged woman plied a mop in the middle of an ornately patterned floor. She looked up in amazement, the fag dropping out of her open mouth as he brushed past.

At the end of the anteroom stood an impressive pair of double doors. Finding them irresolutely locked, Jason ducked into a small room off to one side where a window looked out onto a busy London street. He forced it open, climbed outside, dropped to the pavement and lurched away, startling passersby.

Rounding a corner he knew at a glance where he was. Traffic passed on both sides. From a nearby pub or bar drifted the opening chords of *Informer* by Snow. A taxi still waited patiently on the far side of the road. Jason crossed over.

The Sikh driver was finishing the Guardian crossword. Urgently Jason tapped on the window with his fingernail. The Sikh looked up, smiled, and opened the door.

"Back to the hotel, is it, squire?"

Jason glanced over his shoulder, uncomfortably aware of the muddy stains on his clothes. No sign of any robed figures in pursuit. But what was he thinking? If they followed him, they wouldn't come looking like the Ku Klux Klan. They were more subtle, more insidious than that.

"Just drive," Jason urged him.

They screeched off round the corner into Long Acre, exceeding the speed limit. At the junction they passed the pillared portico of Freemasons' Hall, where a group of men clustered, looking suspiciously around them. Two were speaking to a woman who held a dripping mop. One man was talking into a mobile phone. Jason sank back when he thought he recognised another.

But Mike Blake showed no signs of noticing him.

## 2   Follow the Van

Jason got back to his hotel in Seven Dials shortly afterwards. Having paid the taxi driver—Tracy was going to have to cover that, and no mistake!—he splashed across the wet pavement and entered the little place, possibly the pokiest hotel in all

London.

"Any messages?" he asked the plump, middle aged hotel receptionist.

"Oh yes, Mr Steele." She went to his pigeon hole. "You received a phone call. A girl called Tracy." She winked roguishly. "Wanted you to ring back."

"Gladly." Jason went to the payphone and inserted his phonecard. Ringing Tracy, he found himself connecting with her answerphone.

Tersely he spoke after the beep. "I followed Mike. He went to the Freemasons' Hall. No surprise there. What went on in there...! Well, you'd better ring me back. Who knows who's listening."

He put the phone down and emerged from the booth. The hotel receptionist darted away to fuss around with a carousel containing tourist leaflets. After giving her a hard stare, Jason hurried upstairs to the room he was sharing with Professor Flint.

The professor was sitting in an armchair, alternately eating Welsh rarebit and puffing at his pipe, while leafing through his notes. As Jason entered, he looked up, his brow creased with concern. Brushing a few crumbs off his tweed suit, he clambered to his feet.

"I'm so glad to see you, Jason!" He shook his friend's hand vigorously. "When I came back from the British Museum and found you missing, I feared the worst. I know you mock my fears. But these Freemasons..."

Despite what Tracy suggested, Jason and the professor were hardly a Holmes and Watson double act. On their first meeting, Flint, now an independent researcher, had told him he had been a professor of anthropology until he was sacked due to a Satanic-Masonic occult conspiracy.

"I'm sorry I ever laughed, professor." Jason rang for room service. "Large scotch, please." He sat down on the sofa, then glanced inquiringly at Flint, who mouthed *just a small one for me.* "And a small one."

He went into the tiny bathroom, had a wash and brush up. Somewhat refreshed he came back into the main room, sighed and settled down on the sofa. Flint perched on the edge of the armchair.

"What happened while I was researching?" Flint asked after a moment's silence. "Did you find Sergeant Blake? You said you'd be keeping his taxi under surveillance."

"I got there just in time," Jason replied. "He was getting into a cab himself as I turned up. I was pretty sure it was him. And I was right. I followed him to Wild Street, just beside the Freemasons' Hall…"

Just as Jason was finishing, a discreet knock came from the door. The professor went to answer it. He returned shortly afterwards with two drinks. Jason drank his scotch in two swift gulps.

"That's quite a story," the professor said, sipping at his own drink. "So Sergeant Blake is indeed being forced into carrying out some kind of political murder. Exactly the kind of intrigue I would anticipate from the Freemasons."

"They said something about the Trojan Rite," Jason replied. "What's that?"

Flint shook his head. "Freemasonry has a Scottish Rite," he said, "But I've never heard of any Trojan Rite. However, my researches have uncovered some information that could be relevant."

Jason leaned forward. "What's that? About Masons? Occultism? Murder?"

Flint laughed. "Not quite. I had very little to go on. Much ink has been spilled, covering reams and reams of paper, to the effect that the Freemasons are a dubious organisation. They have been linked with events stretching from the French Revolution to the assassination of John F Kennedy."

Jason raised his eyebrows but Flint went on. "Some trace them back to the builders of Solomon's temple, and it's said that Solomon himself had occult powers, due to congress with demons. As for ritual murder, well, there's little to go on when it comes to hard, concrete fact." He scowled. "Simply numerous allegations."

"This gang Mike's mixed up in, they want him to murder someone," Jason told him. "I saw the knife they gave him."

"One of the leads you mentioned," Flint went on after digesting this, "was the name 'Corineus', which Sergeant Blake let slip in his sleep. According to legend, Duke Corineus was one of the leaders of the Trojan settlers in Britain. It's said that he fought against a race of giants, whose leader was one Gogmagog, for control of the island..."

"Wait a minute!" Jason interrupted. "The Grand Master said something about this Corineus too." He was remembering. "... *in the form of serpents*. Not giants, but serpents. It's these serpents who Corineus fought. These serpents survive, wearing new faces, and Mike's lodge have to hunt them down and destroy them. But what does it all mean?"

"Mystification and balderdash is what it means." The professor grimaced. "*Serpents*... it's a codeword. A reference to their enemies. Politicians or business men who cross the Freemasons. That's who Sergeant Blake is expected to kill. It's an initiation, if you like."

"I see that." Jason nodded. "A lot of gangs have the same kind of rigmarole. A new member has to commit some crime, murder being favourite, in order to join the gang. He's a good copper. But soon he'll be under their thumb."

"He's signed a Faustian pact," the professor agreed. "Ambition is laudable, but it can land a chap in hot water."

"We've got to get him out of their clutches, somehow..." Jason broke off at a knock on the door. Answering it tentatively, he recognised the hotel receptionist.

"Phone for you," she announced, "in the lobby."

Jason thanked her, and popped back to tell the professor. "It's probably Tracy ringing me back." He paused awkwardly. "Thing is, when I rang earlier, I thought that the hotel receptionist was listening. And how long was she outside the door?"

"She could have heard everything." The professor was gloomy. "These Freemasons have agents everywhere."

Jason went downstairs. The hotel receptionist was back in her cubbyhole office off the lobby, but she appeared briefly to indicate the phone booth. He found the phone lying on its side, and picked it up.

"Hello?"

*"Is that you, Jason?"* came Tracy's voice, a faint, windy crackle. *"Babe, what's going on? I got your message, but..."*

Jason cupped the receiver. Speaking quietly, looking up the lobby, he told her, "He's joined them. I witnessed a rite. They want him to kill someone."

There was silence from the other end.

"Hello? Hello?" Jason shook the phone, afraid they'd been cut off.

Tracy squawked, *"What did you say? They want him to… to kill someone? Who? Why? When?"*

"I don't know," Jason murmured. "I had to run for it. I think… well, people could be listening. What do you want me to do?"

More silence. *"You've just got to talk to him,"* she urged him. *"Find out what's going on. Stop him. I don't want him getting into trouble."*

Easier said than done. "He's one of them now," Jason whispered, looking cautiously around. "Do you think I'll be able to stop him? He'd listen to you sooner than me."

*"I can't get the time off work right now."* Tracy sounded desperate. *"This is what I'm paying you to do, babe. Stop trying to wriggle out of it."*

"That reminds me," Jason added. "More expenses." He told her about the taxi. Further silence.

*"Do me a favour!"* she squawked at last. *"How could you run up that much?"* She was incredulous, not to mention suspicious. *"Where did you go, John o' Groats?"*

"The taxi driver waited outside. I'd not have got away if it hadn't been for him. Can you pay the money into my bank account? There's also the hotel bill…"

*"Jason!"* she said warningly. *"You'd better hurry up and get this finished. I can't pay for you to stay in a London hotel indefinitely! And in future, don't let taxi drivers rip you off. You know what these Londoners are like."*

Jason stared at the wall, imagining Tracy's face. She'd have that look again. He remembered it only too well from when they had been together. Cold eyes, mouth a thin line...

"I'll go to see Mike tomorrow," he said at last. "Maybe he'll listen to me. Maybe he'll listen to reason. But look, you wanted me to find out what he was doing. Well, I've found out. This... wasn't in the contract."

"*Jason!*" she crackled again.

"Okay, okay! Bye!"

He rang off. By rights he should increase his fee, he thought. Tailing a man was one thing, breaking and entering in the furtherance of his work was only a bit worse, but how was he supposed to talk Mike out of this? That asked for skills he did not possess.

Going back upstairs, he told Professor Flint the results of his phone conversation.

"Do you want me to accompany you tomorrow?" the professor asked.

Jason shook his head. "You try to find out more about Masonic assassinations. I'll go and talk to him on my own."

It was still on his mind the following morning, after breakfast, when he went out for a run.

Few people were about on the backstreets, but the roar of the early morning rush hour was audible from New Oxford Street. A few puddles lay on the pavement like carelessly dropped mirrors, but the sun was shining, birds were singing.

He felt strangely relaxed. The idea that only twelve hours earlier he had been witnessing sinister goings-on in Freemasons' Hall seemed absurd.

His feet slapped the pavement as he ran. No one seemed to be about, no pedestrians, no drivers. He passed a series of phone boxes, their interiors layered with tart cards.

A car engine broke the hush. Turning his head, he saw a white van speeding up the road. Running on, he noticed a blue Ford Taurus screech out of a side turning and head in the direction from which the van was coming.

With a squeal of brakes the Ford mounted the kerb, skidding to a halt in front of him. Jason halted. He was about to give the driver a serious piece of his mind when the van pulled up, the back doors opened, and four men leapt out, wearing balaclavas and drab, anonymous overalls.

They seized Jason by the arms, and before he could do much more than protest, bundled him into the back of the van. As the vehicle took off again they forced him to lie face down on the floor.

The floor of the van was hard metal, and the place stank of sweaty bodies. All he could see was two lines of scuffed, muddy black boots. He couldn't move. The pressure on his back was like a lead weight.

"You're breaking my arm," he grunted.

"Let him sit up," someone snapped.

One of the men had been holding him down with a knee to the small of his back and his right arm twisted behind his back. The pressure lessened, and Jason rolled over, glowering, just as they took a bend at speed.

He lurched to one side, colliding with the bony knees of one of the other men, who sat along either side of the van interior. It was dark in the van, and this, combined with the men's anonymous balaclavas, gave him the sense that he was being watched by the glinting eyes of rodents. The man whose knee he had headbutted leant over, whipped off the balaclava.

"Car Narmer Carr Ledger Rama!"

It was Mike! But he was talking gibberish.

Jason blinked in confusion. "What was that? What did you say? Mike, I..."

"Car Narmer Carr Ledger Rama," Mike repeated urgently. "Say it, Jason. Say it! Car Narmer Carr Ledger Rama."

"*What* was that about Bananarama?" It was a joke, it must be. Mike was always a joker.

"Don't mess about." Jason had never seen Mike so serious. "Say it after me: 'Car Narmer Carr Ledger Rama'."

"He can't say it," growled another man, leaning over. "He's one of them. Shoot him now before he changes."

He whipped out a Glock 17 from a shoulder holster and put it to Jason's brow.

Jason's blood ran cold as he met the man's white rimmed, crazy looking eyes. How could this be happening? He had just gone out for a run after breakfast and now here he was, bundled into an unmarked van and about to be shot.

"Mike?" he said uncertainly.

"Fuck's sake, Jason, stop pissing about." Mike was furious. "Repeat the words. Car Narmer Carr Ledger Rama."

"Car Narmer Carr Ledger Rama." Jason repeated the nonsense as best he could. "Is that it?"

"That's good enough for me." Mike looked at the gunman. "Constable, put the gun away."

Sullenly the man obeyed. Jason shuffled over to sit by Mike. Sweat trickled down his face and ran down under his shirt.

"Just what's all this about? You know, Tracy's worried sick about you. You've joined the Masons, she says. And what was all that you were up to last night?"

"Never mind what *I* was up to," Mike told him. The van had taken a turn of speed, as if they were driving down a main road, maybe even a motorway. Jason heard the roar of other vehicles. "What did you think *you* were doing, gatecrashing a lodge meeting?"

Jason shrugged. "Just doing my job. I was hired to find out what you were up to."

Mike stared at him. "What, by Tracy?"

Jason nodded. "I didn't want to, but she offered me..." He shrugged apologetically. "...money. You know business has been poor lately. Yeah, well," he added, seeing the look of incredulity on Mike's face. "If you don't want your girlfriend to put private detectives on your tail, you need to be more open with her. I'm no Claire Raynor, but that's a sure sign of relationship problems."

"I can't speak about it." Mike glanced around at the silent, balaclava clad men who sat watching their exchange in grim silence. The one who'd pinioned Jason, Mike had addressed him as 'constable'. Were they all in the police? In that case, what were policemen doing snatching people off the street?

"Why've you kidnapped me?" They must have followed him to the hotel last night. They had been waiting for their chance ever since...

"We've not kidnapped you," said the constable contemptuously. "We're taking you to meet someone. To explain what you saw last night. Now that we know you're on the level, even if you're not on the square."

Jason laughed coldly. "All that Car-Narmer bollocks? Some Masonic codeword? If this is a Masonic meeting you're going to, you'd better drop me off. I don't even know the funny handshake."

Mike gripped Jason's hand, pressing down with his thumb on the knuckle of his forefinger. "That's it, if you're really that curious." His hand was warm and sweaty. "Look, Jason. You know too much, but I can vouch for you. Now I know that you're not one of *them*, in... in disguise. *They* can't say those words, you see."

"One of *them*?" Jason's mind hurtled back to the Trojan Rite. "You mean these so-called 'serpents'?"

"The snake that speaks," muttered another of the balaclava warriors.

"But what does it really mean?" Jason asked. "What—who— are your real enemies? Who is it you're going to have to kill, Mike?"

Silence fell, broken only by the roar of the engine. The eyes of all the policemen were on Jason. The smell of petrol drifted in through the van doors. Before he could say any more, the van braked to a halt, and the engine stopped. A passenger door could be heard opening, then a fist pounded on the outside of the van.

"Everybody out," Mike told them. "You too, Jason."

The man closest to the van doors opened them. Cold light filtered in. Jason followed the others outside to find that they were parked in a grimy yard at the back of a large, unkempt Georgian house. The Ford Taurus that had mounted the kerb was parked behind them. Three uniformed policemen stood beside it.

The man who had been driving their van came round to greet them.

"Were we followed?" Mike asked one of the coppers from

the car, a tall man with a gaunt, sepulchral face.

"Two cars on our tail," he replied. "We shook them off. Best get him inside. The minister wants to speak to him first."

He was the man who had greeted Mike outside the Freemasons' Hall last night. Unlike the men who had abducted him, these newcomers wore no balaclavas. His own captors had removed theirs, and climbing out of their overalls they revealed police uniforms underneath.

"There's been a mistake, Inspector Truegood," Mike told him. "He's not one of them. No, listen! He can say the words."

"Save it for the minister."

Jason was marched inside. A smell of rot and neglect hung in the air, which was cold for the time of year. They passed several rooms filled with dustsheet covered furniture before halting at a panelled oak door. Mike knocked and a voice from within said, "Come."

The room inside was furnished. An electric fire in one corner gave it a welcome warmth. Filing cabinets were ranked along the walls, a decanter and several glasses stood on a bookshelf crammed with musty old volumes, their spines cracked with age. Paintings hung on the walls. Jason thought they looked like originals, not prints. A big desk took up the far side.

Behind it sat a balding man in his early fifties, wearing a charcoal black Saville Row suit. Something about him reminded Jason of the Mekon from the old Dan Dare comics. He had iron grey hair, conservative yet expensive spectacles, and an ingratiating expression. Like a movie star or singer, he somehow radiated presence, seeming much larger than he truly was.

As Mike led Jason inside, the Mekon nodded to the others.

"Please stay outside. But remain alert. You're all armed?"

Jason recognised that voice, that face. From radio, from TV. He wasn't a sci fi baddie, he thought, but...

"But aren't you...?"

The man nodded. "Secretary of State for the Home Department," he said, raising a quizzical eyebrow. He spoke in the mild, slightly camp tones of an Oxbridge man. "And you," he glanced cursorily at a yellow document wallet marked *Top Secret*, "must be Jason Steele. Proprietor of Steele Investigations, former officer in the Essex Police." His eyes narrowed. "Or are you?"

"He's the real Jason, sir," Mike said loyally. "He can repeat the Valusian Catechism."

"Can he indeed?" the Home Secretary asked. "For that matter, can you? How do I know you're who you seem to be? You look like Detective Sergeant Blake, but..."

Mike nodded reluctantly. "Car Narmer Carr Ledger Rama. Jason, you repeat it."

Jason did so, feeling like he was in a nightmare. "What's all this about, sir?"

The Home Secretary visibly relaxed, but, in true politician's style, he evaded the question. "Why were you spying on our meeting last night, Mr Steele?"

Jason was about to answer when he heard a commotion from outside the door. Men were shouting, shots were fired. The door burst open and three uniformed policemen strode in.

At their head was the gaunt man Mike had addressed as inspector. The other two had been in the car with him. All carried Glock 17s. They were training them on the Home Secretary.

## 3   Tired of Life

Jason seized the nearest policeman by the gun arm, trying to wrestle the gun away but it went off, ear-piercing in the small space. Inspector Truegood collapsed, brainpan obliterated, the oak panelled wall lacquered with a jammy porridge of blood and brains.

With the knife he had been given the night before, Mike stabbed the third policeman, who fell backwards into the passageway. Jason dealt the first policeman an uppercut that would have felled an ox but he shrugged it off and trained the gun on him. Mike seized him from behind and slit his throat. Spraying crimson, the man fell dead to the floor. Blood soaked into the priceless carpet.

"The fuck is going on?" Jason shouted, half deafened from the shot. "Who were they?"

The Home Secretary took off his glasses to wipe blood from the frames. "They are serpents."

The carnage had been over in seconds. Jason had not known Truegood for more than a quarter of an hour, but he had never seen a man shot at such a close range. And it had been his fault. His stupid fault for grabbing the other man's gun arm. "What do you mean, serpents?"

Mutely, the Home Secretary indicated the corpse lying by his desk. Jason rolled it over with his foot and stared in shock at the reptilian face revealed. He felt his skin horripilate.

Shaking, he forced himself to crouch down beside the corpse. Where moments before had been the beefy features of a policeman he now saw a scaled face, a fanged mouth from which lolled a forked tongue. Yellow snake eyes rolled in their sockets, a nictating membrane half covering each. It wore a policeman's uniform, it had died from a single stab wound, but it was by no means human.

A chill ran down his spine. He licked lips that were unaccountably dry. It was true. All true. The professor had made a mistake. *Serpents* had been no codeword. It was the literal truth.

Jason rose, glanced unsteadily at the Home Secretary who was watching him in silence, then crossed over to examine the inspector. His face was pale and slick with cold sweat. Although the top of Truegood's skull was a gory mess, the same dead snake eyes stared sightlessly up at the white ceiling.

Jason went out into the corridor, passing Mike, who was cleaning the blade of his dagger.

The third policeman half sat, half lay against the far wall, his face now the glassy eyed face of a snake. Looking up, Jason saw several more prone figures in police uniforms scattered about the corridor. But these had been shot, and they retained their human features.

Jason returned to the Home Secretary's office. "The snake men... They were in the car escorting us. I recognised that one. He led them." He pointed at the corpse of the man who Mike had addressed as inspector.

"We must have been infiltrated from the beginning," Mike muttered. "They gunned down the other men and came for us."

"Came for *me*, sergeant," the Home Secretary corrected him with an obsequious little grin. "I hate to sound conceited, but it's me they want to kill."

"Why? Why do they want to kill you?" Jason flushed when the other two looked at him in incredulity. "Oh, I understand that you're important, a government minister and all the rest of it. But what have snakes got to do with the government? Is it something to do with... the Trojan Rite?"

The Home Secretary looked frowningly at Mike, who shook his head. "I've said nothing!" he said. "Jason was spying on us in the Grand Temple, sir. Remember?"

The Home Secretary fixed Jason with his eye. "What have you worked out so far?"

"Very little." In that room filled with the reek of blood and cordite and monstrous corpses, Jason knew that he understood absolutely nothing. "Something about ancient kings of Britain who don't appear in the history books. Trojans. They came to Britain only to find the place ruled by serpent men, and so they fought against them, drove them out. Or at least they thought they had."

Mike nodded approvingly but said nothing.

"They have the power to change their appearance." The Home Secretary's voice was flat, dispassionate. As if he was discussing nothing more fantastic or grotesque than the government's latest policy on prison reform. "They could look like you. Or like me. When Atlantis was an island of savage tribes, they ruled the mainland until they were driven out by King Kull of Valusia. And yet they returned in disguise. They ruled this country in prehistoric times, they seek to regain power..."

Jason listened in bewildered confusion. Was this true? Or some kind of conspiracy theory? He glanced at the serpent headed corpse by the desk.

"Only the Lodge of the Trojan Rite has been able to fight them," the Home Secretary went on, "because it has remained clandestine, inviolate. Over the centuries it has passed down the imperative to hunt the serpent men wherever they may be. The Lodge has never been infiltrated. Until now."

Jason was baffled. "What are they trying to do? Take over the government?"

"Oh, they've done that time and again," the Home Secretary told him. "All the great tyrants of British history, Richard III, Bloody Mary, Charles I, all were of the serpent man bloodline."

Jason grimaced but the Home Secretary continued. 'When the monarchy was sidelined and power came into the hands of Parliament, the serpent men turned their attention to powerful ministers, murdering them and replacing them. All but one of my predecessors was replaced by a serpent man shortly after becoming home secretary."

"It's obvious, when you think about it," Mike added. "Whenever a minister becomes home secretary, they change completely."

The Home Secretary was peering down at the one Jason had inadvertently killed. "And this," he said proudly, "is one of the worst. You've bagged yourself the crown price, old man. See these markings?" Upon what remained of the serpent man's scaly brows was a white blotch reminiscent of a crown. "He was an important leader. No doubt it was he who would have taken my place. If not for you."

A car pulled up outside. Car doors slammed, footsteps tramped. Mike gestured urgently to Jason to pick up one of the fallen guns. The Home Secretary snatched up the other, gripping it like a gangster. They waited on either side of the door as the footsteps drew closer. Jason felt his heart hammering. Mike had his dagger at the ready.

The footsteps paused as if their owners were surveying the bloodbath. A tall, gaunt policeman appeared in the doorway, flanked by two more. Panting, Jason raised his gun.

"No!" Mike knocked down his gun arm. He turned to the newcomer who wore the form of Inspector Truegood. "Car Narmer Carr Ledger Rama," he shouted in challenge.

"Car Narmer Carr Ledger Rama," replied Truegood. "What happened here?"

"What happened to you, man?" the Home Secretary demanded. "You were supposed to be following the van."

"We were, sir." Truegood stepped over a dead serpent man and they shook hands—the Masonic handshake, Jason saw with a grim smile. "But we got separated in traffic. I saw a car out there—identical to ours, even down to the plates."

"The cunning devils," muttered the Home Secretary.

"What happened?" Jason asked, feeling stupid. "I thought he'd been replaced."

Mike shook his head. "The serpent men—they must have known what car Truegood would be driving. Not only did they take on his appearance, they even copied the car. They must have been responsible for the inspector being delayed too. No wonder I was fooled."

"We'd better do something about these bodies," Truegood announced. "And the shooting. People will have heard. A story's needed. We can blame it on the IRA again." He issued orders to his men.

"How did you know where I was?" Jason asked suddenly. "From one of your agents? Have you been spying on me?"

"I followed your taxi after you were seen on Great Queen Street." Mike was impatient. "We waited until morning. You were seen leaving the hotel. We decided to bring you in."

"You don't have an agent at my hotel?" Jason's eyes narrowed. "An old bat who works there as a hotel receptionist? She's been spying on me, I'm sure of it."

"She must be one of them." Truegood was indifferent. "Ask her to repeat the Valusian Catechism, she'll soon show her true colours."

"But score one to us," added the Home Secretary. "Mr Steele killed the crown prince. One of the most important of the serpent hierarchy. Second only to the king."

The others grinned in approval. A thought struck Jason. "But the professor's still there. He's vulnerable without me. He's in danger."

"You've been of inestimable service today, Mr Steele," the Home Secretary announced. "If not for you I might well be dead, replaced by a serpent man. But I'd like you to do something else for me."

Jason shrugged. "What's that?"

"Tonight I am booked to address a meeting of the Grand Lodge. Every home secretary is invited to do this when they first take up office. Many of the people I will be working with are members. I will be giving a speech concerning my intentions to reform the police and prison service. If I can do this *as myself*, it may well be that the United Kingdom will become a fairer, more tolerant country. But if I am replaced..."

"What's this got to do with me?" Jason asked.

"You have shown yourself to be an able bodyguard," the Home Secretary told him. "I would like you to accompany me to the Freemasons' Hall. Make sure that the serpent men have no opportunity to replace me with one of their own."

And him a mere private detective whose annual turnover was so inadequate he needed to apply for housing benefit. "Th-thank you, sir," Jason stammered. "I'll be sure to go with you."

"For the moment, however, I think you had better return to your hotel," the Home Secretary said. "Check on this friend of yours; he could be in danger. DS Blake, will you run our young friend back to his hotel? Please?"

"Yes, sir, of course," said Mike, and at the Home Secretary's command, Truegood handed over a set of car keys.

At the back of the house another car had joined the other vehicles, of identical make, colour, and even registration number as the first car, a blue Ford Taurus. Mike unlocked the door and got into the driver's seat.

"Come on, Jason. You want to make sure your professor friend's okay, don't you?"

Jason got in the passenger seat and Mike started up the engine, reversing back onto the road. Soon they were turning on to the main road and heading back towards Jason's hotel. Mike overtook a big red London bus of the kind so beloved by tourists and Jason was reminded how much he hated the city. It was too big, too crowded. Too full of idiots in cars beeping their horns. Only important business ever took him to London. He was a small town boy.

"You said that Tracy's worried about me," Mike probed anxiously.

Jason nodded, glancing at him. "Worried enough to pay for a private detective to tail you. Why couldn't you have told her what was happening? At least enough to put her mind at ease."

"I suppose because my own mind's not been at ease." Mike

halted at a red light. "I've had a lot on my plate. I suppose I might have... snapped at her once or twice."

"She did say you got nasty when she asked you what was going on."

"I'm sorry about that, truly I am." The light changed and Mike drove on. "Bet you're not, though. Right, Jason?"

"Don't know what you mean," Jason replied awkwardly.

"Oh, come on, Jason. We're mates, but you still have... feelings for Tracy. Don't you? Must make you happy to see we're having problems."

Jason shifted in his seat. "Me and Tracy are finished."

"But when she asks you to do something like this, you come running."

"She's paying me," Jason insisted. "This is business. She's worried about what you're getting yourself into. She couldn't get a straight answer out of you so she hired a private detective. Just so happened she hired her ex. I doubt she knows many private detectives."

"She could have looked them up in the Yellow Pages."

Jason shrugged and changed the subject. "So what got you into this in the first place?"

"I met Truegood at a conference. He was impressed by my record. I've done okay for myself—some of it with your help, like that trouble we had down in Dunwich. He sounded me out about joining a group. A secret group with what sounded like political agendas. I was worried, thinking maybe it was Combat 18 or something dodgy like that, but he said he could make sure I got the promotion I wanted. Youngest inspector on the force, that was what I was promised."

Jason glanced at him. Mike's face was pensive. He took a

right turn up a narrow backstreet with parking on either side.

"You could make it, Mike," he muttered. "You don't need to join the Masons. You're good enough without them."

"Nice of you to say so, mate. But I thought it was best to have friends in high places. Yeah, it's corruption. But that's how people get on in this country." He changed gear. "I now realise that a lot of it can be blamed on the serpent men. But the Lodge is opposed to them. Opposed to their corruption. Can you imagine what the country will be like if they replace the Home Secretary with one of their own?"

Jason grunted. What he'd seen of the government over the last few years, it might as well have been under serpent man control. The Home Secretary had suggested that all but one of his predecessors had been replaced. So who had been the odd one out?

They turned a corner and Jason recognised the street. His hotel was near the far end. Mike couldn't find a nearby parking place, so they had to get out a five minutes' walk away and double back.

The same hotel receptionist was on duty this morning. Jason greeted her politely, wondering if she ever went off duty. She glanced at Mike and then at him.

"Mr Steele?" she said.

"Yes?"

She seemed normal enough. No hint of scales, except a nasty patch of eczema on the back of one hand. She was somewhere between forty five and fifty at a guess, with ruddy skin that suggested she'd been a bit of a raver in the early seventies. Her eyes were a cold emerald. Perhaps that was it. They were strangely hypnotic. Like the eyes of a cobra.

She glanced at his pigeon hole. "Oh!" she said, flustered. "I thought I had a message for you, but it's not here. Now, where could he have put it? My husband, you see. Never puts things in the right place..."

"Thanks, er," Jason struggled to recall her name, "er, Mrs Hislop. If you can find it by the time I come back down..."

"Of course." Surveying the pigeon holes, she scratched her head distractedly. Dandruff flaked off in a little cloud.

Jason led Mike up the stairs. Reaching his room he slipped the key into the lock and opened it, revealing a room entirely devoid of any professors.

"Professor Flint?"

When no reply was forthcoming he exchanged a worried glance with Mike, then knocked on Flint's bedroom door. No answer. He tried the bathroom but the door swung open to reveal that it was empty. "Professor!"

"Professor Flint!" Mike echoed his calls. "Professor? Jason, mate, he's not here."

Jason saw a sheaf of notes lying scattered on the floor by the sofa. "That's odd. Professor Flint's normally tidier than that."

He picked up a couple of pages, glanced at Mike. "He's not here," he said flatly.

"Maybe he's gone out." Mike shrugged.

Jason sniffed. "Strong smell of pipe smoke. He's been here recently.

"Have a closer look round," he added. "You might find something to suggest where he might have gone. I'm going down to speak with the hotel receptionist. Maybe that message she was talking about was from Flint."

"Okay, mate." Mike produced an elaborate dagger. "But keep

this on you when you go down. Forged to pierce the scales of you know who. Just in case you run into one of *them*."

After concealing it under the waistband of his trousers, Jason thundered back down the stairs, pausing on the first landing to allow a girl to enter a room, along with the tired looking businessman who accompanied her.

Reaching the lobby, he crossed over to the desk.

"You should get a lift installed in this place, Mrs Hislop," he said cheerily. "Who needs exercise!"

"Mr Steele," she acknowledged. "I'm so glad you've come back. I was just about to call you." Inquiringly she looked past him. "Your friend isn't with you?"

"He's still upstairs," Jason replied. "Have you found the message yet? Who was it from?"

"Professor Flint," she explained. "He had to go out not long after you left. He did wait for you, he said, but after a while you showed no signs of returning, so he went, but he left a message with Mr Hislop."

"Great." The professor had just gone out, no doubt to the Reading Room at the British Museum. Jason looked at the pigeon holes meaningly. "Can I have it now?"

"Oh, it's not here," she replied. "My husband left it in the office. On the desk, he said. If you step this way, I'll find it for you."

Jason followed her to the door of the little cubbyhole. She eased her bulk around the tiny desk, searching through the papers that lay piled up on it. A half-eaten plate of sausage and beans acted as a paperweight. "Somewhere here, he said. I don't see it. A small piece of notepaper, torn from one of them spiral bound pads. Can you see any sign of it, Mr Steele?"

As Jason crossed the threshold to help her there was a flash of movement from behind the door. He turned, caught a brief glimpse of scaly flesh. Then felt a blow to his head. A rocket seemed to explode in his mind, and went soaring upwards into dark skies of infinity.

And Jason fell, fell, fell into a black void like a deep, deep well.

## 4   Snake Eyes Watching You

Professor Flint was a worried man. So worried, in fact, that despite the reverential hush of the Reading Room, he found it almost impossible to concentrate on the volumes piled up on the desk before him. Regardless, never one to procrastinate, he opened another book, a history by one Richard of Westminster. The medieval Latin was in a crabbed, monkish hand, and Flint scowled as he attempted to decipher it. His disciplined mind began, inevitably, to wander.

What on earth had happened to Jason?

When the boy had failed to return from his post breakfast run, Flint hadn't known what to do. Had Jason been delayed? Or had it been a sign of something altogether more sinister? Flint had considered phoning the police, but even as he picked up the receiver he realised that the idea was bordering on the hysterical.

Assuming the police were not themselves involved in this Masonic conspiracy, they would only suggest he wait twenty four hours before reporting a missing person. In their eyes he'd be jumping the gun.

But Jason had been following a dangerous course. It had pained Flint when he was unable to accompany the young man on his escapade, his tailing of Sergeant Blake that had resulted in such hi jinks in the Freemasons' Hall.

But at Flint's time of life, he had to face up to the fact that he would be nothing but a burden in such an action packed exploit. He was better here, buried deep in research. So, after waiting two impatient hours, bidding his fears bedamned, he had hurried out, caught a cab on Neal Street, and spent the rest of the day in the Reading Room at the British Museum.

No doubt Jason would turn up.

Much of detective work was like this, he had discovered; desk bound, poring over documents. Seldom was it as glamorous as it seemed in *Inspector Morse*. Although he had only been involved in detective work, (amateur of course), for a short while, he had a lifetime of research behind him to draw upon.

Fortunately, at one point in his academic career, he had studied Medieval Latin. All the same, Richard of Westminster's account was hard going to say the least. Flint was about to turn the page when his eyes fell upon the word "serpens". Serpens! The Latin for snake, or serpent!

He read closely now, no longer skimming the medieval script. Sweat ran down his brow and he paused to mop it away with his handkerchief. Irritably, he glanced at the *No Smoking* sign on the wall nearby. What he really needed was his pipe.

He read on.

This was it! This was what he had been looking for. Documentary evidence to back up these rumours and hints of Trojan Rites and Gogmagog. Gogmagog he was familiar with, having holidayed in the Gog Magog Hills as an undergraduate at Cambridge. And the name was replicated in Gog and Magog, the two giant images in the Guild Hall. But in earlier times, there had been an image named Gogmagog, and another... called Corineus!

His was a name to be found in no modern history book. Since the eighteenth century, doubt had been cast upon the whole legendary history of Britain. Anything prior to Julius Caesar's invasion had been consigned to the rubbish dump. But memories persisted, in odd, out of the way corners. Corineus, champion of the first British king, Brutus, who fought against the non-human inhabitants of a Britain that must have just been emerging from the Stone Age.

Depicted as a giant, a fairy tale ogre, in later accounts, Gogmagog was mentioned here as "serpens", and "draco". *Snake* and *dragon*. And here was another name, the pagan god Gogmagog had worshipped: Yig. "Yig, ille serpens deus" said Richard of Westminster. *Yig, that serpent god...*

*Yig.* That had been another of the names Sergeant Blake had uttered in his sleep.

Flint read on, eyes growing wider as he did so. Enthralled, he barely heard a heated discussion from the front desk. Running footsteps sullied the tranquillity of the Reading Room.

A broad-shouldered man loomed over him. "Are you Professor Flint?" he asked. Flint started back in fear.

Gradually, with no very clear idea of where he was, Jason awoke with a throbbing head. It was pitch black. He was lying on a hard stone floor. Not only was his head throbbing, his body was aching. What had happened? The last thing he remembered was going downstairs to see if Professor Flint had left a note. Then everything was a confused blank.

He felt a twinge of pain from the crown of his head. Putting his hand to his hair, he felt a sticky wetness. Blood? He sniffed at it queasily. Yes, he recognised the rank, coppery odour of blood. If he had been able to see, his fingers would be stained red.

But it was too dark.

Where the fuck was he? Wherever it was, it was bloody cold. And silent. As silent, to coin a phrase, as the grave. He remembered a story he'd read in his teens, by Edgar Allan Poe. Had he been buried alive? He panicked wildly, convinced he was trapped in a coffin, and tried to sit up.

To his relief, there was ample room. He felt a cold draught wafting from somewhere. He was in the dark, that was for sure, but it wasn't an enclosed space like a coffin.

But it didn't really matter where he was! What mattered was whether or not he could get out of here.

Gingerly, he tried to stand up. He tottered on unsteady feet, staggered, tried futilely to grab onto something that wasn't there, and fell flat on the cold stone floor.

He lay there a while, trying to rack his brains as to how he had wound up in this place. He had been on a case... On a case, trailing Mike Blake. Mike? Why had he been trailing Mike, of all people?

He sat up again. Then flailed outwards with his hands. He cursed in pain as he struck a brick wall with his knuckles. Sucking them, he wondered where he could be. Somewhere dark, perhaps underground. With brick walls. That reminded him of something. Something... If only the throbbing in his head would go away he might have a hope of remembering!

Using the wall to steady himself, he clambered to his feet.

Now he moved along the wall, never taking his hands from it. He came to a corner. A right angled corner. He followed it round and traversed another wall. Then the brick ended. He had found a wooden door. Reaching down, he felt a doorknob, and turned it, but the door was locked. Hammering on it he shouted for help.

To his surprise, after only a short while a key grated in the lock and the door opened. Outlined in the doorway was a burly figure.

"Mike!" Jason said. "Mike, what are you doing here?"

"I could ask the same of you," Mike said in a low voice. "I didn't know where you'd be, then I heard you shouting. I came to find you."

Jason's head was swimming, but he gripped Mike's hand in friendly welcome. He shook his friend's hand vigorously and suddenly everything seemed a lot clearer.

"Well, come on," said Mike. "You've got a job to do tonight. Remember? Security work for the Home Secretary himself."

Jason put a hand to his head. Something didn't seem to be making much sense. "Do you really think I'm in a fit state, Mike? I don't even know how I got here."

Mike seemed unsurprised by his reaction. "They knocked you out, and they must have imprisoned you down here. That woman at the hotel and her husband."

A flash of memory. Someone had been hiding behind the door. Scaly flesh. Pain, blackness... Oblivion.

"I've been trying to find you all day," Mike added. "It's about time you were at the Freemasons' Hall."

Jason's guts twisted. "Freemasons' Hall?"

"You remember! The Home Secretary has been invited to a

dinner event where he'll give a speech to all the top Masons. You're needed there as his bodyguard."

Jason nodded wryly. "Quite a responsibility. Especially with this splitting headache."

"Look, if you get in the Home Sec's good graces," Mike told him, "who knows what might happen? You might be welcomed back to the force. No more of this arsing around trying to be Sam Spade. You can be a real detective—in the CID. Come on!"

Still clutching at his head, Jason followed Mike from the room. He saw little of what followed. They seemed to be underground, following a winding series of brick tunnels. Suddenly they were standing in front of a door. Mike opened it and they stepped out into a brightly lit corridor.

The sound of people talking drifted from the other end, where a pair of double doors stood open. Mike led Jason through them and there they were, in the yawning immensity of the Grand Temple, the huge room where he had been the other night. The seats that had lined it had been replaced by dining tables filled by men in sober suits, many of whom looked vaguely familiar to Jason. From the TV, though, not real life.

At the far end, upon a throne, sat the Home Secretary. Mike led Jason right up to them across a chequerboard floor.

That walk seemed to take forever. He had a chance to take in the Grand Temple, seeing details that had escaped him on his previous, furtive visit. Balconies stood along three walls, lined with seats like a theatre, while the whole place had the air of a theatre, or one of the grandiose cinemas of the twenties and thirties.

Running round the walls above was a fresco that seemed to show the Sun God in all his majesty. The men at the tables whispered amongst each other, watching Jason as Mike led him towards the thrones. It felt oddly like an Oscar ceremony. But Jason's eyes were drawn by the Home Secretary.

He remembered the fight in the Georgian house. How he had killed the man who had turned into a snake. The Home Secretary's approval. He had chosen Jason to be his bodyguard. An honour Jason could never have anticipated working for Essex Police.

"Mr Steele!" The Home Secretary greeted him warmly. "So glad you could make it. Here, stand by me."

"Car Narmer Carr Ledger Rama," Jason muttered.

"What's that, mate?" Mike said, startled.

"Say it," Jason demanded. "Say it! You too," he told the Home Secretary. "Car Narmer Carr Ledger Rama."

"Cuff him, Sergeant," the Home Secretary commanded. "There's something wrong here."

Mike groped for his handcuffs. Jason plunged his dagger into Mike's chest.

Cries of outrage and horror burst from the seated guests as Mike fell to the floor with a thud. Jason gazed in sick horror at the blood that stained the blade.

"You—you just killed him!" the Home Secretary cried. "What... what is wrong with you?"

He lunged for Jason. Jason dodged aside, bloody dagger still in his hand.

"Drop that!" the Home Secretary shouted.

The diners all spoke amongst each other, hissing in disapproval. Mike's corpse shimmered, like a ship seen on the horizon. His bluff face vanished, and in its place leered the scaled, reptilian head of a giant snake, tongue lolling from its fanged jaw.

"Mike was a serpent man all along." Jason turned towards the Home Secretary, who crouched, fingers crooked like claws. He no longer resembled an important government minister, but rather a repellent monster. With a cry, Jason flung the dagger. "And so are you!"

Like Mike before him, his face seemed to shimmer. Scales multiplied across his pale skin, his eyes became slits of reptilian malice, fangs jutted from a mouth that had elongated into that of a snake. Blood trickled from that serpentine jaw. The hilt of the dagger jutted from a scaled chest.

The shimmering seemed to spread, to pool out across the Great Temple. Jason turned in bewilderment. The other diners had vanished. The walls were now ancient brick. The ceiling was lower. Candles flickered in the corners. A flight of steps led up to a door on the far wall.

He was not in the Grand Temple after all, he realised, but in the cellars beneath. For a long moment, he stared around himself in bewildered dismay. It was cold, it was dank. How he had found himself in this gloomy place he barely knew. He stared at the reptilian corpses that lay at his feet.

Footsteps rang from somewhere outside. The door burst open and people flooded down the steps. At their head was Inspector Truegood, Mike Blake at his side. With them were several other policemen—and Professor Flint.

"Jason!" the professor shouted. 'There you are!'

Jason tottered and almost fell. Flint seized him and helped him to sit down. The others gathered round them. Mike seized his hand.

"Jason!" he said. "I'm so glad you're alive. What happened

here?" He gestured at the reptilian corpses.

"That's how I knew." Numbly Jason gripped Mike's hand and stared at the bloody dagger he had dropped on the ground. "That's how I knew it wasn't you." They could change their appearance, these snakes, but they couldn't change the fact that they were cold blooded. Their flesh was cool to the touch. Mike's was warm.

He looked up. "Car Narmer Carr Ledger Rama," he said.

Mike removed the dagger from the scaly carcass and wiped it clean. "Car Narmer Carr Ledger Rama." He laughed. "You know, this was supposed to be my job? But I'd never have worked out what was going on if I hadn't found the professor."

Jason turned to Flint. "How do you come to be here?" he asked. "I thought they'd got you. The mess in the hotel room... It looked like you'd been abducted."

"I thought the same about you." The professor chuckled. "And I was right. When you didn't come back, I was worried, but I went to the Reading Room all the same. In something of a hurry, I suppose, which would explain the aforementioned mess.

"A good thing that I did go to the Museum, since it was there that I learnt about this underground temple built long ago by the serpent men, used for rites of human sacrifice. Perhaps the Freemasons chose this place to erect their temple knowing its earlier history. When Sergeant Blake told me you had been snatched... Somehow I knew that they would have taken you here."

Jason felt a chill. "How could they know I killed the crown prince?"

An uneasy silence was his only answer.

"We came looking for you," announced Inspector Truegood. "But it seems that you were capable of looking after yourself." He eyed the two serpent corpses. "Now you've got another job to do."

Leaving two of their number to dispose of the serpentine corpses, Truegood led them out of the subterranean temple. In the vestibule they found the Home Secretary waiting impatiently, reading through his notes. He looked up, and seeing Jason, his face brightened.

'Ah, Mr Steele,' he said breezily. 'You're just in time. Whatever kept you?'

Shortly afterwards they were in the Great Temple, where the Home Secretary was greeted by a round of thunderous applause.

Mike and Jason stood on guard behind him as he addressed the throng. Mind awhirl, Jason barely heard his speech. He remembered the Masons he had seen in the subterranean temple, under the misapprehension that he was here. It had all been so real. It was almost impossible to believe that everything had been... what? Some kind of magical spell cast by the serpent men? Was that possible?

He glanced at Mike, who smiled back. The plot of the serpent men had failed. He was all set to become a popular hero.

He might even get his old job back.

### Epilogue

The following Saturday Tracy was all of a fluster. They had an important guest. No, really, a very important guest. She rushed round the front room, dusting manically, wearing her classiest frock, her bottle blonde hair held back by a bobble.

On the sideboard she had the decanter ready. All very posh, not like her at all. At the last minute, the sun came out, and she insisted on moving everything out into the garden.

Jason had been invited, of course. He sat by the picnic table with Mike, drinking a bottle of Budweiser. He didn't really believe that their guest would come. Important work must inevitably drag him away.

Mike grinned at Jason as he put down his empty bottle. 'Another?'

'I don't want you boys getting drunk before he turns up.' Tracy looked disapproving.

'Thanks.' Jason ignored her, and Mike got him his drink.

It was good to be in the sunshine, feeling a little hazy from his first beer. Professor Flint had been invited as well, but he was away, carrying out research elsewhere, looking into legends of serpent demons in Western Ireland. 'So when are you going to be made inspector, Mike?' Jason asked.

Mike shrugged. 'It's all up in the air,' he replied. 'But all this can only look good in the eyes of the promotion board. And what about you? Maybe the Home Sec can get you some kind of plum job.'

Jason laughed. 'That would be good.' He considered mentioning his real concern. Surely the serpent men would make some fresh attack now that he had foiled their plans. He had killed the crown prince of the serpent men. He no longer felt entirely safe with anyone.

At last, long after the hour when their guest was supposed to turn up, there was a knock from the front door. Tracy hurried into the house, returning soon after, leading him through into the garden. With their important guest was a tall, muscular, silent man in a suit, who carried a briefcase.

Mike sprang to his feet. A little more lazily, having sunk a couple more beers, Jason did the same. He burped. "At ease, men," said the Home Secretary with a tolerant smile.

Tracy showed him to a garden chair by the picnic table, and found another chair for his mysterious unspeaking companion. "I'm so glad you could make it." Her words tumbled over themselves. "Can I get you a drink? We've got sherry, whisky and soda, gin and tonic? Or beer."

The Home Secretary accepted a G&T. "Thank you for inviting me," he said. "Is this where you live, Mr Steele?"

Jason laughed a little too loud. "You don't want to see my flat. No place for entertaining." The Home Sec was surely a man with broad horizons, but Jason doubted he was broadminded enough for a can of super strength lager and a curry-con-carne. "This is Tracy and Mike's place. I thought it was the best place to see you, sir. You've met Tracy."

The Home Secretary gave Mike's girlfriend a charming smile and spoke glowingly about the garden. She drained her gin and tonic at a gulp and talked rapidly and to little purpose.

"I'm afraid I won't be able to stay long," the Home Secretary added, when Tracy finally paused for breath. "Work must go on, even at the weekend, for we politicians. But I wanted to thank both of you. And also the charming Tracy, who I understand was so concerned for Sergeant Blake that she sent Mr Steele to shadow him. No!" He put up his hand, as she protested. "I'm glad you did, dear lady. Without you, it's possible that I would be dead. And the country would be much worse off. So I'd like to thank you as well." A discomfited expression crossed his face. "But there's something else."

He signed to the silent man, who opened up his briefcase and took out several pieces of paper. "I'm afraid I'm going to have to ask you to sign the Official Secrets Act. Personally, I would prefer to reward you all highly, especially Mr Steele. But it's politically impossible. The whole matter must be forgotten about. It's not in the public interest for rumours to spread of a reptilian conspiracy."

Numbly, Jason found himself signing the document. He'd been more than half hoping for rewards, medals, honours. At the very least his old job back. But all of that had gone by the board.

"Thank you," said the Home Secretary fulsomely, rising and shaking Jason's hand, then Mike's. He kissed Tracy's blushing cheek. "I won't forget what you've done for me. But sadly, that is exactly what you are going to have to do."

With that, he and his minder departed. Silence settled over the garden. A bee buzzed around the hollyhocks. Tracy looked meaningly at Mike. Mike glanced at Jason, but he didn't speak.

"Do me a favour!" Tracy sighed in disappointment. "Is that all you get, babe? *Thanks, but you've got to sign the Official Secrets Act?*"

Jason was rubbing his hand thoughtfully, too deep in thought to answer. He should be disappointed. It looked like he wouldn't be back in uniform any time soon. But maybe that wasn't so bad. He'd got used to getting up late. That was one good thing about self-employment, you could choose your hours. No more commuting for him.

But what an icy grip the Home Secretary had, he told himself. *It was almost as if he were cold blooded.*

*In the far distance a series of drab
monoliths broke the surface like
giant cetaceans breaching the ocean,
rising to impossible heights, kissing
the corona of the sky.*

# THE PIERCER OF THE VEILS

*JOHN HOULIHAN*

Green-brown waves lapped against the shore beneath slate grey skies as Darke ducked beneath the cordon and onto the foreshore. A few early morning mudlarkers regarded him curiously, but he ignored them as the shingle crunched beneath his shoes. Behind him, the central span of Tower Bridge has risen to accommodate a passing tall ship and in the distance, the towers of the City were a blocky intrusion into the low hanging cloud. Old wharves stood here once, but now the metal and chrome of a wealthy apartment block rose above eternal Father Thames. Nevertheless, the exposed beach was a liminal space, hidden by the waters but uncovered now at low tide, a halfway point between the old and the new.

The shoreline reeked of bilge and centuries of accumulated filth, but there was something else too, a faint afterimage, an echoing remnant that made his sight twitch. Something macabre had happened here, he knew it instinctively, even without the cordoned tent which stirred in the stiff river breeze. There was a presence here, distinctive, old, malevolent...

'Hey! Hey! You can't be here. Get back behind the barrier.' Darke narrowed his eyes, regarding the policeman, irritated by the interruption in his train of thought. He was just on the point of a withering reply, when a voice from behind him said.

'It's alright sergeant, he's with me.' A tall Asian woman in a long raincoat displayed an ID which silenced the sergeant's objections.

'Chanda. It's good to see you.'

'Darke.'

'Ah, so we're being formal, are we? Okay, DI Parris, what can I do for you?'

'Don't be such a prick, Marcus. Come on, he's this way.'

Inside the tent, the hi-vis skin lent everything a glaring fluorescence but shielded from the elements it had a residual warmth. Outside, a light drizzle had begun to soak the foreshore and the assembled police officers were huddled up beneath umbrellas, nursing hot teas and rubbing their hands to fend off the bleak January cold.

A body lay there, on its back, although lay was not quite the right word. It looked like it had been pressed into the mud and slime of the beach.

'The doctor's been, we're just waiting to wrap him up and ship him off to the morgue,' said Parris.

'So why call me in?'

'You specialise in this freaky shit.'

'I do.'

'Well, that makes you the closest thing I've got to an expert. So go ahead, do your thing. Then tell me what you discover.'

Darke slid on a pair of latex gloves with practised ease, bent down and began to examine the body. Even as he went through the routine, his mind was churning. This is what he had sensed, where that unusual energy had been focused. The evil had concentrated itself here and imposed its will on this individual. He could feel Parris' impatience, but didn't rush.

When he finally stood up, Parris waited expectantly, but he took a moment to compose himself.

'So?' she said.

'I presume you've covered all the basics so let's focus on what stands out. First, no obvious marks or cause of death. The facial expression is unusual, unsettling, like someone caught between abject terror and an irresistible joke. The eyes, closed tightly, like he laughed himself to death while in the throes of some horrible fear spasm.'

'Go on.'

'Then there's the posture, like he was pushing himself away from something, something so horrible, he was trying to burrow into the earth to escape it. No defensive wounds or anything of that nature, nothing unusual under the nails either, it seems like he didn't fight back or try to fend it off.'

'Not bad, but you missed something.'

'Enlighten me.'

'The eyes. They're both missing. No wounds either, they're just gone, as if they vanished clean out of their sockets.'

'Shit,' said Darke, 'his eyelids are screwed up so tightly, I didn't look.'

'Good to know I can still surprise you.'

'You can do a lot more than that if I recall?'

'Yeah, well, let's focus on the case... so?'

'Fair enough. Well, without wanting to state the obvious it's a bizarre way to go. No blood or signs of trauma around the eyes, so doubly weird.'

'Well, that's something you apparently know, but what else

can I tell you? Time of death was between midnight and two in the morning. No witnesses, one of the mudlarkers discovered the body when it got light, but no reason to suspect anything there. What do you make of it?'

'You were right to call me in. It's something uncanny, nothing I could put a name to... yet. I'll need time to think about this, Chanda. Leave it with me. The tattoo is probably significant though.'

'Tattoo?'

'Yeah, the one on the back of his neck, the black circle with the spiky radials coming off it. Hidden by that impressive head of hair, you caught that, right?' A flicker of annoyance told him she had not.

'Hm, okay, so the design is very particular, it rings a bell, but I'm not sure from where. I'll need to do some research.'

'Okay.'

'Did he have any ID? Do we know who this guy is?'

'We're working on it.'

'Okay, so let me know when you find out.'

'Don't take too long, Marcus. I need answers on this one. We can't have someone running around scaring people to death and removing their eyeballs. It doesn't look good on the clear up statistics.'

'Nor on the front pages either, I imagine?'

'Don't even... I don't want the press getting hold of this, splashing lurid headlines.'

'Why would they? He's only just been discovered and I don't see any of the usual hacks amongst the onlookers.'

'Because this is the second one we've found in the last few days. Same MO, eyes removed, victim looks terrified. Best guess is heart failure, but heart failure doesn't cause your eyes to just disappear. I don't have to tell you, that's no coincidence.'

'No, it is rather singular. Alright then, so you want me on board?'

Parris sighed, 'Not particularly, but we need your specialist knowledge, so I guess I'm stuck with you. Your fees will be buried in miscellaneous expenses.'

'The usual rate then?'

'The usual rate.'

'Okay, count me in.'

Darke lounged in his office, took a long pull on a joint and exhaled a gout of fragrant, resinous smoke. Outside, the London traffic was a constant background hum which washed over him like white noise, focusing his mind while he poured over the files Parris had left on the secure server. They made for interesting reading but he was struggling to find any connection between the two victims.

The first was a Romanian woman, Daria Balan, mid fifties, lived in the UK for about ten years, moved here before 2016's great divide. She had been found in the undergrowth of Wapping Woods by a patrol in the early hours of Friday morning. She worked several jobs, carer, laundress, one of those anonymous souls who quietly oil the wheels of society for low pay, long hours and very little thanks. A worthy life but an unremarkable one in an esoteric sense, nothing that might have attracted the attention of a murderer. No strange tattoos or other unusual marks, except she had a hundred and twenty pounds in cash in her purse. Untouched too, which was notable. Looking at the coroner's photograph, she had died in just as much abject terror as the second victim.

The man on the foreshore was a very different kettle of fish altogether. Andrew Leith-Forbes worked in the City as a financier, banker and hedge fund manager, and was a very wealthy man and an unpleasant one too. He had not endeared himself to many by betting against the pound and making himself a small fortune after the referendum. A quick search on the web and across his socials suggested he was an important one too. Donations to right wing think tanks, links with some of the more lunatic fringe backbench MPs, black tie pictures at galas and fundraisers, a picture with a gauche minister. An influential man then, interwoven into the fabric of London society and well acquainted with the corridors of power.

So what linked a foreign carer and a powerful financier? Nothing he could see immediately other than the bare facts that they had been killed at night and within half a mile of each other in the same macabre manner. He rested the joint on the tray and let the end burn down, while he tried to free his mind to roam. What did that tell you? Only that the killer liked to keep things local and preferred to operate under the cover of darkness. Not exactly revelatory stuff, dark deeds are usually best performed when there's no one around to witness them. The open sky might be significant though, was this a particularly propitious time astronomically? He should look into that.

Then there was the modus operandi. How the hell did you remove someone's eyes without causing any sign of injury around the face? Daria Balan's autopsy was already available and revealed some intriguing facts. The eyes had been taken premortem but there was no evidence of trauma, there had been no bleeding or shock, it was as if they had simply been teleported away somehow, which was freaky enough in itself.

Actual cause of death was listed as unknown but most likely heart failure, the coroner couldn't be certain, but it appeared the shock of the experience had just made her heart stop beating. No doubt Leith-Forbes' would read the same when the results came back. It didn't explain the haunting expression on her face from the coroner's photographs though, nor his, both of those would stay with Darke for a long while.

But who or more likely what did all this point to? A person or entity able to remove someone's eyes through esoteric means. But why exactly? Was it symbolic, but then what was it meant to symbolise? A threat? A warning? A warning about what? The things we shouldn't see?

This was getting him nowhere, so he took another drag and tried a different line of enquiry. Perhaps the eyes removal played a more practical role? Perhaps whatever was removing them was feeding on them in some way? Cannibalistically, or as a source of power? Eyes were the gateway to the soul supposedly and the most direct method people used to perceive the world, but Darke wasn't aware of any particular entity or ritual which demanded them.

The tattoo was intriguing, but was it significant? He knew it from somewhere, somewhere obscure, but couldn't dredge up the fragment and even a couple of hours searching and cross referencing his own extensive collection of rare books, tomes and manuscripts hadn't been able to provide an answer. He needed to go somewhere where he could do more detailed research and that would mean calling in a favour or two from a difficult source and the prospect didn't exactly fill him with glee... Questions, questions, feeling unsettled and dissatisfied, he let the darkness of the London evening envelop him in its bleak shroud, falling into a deep sleep where his dreams were troubled by a sense of unease.

*Long have I slept and long have I waited while the galaxies wheeled and the stars fell into alignment again. The sleep of centuries is but a blink of the eye for a cosmic traveller. Now I have reawakened once more from Albion's dreaming to discover the world has turned again, and England, my England, is awash with invaders and interlopers. Long has she ruled the waves but they have washed up a scum of detritus onto these shores which must be purged and cleansed. I did not baulk from it then and I will not baulk from it now. I must finish the work I left undone in the first Elizabeth's time. Then that mountebank Dee and his men foiled my plans, but this era shall be different.*

*Our destiny eternally conjoined, the creature has awoken alongside me and this time I will bend it to my will, we will become one and all the power and glory will be mine.*

*This is a time of strange technological magics and undreamed of marvels but it lacks the mystical knowledge and defences to prevent my ascent to power. Stand strong Albion, you do not have long to wait now, for when we are one again, Ezekiel Ferris will take his rightful place as your ruler, the Seeker will find the sun's gift and the Heir of Albion and will shape this nation's destiny and lead it to greatness.*

Parris had readily agreed to provide him with access but it was not a task Darke was particularly looking forward to. The mortuary was cold and sterile with harsh fluorescent lighting. Isla Lang, the coroner, led him in, sombre and respectful but detached behind her gown and mask. She showed him to the slab where the body had been laid out and raised an eyebrow. He gave a nod and she pulled back the sheet and he looked on the mortal remains of Daria Balan.

Pale and rigid, she was a little overweight and starting to show the wear and tear of a lifetime of work but there was nothing particularly notable about her middle-aged body. Her eyelids had been closed to conceal the missing orbs, although they hadn't been able to entirely hide the look of stark, manic horror which had enveloped her face in her final moments. It would be a closed coffin then to spare her relatives.

Darke approached and his sight triggered right away. There were two distinct sensations: the first a fleeing impression of something bitter, an echo of some spell or enchantment, but faint, so faint it was nearly undetectable.

The second was the overpowering sense of the evil that had consumed the unfortunate woman. It was so overwhelming, he felt it like a blow, staggering back, reeling from the strong emanations, the same signature he had felt on the foreshore. For a moment he caught a glimpse of something, an impression of dozens, no, hundreds of eyes and he cried out, falling, tumbling into an abyss where he was stared at, through, dissected for all eternity.

The next thing he knew, Lang was helping him back to his feet. He had fallen to one knee as he forced the vision out of his head, but the texture of it still lingered like an awful aftertaste.

'Thank you,' he said as Lang helped him up.

'Are you alright?' she said, 'don't worry, seeing a dead body like that can take some people the wrong way.'

'Thanks, I'm quite used to it. This was something different altogether.'

'Would you like a glass of water?'

'No, that's okay. You can cover her up now, I'm done.'

As Lang extended the white sheet over the recumbent form Darke made a silent vow. Whoever, whatever, had done this to Daria Balan, he would make an end of it.

Clarity may begin at home but Daria Balan's flat had added little to his understanding of the case. It was a small, rented studio in a cheap part of Whitechapel, a modest bedsit in a shared house of immigrants and gig economy workers. Darke had waited until the front door opened and simply strolled in. The outgoing occupant, a uniformed man on his way to a maintenance job, didn't even bother to glance at him as he slid inside. A transitory place it seemed, where people kept themselves to themselves and didn't ask too many questions.

The lock was uncomplicated and he was able to ease himself inside with the minimum of fuss. It was a simple but homely place and the police had evidently managed to restrain their usual ham-fistedness when searching it.

The main room was small but immaculately kept and he paused to study an old picture of Daria Balan with her arms around two dark haired children, happy, smiling, proud. A few pictures of saints and religious icons in the eastern orthodox style were also dotted around the place with a prominent crucifix on the old fireplace. A pious woman too, then.

What good did they do you? thought Darke, as you died howling in that park? Methodically he searched the rest of the flat but turned up nothing of interest apart from a cupboard stuffed with an extensive supply of colourful cloths, dusters and other cleaning materials. There was no reason for someone like Daria Balan to attract the attention of such an unusual killer. The flat was old but he didn't sense any lingering malevolence here. So much for a paranormal motive, Daria Balan was exactly what she appeared to be, an honest widow toiling away, sending money back to her children in Romania, hoping to earn them a better life through sacrificing her own.

So much for the who, was there any mileage in the why and the where? What was she doing walking through Wapping Park on a cold January night? Time of death was between 10pm and midnight according to the report which was a wide enough window. The police had no clue what she was doing there, nor had any of her housemates. She didn't seem the type to be out drinking late, or for some illicit romance, besides, she had been found in her work clothes. On her way home from somewhere? Darke called up Google Maps and plotted a course. Wapping Park was in almost a straight line between where they had found Leith-Forbes and her home here in Whitechapel. She had walked through it late at night and there met her grisly fate.

If he could find out what she had been doing out at that time of night then that might provide some insight into the case. It was a small breakthrough, but perhaps a significant one, one small piece of the puzzle dropping into place. Darke gathered his thoughts and took one last look around the flat and the picture of Daria and her children. He gave a small nod of acknowledgement, he would make sure he found who or what was responsible for this and make sure they could never do it again.

*The Chancellor was a fool, easily lured to his death by his vanity and his self importance, his belief in his own infallibility. How simple it was to play upon his pride, inflate his ego, appear so humble and servile, a relic from history, whose ultimate ambition was simply the honour of serving him.*

*I am the master, the heir, never the retainer.*

*How I loathe such creatures with every fibre of my being, those whose god is mammon and who worship money and wealth, not recognizing them as merely passing fancies, pale echoes of where true power resides.*

*The Piercer requires fresh fodder and it must be sated, for its hunger is eternal and it must be fed to open the way. Only then, when the Congregation is finally assembled, the ritual performed and the joining taken place, will the true heir of Albion emerge.*

'I'm still not sure how you talked me into this, Darke.'

'Oh, I can be a persuasive man when I need to be.'

'That I remember.' Parris said, 'how did you even manage to find this place?'

'It wasn't particularly easy. Leith-Forbes was an influential man but a secretive one too, a real Janus, one very public face, another very private one. He usually resides on a huge estate down in the Cotswolds, but I figured a man who spent this much time in the City might have a little *pied-à-terre* secreted away somewhere in town. Oh, it led me on a merry dance through multiple holding and shell companies, but eventually I managed to dredge up the name of the Infinite Beyond Asset Management Company and discovered they owned the penthouse in this newly developed block. A block which was only completed three years ago and which is just two minutes walk from where you found Leith-Forbes's body.'

'You should have joined the force, Darke,' said Parris.

'That's meant to be a compliment, right?'

'Take it whatever way you like. So what exactly are we doing here?'

'I need to take a look inside Leith-Forbes' flat before your boys in blue blunder in...' her eyes narrowed.

'Sorry, I mean before your forensics team tear it apart. By the time they're done, they'll contaminate all traces of anything useful... to me anyway.'

'Better, Darke.'

'Let's not fight, Chanda, we've already wasted enough time doing that.'

The concierge was an officious, tightly wound fellow, neatly dressed grey hair with a pencil moustache, nodding obsequiously at the well-dressed couple who ignored him completely as they shimmered through the doors of the lift. If he'd had a forelock, no doubt he would have tugged it. The embossed name badge identified him as Mike Shovlin – Building Supervisor, a fancy name for a doorman.

'Can I help you, madam?'

'My name is Detective Sergeant Chanda Parris and this is my ... associate. I believe you have a penthouse suite here. I need you to open it up for me.'

'The penthouse? You mean Mr Leith-Forbes residence?'

'Correct.'

'I'm afraid I can't just let you in without authorisation. We have certain standards here at Infinite Towers, certain protocols. Our residents expect discretion, they're very protective of their privacy.'

'Does that privacy extend beyond death? After they've been brutally murdered?' said Darke.

'Murdered? Mr Leith-Forbes? Oh, my goodness... when did this happen?' Shovlin seemed genuinely shocked.

'The details aren't public yet, but this is an ongoing and as I'm sure you'll appreciate, a highly confidential investigation. You'll understand the need for urgency and discretion...' said Parris.

'Well... of course... but Mr Leith-Forbes... I'm not sure... do you have a warrant by any chance? I mean it could be my job if I....'

'We don't need a warrant to search a crime scene, especially one where we might find the evidence we need to convict the killer,' said Darke.

'But... there's... '

'Charges of obstructing justice won't sit well with your employer either will they? Not a good look on the CV, especially if you find yourself looking for a new job?' said Darke. Shovlin considered this for a moment, frowned, then reached underneath his desk.

'Please, come this way...'

The apartment was spacious and modern, a gleaming vision of glass and chrome, white walls and sparse minimalist furniture in contrast to the muddy brown of the Thames which meandered along outside. The balcony offered extensive uninterrupted views of both Tower Bridge and the old wharfs which had been converted into tower blocks and commercial centres opposite. The only features which distinguished it from a thousand and one other bland luxury flats were some rather curious folk artefacts mounted on pedestals around the place, stylised animal masks, a faintly sinister green man and other less identifiable idols.

'Curious taste,' said Parris, studying a fawn-like statuette in contorted congress with a wood nymph.

'Money doesn't necessarily buy you taste,' said Darke, 'but these are strange: crude folk art, rather out of place for a man of such sophisticated tastes.'

They moved through the rest of the rooms but nothing leapt out at him as unusual, just the routine objects and ephemera you might expect in a wealthy man's playpen. There was a spartan living room, a separate dining area and a high end kitchen that could have come directly from the showroom it was so spotless. The bedroom had a king-sized bed but it was freshly made and looked like it had not been slept in recently. In fact the whole place was kept so immaculately it looked more like a show flat rather than anywhere someone would actually live.

Ever since he had arrived though, Darke has experienced a tingle, the faintest trace of magika, like a grain of pollen tickling his nostrils. The occult objects and ephemera were a steady low level background noise, but there was something else here too. It was elusive, like a fragrance on a summer breeze, so he closed his eyes, tried to focus, letting his sight lead him as he traversed the space but in the end only succeeded in confusing himself.

'Dammit,' he said, opening his eyes to find he was in the living room. Parris, who had followed, looked on sceptically.

'There is something here, but it's too dispersed, too defuse, to pin down.'

'So what do we do?'

'I'm not sure, but there's something else that's been bugging me as we've wandered around, something about the dimensions of this apartment. There's a dead space between the corridor and the living room. Look at the walls, there should be another room... just... there,' he pointed.

'Are you sure?'

'Not entirely, but there is a weird missing area. These sorts of flats like to have every square foot on display. There must be a concealed entrance somewhere.'

'Somewhere like that by any chance?' said Parris pointing to a wooden bookcase which had a radial design carved into its top shelf.

'Exactly. How did I miss that?' wondered Darke.

'Sometimes what you need is staring you right in the face,' said Parris smugly.

Darke ran his hands over the bookcase, tilting back book after book, seeking for a hidden switch or mechanism. Frowning, he took a pace back and then reached up to the radial and gave it a twist, manipulating it so that it revolved vertically. For a moment nothing happened and then the entire bookshelf swung toward him, revealing the hidden space beyond.

'A secret door in a modern penthouse, that's a new one. I thought these things were confined to haunted Victorian mansions,' said Parris.

'I guess if you own the building, the architect will work in any feature you want.'

'Including a secret study?'

'Especially, a secret study.'

The emanations were strong here, as if the door and walls had some kind of damping effect, sealing away any magical overspill. The room reeked of magika and was awash with dark harmonies, restless energy and a stale, perfumed odour. Inside was a long, narrow room, a windowless space which evidently served as Leith-Forbes' private library and study. There was a large writing desk with a laptop, black candles, incense, and a bowl containing a burnt offering. The walls were stacked with a variety of books and manuscripts and there was a musty smell of ancient paper. A cursory glance revealed studies of ancient texts and books on Viking and Germanic folklore and legends. The far wall contained the very pride of the collection, grimoires and spellbooks of ancient knowledge. Darke whistled as he recognised several infamous tomes.

Rather curiously there was also a mannequin, a plain head and shoulders on a pedestal opposite the desk. He moved to that first, resisting the siren call of the writing desk. Peering closely, he discovered there was a slight impression around the neck made by some kind of heavy chain or necklace. Curious.

Able to resist no longer, he slid over to the writing desk which burned brighter than a bonfire to his attuned sight. He bent and sniffed at the bowl where the ashes had accumulated. It smelt bitter and acrid, some kind of scrying or divining ritual had taken place here and recently too. It absolutely reeked of magika which meant Leith-Forbes had mastered some forms of the darker arts. There was something familiar about it too, something...

'Quite the collector wasn't he?' observed Parris.

'There's some rare, valuable, and downright dangerous works here. Tread carefully,' he said, distracted, trying to focus on that aura.

'Don't freak me out, Darke, it's not funny,' she said, eying the shelves closely but he moved to quickly lay a hand on her arm which was reaching for a particularly malevolent book.

'I'm serious,' he said. 'Don't touch anything.'

Fascinated, Darke delved further. Here Leith-Forbes kept his treasured possessions on display which weren't for public consumption. There was an unsettling series of paintings from early medieval to Elizabethan and Gothic styles: some depicted groups of white robed men consorting with strange entities, others abstract geometries that were unsettling to look at for too long.

But there were more modern pieces too, propaganda sheets, a few tattered remnants of fascist memorabilia and a framed account of the Battle of Cable Street.

'Seems like Leith-Forbes had a side he didn't want the world to know about,' said Parris.

'Looks like he was quite the fascist fanboy on the quiet.'

'Or just a dedicated collector?'

'I think this is a bit more than historical fascination.'

'What makes you so sure?'

Darke moved to the desk and held up the dagger. 'This knife is an *Ehrendolch*, an SS honour dagger.'

'Still could be just a collectible. There's no direct evidence he had links to the far right.'

'They don't all wander around with swastika tattoos heiling Hitler, nowadays, even they are a bit more subtle than that. The clever ones work in the shadows, pulling strings, stirring up division, manipulating others to do their dirty work. Some, like Leith-Forbes it seems, seek to advance themselves through more esoteric means. I've seen more and more of that kind of thing going on lately.'

'An old dagger and some ancient right wing propaganda isn't exactly definitive, Darke. We're talking about a very prominent member of the establishment here.'

'True, and a very well connected one. Didn't I read that he also had links with some of the more rabid newspaper proprietors?'

'That still doesn't prove anything.'

'"First they fascinate the fools… then they muzzle the intelligent". Sounds like pretty accurate reportage of recent history to me.'

'Any direct evidence to support that notion?'

'Bear with me.'

Darke who had been eyeing the laptop meaningfully opened it up. The screen displayed a prompt for a passcode to gain access.

'I'll send that to the boys in the labs,' said Parris, 'they should be able to crack it in a day or two depending on the complexity of the security.'

'Might not take that long.' Darke tapped a combination into the prompt.

'I'm serious, don't get locked out,'

The machine started into life.

'How the hell did you do that?'

'The passcode I used to access his laptop? It was 20041889.'

'So?'

'Hitler's birthday. Still not convinced?'

'You're just showing off now,' said Parris huffily.

Darke scanned the desktop but nothing unusual jumped out at him. 'This will take some digging into.' He closed the screen and tucked it under his arm.

'You can't take that, it's evidence.'

'Just give me twenty four hours with it, Chanda, and I'll...'

Darke suddenly broke off as he noticed a crumpled piece of paper in the wastepaper bin. Smoothing it out revealed parchment-like paper and a cramped, spidery hand.

*As was foretold, so have I returned*

*By my seal thou will thou know me, brother.*

*I invoke the protocol and the obligations of our order*

*When Arcturus reaches its zenith*

*Meet me at the appointed place*

*There to discuss the destiny of the Heir of Albion and the wider Congregation*

*For I bring news of great important*

*And vow to aid thee as thy appointed servant*

*Thou to be crowned as the appointed Heir*

*The Piercer of the Veils stands on the threshold*

*The sun's gift will be retrieved*

*And then a glorious destiny awaits every true Son of Albion*

*- EF*

The letter bore a seal with a familiar black radial design stamped into the wax.

'"When Arcturus reaches its zenith", that would be two nights ago, same night he died. An invitation from the murderer?' he handed Parris the note.

'Or at least one which lured him to the scene. Let's not jump to conclusions...'

'But it clearly...'

'That's enough Darke, I've got to call this in now. We've made some solid progress here, but it's time to let the pros take over. Put the laptop back, you'll have to wait on its contents like the rest of us. Don't worry, I'll make sure you see the full report.'

'But...'

'Don't try to talk me out of it, I know you of old. Remember, you're on this case as a consultant, but I'm still in charge.'

'Okay, one more thing then.'

'Okay...?'

'The books. Some of them are rare, some of them are valuable, I don't care about those. A couple are downright dangerous. Let me take possession for safekeeping.'

'You can't remove evidence.'

'I won't. Trust me they don't have any direct bearing on this case but they could be a real menace if they find their way into the wrong hands. Don't worry. I promise I'll make sure they're looked after properly.'

'Show me which ones.'

He picked out two books, *Magickal Endeavourz* and *Dee's Hidden Treatises,* showed them to Parris and then placed them safely in his bag. While she dialled it in, another caught his eye, a tome called *The True Histories of the Sons of Albion*. Intuitively, he reached for it and slipped it into his bag without her seeing.

As he waited for Parris to finish up, Darke noticed a flash of brightly coloured material poking out from underneath the bookshelves. He bent down and retrieved it, holding it up to the light.

'A team will be here shortly, which is probably the cue for you to make yourself scarce. What's that?' Darke gave a shudder as a piece suddenly fell into place.

'I know that look, Darke. What are you thinking?'

'Nothing, except what an idiot I am.' He dashed off toward the kitchen and opened the door into the adjoining utility room. It was full of expensive looking white goods, a fridge, a luxury washing machine, laundry baskets full of ironed shirts and starched collars, but he ignored all those and headed straight for the cupboard, opening it with a flourish.

'Aha,' said Darke, beaming, 'there we have it.'

'Have what? Am I supposed to be impressed?' said Parris sceptically.

'You should be,' replied Darke, 'look at those brightly coloured cloths and cleaning materials. Exactly the same eastern European brands that I found in Daria Balan's flat. I can't believe I didn't see it before: Daria Balan was Andrew Leith-Forbes' cleaner.'

'Hm, seems a bit of a stretch,' said Parris but didn't sound wholly convinced.

'Does it? Think about it. She wanted extra money, would probably work for cash in hand. He's exactly the type to give it to her for a reduced rate, naturally.'

'There's a million cleaners in London, Darke, these could be anyone's.'

'What about where they found her? Wapping Park is almost on a direct line between here and Whitechapel where she lives. It's no coincidence.'

'Maybe.'

'Definitely. Don't forget she had a hundred and twenty quid in her purse untouched, a week's wages? Oh, and then of course, there's the biggest signpost of all...'

'Which is?'

'The scent of magika in the ritual bowl, it has the same bitter signature as the one lingering on Daria Balan's corpse. That's it, we've found our connection.'

'It all sounds a bit woo woo to me but I suppose I'll have to take your word for it.'

'Forensics will confirm I'm sure.'

'We'll see when they get here. In the meantime, you'd better make yourself scarce. But stay in touch, yeah?'

'Count on it.'

*Now I possess the great seal of office, none can dispute my divine right to lead the Inner Circle or the wider Congregation. Yet, my arrival has not gone unnoticed. I have attracted the authorities' attention just like the infernal Dee and his meddling men, they are now aware of my works. I sense the approach of the Adversary too, the one foretold in the prophecy, who would attempt to stymie my ascension. I must destroy him, nonesuch must be allowed to gainsay me.*

*I feel my powers grow and expand and I must bend my will toward finding the sun's gift, that which will confirm my ascension. The Proctor knows, she will lead me along the path and show me the way to the consummation.*

*But the Piercer grows stronger too, when it manifests I feel its tendrils wrapping themselves around my mind and I struggle to contain its influence. The joining must come soon, so it can be properly harnessed and its energies pressed into service. Even the mightiest sorcerer would be taxed by being a vessel for such a creature, for it constantly whispers and pleads, insinuates and promises, offers glimpses and insights into this world and those beyond. When it is fully manifest, when our destinies are joined, none will be able to withstand me.*

It took Darke nearly a whole day to absorb his findings and begin contemplating what he had learned. He smoked a couple of spliffs and then took to the Underground, riding the trains without a specific destination in mind, letting them carry him along, losing himself in the ebb and flow of the crowds, the rocking rhythm of the carriages, the play of light and dark over the concrete and steel cityscape. As he was ferried between the heights and depths, through the veins and arteries of the brooding urban landscape, he realised the revelations at the apartment had shone a little light into the void. But he needed time to digest them, assemble them into a coherent order, bring some shape and form to events.

First, Daria Balan. Even though he had established a link between her and Leith-Forbes, her death was still curious, accidental almost, like an afterthought, an outlier. Even with his nationalist tendencies, Leith-Forbes had entrusted her enough to know about the contents of his secret study. He probably saw her as inconsequential, irrelevant, just another foreign minion he could pay to do his bidding.

After pondering the matter deeply, Darke's best guess now was that she had been cleaning the room, accidentally touched the bowl and had picked up a faint trace of the magical aura of the ritual he had conducted. It had been enough to attract the attention of whoever or more likely whatever it was that had ultimately killed her.

Then there was Leith-Forbes himself: his outwardly respectable aspect was a veneer for some pretty unpleasant politics and enthusiasms, and he also had a sideline as a serious practitioner of the occult. Darke had begun to study the book he had purloined, *The True Histories of the Sons of Albion,* and it made for some pretty uncomfortable reading. A lot of it was in code and a lot was hard to decipher due to the archaic language, but it stretched from Elizabethan times through to the Thirties and encompassed all the tropes and propaganda calculated to press the tin foil hat brigade's bigot buttons.

There was a lot about the 'pure blood of true born Englishmen', how Albion could only embrace its destiny once it had thrown off the shackles of foreign interference and the malign influence of traitors and turncoats. It was crude nationalist stuff for the most part, but had been cunningly woven with native myth and legend and sprinkled with a pinch of true occult practice to appeal to the more easily led or hard of thinking. As far as he could tell, these "True Sons of Albion" as they styled themselves were destined to lead the nation into a glorious future once all the usual obstacles and impediments had been swept away.

But in between the nationalist fervour and the crude

propaganda there was one fragment which caught his attention. This told of the Seeker, "A man of *history*, of *destiny*", who would return like the long lamented Arthur to lead the Sons of Albion and the wider Congregation. His ascension as the Heir of Albion would finally slay all the dragons and shibboleths which had long held Albion chained.

That strange note had also mentioned a Congregation, so there was a connection there, but who were these Sons of Albion?

That led him on to contemplating the identity and motivation of the killer. Who was EF? Why had he killed Leith-Forbes? He professed to be a servant but that was obviously a ruse. He had lured Leith-Forbes to the shore and his death and taken something from the body, something significant, most likely the thing that hung upon the mannequin. But what was it and what did it signify? Some kind of chain of office perhaps?

More importantly what method was he employing to slay his victims in such a gratuitous and gruesome manner? Why on Earth or beyond it did he need their eyes? Was it symbolic or practical? What did he do with them once extracted? There were too many unanswered questions, too many parameters, and as afternoon bled into evening, Darke's head began to throb with all the permutations. Time to retreat and get some rest. As darkness enfolded the capital, he came back to the present and found himself on the outer fringes of the Metropolitan line. With a weary sigh he hopped out at Harrow-on-the-Hill, consulted the glowing boards and began to plot his course back home.

*The old woman was an accident, a slip of fate. As the Piercer first materialised into this world it fed on her instinctively before I could direct its appetite, but it matters little. She was just a serving wench, not of the true blood, so what of it? Her essence provided barely a morsel. It was not fully sated until it had feasted upon the Chancellor, the fool who sat in my place as the leader of the Inner Circle.*

*As the Piercer of the Veils opens the ways, so my vision clears and I begin to see more of my Adversary. A dark man, a haunted man, but a man of knowledge and vision. I sense him as he too begins to apprehend me. Perhaps he might be converted to the cause? He could become a powerful ally with the right ... motivation. I must learn more of him.*

Darke walked through an endless plain ringed by the fangs of amber mountains. Overhead, a purple-black sky wheeled and churned, rotating a slew of unfamiliar stars and unknown constellations. His bare feet trod on parched earth, a sea bed long dried up, cracked and bereft of water, throwing up little clouds of nebulous dust which span away in small cyclones.

Well, this is different, he thought as he trudge-traversed the desiccated waste, plodding through a surreal, featureless landscape. This isn't real, perhaps a projection of someone else's mind or my own?

In the far distance a series of drab monoliths broke the surface like giant cetaceans breaching the ocean, rising to impossible heights, kissing the corona of the sky. I am asleep but this is no dream he realised: it is a construction, a meeting place, a unity made by shared consciousness.

Intriguing.

He became aware of a distant pounding like the rumbling

press of jackhammers growing louder. There, on the horizon, a speck formed and took shape, accelerating toward him. In a moment-hour-heartbeat it was upon him, towering above him like a gigantic cyclone, comprised of spokes and tendrils overlain on an impossible sky.

It blinked and numberless eyes open as it rotated into a new configuration, the jagged radial spokes solidifying into a familiar design which then resolved into a baleful glowing eye.

He tried to speak but found he had no mouth and then it began to emit strange sounds, weird pulsating music in a chilling harmony setting off vibrations that seemed to pierce his very being. The unholy symphony swelled and grew to a thunderous crescendo, now growing harsh and discordant, overwhelming, overbearing, overpowering.

It was trying to blot out his identity, his very existence.

Darke felt himself battered beginning to succumb to the ferocious, numbing assault, but as it passed through him, it also threw up a series of strange visions: horrific murders, summary executions, numberless victims.

He recoiled, seeing bloody hands which were not his own.

The force of the emanation floored him and he lay on his back, pressed into the earth as the thing attempted to crush him. He tried to fight back, but the being just pushed harder, increasing the pressure, forcing him down so that his body compressed, his bones cracked, his eyes threatened to leave their sockets.

Then he knew what he must do and instead of resisting, he let it pass through him, permeate him, saturate him until he had absorbed all of its malevolent energies and then he released them, letting them go like a flood upon the fields. In an instant he was awake, bathed in sweat, disconcerted by a persistent ringing in his ears. It took him several moments to realise it was the sound of his phone.

'Chanda?'

'Marcus, sorry to call so late, but I couldn't sleep.

'Me neither, but probably for very different reasons.'

'You okay?'

'I'm not sure. Think so. Just been attacked, assaulted...'

'What?! Let me get a unit around there...'

'Not physically, mentally, psychically. Someone pushing the boundaries, testing my defences... fortunately, they held. Just.'

'Who?'

'Well, they didn't exactly leave a calling card, and it was cloaked in some kind of psychedelic dream space. But I'd be willing to lay odds it was our killer. He knows I... we're on to him somehow and decided to pay me a visit.'

'Are you alright?'

'I'll live, but it works both ways. Just as he's found out about me, so he's revealed a little of himself, a little more than he intended probably. Glimpses slipped through, past times, places, personas. It's all a bit hazy at the moment, but I saw things... terrible things... this isn't the first time he's done this. I'll need a little time to figure it all out.'

'Shit.'

'Yeah.' There was an awkward silence for a moment.

'Thanks for the call though,' said Darke. 'It helped pull me out of it.'

'That's okay.'

'Question: why were you ringing me at this time of night?'

'I... it doesn't matter now. Take all the time you need... I'm glad you're safe, Marc...'

'Marc?'

'Don't spoil the moment, Darke. Get some sleep, we'll speak soon.'

Another twenty four hours passed but Parris hadn't called, so Darke was left to his own devices. He slept in, rose late and once he'd showered away the lingering remnants of the dreamland encounter, he ate breakfast, made himself a large pot of coffee, rolled a joint and sparked it up. Blowing smoke rings, he stared at the cover of *The True Histories of the Sons of Albion* but decided he'd had enough of its racist rhetoric and decided to pursue another line of enquiry.

Setting to work he fired up his desktop and scoured the web, but to little avail initially at least. The internet was a wonderful thing, but had its limitations, and what he was after required a deeper, more detailed delve into history. He connected to the British Newspaper Archive and a few more specialist sites and began digging. It took a couple of hours but eventually he was able to ferret out some pertinent information.

Darke was certain those flashes he had experienced during the night time incursion were real and so he attempted to trace their origins back through the ages or at least as far as the newspaper archives would allow. He had found the first report in one of the more lurid Victorian Penny Dreadfuls, a breathless sensationalist account of strange disappearances in the heart of London in 1875 under the screeching headline "Eye Snatcher Stalks East End!". The perpetrator had accounted for multiple victims with some vague occult connections between them before the killings abruptly stopped. The culprit mysteriously disappeared, never to be heard of again, or at least in that century.

The second instance came from September 1936 when several prominent antifascists and trade union officials had gone missing in the lead up to the events in Cable Street: the battle between Mosley's Blackshirts and a united East End. Police suspected some form of political assassination, but only one body was ever discovered, Jacob Swanson, a Jewish activist who was found floating face down in the Thames. The corpse was bloated and distended from its prolonged exposure to the water, but the medical examiner remarked on the "hideous rictus grin" on the victim's face and that Swanson's eyes were missing, presumably nibbled away by creatures in the water.

Similar murders spanning nearly one hundred and fifty years apart might have shocked more conventional minds, but Darke was not particularly surprised. It wouldn't be the first time he had encountered such phenomena.

It could be some form of copycat killings of course, and in the interests of keeping an open mind he shouldn't rule that out. But he could not escape his instinct that this EF was the force behind these historical killings too and had now reemerged again to continue his reign of terror. Finding out just exactly who EF was should be a priority and that would require asking a favour, a favour from an old acquaintance with whom he wasn't exactly on the best of terms. Unpalatable though it was, he'd just have to suck it up: sometimes you just had to bite the mystical bullet.

Finding the Repository of Books, Antiquities & Curiosities was not easy, even for those who knew where to look. It was down one of those narrow, enclosed, cobbled passageways that belonged to a different London, one populated by sallow Victorian urchins, gin-soaked molls and dangerous ne'er-do-wells, who would slit your throat for so much as a farthing. Darke suspected that the proprietress maintained some kind of specialist glamour to dissuade the unwary and keep unwanted visitors away, for this was a very specialist and exclusive emporium, one that dealt in the rare, occult, obscure, and esoteric.

The exterior looked like a long abandoned storefront, but he ignored the drab, featureless façade and pushed against the door, which eventually yielded with reluctance. The bell croaked rather than tinkled as he entered but once inside, the interior was rather different with a warm, cosy atmosphere generated by the glowing fireplace. The embers threw a red-gold light upon the dozens of curios, artefacts, trinkets, and baubles which competed for space on every possible surface. Stacks of books and manuscripts stretched back in rows of shelves behind the counter and everywhere were objects to delight, bedazzle or baffle the senses. A fat ginger cat, curled into a neat circle on a plump cushion, opened one pale green eye, and apparently satisfied, promptly went back to sleep again.

Darke was prepared for a hostile reception, but to his surprise it was not the proprietress who awaited him behind the teak counter, but a willowy young woman, in her late teens or early twenties, with sharp features and several green plaits woven into her long blond hair.

'Help you?' she enquired.

'I hope so,' said Darke.

'Good, we don't get many of your kind in here...'

'And what kind is that exactly?'

'Tall, dark, kind of handsome... certainly an improvement on the usual clientele.'

"You're new."

"I am."

"Darke."

"That your name, or your outlook?"

'It's my name, Marcus.'

'Sunniva... I usually go by Neve.'

'Well it's nice to see some new blood about the place, Neve... is Mrs Ó Fey around?'

'I thought I told you never to come back?' An older woman bustled in, materialising from the backroom and manifesting with all the aplomb of a magician's assistant and all the attitude of an attack dog. She was short and round, grey hair styled up into an imposing aurora and she sported a shawl overlaying a two-piece outfit of chequered green tweed. Bulbous glasses inspected him and the overall impression was of a rather imposing, wise, yet distinctly hostile bullfrog.

'You didn't really mean that, Jacintha.'

'You damn well know that's not true, Darke,' she said with an Irish brogue. 'Go on, get out of here, , I'm surprised my wards even allowed you to slip in.'

'Maybe they know something you don't?' said Darke.

'What did he even do, may I ask?' enquired Neve.

'You may not,' said the old woman curtly.

'Come on, Jacinta, I come in peace, ready to bury the hatchet. Besides I have ... what shall we call it, an incentive to show my good faith and make nice.'

'There's nothing you can do, you little bollox...' Ó Fey said sourly, but when Darke brandished the copy of *Magickal Endeavourz* he had purloined from Leith-Forbes apartment, her acquisitive gaze told a slightly different story.

'This needs a home,' said Darke. 'Somewhere secure, somewhere safe. Honestly, I couldn't think of a better berth than your private collection.' Age-spotted hands reached out to grasp the tome, but he held it just out of reach.

'But I do need a favour in return... a little research in that collection of yours.'

'What makes you think, I'd let you anywhere near my precious books, Darke?'

'A few hours... maybe a day, tops, is all I'll need.'

'Well...'

'Come on Jacintha,' said Neve. 'He might be fun to have about the place.'

'It's not only against my better judgement but all I hold dear...'

'This would be yours, to keep, remember, forever. All I'd ask is that it stays with you. No selling it on. I'd be entrusting it to your safekeeping.'

'Naturally. You don't think I'd be daft enough to sell something as rare as *Magickal Endeavourz* now do you?'

'Fair enough.'

'One more thing.'

'What now?'

'An assurance that this makes things right between us?'

said Darke. Jacintha Ó Fey hovered for a moment torn between aversion and acquisitiveness, but eventually acquisitiveness won out.

'Oh... oh, alright. Done deal. You always did strike a hard bargain, Darke. But when you tease her with treasures like this, well, what's an old gal to do?'

The morning passed quickly and in a welter of fruitful research and by the time he was done he had a much more complete picture of the nature of what he was facing. Jacintha Ó Fey had led him through a secure portal into her private library and made him comfortable with a cup of tea, which he took as both a peace offering and a sign of a thaw in their strained relations. Yet he also could tell she was impatient and at the first opportunity, she disappeared off to devour her new acquisition in private. Which was fine by him, Ó Fey boasted one of the finest private collections of occult books and esoterica in the country, if not the world, so to be back in her good books, both literally and figuratively, was a major coup.

At first he had struggled to refine his search but a footnote in a historical tome led him to one of the wilder histories of Elizabethan occultism, *Sorcerie During the Reign of the Virgin Queen.* It was a rambling tome, but it made for some enlightening reading and he was soon deep into the heart of the work. One name particularly stood out, an individual known as the Seeker, a lay preacher from Norwich who had risen from obscure origins to attract a legion of devoted followers. His message of strict Protestantism and an extreme hatred of foreigners had found fertile ground during the great scare of the Spanish Armada. This Seeker had also claimed to have had a hand in the destruction of the great fleet saying he had caused "God to blow and it was scattered". A lie of course, but it had won him many admirers at court. More than a few enemies too, although they seemed to have had a habit of disappearing, or turning up dead and eyeless.

In the years that followed this Seeker became one of the best connected men in England for he had a formidable talent for uncovering both useful information and the hidden secrets which men cleaved to their hearts. It was said that he had also formed a "*Society of all true Englishmen for the betterment and advancement of Albion and the establishment of a new commonwealth*". Many who flocked to his cause were drawn from the nobility and influential merchant classes, not surprising since according to this Seeker's creed they would be the ones entrusted with the governance and destiny of the nascent British Empire. The lower orders were welcome too as part of a wider but infinitely more subservient congregation.

Alarmed by the growing influence of this individual, the queen's confidant John Dee began to take a close interest in this Seeker and the arch spymaster soon proved worthy of his reputation. No mean magician himself, Dee soon proved that it was not the nation's best interest but magic which had fuelled this Seeker's rise for he had made a pact with a darker entity with whom he consorted, using it to power his rise to the top. Dee quickly recognised this Seeker's true ambition, which was to replace the Queen with an Inner Council of the nobility of which he would be named lord president and first minister. When the truth was discovered, retribution was swift and the Seeker and his circle were brought down in a night of violence and blood.

This Seeker meant to crown his ambition with a conjuration of his damnable master, the Piercer of the Veils, during which he would be wedded to the sun's gift, whatever that was, and become the Heir of Albion, united with its infernal power to rule the hearts and minds of men.

The ritual to conjure this diabolic power took place in the barren lands to the east of London, but nearing its completion, it was raided by Dee and his Queen's Men. Those of the Congregation who resisted were put to the sword, the more influential sent to the Tower, and the remainder dispersed with a stark warning to never assemble again on pain of death. Many fell that night, but the Seeker himself evaded capture, apparently stepping into a well of darkness, dissolving into the very air itself, though the witnesses who made such a claim were considered unreliable. The full story of his devilment was swiftly obtained through the rack and the fate of the conspirators served as a blunt warning to never plot treason against Gloriana again. The whole episode was purged from the history books and as is often the case with the most inconvenient truths quickly forgotten especially with the advent of the first Elizabeth's golden age.

Quite the tale, though Darke, and if ever there was a prime candidate for this Seeker, it had to be EF...

'Good book?' lost in thought he had not heard the girl enter.

'Good? No. Enlightening? Definitely.'

'Are you looking for something specific?'

'Someone, actually, a sorcerer from another time who may have returned to this one.'

'Oh, I love a mystery.'

'Sadly, this isn't a very wholesome one. He not only terrifies his victims to death but he steals their eyes in the process.'

'Ouch, horrid. Remind me never to answer the door to him.'

'You seem to take all this talk of magic and wizards very matter-of-factly.'

'Yeah I kinda grew up around this sort of thing. My parents weren't exactly what you'd call the conventional type. We didn't get on, which is why I left. Wandered aimlessly for a bit, got into trouble, got out of it again... just about and somehow, I ended up finding this place. Jacintha took me in, gave me a home, gave me a job when few would.'

'Hm, I'd like to hear the full story sometime.'

'Sometime I might tell it to you, but you shouldn't mind Jacintha. She's a sweetheart really.'

'Sweetheart? That's not the first word that springs to mind when I think of Mrs Jacintha Ó Fey.'

'She's... nice, kind even, when you get to know her, once you get past that prickly exterior.'

'Never have, but I'll take your word for it. Still, I'm glad we've brokered a truce, even temporarily. She's a good woman to know in a professional sense as well. It's been a couple of years since I was here last, so a lot has changed. Some things for the better it seems. Maybe you're a good influence, mellowing the old bat out?'

'Not a very flattering label for a venerable old lady.'

'Don't let her hear you call her that. She'll have a fit,' said Darke.

'Call me what?' said Ó Fey appearing from the ether.

'Kind, nice...' said Darke, 'seems like your assistant here is smitten.'

'Darke, still here are you? Don't test my patience. It's been tolerable enough to see you again, but let's not overdo things. Off you fuck, now.'

'Okay, I know when I'm not wanted, I won't outstay my welcome. Enjoy the book, Jacintha. Good to meet you, Neve.'

*The Congregation has assembled and I have declared myself and been accepted and acclaimed. Long have they waited while the members of the Inner Council dithered, grown lazy and complacent, enjoying the trappings and privileges of power without the duties and responsibilities of wielding it. Many groundlings now thirst for the action and decisive leadership, which will begin the restoration of Albion as one of the true powers of the world.*

*Few dared oppose me although that fool Davis will have no use for his eyes... or his life now.*

*It was a convenient demonstration of my powers and both Council and Congregation were impressed. They will make ample foot soldiers, crucial cannon fodder for the battles to come.*

*Yet, the Proctor was missing and she is vital to my scheme, for only she knows the true location of the sun's gift. Perhaps she has heard of the Chancellor's fate and fled? But none can truly hide from the Piercer of the Veils. Now I will bend its will toward finding her and when I do, my consummation as the Heir of Albion will be imminent.*

Nice kid, thought Darke, though that sunny disposition conceals a world of troubles. Unless I miss my guess, that's a girl with a past. How she had ended up at the Repository probably formed a tale in own right, and how she had persuaded such a dedicated misanthrope as Jacintha Ó Fey to take her in spoke to her considerable charm no doubt. Perhaps the old biddy was training her up to be her successor? Even one so long lived and steeped in magical practices couldn't live forever, though Ó Fey seemed intent on actively trying to disprove that theory.

There was something different about this Neve though, something even his normally perceptive sight couldn't penetrate. She was a latent, that was certain, a powerful one too, or Jacintha wouldn't have taken her in, but she seemed blissfully unaware of her powers. It came through in her warmth and charm, so some sort of powerful empathic ability perhaps? Maybe that's what had worked its magic on Ó Fey, bypassing her normally sardonic inclinations? Well, it was a mystery that would keep for another time, there were more pressing concerns right now.

The Sorcerer's Knuckle was an ancient coffee shop which had been around since Samuel Johnson sampled his first cup of arabica and was a known haunt for those of an esoteric persuasion. Darke nodded acquaintance with several of its regular patrons and recognised several characters of a more dubious persuasion lurking in its shadowy recesses. As well as serving world-class coffee and a selection of exotic cakes and pastries, the Knuckle was certified neutral ground and a long held and strictly enforced truce meant that it was a secure spot for business or pleasure.

'Why did we have to meet here?' said Parris as she pulled up a chair and signalled for an Americano from the disinterested barista.

'Because I like it and it's one of the safest spaces in London.'

'Oh?'

'Yeah, and there have been a few developments, shall we say, which I thought you should know about.' Darke brought her up to speed on the psychic attack and his subsequent research.

'Also, I'm pretty sure I'm being followed. Whoever is behind this, I think it goes way beyond a few horrific murders. There's history here and a larger purpose to whatever he's planning.'

'That's quite a lot to take in. I'll need some time to digest.'

'You called me in on this, how did you expect it to go?'

'Well, I didn't expect it to be quite so big, to reach quite so far. But it all ties in with a new victim. Darren Davis, populist online commentator and notorious social media star. The exact same MO as Daria Balan and Leith-Forbes. He even had the same tattoo, but on his shoulder. I'm not entirely sure we can keep a lid on it this time. He was well known and admired by the more rabid right-right wingers and almost universally disliked by everyone else. When his socials go quiet for a few days, it's going to be noticed.'

'Time's ticking then. Anything else I should know?'

'On Davis? No, but the laptop has yielded a few interesting results. A lot of it's encrypted, but the tech boys managed to dredge out some pertinent information. There's a lot of murky stuff, mainly involving nationalism, xenophobia, all that kind of outdated nonsense. But from what we can tell there seems to be a network of people like Leith-Forbes, all in the upper echelons, all on the far right fringes, all pulling strings from behind the scenes for their mutual benefit. They don't get their own hands dirty of course, but work through think tanks, social media programmes, funding for political candidates, cash for street level agitators. They call themselves...'

'Let me guess... the Sons of Albion?'

'What? Are you psychic?'

'Not in that way, which is a shame, as it'd make this job a whole lot easier. No, just one of the names that came up in my research. Please, go on.'

'The other most relevant thing is some email traffic between Leith-Forbes and one Angela Parker, you'll know her or of her, I'm sure. They refer to themselves by fancy titles, he, the "Chancellor", she, the "Proctor". I'll forward the rest but there's one final exchange on the evening he was murdered, about the prophecy, the ritual of joining and the sun's gift. Any idea what any of that means?'

'No.'

'Okay, well, let's keep at it. Anything else I should be aware of?'

'Not much other than I'm pretty certain I'm being tailed.'

'Do you need protection?'

'No, it's okay, they don't know I know. It's nothing I can't handle.'

'Okay, keep me apprised and... take of yourself Marcus.'

'You too.'

'And next time, let's meet somewhere a little less out there... okay?'

Angela Parker then would be key to cracking this case. Fortunately, she was not too difficult to find, the senior executive of a major news group which hovered just about on the saner end of the spectrum. Powerful and well connected, she had the ear of several media moguls and members of government and was a regular amongst the great and good London society.

Actually getting close enough to talk to her would be the real issue. Darke tracked down and visited her address but it was on a gated fortress of an estate in Chelsea and admitted no causal visitors. Thankfully, she was a classical music lover and consulting an appropriate posh diary column, Darke found she was due to attend a swanky orchestral recital in Kensington that very evening. He made it his business to be waiting as the attendees poured out and her limo pulled up.

'Ms. Parker... Ms. Parker? Could I get a quote about the performance this evening?' he lied, approaching the car, but a burly bouncer intervened.

'Sorry, I don't give interviews.'

'What if I want to discuss the Piercer of the Veils?' The briefest flicker played across her face, but she motioned the bouncer aside and said, 'Get in.'

Inside, she looked at him with all the hauteur one would expect upon detecting a piece of excrement upon one's high heel.

'What do you want?'

'No, "Who are you?"'

'I don't care who you are. Get to it...'

'Well, my name's Marcus Darke and I'm investigating the deaths of Daria Balan...'

'That name means nothing to me.'

'...and Andrew Leith-Forbes.' A little flash of recognition there before the mask descended again. 'It's led me down a curious, meandering path which involves the Sons of Albion, a sorcerer out of time and the Piercer of the Veils...'

'Hm, you're not as stupid as you look.'

'I scarcely could be, could I, Madame Proctor?'

Another flash of annoyance this time. 'Ask away then,' she spat, but he noticed the corner of her mouth trembled a little.

'You're one of them aren't you? One of the Sons of Albion.'

'Yes, a fully paid up member, a senior one too, see, I even have the brand,' she slid the shoulder of her dress aside to show him the radial tattoo, 'even though I don't subscribe to any of the wilder claims or that nationalist nonsense. Still, it's a handy tool for manipulating the foolish and a useful means to insert yourself into the corridors of power. I wasn't always who I am today. Once I was a lowly hack working away on an obscure provincial newspaper. I got a break to come up to the big smoke and work on the tabloids. When I was offered a chance for advancement by Andrew, I took it.'

'And now you're starting to regret it? I've done a little research of my own, read your correspondence with the Chancellor, Proctor. What is the Piercer of Veils? Who is this Seeker?' The candour of her answer surprised him.

'His name is Ezekiel Ferris, the founder of the Sons of Albion apparently and reputedly a formidable sorcerer. From what little I know, he's reawakened periodically through the ages, attempting to revive the cult and lead it to its true destiny, but he's always failed up until now.'

'Why's that?'

'I don't know, I think it has something to do with the Piercer of the Veils.'

'Which is?'

'Ferris's servant? His master? It's unclear, an entity of formidable powers and somehow aligned, intertwined, conjoined with him? Andrew was the real historian, the real sorcery superfan, he knew much more about the lore and history of these things. It's a bit late to ask him now I suppose. Aside from the performative functions necessary for my role, I didn't like to get too involved with the occult side of things. All I know is this thing demands terrible sacrifices and if it doesn't get them... well...'

'You're liable to end up eyeless and howling into the void?'

'Andrew once gleefully told me it didn't actually kill anyone, just took their eyes while exposing their mind to the true horrors of the universe. That's what actually killed them. I told him to shut the fuck up, I didn't want to know anymore, but he insisted anyway. He wanted to inherit the mantle you see, wanted to control the Piercer himself, but he didn't have the ability, the natural magical talent to fulfil the prophecy. Every attempt he made died stillborn.'

'The prophecy?'

'You'd have to dig deeper for the specifics, again not my area, but I do know it's one of the founding myths of the Sons of Albion. Fulfil the prophecy and you'll become the Heir of Albion, gain unparalleled power, ultimate control, the ability to sway the masses, extend the Congregation countrywide, restore fallen England to her former greatness again. Blah, blah. It all sounds like complete bollocks to me, but it played well with the grassroots.

'It's unnecessary anyway, you can do all those things by far more conventional means without compromising your immortal soul. Don't know if you noticed, but we've already achieved quite a lot of that without the help of any supernatural entities.'

'You're surprisingly forthcoming. Why confess all this to someone you've only just met?'

'Because you're looking at a dead woman, Mister Darke. Ferris and that thing are coming for me next and there's nowhere left to hide.' Suddenly she seemed fragile, brittle, her uncompromising front replaced by genuine fear.

'Why you? Why not just play along?'

'Because I have something he needs, something I know he desperately wants.'

'Which is?'

'Believe me, you're safer not knowing. I'm not giving it to him and if I told you it would be just one more way for him to find out. It's knowledge that's best kept buried... deep underground. Learn more about the prophecy and maybe you can figure it out. Now, I think that concludes our business?' She touched a button and instructed the chauffeur to pull over. Darke was deposited amidst the bright lights and bustle of Shaftesbury Avenue. As he watched the limousine's lights pull away, he wondered if he'd ever see Angela Parker again.

They were no amateurs, that was certain. The next day he had slept late again and spent a few hours in fruitless research before finally admitting defeat and concluding what he had known all along: he would need to pay the Repository another visit. Both his own library and the internet had proved inadequate, yielded nothing further and so as the drizzle began to fall on another metallic-grey January afternoon, Darke had packed his bag and set out to make his way to the emporium. At first, preoccupied, he hadn't even noticed the watchers, which was some feat of their part, for he was preternaturally sensitive to such things. It was only when they got slightly too close, overplaying their hand, that he finally detected their presence.

After that Darke had steered a rambling and eccentric course, determined not to lead them anywhere close to his true destination. They were skilled though, never showed themselves directly and he had to use his sight and enhanced senses to keep them under surveillance. He led them on a merry dance into a maze of back streets, alleys and dead ends until having lured them far enough away, he turned a corner, and quickly ducked into a derelict shop doorway. There he touched a very particular charm hung around his neck and in an instant became one with the shadows. He watched as a couple of smartly attired, shaven headed men rounded the corner then became increasingly desperate as they realised they had lost him. After he was certain they had gone, he reversed his course and headed back the other way.

This time the door yielded more easily but the shop bell complained like a dyspeptic warthog as Darke entered the Repository. The counter was empty, but his arrival was unlikely to go unnoticed, so he simply wandered over to the footstool on which the cat was perched. The ginger tom yawned, rose and stretched on its cushion, settled and watched him with interest.

'Hello Clive,' he said, scratching it behind the ears, whereupon it began to purr contentedly.

'Well, not so much a bad penny, more like a dodgy thirteen

pound note. We don't see you for years, now we can't keep you away.'

'Jacintha, nice to see you again.'

'I doubt that. Come on, let's dispense with the pleasantries and get down to business. What can I do for you now, Darke? Or perhaps more importantly, what can you do for me?'

'I'll get straight to it then. I need access to your library again.'

'You do now, do you?'

'This is important, Jacintha. I wouldn't come to you cap in hand if it wasn't.'

'How so?'

'State of the country, fate of the nation, important. There's a sorcerer out there aligned with some god-awful creature taking peoples' eyes and drinking their souls. Unpleasant, undeserving souls it's true, but that's just for now, it won't be long before innocent ones start getting caught up in this too. He's planning something large, something terrible if I don't miss my guess and I need to find out what.'

'And why should I care?'

'This is something that will affect all our kind, anyone who belongs in our little community of freaks, weirdos and lost souls.'

'Well...'

'Oh, and did I mention he despises foreigners and immigrants too. Irish included.'

'Feck, who doesn't like the Irish? We're delightful.'

'Exactly and besides, if you needed any more convincing, I've also bought you another gift, let's call it a donation... to a worthy cause.' He produced the copy of *Dee's Hidden Treatises* and waved it seductively.

'Go on then,' she said, sighing, but taking the book anyway. 'If you must.'

It took him most of the day but his research was starting to finally show some results. He had returned to *Sorcerie During the Reign of the Virgin Queen* which had led him on in turn to an obscure memoir written by one Matthew Hawkings esq., a fierce and devoted lieutenant of the spymaster Dee. Not only had Hawkings been involved in the raid on Ferris's ritual, but he had also been one of the chief inquisitors in the subsequent interrogation of the ringleaders of the cult.

Firstly, Darke concentrated on seeking to understand this entity, the Piercer of the Veils and piece together some facts from the fragmentary, incoherent and scattered accounts which had been obtained under duress in the Tower. None of his fellow conspirators knew much about Ferris's origins, or where he had first encountered the creature, but all agreed it had become his own personal familiar and was bound to him by ties of blood. It was variously described as a *"creature of the outer dark", "one of Satan's vilest devils"* or a *"sultry demone from the lowest inferno".*

What they could agree on was that it could reveal men's innermost secrets, access long forgotten knowledge and open gateways to other worlds and dimensions. The price for this bargain was paid with its insatiable appetite, which was fuelled by a bizarre thirst for men's eyes—and that each victim it took increased both the Ferris's power and its own. Few had actually seen the entity, or desired to, for that was often the precursor to madness and death, but it was not entirely of this world and only seemed able to manifest itself on specific occasions. One of Ferris's inner circle who had seen it described it as a "great swirling ebony cloud composed of eyes, orbs and other darker materials".

Not exactly the kind of thing you'd want living rent free in your head, thought Darke, attempting to leaven the grimness of his discovery with humour. No wonder this Ferris seemed on the brink of madness as each successive victim increased his connection with the creature. But it didn't answer why he had appeared and disappeared, seemingly failing in both Victorian times and the Thirties, or indeed why he had returned now.

'Hello, again.' Darke turned to find a smiling Neve regarding him. 'Jacintha seems to have forgotten her manners. Thought you might like some tea?'

'Thank you, all this digging into the dusty archives has worked up quite a thirst.' She had made herself a cup too and sat down next to him.

'What are you working on?'

'Oh, same case as before, although it's getting stranger and more unnerving the more I learn.'

'Sounds intriguing. Mind if I take a hit on that?' she pointed to the half smoked joint he had left in the ashtray.

'Sure,' said Darke as he watched her blow out an elegant succession of smoke rings.

'Jacintha says you're an eldritch detective, specialising in the occult, the unusual and the just plain weird. A good one too, she says.'

'Wow, well, first I'm surprised and a little flattered by her opinion. She never has a good word to say about me normally.'

'I think that harsh exterior is a front, I think she's secretly sweet on you.'

'Now that is wildly implausible.'

'How did you get into it? Being a detective I mean.'

'I don't know, it's just I'm not really sure I could do anything else. I've always had an ability to get to the heart of things, you know? A little innate magical talent too, but nothing you'd write home about. I do have the sight, but it's mainly instinct, intuition, overthinking things, plus a lot of caffeine and a little bit of weed. But I am pretty good at figuring things out... especially the weird and less than wonderful.'

'I didn't know you could make a career out of that. Maybe I'll give it a try some day?'

'I wouldn't advise it. It can be a hard road.'

'I've walked enough of those already. Perhaps I'll just stick with bookshop assistant for now... the hours are good, the tea plentiful and there's some interesting people to talk to.' They both smiled. 'Right, I'd better get back to it,' she said briskly, 'there are books to be shelved and dusting to be done.'

'Good to see you again, Neve.'

'You too, Marcus.'

As well as her other merits, the girl had a talent for making a cup of tea and the brew refreshed him sufficiently to take a further plunge back into his research. There he discovered that Hawkings had, with the aid of coercion, found the key to a secret cipher which the Sons of Albion used in their communications. The key was reproduced in the appendices and he took several pictures of it and filed them away for later use.

Next he focused on the strange prophecy with which the sorcerer seemed so obsessed. One thing that the varied accounts agreed on was that Ferris had been right in the middle of trying to fulfil it when Dee's men's raid had brought an abrupt end to his plans. It had taken place somewhere in the lands to the east of London, somewhere called the Mount but just on the point of being apprehended, Ferris had disappeared, literally vanishing into the ether, never to be seen again.

After turning the matter over in his mind, Darke had eventually come to the conclusion that Ferris had meant to bind the Piercer of the Veils permanently to him, becoming its host, so he could share body, mind and destiny and fulfil the prophecy as the true Heir of Albion

But apparently to make this insane arrangement irrevocable he would need to be joined with something called the sun's gift, a consummation that would grant him knowledge and power beyond earthly comprehension. Frustratingly, the texts didn't specify what this sun's gift actually was, some kind of powerful object or artefact maybe? Whatever it was, he would presumably now be trying to track down its whereabouts in this century.

But how would he do that? It could be anywhere by now, who knows how the intervening centuries had treated it or where it was buried?

Darke took another sip of his cold tea and a pull on the last gasps of the joint. He was just on the point of rising to hunt out another brew when the revelation came and he almost dropped the cup in surprise. Could that be what Angela Parker had meant? That was the great secret she was concealing, she knew the location of this sun's gift!

*She was foolish to think she could stop me, for there is no hiding place from the Piercer of the Veils, no secret it cannot uncover. Locks, bars and the highest walls are no hindrance to one who wields such powers. A spirited woman though, this Proctor, for she was determined not to give up her secret, struck me hard, spat in my face, but she could not fully conceal her fear. I could see it in her eyes, smell it leak from every pore of her skin.*

*Yet despite her defiance she died like all the others, sightless and mad, driven insane as she finally comprehended the true nature of the universe. And as she was devoured by the Piercer, all her memories and knowledge became mine.*

*Now the sun's gift is within reach, the ancient gateway can be opened and the ceremony begin. Even though the Mount has been lost beneath the sprawl of this new city, the sacred space beneath it is preserved.*

*It must be prepared and anointed, made ready for the consummation. There can be no delay. For long centuries have I slept, myriad false starts have I suffered, long aeons have I waited for the clockwork of the celestial spheres to align once again. The Adversary may try his utmost, but this time, I will not be denied.*

*When we are one and I have ascended to my rightful place, then the clarion call can ring out. Turncoats and traitors will be expelled, the Sons of Albion will become my instruments and my will and the message sent to every corner of the land.*

*Once we are purged of such impurities, then the true work, my true calling can begin. When England has been freed from the chains that bind it, I will lead it to its pre-ordained greatness again, its manifold destiny as the foremost nation in the world.*

Angela Parker wasn't answering her calls and Darke was starting to get worried. He had phoned her regularly all the next day leaving a variety of increasingly desperate messages and stressing the urgency of getting a reply. But his own phone had remained stubbornly silent. Meanwhile, he had brooded and cogitated over all the information he had acquired and tried to sort through the various permutations. He couldn't help but feel events were spiraling, snowballing towards some sort of awful climax, yet as long as this sun's gift remained out of Ferris's reach, then perhaps there was hope. If only Angela Parker had confided in him, there might be some way to protect this thing, conceal it, keep it out of the sorcerer's clutches? It would help to know what it was of course.

He dialled Parris and brought her up to speed with everything he knew, but he could tell this was starting to go beyond anything her eminently practical mind could process. When he had concluded his little oratory, he knew she was struggling to formulate a response.

'We'll check on Angela Parker. I'll see if her employers can tell us anything. We might even be able to check her home, but those estates are notoriously unhelpful.'

'Thanks, that'd be appreciated.'

'Is there anything else I can do, Darke?'

'I don't know: hope, pray, think good thoughts, send positive vibes?'

'Not really my area of expertise.'

'Mine neither.'

'Well, if anything else occurs, just call.'

'Thanks, I will.'

While he waited, Darke went back to *The True Histories of the Sons of Albion* again. The cipher he had copied from Hawking's account was the same one used in the book, so he lit a small joint and got down to it. While he had a talent and inclination for such work, its long, rambling, disjointed nature and archaic language, full of random thoughts and hateful polemic, didn't exactly help matters. Working through the whole thing would take all eternity, so he identified the words "sun's gift" in the cipher and began to scan individual passages for instances. Even so, finding and translating them was a slow, painstaking process and outside, nearly a whole day's worth of gusting winds and intermittent rain passed as he made progress.

The first half of the volume was virtually devoid of the phrase, concentrating instead on the deviousness of conspirators and turncoats, the dilution of pure English blood and the myriad ills and iniquities of foreigners and outsiders.

But in the second half as the tone became more and more vehement, the phrase began to crop up again and again. The words were inexorably linked to the prophecy, an omen of foretelling that the Seeker will become the Heir of Albion and rise to lead the nation to a glorious future, supreme amongst the nations. It was rabid, paranoid, delusional stuff. I don't know if you noticed, thought Darke, but we did pretty well without supernatural aid in the centuries that followed Elizabeth's reign.

Yet the more he absorbed, the more the true answer remained elusive. The Seeker and the sun's gift were to be joined in some way and their consummation would light the way to this glorious future. But what this sun's gift actually was, was never specified, like one of those things that everyone knows about, which was so obvious it was never actually named. Frustratingly, he knew his mind was hovering close to the answer but wasn't quite able to grasp it. Then something seemed to coalesce and he was on the verge of articulating it when his phone rang again.

'What?' irritated, he answered without thinking.

'Marcus?'

'Chanda? Sorry, I was right in the middle of something. I'm close here, I can sense it, but the breakthrough just won't come.'

'Well, just to add to your woes, we've found Angela Parker, or what's left of her. She was home on that high-security estate but it didn't make any difference. Same as the others, eyes missing and a look of mortal horror on her face, like she had been terrified out of her mind.'

'Shit.'

'There's no way of keeping a lid on this one. We've cordoned it off, but I've already had the tabloids sniffing about. I've had to let the husband know of course, but he's overseas.'

'Husband?'

'Yeah, she is... was married to an American businessman, David Parker. That important?'

'Yes... no... not him... but who, what he was... that's it!'

'That's what?'

'I'm going to text you an address, meet me there.'

'What?! I'm in the middle of something, I can't just...'

'Sorry, no time to explain, just get there.'

He hurried towards the Repository and this time its door yielded without a struggle although the bell parped its familiar refrain. Behind the counter, Neve had her head buried deep in a tome of arcane lore but she glanced up and brightened when she saw him.

'Marcus, three visits in a week? Any more and a girl could get to thinking you're some kind of stalker,' she laughed. 'More research is it? Shall I get us some tea?'

'No, but thanks. Sorry this is urgent so I'm going to dive straight in.'

'Go ahead.'

'You told you didn't get on with your parents?' A frown crossed her face.

'Yeah, we never exactly saw eye to eye. What's this about?'

'Sorry, humour me. When did you last see them?'

'I left when I was fourteen, so four, five years maybe. I lived with my mum, but I didn't see my dad all that much. They split years ago, but he would visit sometimes. She could be trying, but I really disliked him. There was a whole capitalist bastard thing of course, but he had a weird vibe, strange ideas. It was never explicit but sometimes it felt like he wanted me to be more than a daughter to him, you know? It was beyond creepy. Mum did her best to shield me from him, but we clashed a lot.'

'And did you stay in touch with either of them?'

'I speak with mum once in a while, birthdays, holidays, but we are really not close anymore. As I said they, especially he, have some pretty weird beliefs and I didn't want any part of them. It's why I eventually left.'

'And what were those beliefs?'

'This is starting to make me a bit uncomfortable, Marcus, What's this all about? Why do you need to know so much about my parents?'

'Bear with me, just one more question: your parents, what are their names?'

'My mum's Angela Parker, the newspaper exec, you might have heard of her? Dad's Andrew Leith-Forbes. He's a banker, a real tosser actually...'

'Oh, shit.'

'I told you he was quite the detective,' said Jacintha Ó Fey appearing from the back room.

'These are no revelations to you, are they, Jacintha?' said Darke.

'Not really.'

'It was no accident you took her in either, was it? You knew exactly who she was.'

'I did. I do. Ah, sorry love, we sort of engineered it so you'd find your way here. A little suggestion here, a little nudge there, a little charm to guide your way. I promised Angela I'd look after you, provide a safe haven, a hiding place where they wouldn't find you. Sorry about the deception but it was for your own good, so...'

'But why? Why do I need hiding from anyone? I'm a nobody.'

'No, lovey, you're not. Your mum knew, knew about the prophecy, knew they'd be coming for you one day. Your dad, well he was a true believer, got it all from that book Darke stole off him, isn't that right? You lovey are a pawn and would have been made to well... let's say, it's not a fate you'd enjoy.'

'Ugh, gross.'

'And if it wasn't your dad, it would be someone else from

amongst those fools, or someone infinitely more terrible. When your mum sent you to me, she was trying to protect you.'

'What the actual living fuck?' Neve slumped down on her stool.

'One final thing,' said Darke. 'Your name...'

'Neve? What about it?'

'No, when we first met, you told me your full name.'

'Sunniva? Yeah, it's Anglo Saxon I think.'

'Of course, it is, a true English Anglo Saxon name.'

'I never liked it, that's why I shortened it to the Irish version.'

'I think I already know the answer to this, but what does it mean? Do you know what the actual translation is?'

'Well it means gift, I think... the gift of the sun.'

'The sun's gift... fucksticks. You're it, you're the thing he needs to fulfil that prophecy—or he believes you are—which amounts to the same thing. "When the Seeker is joined or more accurately wedded to the sun's gift, when he becomes your husband, then the Heir of Albion will be revealed and the destiny of the Sons of Albion fulfilled".'

'What the actual fuck?' said Neve.

'Very good, Adversary, I couldn't have put it better myself.' A voice carried over the bell's discordant clang. The speaker was a tall, bearded man of indeterminate age dressed in archaic Elizabethan apparel. Long lank hair bestrode a sallow ferrety face, but his eyes burned fiercely and he carried a general air of malevolence. A group of several shaven headed thugs followed in his wake.

'Thank you kindly for leading me to her, Adversary.'

'Ezekiel Ferris,' said Darke cursing inwardly. He had been in such a hurry to get here, he hadn't taken his normal precautions.

'The very same, sir. But let us dispense with the formalities, I have come to claim my gift,' he leered at Neve.

'Oh, I don't think so,' said Jacintha Ó Fey and moved in front of the counter protectively, small balls of energy beginning to swirl around her fingers.

'It would be wise of you not to...' began Ferris, but then from nowhere a yowling, hissing ginger streak launched itself at his face, a ball of furry feline fury. Clive attempted to claw at his eyes, but Ferris moved preternaturally fast, snatching the cat, holding it up and then hurling it against the back wall where it did not rise again.

'You bastard, I'll...' shouted Jacintha.

'You'll do nothing, witch!' screamed the sorcerer and a darkness erupted from him, a tempestuous swirling thundercloud of blinking eyes and snaking tendrils, throwing all of them backward, taking their feet from under them. Stunned, Darke tried to raise himself up, but his limbs refused to obey him and he slumped helplessly along with the others. As he fell into unconsciousness, the last thing he heard was Ferris ordering, 'Bring her.'

'Darke... Darke...' he was in a great subterranean cavern, watching as a multitude raised their faces, their voices to a platform suspended above them. Suddenly he was aware of being violently shaken. Blinking, he opened his eyes to find Chanda Parris's face occupying his entire vision. Groaning, he heaved himself from the horizontal, his body ached like ten thousand volts had been passed through it.

'Are you alright, Marcus? What the hell happened here?'

'I'll live, I think. Shit, Neve...'

'He took her,' Darke was relieved to hear Jacintha's Ó Fey's voice, but when he turned, he saw the old girl had borne the brunt of Ferris's attack. Clive was sitting on her lap, trying to lick her face.

'Jacintha, your eyes!'

'They were old, riddled with cataracts, I won't miss them particularly.'

'Shit. But what about being exposed to the true nature of the universe?'

'Seen it all before. Wasn't impressed.' Damn, thought Darke, she really was harder than nails.

'Taken who?' said Parris and despite feeling like hammered shite, Darke quickly recapped recent events, 'And if we don't stop him... well...'

'Yeah, the Heir of Albion emerges, cosmic doom, an eternity of suffering under his oppressive rule, I get the picture. Where would he take her to enact this ritual?' asked Parris.

'The original binding was supposed to be conducted at a place called the Mount,' said Darke. 'I saw a vision of it just before you woke me. It's probably the exact same place, trouble is, I've no idea where that is. A lot has changed in London since Elizabethan times, especially around the east end.'

'Whitechapel Mount,' said Jacintha Ó Fey, 'it has to be. He's always kept things local hasn't he? The murders, this shop, all within a mile or so's radius. The Mount was an ancient landmark, some believed it was a plague pit, others a civil war fort, but it's far older than that. The surface site has long since vanished but there's supposed to be an ancient liminal space underneath. The District line runs nearby, if you can get into the access tunnels you should be able to find it with your sight, Darke. If all else fails, follow the smell of evil.'

'Good to see you haven't lost your sense of humour, at least' Darke said.

'No, just the eyes.'

Gaining access to the underbelly of London's infrastructure wasn't easy but Parris's warrant card and the words "national security matter' opened up a lot of doors. Once the ceiling lighting ran out, their torches provided flickering illumination in the maze of abandoned service tunnels to the east of Whitechapel station. Yet once he was unleashed into these, Darke was like a hound upon the scent, his sight easily following the strong residual reek of Ferris and the malign entity which inhabited him. The trail led a twisting course in the semi-dark and Parris struggled to keep up with him at times, but soon the sounds of ranting speech and responsive chanting told them that they were close to their goal.

'Quite the mini-Nuremberg rally they've got going on down here,' whispered Parris as they both gazed over the shadowy natural amphitheatre spread out before them. Down on the cavern floor a heaving mass of foot soldiers stared up, enraptured by the gathering embers of raw magical energy which swirled around the central structure. Above them on an elliptical stone gallery running around a central dais were the inner circle of the Sons of Albion, hooded and masked figures sporting long white cloaks with red crosses.

'Subtle,' whispered Darke.

The Sons of Albion now knelt as one to the figures on the

central raised platform. There Ezekial Ferris, grandly caparisoned in the supreme wizard's robes and wearing his heavy golden Chancellor's chain of office, continued to whip them up with a frenzy of nationalist invective, spitting hatred and bile. Beside him stood a figure in a long white dress with the cross of Saint George emblazoned on one shoulder. Her face was semi-veiled, but it was undoubtedly Neve. She swayed unsteadily and her eyes seemed vacant, as if she had been drugged or ensorcelled. Beyond the pair another masked Son of Albion, acting as the officiant, awaited his cue to commence the nuptials.

'Shit, what are we going to do now?' said Parris.

'I don't know, get closer to them and I'll work something out?'

'And how do we do that exactly?'

'They must keep those robes and masks somewhere.'

Darke and Parris strode towards the dais. It had taken them a little while to find the accoutrements but fortunately Ferris loved the sound of his own voice which had bought them a little time. But as they finally neared the pair the wedding service was in full swing, the officiant solemnly intoning the vows of the ancient rite. Ferris and Neve stood side by side, hand in hand, strange purple-black energies flickering between them before reaching up to feed the sanity-defying discordant shape coalescing in the void above them.

The Piercer of Veils was incarnating as a nightmarish cloud of malignant orbs and glowing tendrils, a thousand wicked eyes blinking in unison as it witnessed the ceremony below. The three formed a triangle of unholy eldritch energy which surged and flickered between them, but it was Neve who seemed to be supplying the power which Ferris relayed to the horror above.

'Shit, that's some serious magical energy. She must be much way more powerful than I imagined,' whispered Darke. 'She's acting like some form of arcane battery. Ferris is draining her and feeding it to the creature.'

'How do we stop him?'

'Working on it.'

They were close now but Darke still didn't have a plan. What had he imagined he was going to do, just walk up and club Ferris around the head or something? But as he was still deliberating his move, the sorcerer suddenly turned and advanced on them.

'Welcome Adversary, and look at you, suitably dressed for the happy occasion too. Did you really think you could approach me without being detected, stop me at the moment of my triumph?'

'I... well... ' Darke was at a loss.

'How charmingly naïve... and how utterly pointless. Shall I have the Piercer feast on your souls now, or would you rather witness my accession first?'

'Feast on this, fucker!' said Parris pulling her pistol and aiming and firing in one smooth motion. But Ferris simply raised his palm and the shot deflected off to impact wetly somewhere behind him.

'Very bold, law woman. But the Piercer allows me to know your thoughts even as you have them. I can anticipate your every move. You cannot harm me.' Ferris flicked a finger and a dark tendril lashed out, bowling Parris over, her head impacting heavily on the smooth stone.

'Now Adversary, all that remains is you and I,' said Ferris, dark energies flowing through him into a flaring halo. More tendrils shot out, encircling and binding Darke, then slamming him brutally, back first, into the ground. On the gantry below the Sons of Albion cheered and the wider Congregation roared their acclaim at their master's imminent triumph.

'Did you really imagine you could challenge me, Marcus Darke? When the Piercer of the Veils grants me such visions, such knowledge, such power? You thought to frustrate me but came with no strategy and no plan. Now I will have it drink your memories, your essence, your very soul!'

Ferris concentrated, directing tentacles of ebon energy and Darke could feel the malignant touch of something very old and very ancient and very evil. He tried to erect defences to withstand it, but the creature easily overpowered them, gnawing at his psyche, eating into his very being. Its terrible touch penetrated through him and slowly it began to consume the very essence of who he was. He cried out in impossible agonies as it began to reveal the glimpses of the strange and terrible nature of existence, horrible cosmic revelations, unpalatable eternal truths, but there was nothing he could do to prevent it. His eyes seemed to melt and he felt madness pressing down upon him like a leaden weight.

And then suddenly the pressure stopped. He had been released. Groggily, he rolled over and groped his way to his hands and knees. Neve was confronting Ferris, blood seeping from her shoulder and all down her arm where the bullet had struck.

'You want this arsehole? Then have it!' she shouted, directing a great surging stream of eldritch force into Ferris who screamed. The sorcerer thrashed and howled, losing control of his body which jerked and danced manically. This sudden supernova burst of power had drawn the Piercer's attention away from Darke and now it turned its full awareness onto Ferris, whose body started to bloat and swell, as he struggled to contain the sudden influx of arcane energy.

'No, no! I am your master! You cannot, or the great work will remain undone... feed on me and your connection to this world is severed!'

But the creature ignored his pleas and began to devour this wondrous new source of power and as it did so, its frenzied throes began to shake the cavern, dislodging rocks and debris, squashing the officiant and falling onto the screaming congregation below. As Neve forced the last of her remaining reserves into him, Ferris howled in mortal agonies but the Piercer only drank deeper, draining him, consuming him in its voracious greed.

Holding her shoulder, Neve staggered toward Darke, helping him up, but not daring to look at the horrible spectacle behind her. The cavern began to be seized by violent tremors which threatened to pitch them all into the abyss below. Together, they managed to raise the semi-conscious Parris to her feet and all three supported each other as they stumbled away from the increasingly unstable platform.

Darke stole one last glance behind him to see that the creature had finished feeding and all that remained of the sorcerer Ezekiel Ferris was a shrivelled husk. The Piercer of the Veils, which had now swollen to a gigantic size, casually tossed it aside and began to feast on the shrieking Sons of Albion on the outer platform. Yet already it was beginning to dematerialise and fade, eaten up by its own unholy greed, as with Ferris's death its connection to this reality was severed.

Once they had cleared the platform, Darke and Parris threw off their robes and all three of them staggered and lurched their way through the tunnels. Darke retained sufficient sight to help find their way and as they put distance between themselves and the cavern, the shaking and tremors began to grow less powerful until they eventually ceased altogether.

Ahead, the trio could see the faint electrical light of an access tunnel and it was such a relief that they embraced and wept and hugged each other, grateful at last to leave the nightmare of that awful cavern and its attendant horrors behind.

# BIOGRAPHIES

**SIMON BLEAKEN** lives in Wiltshire. His work has appeared in numerous magazines, including *Lovecraft's Disciples; Strange Sorcery; Lovecraftiana;* and on the *HorrorBabble Originals* podcast. He has also appeared in several anthologies, including: *Eldritch Horrors: Dark Tales (2008); Eldritch Investigations* (2023) *and Witchcraft and Black Magic in the United States* (2024). His first collection of short stories: *A Touch of Silence* was released in 2017, followed by *The Basement of Dreams* in 2019 and *Within the Flames* in 2021.

**DAVID CARTWRIGHT** was born in 1981, and raised in the Golden Age of Saturday morning cartoons. From that time he has been an avid watcher and reader of Science-Fiction, Fantasy and Horror, encompassing the likes of *The Hitchhikers Guide to the Galaxy, The Walking Dead* and the works of J.R.R. Tolkien and Neil Gaiman. He lives in Hampshire, England with his family, cat and growing collection of flannel shirts.  https://davidcartwriter.art.blog/

**GAVIN CHAPPELL** has been published by Penguin Books, Horrified Press, Nightmare Illustrated, Death Throes Webzine, Spook Show, and the podcast Dark Dreams. He has worked  as a lecturer, private tutor, tour guide, independent film maker, and is editor of *Lovecraftiana* magazine. Influences include RE Howard, Moorcock, HP Lovecraft, and Terrance Dicks. He lives in northern England.

**B HARLAN CRAWFORD**  is a lapsed musician, sub-par artist, would-be writer and purveyor of the sort of low-brow schlock that is ruining this country.  He festers loathsomely at his home in Tennessee with his wife, two cats and two dogs. More of his fevered scrawling can be read at https://thelibraryoftheschlocklords.blogspot.com

**JOHN HOULIHAN** has been a writer, journalist and broadcaster for over 30 years. He's best known for his *Seraph Chronicles* and *Mon Dieu Cthulhu!* book series and *The Constellation of Alarion*. He works as a video game consultant and script writer, and creative lead on the *Achtung! Cthulhu* RPG.    www.john-houlihan.net

**TIM MENDEES** is a writer from Macclesfield whose work has been described as the love-child of H.P. Lovecraft and P.G. Wodehouse. He is the author of over 100 published short stories and novelettes, nine novellas, and two story collections. He has also curated several cosmic horror-themed anthologies. Tim is a goth DJ with a weekly radio show, and a co-host of *The Innsmouth Literary Festival*, and the *Innsmouth Book Club* & *Strange Shadows* podcasts. He currently lives in Brighton & Hove with his pet crab, Gerald, and an army of stuffed octopods. timmendeeswriter.wordpress.com/

**ROBERT POYTON** is the founder of *Innsmouth Gold*, set up as an outlet for his music and literary projects. Robert is a keen musician, and an experienced martial arts instructor. He is co-host of the *Innsmouth Book Club* and *Strange Shadows* podcasts and co-organiser of the *Innsmouth Literary Festival*. Raised in East London, Robert now lives in rural Bedfordshire, where he enjoys making a noise and swinging sharp objects around.

**A.D.RADFORD** stumbled into the mythos just a few years ago when he was given a dog-eared copy of Ramsay Campbell's *The Kind Folk* as a Secret Santa gift. Since then, he has written on and off (mostly off) and recently finished his debut short story, Cell 34. He resides in Taiwan with his ever-patient wife, where he teaches English.

**LEE CLARK ZUMPE'S** short stories and poetry have appeared in *Weird Tales*, *Space and Time* and *Dark Wisdom*; and in anthologies such as *The Children of Gla'aki*, *Best New Zombie Tales Vol. 3*, and *World War Cthulhu*. His work has earned honourable mentions in *The Year's Best Fantasy and Horror* collections. His work as entertainment editor for Tampa Bay Newspapers has been recognized by the Florida Press Association, including a first place award for criticism in the 2013. Lee lives on the west coast of Florida with his wife and daughter.

# Acknowledgements

We would like to give thanks to everyone who helped
make this book possible. To our authors and artist for sharing their
talents, and to all those who backed the project and
helped spread the word, including:

Abe   Adam Alexander   Adam Selby-Martin   Boris Veytsman

Brandy Ybarra   Brian D Lambert   Candace   Cerise Cauthron   Chris

Jarocha-Ernst   CoolWhipKid   Dave G   Eron Wyngarde   FredH

Giusy Rippa   Helena Nash   Isador Sotho   Janine Bourdo   John

Haines   Kieran Pritchard   KLGaffney   KorvusRock   Lisa McEwen

luciano   Matthew Plank   Matthias Ackerl   Michael Fitzpatrick

Michael Ley   Miguel Fliguer   Mike James   Myron Fox   Rebecca

Buchanan   Richard O'Shea   Sebastian Zanker   Simon   Simon Hunt

Stewie   Tony Bradbury


Adam   Andrew Ferguson   Anthony Price   Anthony Riley   Brian

Hanes   Chris Chastain   Chris Kalley   Christopher Henderson   Colleen

Feeney   David Chamberlain   David Chrichard   Edward Abbott   Esa

Eriksson   Fiona Clark   Francisco Vera   ian moore   Ida Umphers   j

william berger   Jack Daniel   Fisher   Kelly McMahon   Kellyn

Kristina   L.E. D.   Mario Santos   Michael Hinrichs   Michelle White

Mordy gofman   Pedro Medellin   Richard Hebson   Riju Ganguly

Robert Compton   Shane Ardely   Simon Mark de Wolfe

Stephanie Barth   Stephanie Heatley   Therese Öberg   Tony Ciak

Tyler

Alec Smith    bobby z    David Heath    Dominick Allen    GhostCat
Kevin Donachie    Matthew Carpenter    Michael Shovlin    Rich
Ruth Beaty    Stefan Von Blon    Thomas Kirby    Tina Good    Tobias
Gasser

If you have enjoyed this book, please
post a review on Amazon. Thanks!

www.innsmouthgold.com

For the latest info on new releases, special offers and events,
sign up to our *Innsmouth Whispers* newsletter.
You'll get a 20% discount voucher on joining!

**http://eepurl.com/hysilb**

# INNSMOUTH LITERARY FESTIVAL

An annual festival celebrating the work of HP Lovecraft and
weird fiction in general.

Full program of events, including:

Author signings and panel discussions
Film screenings
Readings, Trade stands, Gaming
Competitions and photo ops
Innsmouth After Dark evening event

Full details at
http://www.innsmouth.uk/

# THE INNSMOUTH GOLD COLLECTION

## ANCESTORS AND DESCENDANTS

This anthology explores prequels and sequels to
Lovecraftian tales. You will discover the dark history of
the de la Poers, read of the early days of the artist
Pickman, and learn the secrets of Erich Zann. From
downtown Arkham to distant Venus, this unique
illustrated collection expands and explores the rich
legacy left to us by the Father of the Weird Tale.

Lovecraft loved cats! So we
gathered together new weird
stories with a distinctly feline
theme!

From unearthly Ultharians to the humble house
moggy, from temple guardians to witch's familiar, you
might never look at your cat in the same light again...

# Portraits of Terror

New tales of the weird and the Lovecraftian, all based on the theme of the Arts. From doomed musicians, to magical paintings, from lost Shakespeare plays to unworldly sculptures. Thirteen tales that may well change your perspective on Art and Creation...

# CORRIDORS

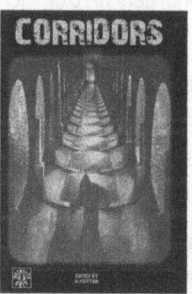

*The world changed. Now, we live underground in labyrinthine complexes, our lives overseen by the Ministry. For only they have access to our Ruler... The King in Yellow.*
13 tales in a new setting based on the King in

# FEAST OF FOOLS

This anthology continues the tradition, of Robert E. Howard, with eleven new sizzling *S&S* tales. The yarns within feature a cast of lucky thieves, avenging barbarians, bold swordswomen, and temple plunderers, not to mention sorcerers, necromancers,and a range of horrors that would freeze the blood of all but the bravest warrior.

# THE PICKMAN PAPERS

1826, and the august members of the Pickman Club gather for their Annual Dinner. As is usual, members are asked to share any recent strange or singular experiences with the group.
Here are those stories, presented for your interest and enjoyment. Be warned! The tales within reveal many disturbing secrets about our world and the things that lie beneath it.
Learn of cursed family artefacts, the dangers of experimenting with exotic drugs. And hearken to the chilling reality revealed by the digging of the Thames Tunnel. The door to the Pickman Club is open...

# THE DUNWICH TRILOGY

**A MODERN MYTHOS TRILOGY!**

**THE DUNWICH NIGHTMARE**

DC Marcus Hinds and journalist Suzy Bainbridge get drawn into a mystery following a series of grisly murders on Dunwich beach. Could there be a connection to the nearby top secret research facility?

**THE DUNWICH CRISIS**

The scale of the conspiracy is revealed as Marcus and Suzy are drawn deeper into the nightmare. Meanwhile, an ancient evil stirs in the depths of the North Sea and the world is about to change forever!

**THE DUNWICH LEGACY**

The true purpose of the Geneva CERN facility is revealed and Marcus plunges into the "world beyond" in order to save his friends and avert global catastrophe.

*"A must read for all Lovecraftians. Check your sanity at the door to the dark realms of Robert Poyton's Lovecraftian Worlds."* - Amazon review

# INNSMOUTH BOOK CLUB

If you are a fan of Lovecraftian books and films, check out our podcast the **Innsmouth Book Club!** Exclusive tours of Innsmouth's cultural sites, including the museum, library and Gilman house, where we talk weird fiction book, film, RPGs, and music ,and chat to Lovecraftian creatives.

Also take a look at **Strange Shadows**, a podcast devoted exclusively to the weird fiction of Clark Ashton Smith!

**www.patreon.com/innsmouthbc**